BURIED TREASURE

The lid opened with surprising ease. Brass hinges, he thought. If they had been iron, they would have fallen to powdery rust long ago. Gently, barely containing his enthusiasm, he lifted it back and peered inside.

The chest was full of pages of manuscripts—written on parchment or vellum that was now brittle and delicate. Gently, he eased one sheet up. The edges crumbled but the center remained intact. He leaned forward, craning to read the closely written words on the page. Carefully, he studied other pages, handling the brittle manuscript pages with expert care, making out names, places, events.

"Audrey," he said, "do you know what we've found?"

She shook her head. Obviously, from his reaction, this was something major. No, she thought, more than that, something *unprecedented*.

"What is it?" she asked.

"We never knew what had become of them," he said, and when she cocked her head in an unspoken question, he explained further.

"The Rangers. Halt, Will Treaty and the others. The chronicles and the legends only take us as far as the point where they returned from their voyage to Nihon-Ja. But now we have these."

"But what are they, Professor?"

MacFarlane laughed aloud. "They're the rest of the tale, my girl! We've found the Lost Stories of Araluen!"

Read all the adventures of

RANGER'S APPRENTICE

And the companion series

BROTHERBAND CHRONICLES

THE
LOST
STORIES

BOOK ELEVEN

JOHN FLANAGAN

PUFFIN BOOKS
An Imprint of Penguin Group (USA)

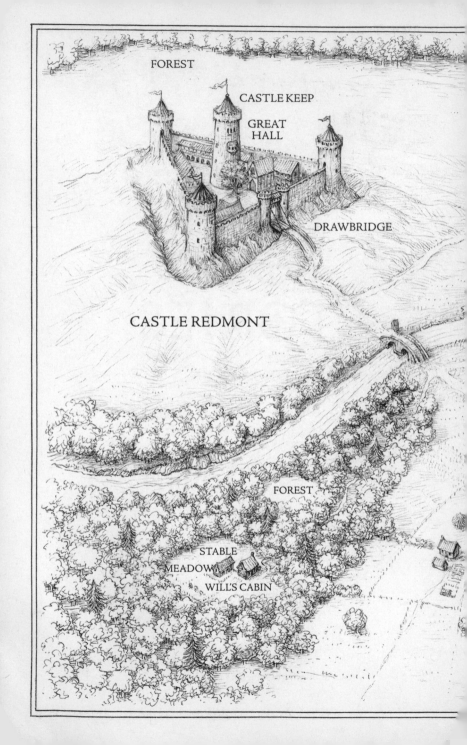

FOREST

CASTLE KEEP

GREAT
HALL

DRAWBRIDGE

CASTLE REDMONT

FOREST

STABLE

MEADOW

WILL'S CABIN

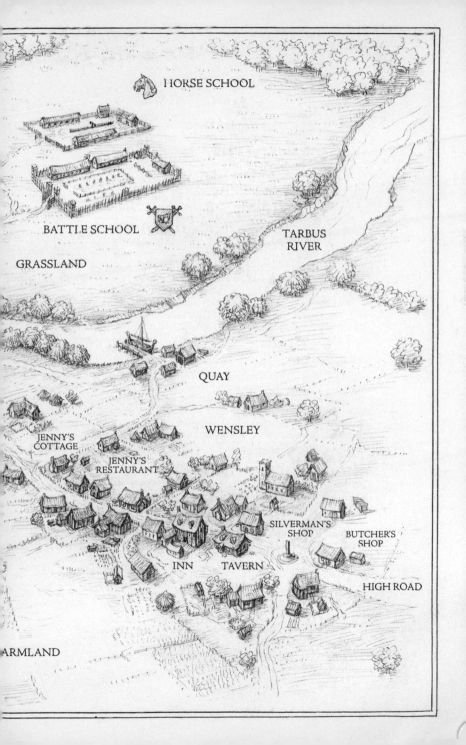

HORSE SCHOOL

BATTLE SCHOOL

TARBUS RIVER

GRASSLAND

QUAY

WENSLEY

JENNY'S COTTAGE

JENNY'S RESTAURANT

SILVERMAN'S SHOP

BUTCHER'S SHOP

INN

TAVERN

HIGH ROAD

FARMLAND

PUFFIN BOOKS
Published by the Penguin Group
Penguin Group (USA) LLC
375 Hudson Street
New York, New York 10014

USA * Canada * UK * Ireland * Australia
New Zealand * India * South Africa * China

penguin.com
A Penguin Random House Company

Published in Australia by Random House Australia Children's Books, 2011
First published in the United States of America by Philomel Books,
a division of Penguin Young Readers Group, 2011
Published by Puffin Books, an imprint of Penguin Young Readers Group, 2013

THE LIBRARY OF CONGRESS HAS CATALOGED THE PHILOMEL EDITION AS FOLLOWS:
Flanagan, John (John Anthony)
Ranger's apprentice : the lost stories / John Flanagan.
p. cm.
Summary: In 1896, an archaeological dig unearths an ancient trunk containing manuscripts
that confirm the existence of Araluen Rangers Will and halt and tell of their first meeting
and some of their previously unknown exploits.
ISBN 978-0-399-25618-9 (hc)
[1. Apprentices—Fiction. 2. War—Fiction. 3. Fantasy.] I. Title.
PZ7.F598284Ran 2011
[Fic]—dc23
2011024267

Puffin Books ISBN 978-0-14-242195-6

Printed in the United States of America

This book is dedicated to those Ranger fans around the world
who have made the last six years so enjoyable for me.
The stories that follow are in response to questions
you have asked me over the years.

Thank you all.

Contents

FOREWORD

Redman County
The Republic of Aralan States
(formerly the medieval Kingdom of Araluen)
July 1896

PROFESSOR GILES MACFARLANE GROANED SOFTLY AS HE EASED his aching back. He was getting too old to remain crouched for long periods like this, gently whisking dust away from the excavated ground before him as he sought to release yet another artifact from the earth that had held it captive for so long.

He and his team had come upon this ruined castle several years ago. They had mapped the outline of its triangular main walls—an unusual shape for a castle. The jagged stump of the ancient keep tower stood in the middle of the space they had cleared. The collapsed tower was barely four meters high now. But even in its ruined state, MacFarlane could see that it had been a formidable building.

Their first digging season had been spent determining the outer limits of the building. The following year, they had begun a series of cross trenches, digging down to discover what lay beneath the build-up of earth and rock and detritus that had collected over twelve hundred years.

Now, in the third season, they were down to the fine work, and beginning to unearth the ancient treasures of the dig. A belt buckle here. An arrowhead there. A knife. A cracked ladle. Jewelry whose design and general appearance dated to around the middle of the tenth century in the Common Era.

On one momentous day, they had unearthed a granite plaque, carved with the likeness of a tusked boar. It was that piece that had identified the castle beyond doubt.

"This was Castle Redmont," MacFarlane had told his hushed assistants.

Castle Redmont. Contemporary of the fabled Castle Araluen. Seat of Baron Arald, known as one of the legendary King Duncan's staunchest retainers. If Redmont had really existed, then surely all the tales of its people might have a basis in fact. Perhaps, MacFarlane thought, hoping beyond hope, he would find proof that the mysterious Rangers of Araluen had actually existed. It would be a staggeringly significant discovery.

But as this season had progressed and the trenches had been dug deeper still, there had been no find as important as that first one. MacFarlane and his people had to be content with the normal fare of excavations—nondescript metal tools and ornaments, pottery shards and remnants of cooking vessels.

They searched and dug and brushed, hoping every day that they would discover their personal Holy Grail. But as the summer digging season passed, MacFarlane had begun to lose hope. For this year, at least.

"Professor! Professor!"

He stood, rubbing his back again, as he heard his name being called. One of the young volunteers from the university who augmented his paid staff was running through the excavation, waving as she saw him. He frowned. An archaeological dig was no place to be moving so recklessly. A slight misstep could ruin weeks of patient work. Then he recognized her as Audrey, one of his favorites, and his expression softened. She was young. The young were often reckless.

She drew level with him and stood, shoulders heaving, as she recovered her breath.

"Well, Audrey, what is it?" he said, after giving her a little time.

Still panting, she pointed down the hill toward the River Tarb.

"Across the river," she said. "Among a tangle of trees and bushes. We've found the outline of an ancient cabin."

He shrugged, not excited by this revelation. "There was a village down there," he said. "It's not surprising." But Audrey was shaking her head and grasped his arm to lead him down the hill.

"It's way outside the village limits," she said. "It was on its own. You must come and see it!"

MacFarlane hesitated. It would be a long walk downhill, and an even longer one back up. Then he shrugged mentally. Enthusiasm like Audrey's should be encouraged, he thought, not stifled. He allowed the girl to lead him down the rough, zigzag path.

They crossed the old bridge that spanned the river. Never one to miss a chance to teach, he indicated to the girl how the supports at either end were much older than the middle span.

"The middle section is much newer," he said. "These bridges were designed so that the center span could be removed or destroyed in the event of an attack."

Normally, Audrey would have hung on his every word. The professor was a personal hero for her. But today she was in a fever of excitement to show him her find.

"Yes, yes," she said distractedly, urging him on. He smiled indulgently as she tugged at his sleeve, leading him away from the remains of the ancient village. The going became tougher as they entered the forest and had to make their way along a narrow path, through the close-growing large trees and unkempt undergrowth. Finally, Audrey turned off the path and, bending double, forced a way through a tangle of vines and creepers. MacFarlane followed awkwardly, then stood in some amazement as he found himself in a small clearing, surrounded by ancient oaks and more modern dogwood.

"How on earth did you find this?" he asked.

Audrey blushed. "Oh . . . I . . . er . . . needed a little privacy . . . you know," she said awkwardly.

He nodded, waving a hand. "Say no more."

She led him forward, and looking where she pointed, his practiced eye could see the unmistakable outline of a small hut or cabin. Most of the structure had rotted away, of course. But there were still a few vestiges of the upright columns remaining.

"Oak," he said. "It'll last for centuries."

The outlines of the rooms and dividing walls could still be made out—faint signs imprinted into the ground itself over the centuries, even though the original structure was long gone. And the flattened, level ground of the interior floor was all too obvious.

"There may have been a stable at the rear," she said, her voice hushed in this ancient place. "I found a few metal pieces—bits and what might have been harness buckles. And the remains of a bucket."

MacFarlane turned in a slow circle, studying the dim outline of the building.

"It's a different layout to the village houses," he said, almost to himself. "Completely different."

He took a couple of steps, intent on making a rough measurement of the cabin's dimensions, then stopped suddenly.

"Did you hear that?"

Audrey nodded, eyes wide. "Your last step. It sounded as if the ground were hollow."

They dropped to their knees together and scrabbled at the dirt and leaf mold. Audrey rapped her knuckles on the ground and again they heard the sound of a hollow space beneath. MacFarlane never moved anywhere without a small hand spade in his belt. He took it now and began tossing the earth aside. Then the blade thumped against something solid—solid, but with a certain give in it.

Working quickly, testing the ground for that hollow sound continually as he went, he cleared a rectangular space, some forty centimeters by fifty. Audrey leaned forward and brushed the remaining earth from the center. They found themselves looking at an ancient, desiccated timber panel. A brass ring was set in one side and Mac-Farlane gently eased the spade under it, lifting it.

The panel came with it, splintering and half disintegrating, to reveal a stone-lined space underneath.

A space that contained an ancient wood-and-brass chest.

Once more, the professor used the spade to edge the lid of the chest open. Audrey put a hand on his to stop him.

"Should we be doing this?" she asked. She knew MacFarlane would normally never disturb an artifact like this without taking the utmost care to preserve it from damage.

He met her gaze.

"No," he said. "But I'm not waiting any longer."

The lid opened with surprising ease. Brass hinges, he thought. If they had been iron, they would have fallen to powdery rust long ago. Gently, barely containing his enthusiasm, he lifted it back and peered inside.

The chest was full of pages of manuscripts—written on parchment or vellum that was now brittle and delicate. Gently, he eased one sheet up. The edges crumbled but the center remained intact. He leaned forward, craning to read the closely written words on the page. Carefully, he studied other pages, handling the brittle manuscript pages with expert care, making out names, places, events.

Then he gently replaced the sheets and leaned back on his haunches, his eyes glistening with excitement.

"Audrey," he said, "do you know what we've found?"

She shook her head. Obviously, from his reaction, this was something major. No, she thought, more than that, something *unprecedented*.

"What is it?" she asked.

MacFarlane threw back his head and laughed, still unwilling to believe it.

"We never knew what had become of them," he said, and when she cocked her head in an unspoken question, he explained further.

"The Rangers. Halt, Will Treaty and the others. The chronicles and the legends only take us as far as the point where they returned from their voyage to Nihon-Ja. But now we have these."

"But what are they, Professor?"

MacFarlane laughed aloud. "They're the rest of the tale, my girl! We've found the Lost Stories of Araluen!"

DEATH OF A HERO

1

It had been a long, hard three days.

Will had been on a tour of the villages surrounding Castle Redmont. It was something he did on a regular basis, keeping in touch with the villagers and their headmen, keeping track of the everyday goings-on. Sometimes, he had learned, little pieces of gossip, seemingly trivial at the time, could become useful in heading off future trouble and friction within the fief.

It was part of being a Ranger. Information, no matter how unimportant it might seem at first glance, was a Ranger's lifeblood.

Now, late in the afternoon, as he rode wearily up to the cabin set among the trees, he was surprised to see lights in the windows and the silhouette of someone sitting on the small verandah.

Surprise turned to pleasure when he recognized Halt. These days Will's mentor was an infrequent visitor to the cabin, spending most of his time in the rooms provided for him and Lady Pauline in the castle.

Will swung down from the saddle and stretched his tired muscles gratefully.

"Hullo," he said. "What brings you here? I hope you've got the coffee on."

"Coffee's ready," Halt replied. "Tend to your horse and then join me. I need to talk to you." His voice sounded strained.

Curiosity piqued, Will led Tug to the stable behind the cabin, unharnessed him, rubbed him down and set out feed and fresh water. The little horse butted his shoulder gratefully. He patted Tug's neck, then headed back to the cabin.

Halt was still on the verandah. He had set out two cups of hot coffee on a small side table and Will sat in one of the wood-and-canvas chairs and sipped gratefully at the refreshing brew. He felt the warmth of it flowing through his chilled, stiff muscles. Winter was coming on and the wind had been cold and cutting all day.

He gazed at Halt. The gray-bearded Ranger seemed strangely ill at ease. And despite his claim that he needed to talk to Will, once the usual greetings were out of the way, he seemed almost reluctant to begin the conversation.

"You had something to tell me?" Will prompted.

Halt shifted uncomfortably in his seat. Then, with an obvious effort, he plunged in.

"There's something you should know," he said. "Something I probably should have told you long ago. It's just . . . the time never seemed right."

Will's curiosity grew. He had never seen Halt in such an uncertain mood. He waited, giving his mentor time to settle his thoughts.

"Pauline thinks it's time I told you," Halt said. "So does Arald. They've both known about it for some time. So maybe I should just . . . get on with it."

"Is it something bad?" Will asked, and Halt looked directly at him for the first time in several minutes.

"I'm not sure," he said. "You might think so."

For a moment, Will wondered if he wanted to hear it, whatever it might be. Then, seeing the discomfort on Halt's face, he realized that, good or bad, it was something that his teacher had to get off his chest. He gestured for Halt to continue.

Halt paused for a few more seconds, then he began.

"I suppose it starts after the final battle against Morgarath's forces, at Hackham Heath. They'd been retreating for several days. Then they stopped and made a stand. We'd broken their main attack and we were forcing them back. But they were rallying on the right, where they'd found a weak point in our line . . ."

2

South of Hackham Heath

"Sire! The right flank is in trouble!"

Duncan, the young King of Araluen, heard the herald's shout above the terrible din of battle. The clash of weapons and shields, the screaming and sobbing of the wounded and dying, the shouted orders of commanders rallying their troops and the involuntary, inarticulate cries of the soldiers themselves as they cut and stabbed and shoved against the implacable enemy formed an almost deafening matrix of sound around him.

Duncan thrust once more at the snarling Wargal before him, felt the sword go home and saw the snarl change to a puzzled frown as the creature realized it was already dead. Then he stepped back, disengaging himself from the immediate battle—physically and mentally.

A young knight from the Araluen Battleschool quickly took his place in the line, his sword already swinging in a murderous arc as he stepped forward, cutting through the Wargal front rank, like a scythe through long grass.

Duncan rested for a moment, leaning on his sword, breathing heavily. He shook his head to clear it.

"Sire! The right flank—" the herald began again, but Duncan waved a hand to stop him.

"I heard you," he said.

It was three days since the battle at Hackham Heath, where Morgarath's army had been routed by a surprise attack from their rear, led by the Ranger Halt. The enemy were in full retreat. By rights, Morgarath should have surrendered. His continued resistance was simply costing more and more casualties to both sides. But the rebellious lord was never concerned with preserving lives. He knew he was defeated, but still he wanted to inflict as many casualties as possible on Duncan and his men. If they were to be victorious, he would make them pay dearly for their victory.

As for his own forces, he cared little for their losses. They were nothing more than tools to him and he was willing to keep throwing them against the royal army, sacrificing hundreds of troops but causing hundreds of casualties in the process.

So for three days, he had retreated to the southeast, turning where the terrain favored him to fight a series of savage and costly battles. He had picked the spot for this latest stand well. It was a narrow plain set between two steep hills, and recent rain had softened the ground so that Duncan could not deploy his cavalry. It was up to the infantry to throw themselves against the Wargals in hard, slogging, desperate fighting.

And always lurking in the back of Duncan's mind was that one mistake from him, one lucky throw of the dice for Morgarath, could see the Wargal army gain the initiative once more. Fortune in battle was a fickle mistress and the war that Duncan had hoped was ended at Hackham Heath was still there to be won—or lost by a careless order or an ill-considered maneuver.

Momentum, Duncan thought. It was all-important in a situation like this. It was vital to maintain it. Keep moving forward. Keep driving them back. Hesitate, even for a few minutes, and the ascendancy could revert to the enemy.

He glanced to his left. The flank on that side, predominantly troops from Norgate and Whitby, reinforced by troops from some of the smaller fiefs, was forging ahead strongly. In the center, the armies from Araluen and Redmont were having similar success. That was to be expected. They were the four largest fiefs in the Kingdom, the backbone of Duncan's army. Their knights and men-at-arms were the best trained and disciplined.

But the right flank had always been a potential weakness. It was formed from a conglomerate of Seacliff, Aspienne and Culway fiefs, and because the three fiefs were all about the same size, there was no clear leader among them. Knowing this, Duncan had appointed Battlemaster Norman of Aspienne Fief as the overall commander. Norman was an experienced leader, most capable of melding such a disparate force together.

As if he were reading the King's thoughts, the herald spoke again.

"Battlemaster Norman is dying, sire. A Wargal burst through the lines and speared him. Norman has been taken to the rear, but I doubt he has long to live. Battlemasters Patrick and Marat are unsure what to do next, and Morgarath has taken advantage of the fact."

Of course, thought Duncan, Morgarath would have recognized the banners of the smaller fiefs on that flank and guessed at the possible confusion that might result if the commander were put out of action. Once Norman was down, the rebel commander had undoubtedly sent one of his elite companies of shock troops to attack the right flank.

Momentum again, Duncan thought. Only this time it was working against him. He peered keenly toward the fighting on the right flank. He could see the line had stopped moving forward, saw his men take the first hesitant step backward. He needed a commander to take charge there and he needed him fast. Someone who wouldn't hesitate. Someone with the force of personality to rally the troops and get them going forward once more.

He glanced around him. Arald of Redmont would have been his choice. But Arald was being tended by the healers. A crossbow quarrel had hit him in the leg and he was out of action for the rest of the battle. Arald's young Battlemaster, Rodney, had taken his place and was fighting furiously, urging the Araluen forces forward. He couldn't be spared.

"They need a leader . . . ," Duncan said to himself.

"I'll go." A calm voice spoke from behind him.

Duncan spun around and found himself looking into the steady, dark eyes of Halt, the Ranger. The dark black beard and untrimmed hair hid most of his features, but those eyes held a look of steadiness and determination. This was not a man who would bicker over command or dither over what had to be done. He would act.

Duncan nodded. "Go on then, Halt. Get them moving forward again or we're lost. Tell Patrick and Marat—"

He got no further. Halt smiled grimly. "Oh, I'll tell them, all right," he said. Then he swung up onto the small shaggy horse that was standing by him and galloped away toward the right flank.

3

ABELARD'S HOOVES THUNDERED DULLY ON THE SOFT TURF AS they drew near to the trouble spot. Now that he was closer, Halt could see that the Wargal attack was being spearheaded by one of Morgarath's special units. They were all larger than normal, selected for size and strength and savagery.

And they cared nothing for their own losses as they battered their way forward. Maces, axes and heavy two-handed swords rose and fell and swept in horizontal arcs.

Men from the Araluen army fell before them as they advanced in a solid wedge shape.

Halt was still forty meters away and he knew he would arrive too late. The Araluen line had bowed backward before the onslaught. Any second now it would crumble unless he acted.

He reined Abelard to a sliding stop.

"Steady," he said, and the little horse stood rock-still for him, disregarding the terrifying cacophony of battle and the awful, metallic smell of fresh blood.

Halt unslung his bow and stood in his stirrups. Then he began to shoot. He had three arrows in the air before the first struck the Wargal leading the attacking wedge. Halt had chosen his most powerful bow for the battle, one with a ninety-pound draw weight at full extension. Forty meters was point-blank range for such a weapon. The heavy, black-shafted arrow slammed through the beast's corselet of toughened leather and bronze plates and dropped him where he stood. Then, in rapid succession, the next two arrows struck home and two more Wargals died. Then more and more arrows arrived, each with a deadly *hiss-thud*, as Halt emptied his quiver in a devastating display of accuracy.

He aimed for the Wargals at the head of the wedge, so that as they fell they impeded the progress of those behind them. It was the sort of shooting no ordinary archer would attempt. If he missed, he might well send his arrows into the backs of the Araluen soldiers facing the Wargals.

But Halt was no ordinary archer. He didn't miss.

Out of arrows, he urged Abelard forward once more. As he reached the rear of the line, he dropped from the saddle and ran to join the struggling troops. On the way, he stopped, tossed his cloak to one side and picked up a round shield lying discarded in the grass—the Ranger two-knife defense was no use against a Wargal's heavy weapons. He hesitated a second, looking at a long sword that lay beside a dead knight's outstretched hand. But it was a weapon he was unfamiliar with and he discarded the notion of using it. He was used to his saxe knife, and its heavy, razor-sharp blade would be perfect for close fighting. He drew the saxe now as he ran forward, forcing his way between the soldiers.

"Come on!" he shouted. "Follow me! Push them back!"

The soldiers parted before him until he was at the front of the line and facing a huge, snarling Wargal squad leader. The brute was only a little taller than Halt but was massive in the shoulders and chest and probably weighed twice as much as he did. Halt saw the red mouth open as the Wargal bared his fangs at this new enemy. A spiked mace swung horizontally at him and he ducked beneath it, instantly coming upright and driving forward with the saxe, sinking it deep into the beast's ribs.

He saw a sword coming from the left, blocked it with the shield, then kicked the huge Wargal off the point of his saxe, sending the dying monster sprawling.

"Come on!" he shouted again, slashing his blade across another Wargal's throat and springing forward. He dodged another sword and stabbed twice at a Wargal facing him, buffeting it aside with the shield as it doubled over in agony. The Wargals were immensely powerful. But they were clumsy, and Halt had the speed and reflexes of a snake. He ducked and weaved and cut and stabbed, carving a path forward. And now he sensed someone moving up behind him, heard another voice echoing his cry.

"Come on! Forward! Push them back."

The hesitation in the Wargals' attack caused by Halt's volley of arrows, and his sudden appearance as he darted forward and took the fight to the enemy, gave the Araluen soldiers new heart. They began to follow Halt and his unidentified companion, moving forward once more.

Halt turned momentarily to glance back. He saw a stockily built sergeant a pace behind him and to his right, armed with a spear. As Halt looked, the sergeant thrust the spear forward, skewering a Wargal so that it screeched in agony. The man grinned at him.

"Keep going, Ranger! You're getting in my way!"

Behind him, others were following, forming their own wedge now and driving deeper and deeper into the Wargal line.

Halt faced the front once more. A Wargal came at him, ax drawn back for a killing blow. The sergeant's spear shot forward over Halt's shoulder, taking the Wargal in the throat and stopping it dead.

"Thanks!" Halt called, without looking. Two more Wargals were coming at him. He sidestepped the sword thrust of the first, felt his foot turn as he trod on the arm of a dead enemy, and tumbled sideways to the ground.

The second Wargal had swung a club at him and the stumble probably saved his life. The club struck only a glancing blow instead of shattering his skull with a direct hit. But it stunned him and he hit the ground, losing his grip on the saxe knife. He tried to rise but was hampered by the shield on his left arm. Dully, he realized that the Wargal with the club was standing on the shield, preventing his rising. He looked up, still dazed by the glancing blow, and saw the club go up again.

So, this is it, he thought. He wondered why he felt such a stolid acceptance of his own death. Maybe the blow to the head had slowed him down. He watched, waiting calmly, fatalistically, for the club to descend.

Then a flicker of light blazed over him, gleaming off a spearhead that buried itself in the Wargal's chest. The force behind the spear thrust shoved the creature backward. It gave a hoarse screech of pain and fell, passing out of Halt's line of sight. The sergeant jumped nimbly over Halt's fallen form, dragged his spear free of the dead Wargal's body and stood with feet braced wide apart, protecting Halt from further attacks. He thrust again with the spear and another Wargal retreated hastily. Then a battleax smashed down onto the spear shaft, and the heavy iron head went spinning away, leaving the sergeant with nothing more than the two-and-a-half-meter ash spear shaft.

Halt's head swam and his vision blurred. The blow to the head had definitely done him some damage. His limbs were weak and he couldn't find the strength to rise. The scene before him seemed to unfold at a slow, dreamlike pace.

The sergeant took one look at the headless spear, shrugged, then whirled the heavy ash shaft in a circle, smashing it against another Wargal's helmet. Holding the shaft in both hands now, like a quarterstaff, he thrust underarm at a second enemy, driving the end deep into the Wargal's midsection.

"Look out!" Halt's attempted shout of warning was nothing more than a croak. He had seen a third Wargal, crouching low and concealed behind his companions, a jagged-edged sword ready to thrust.

One of the injured Wargals grabbed at the spear shaft, dragging the sergeant off balance, and the sword blade shot forward like a serpent striking. Red blood flowed from the sergeant's side where the sword had taken him. But still he didn't falter. He jerked the spear shaft free of the enemy's grip and, with an overhand action as if he were casting a spear, slammed it straight forward, hitting the Wargal who had wounded him straight between the eyes with the blunt end of the shaft.

The Wargal screamed and fell, throwing his hands to his shattered forehead and dropping the sword as he did so. Instantly, the sergeant seized it, tossing the spear shaft aside. Now he struck left and right with blinding speed and opened great slashing wounds in two more Wargals. One fell where he stood, while the other spun away, blundering into his companions, knocking two of them over. The sergeant parried a short iron spear thrust coming from his right. Another stabbed out from the left and struck him in the thigh. More blood flowed. Yet still he fought on. He killed the Wargal behind the spear with almost contemptuous ease. Then he slashed and cut left and right with the sword, taking a dreadful toll on any enemy who came within its reach. A knife thrust cut him in the side. He ignored it and dispatched the knife wielder with a backhanded slash.

Then Halt saw something he thought he'd never see.

As the bloodstained figure drove forward, sword rising and falling, hacking and cutting and slashing and stabbing, a tide of fear swept over the Wargals.

Morgarath's handpicked shock troops, who up until now had feared nothing short of mounted, armored knights, fell back in terror before the bloodied, death-dealing figure with the sword.

And as they did so, the men of the Araluen army found new heart and swept forward in the wake of the sergeant. He was badly wounded, but he continued fighting until his comrades surged past him, slamming into the demoralized Wargals and screaming in triumph.

For a moment, the sergeant stood in an empty space on the battlefield. Then, as the second rank of Araluen fighters poured past him to reinforce the first, and the Wargal line broke and retreated in total confusion, their hoarse, wordless screams filling the air, his knees gave way and he sagged to the ground.

The noise of the battle moved away from them, receding like a tide, and Halt finally managed to free his arm from the shield, still pinned to the ground by a Wargal's dead body. He tried to rise to his feet, but the effort was beyond him. Instead, he crawled painfully to the fallen sergeant, dragging himself over the sprawled bodies of the Wargals the man had killed.

In spite of his wounds, the sergeant was still breathing, and he turned his head painfully as the Ranger approached. He managed a weak smile.

"We showed them, Ranger, didn't we?"

Halt could barely hear the voice, and his own was a croak as he answered. "That we did. What's your name, sergeant?"

"Daniel."

Halt gripped his forearm. "Hold on, Daniel. The healers will be here soon."

He tried to put as much encouragement into the words as possible. But the sergeant shook his head.

"Too late for me." Suddenly the man's eyes were filled with urgency. He tried to rise but fell back.

"Rest easy," Halt told him, but Daniel raised his head wearily and leaned toward him.

"My wife . . . ," he managed to gasp. "My wife and the baby. Promise me you'll . . ." He coughed and blood rolled down his chin.

"I'll look out for them," Halt told him. "But don't worry. You'll be fine. You'll see them soon."

Daniel nodded and let his head fall back. He took a long, shuddering breath. Then he seemed to relax, and his breathing became easier, as if Halt's promise had lifted an enormous burden from his mind.

Halt heard voices then, and footsteps nearby. Then gentle hands were rolling him over and he found himself looking up at the concerned faces of a pair of medical orderlies who were setting down a litter beside him. He gestured weakly toward Daniel.

"I'm all right," he said. "Take the sergeant first."

The nearest orderly glanced quickly at Daniel, and shook his head.

"Nothing we can do for him," he said. "He's dead."

4

HALT WOKE.

For a few seconds, he wondered where he was. He was lying on his back, staring at the canvas roof of a large pavilion. He could hear people moving quietly nearby, speaking in lowered voices. Somewhere, farther away, a man was moaning. He tried to turn his head but a sudden flash of agony greeted the movement and he grunted in pain.

He raised his hand to his forehead and felt a thick bandage there. Then the memory began to come back to him.

The battle with the Wargals. He remembered that. Remembered the club that had caught him on the side of the head. That must be the cause of the flaring headache he now felt. And he remembered a sergeant. What was his name? David? No! Daniel. Daniel had saved his life.

Then he was overcome with sadness as he remembered the words of the litter bearer. Daniel was dead.

How long had he been here? He remembered that as the medical orderlies had lifted him onto the litter, he had lost consciousness. It seemed that it had happened only minutes ago. He tried to rise and the headache speared him behind the eyes again. Once more, he grunted in pain, and this time a face came into his field of vision, looking down at him.

"You're awake," the orderly said, and smiled encouragingly at him. He reached down and laid a palm on Halt's forehead, testing for fever. Seemingly satisfied that there was none, he touched the bandage lightly, making sure it was still tight.

"How . . . long . . ." Halt's voice was slurred and his throat was thick and dry. The orderly held a cup of cool water to his lips, raised his head carefully and allowed him to drink. The water felt wonderful. He gulped at it and choked, coughing so that water bubbled out of his mouth. The action of coughing set his head aching again and he closed his eyes in pain.

"Still feeling it, I see?" the orderly said. "Well, the healers said there's no serious damage. You just need a few more days' rest to let the headache settle down."

"How long . . . have I been here?"

The orderly pursed his lips. "Let's see. They brought you in the evening before yesterday, so I'd say about thirty-six hours."

Thirty-six hours! He'd lain here asleep for a day and a half! A sudden chill of fear struck through him.

"Did we win?" he said. He remembered that the Wargals had retreated ahead of Daniel's attack, but that might have been a localized event.

The orderly smiled, nodding his head. "Oh yes indeed. Morgarath and his brutes were thoroughly beaten. Someone referred to it as a rout. I hear you had a little to do with that, as a matter of fact?"

He added the last curiously, as if interested to hear more about Halt's battlefield escapades. But the Ranger waved that aside.

"So Morgarath is retreating again?" he asked.

"Yes. The cavalry are pursuing the enemy, of course. But the rest of the army is still here. Not for long, though. They'll be moving out soon."

"Moving out where?"

"Disbanding. The war's over. The men will be going back to their farms and their families. And none too soon."

Farms and families. The words stirred another memory in Halt's mind. Daniel had spoken of a wife and baby. And Halt had promised to help them. But now he realized that he had no idea where they were, and if the army was really disbanding, he might never find them. He sat up without thinking and swung his legs over the side of the bed, then doubled over as the crippling pain hit him. The orderly tried to restrain him.

"Please! Lie still, Ranger! You need to rest."

But Halt seized his forearm and managed to stand, swaying, by the bed. He blinked several times. The pain eased a little. But it was still there.

"I don't have time," he said. "Get me something for this headache. I've got to find out where he lived."

He remembered that the men he had been sent to lead were a mixed group from Seacliff, Aspienne and Culway. The soldiers around him when he forced his way through to the front rank had worn the crest of a black badger on their tunics. He had seen the same crest on Daniel's. He had no idea what group marched under that banner, so he headed for the command tent, and the King's Battlemaster.

When he reached the command center, he found the Battlemaster gone. Of course, he was leading the pursuit that was hounding Morgarath and the Wargals back to the southeast corner of the kingdom. But his secretary was still there, making notes as to casualties, replacements and promotions. He glanced up as Halt entered, and smiled warmly. The entire army had heard of Halt's feats during the battle.

"Good morning, Ranger," he said. Then he noticed the blood-stained bandage and saw how Halt swayed as he entered the tent, reaching out to steady himself against the tabletop where the secretary sat.

"Are you all right?" he said anxiously. He rose and hurried to find a bench for Halt. The Ranger dropped onto it gratefully. He blinked several times. His vision was still blurry. He hoped that was only temporary. He couldn't imagine shooting with such poor vision.

"Just a headache," he said. "I need some information. I took command of troops on the right wing in the final stages of the battle—"

"Indeed you did!" the secretary said warmly. "The whole army has heard about it."

"There was a soldier. A sergeant named Daniel. He actually led the charge when I was knocked down. Did anyone mention his full name, or would anyone have a record of where he lived?"

But the clerk was shaking his head. "I don't keep the full roster. Each individual force looks after that for their own men. What unit did he belong to?"

"I'm not sure. They wore a black badger as their crest."

The clerk's eyes narrowed in concentration for a few seconds, then his expression cleared. "A black badger? That'd be Captain Stanton's company, from Aspienne Fief. They're camped over to the north, on a small hill. Stanton was badly wounded before you rallied his men. He's been invalided back to Castle Aspienne. But his sergeant major should be able to help you."

"Thanks for your help." Halt left the tent. He paused for a moment, looking to the north. On a low hill several hundred meters away, he could see a group of tents clustered around a banner. It was too far to make out the device on the flag, but he could see that it was black in color. He headed toward the tents.

As was the custom, the banner marked the position of the commanding officer's tent. As Halt drew closer, he could see that he had been right. The device on the flag was a black badger. He paused at the open entrance. The command tent was larger than the simple four-man units that surrounded it. The commander and his staff worked here, so it was used as a company office. At the rear, a separate section was screened off, forming the captain's living quarters. Now, of course, that would be vacant. But a burly figure was sitting at a table in the front section, frowning over sheets of paper. He was an older man, somewhat grizzled and with an unmistakable look of experience and authority—undoubtedly the sergeant major the clerk had mentioned. He looked up as Halt stepped into the tent, taking in the Ranger cloak and the bandage around his head.

"You look as if you've been in the wars," he said, grinning. Halt allowed himself a faint smile.

"Just one. Same one you've been in. I'm trying to find a home address for one of your men. A sergeant by the name of Daniel."

The grin faded and the sergeant major shook his head sadly. "Daniel? He was a good man. We lost him in the final battle, I'm afraid."

"I know. He saved my life just before he died."

The older man regarded Halt with increased interest. "Oh," he said, "you're that Ranger, are you?" He rose from behind the table and offered his hand. "It's an honor to meet you. My name's Griff."

Halt shifted uncomfortably. He disliked being the center of attention. It wasn't his way. He preferred to move unobtrusively through life, going unnoticed wherever possible. But he shook the man's hand. "I'm called Halt," he said.

Griff waved him to a seat and sat down himself once more. He pursed his lips thoughtfully.

"Not sure I can tell you too much. Everything was pretty rushed when we mobilized the army, and Daniel was new to the fief. He and his wife had moved from Norgate not long before the war began." He indicated the piles of paper and scrolls on the table that was serving as a desk. "We didn't get time to put down all the men's details before we had to march out. I'm trying to catch up on it now."

"Can you tell me anything about him?" Halt asked.

"He had a farm, I believe, somewhere in the southeast part of Aspienne. But where it might be, I have no idea."

"Did he have any friends in the company who might know?"

The sergeant major was shaking his head before Halt even finished the question.

"He may have. Although as a sergeant he would have kept a little separate from the other men. You could ask around. He had command of the sixth squad. You'll find them one row over and halfway down."

"I'm obliged," Halt said. He rose to his feet, wincing once more as the pain lanced through his forehead. He put a hand on the table to steady himself and Griff looked at him with some concern.

"Should you be up and around? You don't look so good."

Halt shook his head—and immediately wished he hadn't. "I'll be fine," he said. "Just a bit of a knock. I'm better off in the fresh air than in a stuffy healer's tent."

"That's true." Griff looked back at the forms and papers on his desk with a degree of disappointment, as if he'd been hoping they'd fill themselves in while he talked. "Well . . . sorry I can't be of more help."

Halt waved a hand in acknowledgment. "Every little bit of information helps," he said.

He strolled down the neat tent lines, cutting through between two tents to reach the next row across. About ten meters farther down, he saw a placard mounted on top of a spear shaft with the numeral 6 on it. He looked down the next five tents and there was a similar marker, this time bearing the number 7. Five tents, four men to each, that made twenty men in the squad. Assuming they had all survived, which he knew they hadn't. Three soldiers were lounging in the sun outside the first tent. They looked up as his shadow fell across them. There was a hint of suspicion in their eyes, but since Crowley and he had re-formed the Ranger Corps, Halt was becoming used to that. Officers and sergeant majors might value the skills Rangers brought to the army, but the rank-and-file soldiers tended to be ill at ease around the gray-and-green-clad figures. He knew there were wild rumors circulating that Rangers practiced sorcery.

"Good morning," he said evenly.

The men nodded, craning their necks to look up at him. They were seated on low stools. One was patching a ripped jerkin, a second was whittling a stick with a knife and the third was chewing slowly on a piece of dried beef. From where Halt stood, it looked as if the beef was winning the struggle. Halt indicated a spare stool, a few feet away.

"Mind if I join you for a few minutes?" he asked.

The man patching his jerkin nodded. "Why not?" he said, his tone neither welcoming nor dismissive.

His companion with the beef jerky was staring at Halt, a frown of recognition on his face. "I know you," he said thoughtfully, trying to place the memory. Then it came to him. "You were at the battle!" he said. "We were being driven back and suddenly you were there, shoving forward and slashing away at the Wargals and yelling at us to follow you. You did an outstanding job. Outstanding!" He turned to the others. "Did you see him? First of all, he dropped at least a dozen of them with his bow, then he darted in among them, slashing and stabbing. And look at him! He's barely bigger than a boy."

Halt raised an eyebrow at that. He wasn't the largest of men, but he knew the soldier was stretching it a little. However, he could see that no insult was intended, so he let the comment pass.

"Your sergeant gave me a hand," he said, and the man nodded vigorously.

"He did! He took them on when you went down. Must have killed a dozen of them too!"

Halt smiled quietly at that. The man was inclined to exaggerate. "He did a great job," he agreed.

The jerky chewer turned to his friends. "Did you see the sarge?"

Both of them shook their heads.

"We were farther over, on the right," the jerkin patcher replied. "All we saw was that the line was about to break and run, then it started to move forward again. Then the Wargals were running instead."

But the question had been rhetorical and the beef chewer was keen to continue his story.

"He did four or five of them with his spear. Then one of them chopped the head off it and he used it like a quarterstaff, spinning it around, knocking them over like ninepins. Then he grabbed a sword and killed eight or nine of them before they got him." He looked to Halt for confirmation. "You saw it, Ranger! How many do you reckon he killed?"

"At least eight," Halt said. He saw no reason to contradict the man. The atmosphere was suddenly a lot more welcoming than it had been at first. "I wanted some information about him," he said. "Any idea where he lived?"

He was disappointed to see the three faces cloud over in a now familiar expression of uncertainty.

"Sorry," said the man who had been extolling Daniel's deeds and courage. "He was new to the unit and the area. Got promoted quickly."

"That's right," said one of the others, laying aside the patched jerkin. "The captain liked the look of him. Made him a sergeant almost immediately. Apparently, he'd had some military experience in Norgate before he came to Aspienne."

"He was promoted so quickly, we didn't really have time to get to know him," said the man who had been whittling. "I think I heard him mention a farm somewhere . . ." He trailed off, unsure of his facts. There was an awkward silence. Halt made a move to rise from the stool, thinking that once again his efforts to trace Daniel's family were doomed to failure. The first man who had spoken, the beef jerky chewer, seemed to come to a decision.

"You could try Kord and Jerrel," he said. "They might have an idea."

"If they'd tell you," the man with the repaired jerkin put in.

Halt looked from one to the other. "I take it you're not fond of these two?"

The three men exchanged glances. Then the one who had suggested the two names answered him.

"They're a pair of liars and cheats. They run a dice game and they tried to make a friend of Daniel initially, playing up to him and inviting him to play. My guess is they were letting him win at dice to get in his good books. But he saw through their scheme before long and they found themselves doing their fair share of fatigue duties. So they dropped him."

"What makes you think they'd know where he lived?" Halt asked, and again there was an awkward pause. Finally, the whittler spoke.

"They always wanted to know where everyone lived. Always asking you questions about where you came from, what you did back home. Can't prove anything, but I reckon they were keeping a record, planning to go back after the war and rob people."

"Particularly those who'd been killed in battle," the jerkin patcher said heavily. "They'd know the families would be easy prey. It's the sort of thing they'd do, all right. They probably know where to find the sergeant's farm."

"The trick will be getting them to tell you," the beef jerky chewer said, and the others nodded. Halt looked around the small circle of faces, seeing the distaste for the two vultures called Kord and Jerrel.

"How would I get to meet these two?" he asked.

The jerkin patcher raised an eyebrow.

"Play dice with them," he said. "But be prepared to lose."

5

Private Jerrel of the Black Badger company was working on a pair of dice. He'd finished the first one and he was almost done with the second. He was filing off two of the sharp corners on the die, rounding them slightly so that they would tend to roll to a pre-selected point, showing a score of six more often than sheer chance would allow. It wasn't as reliable as his alternative method of fixing a pair of dice. That involved carefully inserting weights to make it fall with the selected side faceup. But sanding the corners increased his chance of a winning roll.

In his pocket, he had a pair of counterweighted dice, carefully doctored to show scores of one and two. But weighting dice was a tricky business. It took a long time to remove all signs that something had been inserted in the little cubes. His other pair had been confiscated some days previously by a passing officer. Now he had to resort to rounding the corners to replace them. You needed two pairs of doctored dice to fleece a new victim. You used one pair to get him interested, letting him win the first few rolls. Then, when he thought his luck was in, you suggested raising the stakes. And when he agreed, you switched the dice so he'd roll a losing number.

A shadow fell across the entrance to the tent and Jerrel hastily shoved the die and the small file under a blanket. The entrance to the tent was blocked for a moment as a man entered. Jerrel looked up, frowning. The newcomer carried a kit bag and a sheathed sword and sword belt. He was wearing a soldier's uniform with a black badger on the left breast. He looked around the interior of the tent, saw an empty bunk and dropped his belongings on it.

"Who the devil are you?" Kord asked. He'd been lying back on his own bunk on the opposite side of the tent and the displeasure was obvious in his voice. He and Jerrel had enjoyed having the tent to themselves. Their four tent mates had been killed or wounded in the battle. Now, it seemed, they had a new man joining them.

"Name's Arratay," the newcomer said. "I've been transferred from second squad. Sergeant major said for me to bunk in here."

He was a short man, slightly built but with powerful shoulders and a deep chest. His beard and hair were ragged and unkempt. He had a grubby bandage wound around his head. Above it, the hair was black and the eyes were dark and piercing. Like a bird of prey, Jerrel thought. Then he smirked at the idea. It was more likely that the stranger would become prey for him and Kord—once he had a chance to finish working on that pair of dice. Even so, he didn't want the stranger in the tent with them.

"Find somewhere else to bunk," Jerrel said shortly. "We're full here."

"There's only two of you," Arratay said reasonably, looking around the tent.

"You heard him," Kord said. "Now get out of here."

Arratay shrugged. "If you say so . . ."

"I do," Kord said. "So get out."

Shrugging, the newcomer picked up his kit and left the tent. Jerrel smiled at Kord. That had been easy, he thought. Then his face darkened as he heard a loud voice outside the tent.

"You there! A-ratty—or whatever you call yourself! Where d'you think you're going? I told you to bunk in tent forty-three, didn't I?"

"The tent's full, sergeant major," Arratay replied.

"The blazes it is!" Kord and Jerrel exchanged exasperated glances as they heard heavy footsteps approaching. Then the tent flap was thrown back and the bulky frame of Sergeant Major Griff filled the entrance.

"My aunty's mustache it's full! Get in here!" He glared at the two occupants. "You two make room!" he bellowed.

"Yes, sar'major," Jerrel said sullenly. Kord managed a grunt in reply. As Arratay reentered the tent, Griff stepped in front of him to bar his way, his hands on his hips in an aggressive posture.

"As for you, A-ratty, you can report to the cookhouse and scrub rubbish bins and cook pots for the rest of the day. That might remind you next time to do as I tell you!"

"Yes, sar'major," the small man said. His eyes were down, not meeting the temporary commander's. But as Griff stalked out of the room, Arratay made an insulting gesture toward his back. Then he turned, shrugging, to Jerrel and Kord. "Sorry about that," he said.

They exchanged a look, then Jerrel stood and took Arratay's pack, placing it on an empty bunk.

"Can't be helped. Griff can be a real pain. Better get along to the cookhouse or he'll be at you again." He caught Kord's eye. As soon as Arratay had gone, they'd go through his kit to see if there was anything worth stealing. Kord nodded unobtrusively. The same thought was going through his mind.

Arratay sighed and turned to go. As he reached the entrance, Kord called after him, "When you've finished your work detail, maybe you'd like a little game of dice?"

Arratay smiled at them. "That sounds like fun," he said.

. . .

Kord threw up his hands in mock exasperation.

"Another winning throw! Where does your luck come from, Arratay?"

The small trooper grinned happily as he raked in his earnings. He'd thrown three winning scores in a row and now there was a respectable pile of coins on the low table where the three of them were seated.

"Just my lucky day, I suppose," he said, pushing forward a new wager and shaking the dice in their cup. The bone cubes rattled together, then he cast them onto the table.

"Double six again!" Jerrel said. "I don't believe it!" He looked at Kord. "I think we've got a professional in the tent." Kord nodded gloomily, but Arratay merely laughed.

"Not me, boys. It's just clean living and a clear conscience. Want to raise the stakes?" He said it casually, but he noticed the quick, furtive look that passed between the two men.

Kord agreed, after a brief show of reluctance. "Well, I might be crazy, but why not? It'll give us a chance to win some of our money back."

"Or I'll clean you out sooner." Arratay smiled. He put another bet forward, waited till they matched it, then rolled again. Eleven this time, but still an automatic winner.

"Can't you roll anything but fives and sixes?" Jerrel said.

"Not when I'm running hot." Arratay smiled again, but his eyes narrowed as this time, instead of letting him reclaim the dice, Kord picked them up and handed them to him. He's made the switch, Halt thought. He took the dice, placed them in the cup, shook them and rolled.

The other two gave an ironic cheer as the dice turned faceup to show a two and a one.

"Three!" said Jerrel. "And about time!"

It was a simple game. Eleven and twelve were automatic winners. Two and three were losers. Any other score didn't count. The gambler simply threw again until he won or lost. Halt grimaced as the others scooped in the money he'd bet. The dice passed to Jerrel and he threw a six. Then a four, then a two. Halt won back a small fraction of what he had lost on his last throw. Kord took the dice and fumbled as he placed them in the cup.

He's switched them again, Halt thought. And sure enough, Kord threw an eleven, then a twelve, winning two small hands, before switching the dice once more so that he lost, then handing the dice on to Halt. In the process of handing them over, he switched them again for the winning dice. The two cheats didn't want Arratay, as they thought he was called, losing enthusiasm too soon. The game went on, Halt winning some hands, losing others, but generally staying just ahead of breaking even.

The two cheats kept plying him with wine, which he surreptitiously managed to empty into an old boot when they weren't watching. But he pretended to become more and more affected by the drink, slurring his words and laughing foolishly when he won.

"Big day tomorrow," he said after they had been playing for some time. "We're moving out early and heading south."

His two companions reacted with surprise at that.

"South?" said Kord. "Why south? We're supposed to head home and disband."

Halt shook his head and peered at them owlishly. "Not anymore. Not anymore," he said, tapping the side of his nose with his forefinger. "The Wargals are putting up a stiffer resistance than expected. Morgarath has them under firm control again and Duncan needs extra men. We're them," he added after a pause.

He could see that this news had the effect he'd desired. Kord and Jerrel exchanged a glance. Then Jerrel questioned him further.

"Where'd you hear this?" he asked.

Halt jerked a thumb over his shoulder in the general direction of the administration section of the camp.

"At the cookhouse," he said. "The cooks had taken delivery of extra rations to prepare for us."

Now the two cheats looked thoroughly concerned. Cookhouse rumors were the source of much intelligence among the rank and file. And they had a reputation for accuracy. Halt, of course, had heard no such rumors. But he hoped that the thought of an imminent departure for the south might force Kord and Jerrel's hand. If they were planning to rob Daniel's farm, this might precipitate things.

He leaned forward, peering with bleary eyes at the table.

"Now where are those dice?" he asked. "It's my throw again."

"Here you are," Kord said, passing him the dice and throwing cup. He had just lost the last throw and it was Halt's turn again. Halt was reasonably sure that he'd been handed the losing dice. His suspicions were confirmed by Jerrel's next words.

"It's getting late," he said. "Let's put it all on one last big pot. What do you say?"

Kord pretended to look doubtful. "It's up to Arratay."

Halt shrugged. "Why not?" he said. "I feel my luck's coming back."

They all shoved their remaining money into the center of the table. Halt reached for his tankard and took a deep swig—the biggest he'd had all night. Then, as he clumsily set the tankard down, he spilled the remaining wine on the table, flicking it toward Jerrel so that a red tide flowed across the rough wood and into his lap. Jerrel sprang backward with a curse.

"Look out!" he said.

"Sorry. Sorry," Halt replied thickly. But in the confusion, he'd switched the losing dice for another pair that he'd had in his jerkin pocket. He'd prepared them that afternoon while he was supposed to be at the cookhouse, and they were shaved so that they would show a twelve at each throw.

He shook them, muttering to them as he did so, then spilled them out onto the table.

"Bad lu—" began Kord, already reaching for the money. Then he stopped as he saw two sixes gleaming up at him, like two sets of teeth in two tiny skulls.

"How did you . . . ?" Jerrel stopped as he realized he'd give the game away if he went any further. Arratay might be drunk. But he wasn't that drunk.

Halt grinned foolishly at the dice, and scooped them up. "Lucky dice!" he said. "I love these dice!"

He pretended to kiss them noisily, and switched them once more for the losing pair he'd been handed originally. That done, he slipped his own dice into his pocket and dropped the others back onto the table as he began to rake in his winnings.

"No hard feelings, boys," he said. "I'll give you a chance for revenge tomorrow."

"Yes. Of course. Tomorrow," Kord said. But his tone told Halt that there would be no game the next night. And there'd be no sign of Kord or Jerrel, either.

Half an hour later, Halt lay on his back, breathing heavily and noisily through his mouth as he feigned sleep. His two tent mates were talking in lowered voices. They had waited until they were sure Halt was fully asleep. Kord was testing the dice, rolling them over and over again and constantly getting a losing score as a result.

"I don't understand," he said quietly. "It's simply not possible for him to roll a twelve with these dice."

"Careful," Jerrel told him, casting a quick glance in Halt's direction. But his companion waved his caution aside.

"Aaah, he's out like a light," he said. "Did you see how much he drank? He's full as a boot."

Halt's mouth twitched slightly in amusement. There was definitely a full boot in the tent, he thought. His loud breathing was making it difficult to hear what the others were saying, so he stirred, muttered something and rolled onto his side, facing away from them. The snoring stopped as he was no longer on his back, but he kept his breathing deep and even. Kord and Jerrel hesitated as he stirred, but soon relaxed when it became obvious he hadn't woken.

Once again, Kord tested the dice. Once again, they rolled a three.

"Give it away," Jerrel told him angrily. "It was an accident. They must have hit a crack or a dent in the tabletop. Besides, we've got more important things to think about."

Reluctantly, Kord stowed the dice away in his pocket. "You mean this rumor about us heading south?"

Jerrel nodded. "Last thing we want is to get tied up in another campaign. It could go on for weeks, and we've got places to be. If we're held up, there's a chance that family members will arrive to help the widows and we'll miss our chance."

Turned away from them as he was, Halt could allow himself a scowl of anger. It was true, he thought; the two of them were planning to rob the families of men killed in the battle.

"So what's your plan?" Kord asked.

Jerrel paused, then came to a decision. "I say we pull out tonight. We'll leave an hour or two before dawn and get on the road north. We'll hit the sergeant's farm first. That's the closest."

"We'll be flogged if they catch us deserting," Kord said, but Jerrel dismissed the protest.

"They won't catch us. With all the recent losses, odds are they won't even be sure we're gone."

"Griff will know. I get a feeling he has his eye on us."

Kord snorted derisively. "Griff will be too busy doing his job and the captain's job to worry about us. He'll probably think it's good riddance. Now let's turn in. We'll need to get started early."

"What about him?" Jerrel asked, jerking a thumb toward Halt's still figure. Kord hesitated.

"I'd like to knock him on the head and take our money back," he said. "But if we kill him, Griff will have to take notice of the fact. He'd be sure to send men after us. Best if we leave him."

6

HALT HEARD THEM LEAVE JUST BEFORE THREE IN THE MORNING. They were thieves and they were accustomed to moving quietly. But the Ranger's senses were finely tuned and he was a light sleeper. He listened to their stealthy movements and quiet footsteps as they gathered their kits together and stole out into the night. The moon had waxed and waned hours ago and there was a scattered cloud cover riding on the wind, sending bands of shadows scudding across the silent camp.

Kord and Jerrel had no trouble eluding the sentries. The men on watch were tired and bored as they neared the end of their three-hour shift. And besides, they were more inclined to look for intruders from outside the camp than people leaving from inside. The rumor that the company would be heading south and continuing the campaign was a false one Halt had concocted to force the thieves' hand, so with the company due to return home and disband in the near future, there was little reason for men to desert.

He waited fifteen minutes to give the two time to clear the camp perimeter, then rolled out of his blankets and ghosted out of the tent after them. He retrieved his own clothes from the company command tent. Griff was waiting for him, a shaded lantern throwing a dim light over the interior.

"They took the bait?" he asked.

Halt nodded. He changed clothes and placed the heavy purse containing his winnings on the table.

"You can put this into the company fund," he said. He knew most companies contributed to a fund that was used to help the families of those who lost their lives on campaign. Griff nodded his thanks.

"If you catch them, feel free to bring them back here," he said. "I'd be quite happy to see to their future discomfort."

"Oh, I'll catch them, all right," Halt told him. "And when I do, it'll be up to them how I deal with them."

He shook hands with the sergeant major and went to the rear of the tent, where Abelard was waiting. He swung up into the saddle and trotted out of the camp. He made no attempt at concealment, identifying himself to the sentries as he went.

He found the north road and held Abelard down to a walk. He didn't want to catch up to the two men too quickly. Concealed in his Ranger cloak, they might not recognize him as their erstwhile tent mate, but the sight of a Ranger traveling the same road might panic them into abandoning their plans for the time being.

As dawn came and the first gray light stole over the countryside, he increased his pace. Before long, he rounded a bend and caught sight of two figures trudging along the high road, several hundred meters in front of him. Thankfully, the headache and blurred vision that had plagued him were gone and he had no trouble recognizing the two men—Kord tall and wiry, Jerrel more compact and solidly built. He checked Abelard and moved off the road, where the dark green of the trees would conceal them from view.

When Kord and Jerrel rounded another bend and disappeared from sight, he cantered slowly after them.

He proceeded in that fashion for the rest of the day. As the light improved, he was able to make out their tracks on the dusty road—their hobnailed army sandals left an easily followed trail. He fell farther back, only closing up again when the light began to fail in the late afternoon. As dusk was falling, the two men moved off the highway and made camp.

He spent the night wrapped in his cloak, leaning against a tree and watching the light of their fire. He dozed in brief snatches, confident that Abelard would wake him if there were any movement from the distant camp. He woke cold and cramped in the early-morning light. The fire had died before dawn and there was a thin spiral of smoke rising from it. After half an hour, he saw the two men rising and moving around their campsite. Abelard was back in the trees and there was no need for Halt to seek concealment. Wrapped in his cloak, he would be invisible, even if they looked directly at him. His stomach grumbled as they relit their fire and he smelled bacon frying. After that, the smell of coffee brewing made his mouth water. He contented himself with a discreet mouthful of cold water from his canteen. It was a poor substitute.

The pair was slow in getting moving. Halt shifted uncomfortably a few times, waiting for them to get on the road. Finally, they rolled their packs and struck camp, heading north once more. He waited until they had rounded the next bend in the road, then moved to where Abelard waited inside the trees. He tightened the girth straps—he had left the horse saddled through the night in case of an emergency—mounted and rode slowly after them.

When he reached the bend, he dismounted and went ahead to peer around, down the next stretch of road.

There was no sign of them.

For a moment, his heart raced with panic. This stretch of road was at least three hundred meters long—and there was no way they could have reached the far end before he rounded the bend. Where had they gone? Had they become aware that they were being followed? Perhaps they'd gone to ground somewhere along the road and were now waiting in ambush for whoever was behind them. Or had they moved more quickly than he had judged, and were now beyond the far bend?

He forced himself to calm down. Both those theories were possibilities, he admitted. But it was more likely that they had moved off the high road onto a side track somewhere along the way. They were inside Aspienne Fief now and they could be close to Daniel's farm. He remounted Abelard and tapped his heels into the horse's side.

The temptation was to gallop full out to see if there was, in fact, a turnoff. But doing so would cause noise and would risk drawing their attention. He trotted the little horse gently along the hard surface of the high road.

Forty meters along, he found what he was looking for. A narrow side trail led off from the main road. It was well traveled and seemed to have been established for some time. He glanced along it, but it wound and twisted through the trees and there was no sign of Kord and Jerrel. But as he studied the ground, he saw a familiar footprint. Kord's right boot was worn down on the inside—the result of an uneven stance. There in the sand that formed the path's surface, Halt could see the distinctive track. He swung down from the saddle and led Abelard along the track. It wouldn't do to come upon them unexpectedly.

Presently, he began to smell wood smoke, then the rich and distinctive odor of a farmyard. It was a mixture of manure, fresh-cut hay and large animals that told him he was nearing Daniel's farm. Then he heard a sound that confirmed the fact.

Somewhere close to hand, a woman screamed.

7

HALT DROPPED ABELARD'S REIN AND BEGAN TO RUN. THE HORSE would follow along, he knew. Another scream came through the trees. The first had been a shout of fear and alarm. This one had anger mixed in. He ran faster, the saxe knife and quiver thumping on his hip and shoulder as his feet hit the ground. Belatedly, he realized that he would have been better off remounting and riding Abelard. But no sooner had the thought occurred than he burst into a clearing where a small thatched farmhouse stood, smoke curling lazily from its chimney, several cows moving uneasily in the fenced-off paddock beside the house.

Another defiant scream, then a man's voice raised in anger and the unmistakable sound of a blow. A gasp of pain from the woman.

"My husband will kill you for that!" she cried.

"Your husband's dead!" a sneering voice replied. "And you'll join him if you don't do as you're told. You and the baby!"

Halt heard a quick sob of grief from the woman at these words. Seething with rage, he hit the farmhouse door with his shoulder and burst into the dim room inside.

He took in the details instantly. A woman crouched in the far corner, close to the cooking hearth, her arms spread protectively over a cradle. Jerrel stood over her, his hand raised to hit her again, frozen in the act as the door crashed back on its leather hinges.

To Halt's left, Kord was rummaging through a chest, hurling clothes and household pieces in all directions as he searched for items of value. He, too, froze at the sudden appearance of the Ranger. Then recognition dawned as he made out the dark, bearded face.

"You!" he snarled. "What are you doing here?"

He didn't wait for an answer but lunged to his feet, drawing the cheap sword that he wore at his waist and surging across the room to swing a downward cut at Halt.

The Ranger's actions were instinctive. He sidestepped the savage sword stroke, swaying to his right, and simultaneously drew the saxe knife with his left hand. He was bringing the big knife up to a defensive position when Kord's momentum drove him onto the blade. Kord looked down in horror as the razor-sharp hardened steel slid easily through the rusty links of his chain-mail vest.

He gasped and blood welled out of his mouth. His eyes went dull and his knees gave way. Halt jerked the knife free of the falling body and spun to face Jerrel, who was still trying to take in the rapid sequence of events. Then Jerrel's eyes hardened and he drew his own sword, stepping deliberately forward, not rushing as Kord had done, presenting the sword point first and letting it sway back and forth, threatening the smaller man who faced him.

The woman dropped back on her haunches beside the cot, watching in wide-eyed horror as the scene unfolded before her.

Jerrel advanced another pace. Halt switched the saxe to his right hand and withdrew warily. He was confident that he could handle the soldier, in spite of the apparent disparity in their weapons. Swordsmen often underestimated the lethal potential of a saxe knife, he knew. Still, he was prepared to let Jerrel make the first move, and so draw him into closer range, where the saxe would be effective.

Jerrel feinted with the blade. Halt, watching his eyes, saw no commitment there and ignored the movement. His apparent calm infuriated Jerrel. Halt saw the hot anger welling up in his eyes.

"You're a dead man, Arratay," Jerrel said through clenched teeth.

Halt smiled. "That's been said before. Yet here I am."

He took another pace backward, conscious of Kord's still body on the beaten earth floor of the farmhouse, just beside and behind him.

Jerrel darted the sword blade out at him. This time it was no feint and Halt was ready for it. He flicked it aside with the saxe, the two blades ringing together for a second. The speed and ease of his response raised a worm of doubt in Jerrel's mind. He had the longer weapon. He had the advantage. Yet this bearded figure in the strange mottled cloak seemed completely at ease.

He was thinking about this when Arratay, as he knew him, lunged forward with the short, gleaming saxe. Jerrel leaped backward, yelping in surprise, and managed to swipe his sword across in a clumsy parry, just in time. For the first time, he realized that he might be outmatched. He was about to drop his weapon and plead for mercy when something totally unexpected happened.

Halt felt an iron grip on his left ankle, then the leg was jerked from under him, sending him sprawling awkwardly on the farmhouse floor.

As he fell, he turned and found himself looking into Kord's face. The eyes were filled with hatred, the lips curled back in one last snarl of triumph. With his final breath, Kord had managed to take his revenge on the small man who had ruined everything for them. Now the eyes went blank as the life left his body.

Jerrel, who was never too quick on the uptake, saw that his opponent was, for the moment, helpless before him. With a cry of triumph, he raised the sword in both hands, point down, and stepped forward, preparing to drive it into the prone body on the floor. Halt struggled to rise but knew it was too late. The gleaming sword point began to descend.

Then a figure came from nowhere and crashed into Jerrel, clinging to him and knocking him sideways, sending the sword spinning out of his grasp. Halt dodged sideways as the weapon fell close to him, then realized what had happened.

The woman had launched herself at Jerrel, landing on his back and clinging there like a wildcat as she raked at his face and eyes with her nails.

The thief staggered under the impact, turning so that the two of them crashed into the kitchen table, sending it spinning, then cannoned into the wall, smashing halfway through the close-woven willow sticks daubed with mud. Unable to dislodge the grim, clinging figure on his back, Jerrel twisted so that he was facing her and, drawing his heavy-bladed dagger, struck out desperately at her.

She cried out in pain and released her grip, falling back, hands clutching at the savage wound in her left side. Blood covered her hands instantly, soaking the white cotton material of her shift as she sank to one knee. Then Halt was upon Jerrel, grasping the man's knife hand and forcing it upward while he drew his throwing knife and rammed it deep into his body. Jerrel gave a grunt of pain. The heavy dagger fell from his hand and for a moment he was supported only by Halt's grip on his right wrist. Then, as the Ranger released him, he sagged to his knees, looking up at Halt, his eyes showing shock at the fact that this was the way his life was to end. He fell over sideways, his hands desperately trying to stem the flow of blood from the wound. Halt stood warily for a second, making sure that Jerrel was truly finished. His recent experience with Kord had made him careful. Then, satisfied that Jerrel wasn't about to rally for another attack, he knelt quickly beside the stricken woman.

Her face was white and drawn with the savage pain of the wound. Halt looked at the amount of blood she had lost already and knew she had no chance of surviving. She looked up at the stranger who had tried to save her, whom she had saved with her desperate attack on Jerrel. She saw the sadness in the dark eyes looking down at her and knew the truth. She was dying. Yet there was something she had to know.

"My . . . husband . . . ," she managed to gasp. "Is he really dead?"

Halt hesitated. He was tempted to lie to her, to comfort her. But he knew he could never carry off the lie. He nodded. "Yes," he said. "You'll soon be with him."

He saw the sudden look of anguish in her face as her eyes turned toward the cot in the corner of the room.

"Our son . . . ," she said, and coughed blood as she spoke. Then she made a massive effort and recovered herself. "Don't leave him with the villagers . . . He'll have no life with them . . . We're strangers here . . . They'll work him to death . . ."

Halt nodded. Daniel and his wife were new arrivals in the area. They wouldn't have friends in the village to take care of their infant son. An orphan would be a burden to most villagers. His only worth would be as a worker—a virtual slave.

"I'll take care of him," he said gently, and the woman reached up and seized his hand in a surprisingly strong grip.

"Promise me," she said, and he placed his other hand over hers.

"I promise."

She studied his eyes for several seconds and seemed to find reassurance there. She released his hand and sank back onto the blood-soaked floor. She spoke again, but her voice was so soft, he didn't hear the words. He bent to her, turning his ear to her mouth.

"Tell me again," he said, and this time he could make out the whispered words.

"His name is Will."

"It's a good name," he told her. But she didn't hear him. She was already dead.

8

HE BURIED THE WOMAN IN A SMALL CLEARING BEYOND THE HOME paddock, marking the grave with a stone. He didn't know her name, or the family name. So he inscribed the stone with a simple legend: A BRAVE MOTHER.

Kord and Jerrel deserved no such treatment. They had destroyed a happy, loving family, so he dragged their bodies into the woods, leaving them for the foxes and crows.

The baby slept quietly in his cot while Halt attended to these matters. As Halt sat nursing a cup of coffee in the disarranged house, the infant woke and muttered quietly. Halt noted with approval that he didn't cry.

"I expect you're hungry," he said. He had a warmed bowl of cow's milk and a clean linen cloth ready. He twisted the end of the cloth into a narrow shape and dipped it into the milk, then placed it by the baby's mouth. The lips formed around the cloth twist and the baby sucked the milk from it. Halt dipped it into the bowl again and repeated the process. The system was time-consuming but it seemed to work. The baby watched him as it fed, big, serious brown eyes staring at him over the milk-soaked cloth.

"The question is," Halt said, "what am I to do with you?"

The farm, he knew, would revert to the baron of the fief, who would appoint another tenant family to work it. So there was nothing for the infant to inherit. He couldn't leave him here—as the mother had so desperately pointed out. And he couldn't raise the baby himself. He simply wasn't equipped to look after a baby, nor was he in any position to do so. His work as a Ranger would keep him absent from home for long periods and the baby would be left alone and uncared for.

But an idea was forming. Baron Arald had created a Ward at Castle Redmont where the orphans of men and women who died in his service were cared for. It was a bright, cheerful place, staffed by kind, affectionate people, and there were several recent additions to the ranks of children being cared for there. A baby girl called Alyss, and another boy—Horace, his name was.

Will would know warmth and companionship there. And as he grew, he would be given a choice of different vocations to follow. All in all, it seemed like an ideal solution.

"Problem is," Halt told the watchful infant, "we can't let on that I've brought you there. Folk are suspicious of Rangers. If they thought you were associated with me, they might tread warily around you."

Rangers had an aura of mystery and uncertainty about them. And that could have drawbacks for the child. People often feared things they didn't understand, and he didn't want that fear transferring itself to young Will. Better if his background remained a mystery.

"Which it is," Halt mused. "I don't even know your last name."

He considered that. He could ask around the district. But as he had learned, the family was new to the area and people might not know their names. In addition, he would have to reveal his plans for the baby, and he wasn't sure if what he was planning was exactly legal. Will was the child of two subjects of the local baron and Halt technically had no right to carry him off to another fief.

But then, in his lifetime, Halt had often ignored what was technically legal. Technicalities didn't appeal to him. All too often, they simply got in the way of doing the right thing.

He dipped the cloth in the last of the milk and held it to the baby's mouth. Will sucked eagerly, his eyes still fixed on the Ranger.

"Yes, the Ward is the best place for you," Halt told him. "And it's best if you're anonymous. I'll tell Arald, of course, in confidence. But nobody else will know. Just the two of us. What do you say?"

To his surprise, the baby emitted a loud burp, then smiled at him. A ghost of a smile touched Halt's bearded face in reply.

"I'll take that as agreement," he said.

Four days later, just before the first gray streaks of light heralded the dawn, a dark figure carrying a basket stole across the courtyard of Castle Redmont, to the building that housed the Ward.

Setting the basket down on the steps outside the door to the Ward, Halt reached in and moved the blanket away from the baby's face. He placed the note that he had composed into the basket, at the baby's feet.

> *His mother died in childbirth.*
> *His father died a hero.*
> *Please care for him. His name is Will.*

A tiny hand emerged from the blankets and gripped his forefinger.

"I'd swear you were shaking hands good-bye," Halt whispered. Then, gently disengaging himself, he stroked the baby's forehead.

"You'll be fine here, young Will. With the parents you had, I suspect you'll grow to be quite a person."

He glanced around, saw no sign of anyone watching, then reached up and rapped sharply on the Ward door before melting away into the shadows of the courtyard.

The Ward's staff was already up and about, and he heard the door open a few minutes later, then the cry of surprise.

"Why, it's a baby! Mistress Aggie, come quick! Someone's left a baby on the doorstep!"

Wrapped in his cloak, hidden in the shadows of the huge wall, Halt watched as several women came bustling out, crying out in surprise at the sight of the baby. Then they took him inside, closing the door behind them. He felt an unfamiliar prickling sensation in his eyes and a strange sense of loss.

"Good-bye for now, Will," he whispered. "I'll be keeping an eye on you."

Halt felt that same prickling sensation once more as he finished the story. He turned away slightly so that Will couldn't see the tears that had formed in his eyes.

"But, Halt, why didn't you tell me for all those years? Why did you say my mother died in childbirth?"

"I thought it would be easier on you," Halt said. "I thought if you knew your mother had been murdered, it might make you bitter. And, as I said, I thought it would be easier on you if nobody knew of my involvement. If I'd said your mother was murdered, people would have started asking questions. I didn't want that. I wanted you to be accepted."

Will nodded thoughtfully. "I suppose so."

The older Ranger shifted uncomfortably.

"There was something else . . ."

Will opened his mouth, then closed it. He sensed it would be better to let Halt speak in his own time.

Eventually, his mentor said, in a low voice that Will could barely hear, "I was afraid you'd hate me."

Will recoiled in astonishment at the words. "Hate you? How could I hate you? *Why* would I hate you?"

Now Halt turned back to face him, and Will could see the anguish in his eyes. "Because I was responsible for the deaths of both your parents!" The words came out violently, as if they were torn from him. "Daniel died saving my life in battle. Then your mother came to my aid when I was fighting Jerrel. If she hadn't done so, she'd still be alive."

"And you'd be dead," Will pointed out. But Halt shook his head.

"Maybe. Maybe not. But the fact remains, it was my fault that your family was destroyed, and up until now I was unable to tell you. I thought you might blame me."

"Halt, it wasn't your fault. Who could blame you? You were keeping a promise you made to my father. Blame Morgarath. Blame the Wargals. Or blame Kord and Jerrel. That's where the fault lies. Not on your shoulders."

Watching Halt, Will now saw those shoulders sag with relief.

"That's what Pauline said you'd say," Halt whispered, and Will put an arm around him. It felt strange to be comforting the man who had comforted him so much over the years.

"Halt, you didn't destroy my family. That was fate. You gave me a second chance at having a family. You gave me a whole new life. How could I hate you for that? Besides," he added, "can you imagine me as a farmer?"

He felt Halt's shoulders begin to shake, and for a moment he was afraid the older man was weeping. Then he realized with relief that he was laughing.

"No," his teacher said, "I certainly can't see you as a farmer. Farmers are disciplined folk."

They both laughed at the thought of Will plowing and planting. Then, after a while, the young Ranger grew serious.

"I would like to see my mother's grave," he said, and Halt nodded.

"I'll take you there."

And then they said nothing more, but sat together in companionable silence as the shadows lengthened and the sun finally set.

THE INKWELL
AND THE DAGGER

Author's note: I've had many e-mails from fans over the years, asking what happened to Gilan when Halt and Horace went to Gallica to rescue Will in The Icebound Land. *Here's the answer.*

1

Araluen Fief
The coast road
Shortly after the battle of Three Step Pass

GILAN SAT ON HIS HORSE AND WATCHED AS HALT RODE AWAY, HIS gray-cloaked figure gradually becoming smaller and smaller and merging into the misty rain that had been drifting across the countryside all morning.

The young Ranger felt tears prickling behind his eyes. He shook his head impatiently to get rid of them. Halt had always been a grim figure, and his smiles were few and far between. But today, there had been something intrinsically sad about his manner. Of course, Gilan realized, Halt had only recently insulted and argued with King Duncan, a man for whom he had always shown the greatest respect and admiration.

And, as a direct result of that insubordination, he had been banished from the kingdom for a period of twelve months. On top of that, he had been stripped of his position in the Ranger Corps.

Those two facts would be enough to drive a keen blade of

sadness deep into Halt's soul. But Gilan sensed the real cause was
something else—something within Halt himself.

"He's blaming himself," he told Blaze.

The bay mare pricked her ears at the sound of her master's
voice.

He shouldn't have sent Will to Celtica.

"He thought he was doing the right thing, keeping Will out of
harm's way. Besides, if anyone's to blame for this mess, it's me. I
should never have left Will and Evanlyn alone in Celtica."

There was no reply from Blaze, and Gilan wondered if she
might be agreeing that the capture of Will and Evanlyn by the
Skandians, and their subsequent abduction on a wolfship, really was
his fault. He glanced at his horse, troubled, then decided that Blaze
wasn't the blaming kind. She probably just had nothing further to
add to the discussion.

Halt's gray-green cloak was blending into the mist now, so that
he was becoming harder and harder to make out. Then he reached
a turn in the road and disappeared from view. Gilan continued to
look down the empty road for a few more minutes, then heaved a
sigh and turned Blaze's head toward Castle Araluen.

Fifteen minutes later, he caught up with Crowley. The Ranger
Commandant was easing his horse along at a walk to allow the
younger man to catch him. They exchanged dejected looks, then
Crowley lifted his shoulders in a shrug.

"Nothing to say, really, is there?"

Gilan nodded. Already, they were feeling the absence of the
gray-bearded Ranger. Coming on top of the loss of Will and the
Princess, it was doubly sad for them. The Rangers were a close-
knit group, but Crowley was Halt's oldest friend and Gilan had
been Halt's first apprentice. They felt his loss more keenly than
others might.

The two rode on for several minutes, their horses matching step with one another. Finally, Gilan said, "He wants me to track down Foldar."

Crowley nodded. "Thought he might ask you. I've got his files back at the castle. He made sure I had them before he went around insulting the King in taverns."

"He was pretty organized for someone making an impulsive gesture. You'd almost swear he knew exactly what he was doing."

Crowley glanced sidelong at the tall, young Ranger riding beside him.

"Oh, he knew what he was doing, all right. Halt always knows what he's doing."

Back at the castle, Gilan changed into dry clothes. He was staying in guest accommodations in Castle Araluen and he had a small but comfortable apartment in the east tower. Crowley's office and headquarters were in the south tower, and to access them, Gilan had to return to the third-floor level of the castle and cross over to the south tower staircase.

He smiled as he made his way up the spiraling stairs. Like all castles, Araluen's stairs twisted upward to the right, so that a right-handed swordsman trying to fight his way up the stairs would have to expose his entire body to the defenders above, while the defenders would show only a small part of themselves around the central column of the staircase as they retreated upward. This had been the reason why MacNeil, the swordmaster who instructed Gilan from an early age, had been at pains to make his young student practice his swordsmanship with either hand. Gilan was very good with his left hand. With his right hand, he was an expert.

Crowley's office was three floors up. Gilan knocked at the door, then entered in response to Crowley's call. The office was spacious and airy, like most of the rooms in Castle Araluen. A large window overlooked the expanse of grassland that swept away on a gradual slope from the castle. In the distance, Gilan could see a small village and the orderly squares of cultivated farmland.

Crowley had changed into dry clothes too, and he was now sitting comfortably in a large oak armchair by the window, reading a report. The rain was still misting outside, but the wind was blowing it away from the castle. Like most Rangers, Crowley liked fresh air and light, so he had refrained from closing the wooden shutters. As insurance against the chill of the oncoming evening, however, a fire burned cheerfully in the grate opposite the window.

"Take a seat," Crowley said, and gestured to another oak armchair, not quite as large as his own. Gilan sat and Crowley glanced up from the document in his hand, indicating a pile of parchment rolls, each tied with a plain black string, on the low table between them.

"Halt's reports on the Foldar business," he said. "Have a glance through them." He reached forward and took a quill pen from an inkwell on the table, made a notation on the paper he was reading, then continued to scan the document.

There were a dozen rolls in the pile. Each one was labeled with the name of the fief from which the report had originated. Three were also labeled with the word CLOSED. Gilan selected one of these and unrolled it, glancing through the contents.

As he had suspected, the CLOSED label signified that these were cases that Halt had investigated and found to be false trails.

Foldar was known as a cold-blooded and totally pitiless killer. Confronted by a man claiming to be Foldar, people were more likely to hand their money over without resistance. Because of this, a host of Foldar impersonators had sprung up, trading on the man's notoriety to help them cow their victims into submission.

The report he was reading detailed one of these instances. A common robber, leader of a small band of outlaws, had assumed the Foldar identity and had tried to rob a wealthy merchant and his wife, traveling on a forest road. Halt had intervened, having learned of the plan, and the fake Foldar was now reposing in jail.

It was this proliferation of false Foldars that had led to Halt's frustration. Each case had to be investigated, each criminal tracked down and arrested. The task could take a year or more.

Unless . . .

Gilan tapped his teeth idly with his thumbnail as he glanced quickly through another case study. An idea was forming in his mind. He glanced up at Crowley, still engrossed in the report he was reading.

"Do you mind if I take these away?" he said.

The Commandant looked up. For a moment, his attention was miles away. Then he nodded, understanding the request.

"Be my guest," he said. "The fewer papers I've got in here, the better."

He gestured to a desk in the corner, piled high with rolls of parchment, sheets of paper and linen envelopes containing reports, requests and other official forms from all over the kingdom. It was a mountain of paperwork, Gilan realized. He grinned sympathetically.

"I'll take these off your hands then," he said. Gathering up the parchment rolls, he rose and made for the door.

2

"I LOOKED THROUGH ALL THOSE FILES LAST NIGHT," GILAN TOLD Crowley the following morning. The Commandant gave him a wan smile.

"All of them? Wish I could say the same. Paperwork is the bane of my life."

"It's the price of your exalted rank, Crowley," Gilan told him with a grin. "That's why you're paid the big money."

Crowley looked at the cheerful face beside him. "You know, there are some people who might think it was a good career move to show sympathy for their commanding officer's problems," he said. Then he sighed. "But very few of those people were trained by Halt."

Gilan thought about that for a second or two. "True," he said.

They were strolling through the parkland to the south of Castle Araluen. Crowley often held discussions with his Rangers in the open air. He claimed it was good security. Inside a castle, one never knew who might be listening on the other side of a wall or outside a door. Out here, nobody could come within earshot without being seen.

Gilan suspected that equally important was Crowley's love of open space and fresh air. The Commandant was constantly heard to grumble about being "cooped up indoors all day."

"So, did you discover anything important?" Crowley asked after a brief pause.

"I might have," Gilan replied. "There are nine cases still outstanding. Of them, seven are relatively small matters—a robbery here, a holdup there. Sometimes the thieves stopped single travelers on the highway and robbed them. On other occasions, they raided small, isolated taverns or settlements. In all those cases, the amounts of money taken are relatively small. The largest was fifteen gold royals. It's barely more than petty theft and I just can't imagine Foldar setting his sights so low."

"Fifteen gold royals is a lot for a small tavern," Crowley interposed.

Gilan nodded impatiently. "I'm not saying it's insignificant for the victims. But for Foldar? It's really small stakes. I mean, he was helping Morgarath to overthrow the throne. For a man like that, fifteen royals is hardly noticeable."

"What about the other two fiefs?" Crowley asked. He thought Gilan's point was a good one. Foldar had never been a petty thief. There was little to suggest that he might have become one. He thought in much grander terms.

"One was a very large amount. A merchant was robbed and the thieves got away with a large amount in gold and silver coins."

"That's more promising," Crowley said. But Gilan made a negative gesture with his hand.

"The size of the crime is more in keeping with what we know of Foldar. But the method doesn't fit him. It was done at night, without the merchant or his family hearing anything. They didn't know they'd been robbed until the following morning. The thief even locked the doors behind him when he left."

"I see your point. If Foldar had broken in, chances were he would have killed them all in their sleep, just for the fun of it."

"My thoughts exactly," Gilan said.

"Which leaves one other case," Crowley prompted him.

The young Ranger nodded. "As you say. One other case. It was a raid on a well-guarded caravan of pay wagons in Highcliff Fief, carrying silver and gold to pay the garrisons in outlying castles. Highcliff, incidentally, is currently without its Ranger. He was injured in the war and he's not ready to resume his duties."

"Which might make it an attractive base of operations for Foldar," Crowley said thoughtfully.

"That had occurred to me as well. The caravan was attacked by fifteen to twenty men, all well armed and trained. Half the guards were killed. The others escaped into the trees. The drivers weren't so lucky."

"Now that has Foldar's stamp on it," Crowley said.

"That's what I thought. In addition to the organization of the raid, and the sheer brutality involved, there's a good chance that an informer in Castle Highcliff gave out information about that pay train. It was supposed to be a secret."

"Exactly the sort of thing Foldar would be involved in," Crowley said. "So what's your next move?"

"I thought I'd travel to Highcliff and see if I can think of some sort of trap for Foldar—and his inside informant. I'll need to nose around the place a little before I come up with any definite plan."

Crowley nodded. "It sounds like a good idea to me. Well done, Gilan." Then he frowned. "I'm surprised that Halt didn't reach the same conclusion. He's usually pretty quick on the uptake."

"I thought the same thing. But remember, Halt was distracted, worrying about Will. And he tended to concentrate first on the cases closest to Araluen."

"Which gave him plenty of opportunity to put his case to me and Duncan," Crowley said. "If he was off in the west at Highcliff, he wouldn't have been able to nag at me every second day to let him go."

"Whereas I have no reason not to head for Highcliff Fief and leave you to your paperwork," Gilan said.

Crowley's mouth turned down at the corners in an expression of distaste. "Ah yes, the paperwork. You wouldn't consider trading places? You stay and fill in the forms and requisitions. I'll go chasing after Foldar."

Gilan raised one eyebrow at him. "You're right. I wouldn't consider it."

"I could order you to do it, I suppose," Crowley said wistfully, and Gilan thought he was only half joking.

"You could. And I'd probably insult the King in public and have myself banished," he replied.

Crowley shook his head. "I sometimes wonder if it was a good idea having Halt train apprentices. He seems to teach them no respect for authority."

"Oh, he teaches us to respect authority," Gilan said innocently. "He just teaches us to ignore it when necessary. I'll get going this afternoon," he added, and Crowley nodded agreement.

"The sooner you leave, the sooner you'll be back," he said. It was the Ranger way, after all. No sense letting the grass grow under your feet if there was work to be done.

"There's that. And besides, I should get going before you decide to order me to stay."

3

CASTLE HIGHCLIFF WAS APPROPRIATELY NAMED, GILAN THOUGHT.
He checked Blaze's easy canter and slumped in the saddle, studying
the castle.

There was nothing remarkable about the building itself. It was a
solid granite structure, with the usual four corner towers, joined by
crenellated walls. A single, taller tower stood in the center of the
enclosed space. That would be the keep, he thought, where the castle's eating, sleeping and administration quarters were located. But it
was the site on which the castle had been built that gave it its name.
The coastline in this part of Araluen was formed by high, rocky cliffs
of white chalk. The castle had been built on a high outcrop, a peninsula joined to the coast by a narrow, winding neck of land barely
twenty meters wide. On either side of this path, steep cliffs dropped
away to where the sea crashed constantly against the rocks, sending
tall columns of spray skyward and creating a rhythmic booming
sound. Tumbled piles of chalky rock at the base of the cliffs showed
where the path was being constantly undermined and eaten away by
the waves' incessant attack. In time, he thought, the path would disappear completely, leaving Highcliff to stand on an island.

As he watched, he saw men patrolling the castle walls. In one of

the towers on the landward side, he could make out a tiny figure
leaning his elbows on the parapet. As Gilan watched, another figure
joined the first, arm outstretched, pointing at the spot where Gilan
and Blaze stood motionless. The first guard straightened up from his
relaxed position and turned away, doubtless calling an alert to someone below.

"They've seen us," Gilan told Blaze.

We are a little obvious, silhouetted against the skyline like this.

"I wasn't trying to creep up unobserved," Gilan said, and Blaze
sniffed disdainfully. She had a habit of doing that, Gilan thought.
Knowing he would never manage to have the last word with his
horse, he urged her forward and she picked her way carefully down
the rocky path to the beginning of the isthmus leading to the castle.

There was a sentry point there, manned by two bored-looking
soldiers. Gilan identified himself, although the Ranger cloak and
massive longbow left little doubt as to who or what he was, and the
senior man present nodded to him.

"Just wait a moment, please, Ranger," he said. His voice was respectful, even wary. The Ranger Corps' reputation was the reason for
the twofold reaction. The soldier nudged his companion with an
elbow. "Run up the yellow flag, Nobby," he said. Without a word, the
second man stepped to a mast nearby, where Gilan could see there
were two flags attached to halyards, ready to be run up. One was yellow, the other red. Nobby selected the yellow and hoisted the square
of colored cloth to the top of the mast. The flag vibrated in the stiff
ocean breeze, standing out from the flagpole. After a few seconds, an
answering flag appeared at the castle gate.

Presumably, thought Gilan, had he been identified as an enemy,
the soldiers would have signaled with the red flag. Had he been an
enemy, of course, he might not have given them the chance, although
he supposed no signal would be taken to mean the same as a red flag.

It was probably better for the sentries' morale to believe that they had a chance of signaling if an enemy were to arrive at the guard post.

"Go on across, Ranger," said the soldier. Gilan waved a hand in acknowledgment and started Blaze forward.

He let the reins go slack, allowing the horse to pick her own way. The isthmus wasn't particularly narrow for a single rider, but he was conscious of the steep drop-off on either side to the sea below. As he approached the castle gate and portcullis, the track narrowed considerably, so that there would have been room for no more than four men abreast to approach the castle entrance.

He touched the reins lightly as they reached the portcullis and Blaze came to a halt as a sergeant stepped forward. His keen gaze took in the cloak and the longbow Gilan carried across his saddle bow. He also noticed the long sword hanging at the Ranger's left side and frowned. Swords were not normally part of a Ranger's weaponry. Gilan nodded approvingly. The two outer guards hadn't noticed the weapon or, if they had, they had attached no significance to it.

He produced the silver oakleaf that hung on a chain around his neck and leaned forward so that the sergeant could see it clearly.

"Ranger Gilan, temporarily detached on special duties," he said.

The sergeant studied the amulet, glanced once more at the sword, then came to a decision. He signaled for the single pole barrier across the gateway to be raised, then stepped to one side.

"Pass through, Ranger Gilan," he said. "The seneschal's office is straight ahead, on the ground floor of the keep."

Gilan nodded and urged Blaze forward through the shadows of the massive gateway. Her hooves rang loudly as they passed onto the flagstones of the castle courtyard. As Gilan dismounted, a stable hand materialized beside him.

"Can I look after your horse, Ranger?" he asked.

Gilan considered for a second or two. It was his normal practice to tend to Blaze himself. "That would be kind of you," he said. "We've come a long way, so please give her a good rubdown and a measure of grain."

The stable hand nodded and reached for Blaze's bridle. As Gilan handed it over, he said to the bay, "Go along, Blaze."

Thus instructed, his horse turned and clip-clopped after the stable hand, toward the wooden building by the north wall that housed the stables. Gilan smiled quietly to himself. Had he not said those three simple words, she would have been as immoveable as the north wall itself.

He entered the keep. The ground floor was largely open space. In the center was a large wooden staircase leading to the next level. In the event of an attack, the stairs could be burned or smashed down once the inhabitants had escaped to the higher floor, leaving attackers with no way to access them. From there, access to higher floors would be by the same right-hand spiraling staircases he had remarked on at Araluen. On the left-hand side, a large area was closed off by a timber wall. He guessed it was the guardroom, where sentries could relax or sleep while not on duty. On the right-hand side, another wall separated a slightly smaller area. This would be the seneschal's, or castle manager's, office. As a Ranger, Gilan could simply head for the higher levels, where he would find the Baron's quarters. But it was good etiquette to approach the seneschal first and he saw no reason to ruffle any feathers just to prove his own importance.

A slightly overweight man sat at a table outside the large brass-bound door to the office. The sleeves of his jerkin were clad in black cloth to protect them from ink stains, and he was copying a list of figures from a parchment sheet into a large journal. He looked up at the sound of Gilan's boots on the flagstones.

"Can I help you?" he said politely.

Gilan tossed his cloak back over his shoulders and proffered the silver oakleaf once more.

"My name is Gilan. I'm a King's Ranger," he said. "I'd like to see the seneschal, please."

"Of course. Please wait a moment." The clerk set his quill pen down and rose, hurrying to the door that led to the inner office. He disappeared inside for less than a minute, then emerged once more, beckoning to Gilan.

"Please come in. Seneschal Philip is at your service. Can I get you some refreshments?"

Gilan hesitated. It had been a long ride and the sea breeze over the last ten kilometers had been chilly. "Coffee, if you have it," he said.

The clerk bowed and gestured him through the doorway.

"I'll bring it right away," he said as Gilan entered the office.

The seneschal was an elderly man. His long hair was completely gray and his face was lined. Although, thought Gilan, that might be the result of the rigors of his office, rather than age. He was rising from behind his desk as the Ranger entered, his hand outstretched in greeting.

"Welcome to Highcliff, Ranger Gilan," he said. "It's an honor to have such a distinguished guest."

The words could have been obsequious, but Philip seemed genuine enough. Yet there was something about him that bothered Gilan. He seemed ill at ease in Gilan's presence. He ushered Gilan to a chair in front of his large desk.

"Please sit down, Ranger. I'm sorry to say you've caught us unprepared. Baron Douglas is out hunting. He won't be back for several hours. But if I can help you in any way?"

Gilan waved the apology aside. "I'm in no rush," he told the man. "I'm happy to wait for the Baron's return. In the meantime, you might be able to provide me with some information."

As he said the words, Gilan was sure he saw the beginnings of a guilty start, hastily covered. His eyes narrowed slightly. Philip was definitely nervous about something. And Gilan already had suspicions that there was an informant in the castle—someone placed high enough to have known about the recent pay convoy and its route.

"Information?" Philip said. By now he had his reactions under more control and his voice was steady and his manner noncommittal. "What would that be about?"

There was a tap at the door and the clerk entered, bearing a tray with a cup of coffee. Gilan decided not to answer immediately. He wanted to give the other man time to wonder what information he might be looking for. He accepted the cup, added sugar and took a deep, appreciative sip. He nodded his thanks to the clerk, who withdrew from the room. As the door closed behind him, Gilan turned back to Philip.

"I'm trying to track down a man called Foldar," Gilan said. "You may have heard of him."

Now Philip's face darkened, anger replacing the former nervousness. "Foldar?" he said. "I've never known a man so evil. In my opinion, he was worse than Morgarath himself."

Gilan looked up quickly. "You knew him?"

Philip nodded several times before answering. When he did speak again, his mind was obviously far away. "Oh yes. I knew him," he said. "Knew both of them, as a matter of fact. Evil, they were. I suppose that's what attracted Foldar to Morgarath. As they say, like clings to like."

"How did you come to meet them?" Gilan asked, fascinated. He hadn't met many people who had actually known Morgarath, even though the former baron's shadow had loomed over Araluen for so many years.

Philip's eyes rose to meet his.

"At Castle Gorlan," he said. "I began my training in service there as a junior steward. Of course, I wouldn't actually say that I *knew* them—not in the sense of sharing time with them or meeting them. But I saw plenty of them around the castle. And that was enough for me. I couldn't wait to leave the place."

"When was that?" Gilan asked. He was feigning only polite interest, but his senses were tingling. In spite of Philip's claim that he couldn't abide Morgarath's former lieutenant, he had admitted that he knew Foldar in the past. Perhaps that had been enough to secure Philip's current services for the outlaw.

"Must have been three or four years before Morgarath's revolt," Philip told him. "I could see something bad was coming and I wanted no part in it. So I got out. Cost me a year's seniority and three months' pay, but I figure I got the best of the deal in the long run."

Interesting, Gilan thought. The man would have little reason to be loyal to Morgarath or Foldar. But then again, he might have been a carefully placed agent, with his departure from Gorlan Fief a cunningly planned ruse. Morgarath had been a man more than capable of such devious planning and advance plotting.

"What makes you think Foldar is anywhere in this region?" Philip asked, interrupting his thoughts.

"There was a report of an attack on a pay convoy. Men killed in cold blood, gold stolen. It had all the hallmarks of the sort of thing Foldar would get up to."

Philip nodded thoughtfully.

"Yes. I remember that," he said. "I was the one who sent in the report. At the time, I never associated it with Foldar. Although, come to think of it, one of the survivors did say that the leader of the bandits wore a black cloak. Still, it seems a pretty thin connection to Foldar. Are you sure it was him?"

"No. Not at all. I'm chasing down leads all over the kingdom. This seemed one of the most likely. I'll stay a few days, nose around the area, ask people if they've seen any suspicious gatherings of men, do a bit of scouting through the forest. If there's a robber band any-where in the district, that's where they'll most likely be. I'll see what I come up with." *It all sounds vague and indefinite*, he thought. He didn't mention that he was hatching a plan to entrap the bandits. He wasn't sure yet where Philip's loyalties might lie. The seneschal shrugged.

"I suppose that's all you can do," he agreed. "Who knows? Some-thing might turn up."

"My thoughts exactly," Gilan replied. He set his cup down and rose from his chair. "Now, if you can have someone show me to my quarters, I'll let you get back to work."

Philip rose also, accompanying him to the door.

"My clerk will show you to your rooms," he said. As he opened the door, the clerk looked up. "Take Ranger Gilan to the guest apart-ment on the fourth floor," Philip told him. Then, turning to Gilan again, he said, "I'll send word when the Baron returns from hunting. I'm sure he'll want to see you immediately."

The guest accommodation was a comfortable suite of three rooms, overlooking the ocean. In a building like this, Gilan thought, sited as it was, most rooms would overlook the ocean. A clean salt breeze swept in through the open windows, sending the heavy curtains bil-lowing out. There were shutters but Gilan chose to leave them open. He liked fresh air, and the cold that accompanied it didn't bother him.

After he'd settled in, he went to the stables to check on Blaze. There was another bay—a gelding—in one of the stalls near the entrance. For a few seconds, in the dim interior, he mistook it for

Blaze. Then he heard her familiar nicker and realized she was stabled four stalls away.

The stable hand had done a good job and Blaze was comfortable in a dry stall, with plenty of fresh straw and a bin half full of grain. The water in the bucket hanging from a hook was fresh and clean. Nodding approval, he patted her muzzle and then turned away just as a castle servant entered, looking for him.

"The seneschal said to tell you Baron Douglas has returned. He'll see you now."

Douglas had his office and sleeping quarters on the third floor. Gilan frowned slightly at that. A careful commander would site his command position high in the tower, not in the more easily accessible lower levels. Douglas had possibly grown lazy, he thought, and maybe had an aversion to climbing too many stairs.

His first sight of the Baron of Highcliff confirmed the guess. Baron Douglas was seriously overweight. Gilan knew that other barons, like Arald of Redmont, struggled to maintain their waistlines. But Douglas seemed to have no such inhibitions.

He was tall—about the same height as Gilan—and his hair was thinning on top. As if to compensate for that fact, he kept it long on the sides. Gilan guessed that on formal occasions, he might well comb it over the top to disguise the pink scalp showing through. He was clean shaven, fleshy in the jowls, and his blue eyes were set close together. That gave him a slightly shifty look, Gilan thought. Then he discounted the idea. Douglas couldn't be blamed for the positioning of his eyes any more than he could be blamed for his tendency to baldness.

The baron spoke a little too loudly, as if he were conscious of his own importance and constantly trying to assert it. His manner was abrupt, although he stopped short of actual rudeness. No wise man was ever rude to a Ranger.

"Philip tells me you think that devil Foldar is somewhere in Highcliff," he said, after they had gone through the polite formalities of introduction.

Gilan shrugged. "I'm following leads," he said. "There's a chance that he could be here. I'm sure Philip mentioned the raid on the pay convoy some weeks back."

Douglas snorted. "That? Shouldn't think that was Foldar. Just bandits if you ask me."

"You're probably right. Although your seneschal did agree that the attack was the sort of thing Foldar would organize. Apparently he knew him some years back. How about you? Did you ever meet him?"

Douglas sat upright. "Me? No. Never laid eyes on him. I never want to either. Why do you ask?" he added, leaning forward suspiciously.

Gilan waved a hand casually. "I'd be interested in getting a more complete picture of the man. The more I know about him, the easier it might be to predict his moves."

"Well, I can't help you there," Douglas said, his tone indicating that he felt this interview had gone on long enough. "Anything else I can do for you, just ask. Better still, ask Philip. He's the man to get things done."

"I'll try not to be too much of a bother," Gilan said, smiling. Douglas shook his head emphatically. He did most things emphatically, Gilan thought.

"No bother. No bother at all." Already he had dismissed Gilan as a concern.

4

The temporary absence of the local Ranger, Gilan thought, might well have influenced Foldar's decision to choose Highcliff as a site of operations—assuming that he had, in fact, done so.

A day had passed since his arrival and he was riding through the farmland surrounding the castle. It was good, rich land, with the majority of farmers concentrating on dairy cattle. The countryside seemed peaceful enough, and when he stopped for his midday meal at a small village inn, the people seemed content and welcoming.

It was a sunny day and he chose to sit at a table outside the inn. The innkeeper was an attractive woman, around thirty years of age. She had a friendly nature and she smiled as she took his order. He noticed she was wearing a plain ring on the third finger of her left hand, but there was no sign of a husband anywhere in the building. When she returned and set a tankard of ale down in front of him, he looked around the inn.

"Is your husband away?" he asked, and the woman's smile faded. Sadness filled her eyes.

"He was killed in the war," she said.

Gilan shook his head in apology. "I'm sorry," he said, regretting that he'd caused her pain. "I shouldn't have asked."

She shrugged philosophically. "I'm not the only woman left without a man," she said. "And I'm better off than most. At least I have a business that I can run. Some widows are left with a farm to tend on their own, and that's no work for a woman." She smiled again, not quite as brightly as before, and changed the subject. "So what brings you to our doorstep, Ranger?"

"Please, call me Gilan," he said, and she reached forward to shake hands.

"I'm Maeve," she told him. She studied him frankly. He was tall and good-looking, with a hint of humor, or even mischief, in his eyes. And he had an air of confidence about him. Quiet confidence, not arrogance like some young men. He was probably a year or two younger than she was. But it wasn't a great difference in age and she wondered if he was married.

"You were saying?" she prompted, and Gilan remembered her question.

"Oh . . . just a little business at the castle," he said carelessly. "Administration details really, getting things back in order after the war." He paused, then added, "Do you know Philip, the seneschal, at all?"

In the past, he'd found that innkeepers were usually well informed about local gossip. And they were often more than willing to share their knowledge. Maeve proved to be no exception.

She nodded. "A good administrator," she said, "if he can keep away from the dice."

"He gambles?" Gilan asked, and she paused, pursing her mouth thoughtfully before she answered. She liked Philip and didn't want Gilan getting the wrong idea about him.

"He used to. He and some of the local merchants used to

gamble regularly in the Swan tavern." She jerked her head toward a single-story building on the far side of the village's main street. "But I haven't seen him there for the last month or two. I think he's sworn off it now. He ran up quite a debt with the other players. Some of them were going to report him to Baron Douglas, but he persuaded them not to."

"That wouldn't have done him any good," Gilan said. As seneschal, Philip would be in charge of the castle's treasury. Douglas would hardly be comfortable if he knew his financial administrator was running up gambling debts in the village.

"Agreed. Not that anyone around here has much time for the Baron . . ." Maeve stopped warily as she realized she might be speaking out of turn.

Gilan smiled sympathetically.

"I've met him," he said. "He's a little pompous, isn't he?"

Maeve seemed to relax. "As I say, none of the others felt they owed him any favors. They already owe him enough in taxes," she added darkly. "He's somewhat heavy-handed when it comes to taxing local businesses."

Gilan nodded, keeping a straight face. But inside, he was smiling. He was yet to meet a trader who didn't think he or she was being asked to pay too much tax.

"So . . . Philip doesn't come to the village much these days?" he asked.

She shook her head emphatically. "Not to the Swan," she said. Then she paused. "But I have seen him a few times recently, late at night. I'm a light sleeper and I'll often sit at my window, watching the street outside." She didn't add that her lack of sleep was caused by loneliness in the small hours. It was then, with nothing to occupy her mind, that she felt the loss of her husband most keenly.

"Where was he going?" Gilan asked.

She hesitated for a few seconds. "If it was him. Although I'm sure it was. I never actually saw his face, but he has that way of walking, with his head thrust forward and his shoulders hunched. He seemed to be heading for Ambrose Turner's house, at the end of the high street. Strange, I thought, since Ambrose was the one he owed the most money to."

"Did he manage to repay the debt?" Gilan asked.

"I don't know. He must have. He'd hardly be welcome at Ambrose's house if he hadn't, would he?"

Gilan frowned. "No. He wouldn't be," he said thoughtfully. Maeve, who had been perched on the edge of his table as they spoke, glanced up as a group of customers arrived, calling cheerfully to her as they went into the taproom.

"I'd best see to them," she said. "Your meal will be here shortly. Nice to talk to you, Gilan. Call by again," she said. There was a slightly wistful look in her eyes as she said it.

"I'll do that," Gilan said, smiling. But his mind was working overtime as he mulled over what she had told him. He had a lot to think about.

He rode back to the castle slowly that afternoon, still thinking on the information he had gleaned, assembling the facts in his mind.

The seneschal was, or had been, a heavy gambler. Worse, he was an unsuccessful one and he'd run up a large debt with some of the local traders. That was a dangerous combination. As seneschal, Philip had access to the castle's funds. If he had repaid the debt— and as Maeve had said, he'd hardly be welcome in the village if he hadn't—then his most likely source of money was from the castle treasury.

There was another possibility. Philip's gambling made him a prime subject for blackmail. If the Baron discovered that he was a gambler, and that he owed money to local merchants, he would be dismissed immediately.

Suppose Foldar had discovered Philip's secret? He might have paid the debt for him, then threatened to expose him. Once he had the man in thrall, he could well have forced him to become his informant in Castle Highcliff, telling him when pay convoys or tax payments were being transported through the fief.

Tax payments! The quarterly tax payment to the King would be due in a week. Had Philip been passing information to Foldar about the amount of money that would be sent to Castle Araluen? Or about the date of departure or the route the wagon containing the money would take?

That might explain his late-night, clandestine trips to the village. What if he were not visiting the merchant Ambrose, but meeting with Foldar or his agents? After all, Maeve had never actually seen him go into Ambrose's house, and it was at the end of the high street. Philip may well have passed through the village and kept going to a rendezvous with Foldar.

His mind whirling, Gilan nearly missed Blaze's warning rumble and the toss of her head to the left. Fully alert once more, he glanced left and saw two figures rising from behind the cover of a fallen log on the far side of the stream he was riding alongside. He registered the men and, a fraction of a second later, the fact that they were both armed with crossbows, and those bows were aimed at him.

Kicking his feet from the stirrups, he hurled himself sideways from the saddle, diving to his right so as to keep Blaze between him and the two ambushers. He heard a wicked buzz close to his head as he dived, and felt something pluck viciously at his cloak. Then he hit the ground on his side, rolling to cushion the fall.

He grunted at the impact, then called softly, "Blaze! Panic!"

The bay pricked her ears as she heard her name. Then, at the second word of command, she went into a remarkable performance. She whinnied loudly and reared onto her hind legs, her forelegs thrashing at the air. As her front feet crashed back to the ground, she whirled in a circle, still whinnying and neighing. Then she ran a few meters back the way they had come, stopped, hesitated and ran in the opposite direction, curving in a large circle, tossing her head and mane as she did so.

It was a carefully rehearsed routine, one of many that Rangers and their horses practiced from their first days together. The noise, the movement, the apparent panic were all designed to provide a distraction. As Gilan left the saddle and dropped to the ground, it was almost impossible for an observer not to take his eyes off the Ranger and look instead at the plunging, rearing, neighing horse.

That gave Gilan time to roll over several times, wrapping himself in his cloak as he did so. He realized that his cowl had fallen back from his head as he jumped. There was no time to replace it, so as he rolled, he pulled a fold of the cloak up over his face as a mask. He came to rest lying flat on the ground, facing the direction from which the attack had come. Then he lay absolutely still, barely breathing, as Blaze apparently recovered from her sudden panic and stopped, head down, ten meters away from him.

Trust the cloak. It was a mantra drummed into all Rangers during their years as apprentices. Gilan followed the rule now, lying unmoving in the muddy grass, the gray-and-green pattern of the cloak rendering him, to all intents and purposes, invisible.

His attackers were barely thirty meters away, with the deep creek between him and them. He could hear them clearly. "Where's he gone?"

"I got him. I know I got him." The second voice was excited. The first, when he spoke again, was heavy with sarcasm.

"Then where is he? There's no sign."

"There must be. I know I . . ." The voice trailed off.

Eyes slitted above the cloak, Gilan watched as the two men moved out from behind the cover of the fallen log and advanced cautiously to the edge of the stream. The senior of the two men, the sarcastic one, looked doubtfully at the dark, swift-flowing water.

"Hop across and look for him then," he ordered, but the other man snorted indignantly.

"Hop across? Not likely! That water must be three or four meters deep and I'm no swimmer! Hop across yourself."

Belatedly, the two would-be assassins realized that they hadn't reloaded their crossbows. They did so now, grunting with the strain as they heaved the heavy cords into place. Gilan looked to where his longbow lay, a few meters away. He'd released his grip on it during his fall, in case he landed on it and broke it. For a moment, he considered his next move. He could rise and move in seconds to retrieve it. Another two seconds to draw an arrow from his quiver and nock it. Then a half second to draw, aim and shoot. And that assumed that his cloak, wound around his body as it was, had left his quiver free. More likely, the quiver and its arrows would be hopelessly tangled in the folds of the cloak, adding precious seconds to the time it would take him to shoot.

No. He'd missed his opportunity while they stood with their bows unloaded. If there were one of them, he might chance it. But with two crossbowmen at such short range, the risk was too great. A second after he made this decision, he was glad that he had. A third voice joined the discussion.

"You two! What's going on?"

The voice was cultured but the tone was sharp and demanding. Gilan's eyes flicked in the direction that it came from. He daren't move his head. He could see a dark figure right on the edge of his vision. Whoever it was, he appeared to be dressed in black. Then his identity was made clear as the first of the crossbowmen answered his query.

"Just checking, Lord Foldar."

Gilan stiffened. So Foldar was here after all, he thought.

"Checking? Checking what? Did you get him?"

The two shooters exchanged a worried glance. Then the senior man called again.

"Yes. We got him, my lord. He's down, well and truly."

"Then make sure of him!" Foldar ordered angrily.

Again, the two men exchanged a worried glance. If they couldn't see Gilan, how could they make sure he was dead? Then the senior man shrugged slightly. "Very well, my lord," he called, and raised his bow. He aimed at a random spot three or four meters to Gilan's left and squeezed the trigger lever on the bow. There was the usual ugly smack of the crossbow mechanism releasing, then a *hiss-thud* as the short quarrel buried itself in the ground.

Gilan decided that this had gone on long enough. Blaze was still standing some meters away. He whistled softly, a pulsing, three-note whistle that was another prepared signal. Quiet as it was, the bowmen across the stream heard it and looked up suddenly, not sure where the noise had come from.

"What was that?" the younger one asked. But then Blaze took a hand once more. She raised her head, ears pricked, and looked away from Gilan, into the nearby trees. She whinnied and began trotting in the direction she was looking.

"Someone's coming!" said the senior bowman. "Let's get out of here!"

Gilan watched as they crashed clumsily through the under-growth on the far bank of the stream. He heard a brief, angry exchange between them and Foldar, in which they assured their leader that Gilan was dead. Then all three figures merged into the trees on the far side of the stream.

Gilan waited a few minutes, then slowly sat up. He whistled and Blaze came trotting back to him.

How was I?

"You were remarkable," Gilan told her. "In fact, I'm wondering if you weren't really panicking."

Blaze snorted in derision. *Me, panic? Over two ham-fisted crossbowmen? Why didn't you shoot them?*

"I dropped my bow," Gilan said, and immediately wished he hadn't. Blaze turned her head sidelong to look at him.

Of course you did.

He remounted and rode off thoughtfully. After a few kilometers, he voiced his thoughts aloud. "Why would Foldar send men to ambush me? It's hardly a good plan if he wants to remain unobtrusive. You don't try to kill a Ranger and expect it to go unnoticed."

Maybe he just doesn't like Rangers.

"Possibly. It's more likely he knows that I'm hunting him and he was trying to get in first."

How could he know that? Unless someone told him about you. And only two people know what you're doing here.

"Exactly," said Gilan.

5

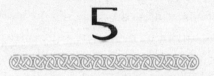

IT WAS SEVERAL HOURS AFTER MIDNIGHT WHEN PHILIP EMERGED from the large house at the end of the village. He moved furtively, staying in the shadows cast by the houses. In his right hand, he carried a large white canvas sack.

Gilan watched from his vantage point in a side alley as the seneschal went past him, barely three meters away. Philip never noticed him, but he was close enough for Gilan to hear the unmistakable chink as Philip swapped the sack to his other hand. Money, he thought. And quite a lot of it.

As the seneschal moved away, Gilan ran lightly to the back of the alley. Staying parallel to the village high road, he continued to move at a run, his feet making barely any sound on the soft earth. By the time he reached the end of the village, he had already overtaken Philip and was now some ten meters ahead of him.

Philip was walking slowly, head down, burdened by the heavy sack. He was taking no interest in his surroundings. At this time of night, he expected to see nobody, and be seen by nobody. Nonetheless, Gilan branched off at an angle and found the cover of the trees. He continued to run, still staying parallel to the high road, heading back to the castle and moving farther and farther ahead of the plodding figure behind him.

After sunset, the outer guard post on the isthmus wasn't manned. The guards withdrew inside the castle and the heavy portcullis was lowered to bar entry. But there were still sentries on the battlements, and the road across the isthmus was in plain view. However, when Gilan had followed Philip from the castle earlier that evening, he had watched the seneschal climb awkwardly down the rubble-strewn slope beside the road for several meters, where a rough and almost indiscernible track ran through the tumbled rocks. Here, he was hidden from the sight of the castle sentries. Gilan moved along the track now until he was only a few meters from the towering castle walls. Then he slipped quickly back up to level ground. Pressing himself against the rough stone, he moved to the left, rounding one of the corner towers. A few meters on, he came to the small wicket gate Philip had used to leave the castle.

"There's always a secret way in and out," Gilan had mused when he had seen the seneschal unlock the gate earlier in the evening. This was the reason for his running ahead of Philip. When the other man reentered the castle, he would be sure to lock the gate. Gilan pushed it shut behind him and moved stealthily to the keep tower. Once inside, he concealed himself behind a high-backed chair, where he had a view of Philip's office and the massive door to the strong room where the tax money was kept secure.

He'd been in place for several minutes when the outer door creaked open and Philip slid around it to enter the keep. He glanced around, making sure there was nobody watching, then hurried to the strong room door. Again, Gilan heard the chink of coins as he set the white sack down and fumbled with a key ring to unlock the strong room.

Several minutes later, he emerged once more and busied himself with the multiple locks on the strong room door. He tested the door to make sure it was secure. Then, with a weary sigh, he made his way to his office and went inside. Gilan knew that Philip's private quarters were located behind the office. He also noticed that, when the seneschal had emerged from the strong room, he wasn't carrying the sack of money.

"Fascinating," Gilan said to himself.

"It's a big risk," Baron Douglas said, frowning, as Gilan laid out the first part of his plan. "You plan to send the tax money in one small cart, with no escort? I don't like it."

"It's not exactly unescorted," Gilan said. "After all, I'll be traveling in the cart."

Baron Douglas looked unconvinced. Ranger or not, one man would make little difference if Foldar's band decided to attack.

"The point is," Gilan continued, "Foldar will think the tax money is in the usual convoy. We'll organize things so it leaves ten minutes after the small cart, with the usual escort."

Baron Douglas leaned back in his chair, shaking his head doubtfully.

"If Foldar does decide to steal the tax money," he said, "he'll be watching the castle. And he'll see the small cart leave, with you aboard it, a few minutes before the large wagon and its escort. He'll know you wouldn't let the money out of your sight and he'll smell a rat. He'll see through your plan. He's no fool, you know."

"I'm banking on it." Gilan smiled. "Because I'm planning a double bluff. The money will actually be where it's supposed to be— in the large wagon with the escort. So while Foldar's busy attacking the small wagon—and giving me a chance to capture him—the real tax wagon will be miles away, and safe."

For a moment, Douglas was speechless. His lips moved wordlessly as he pieced together the convoluted working of Gilan's mind.

"So the large wagon, which is supposed to be a decoy, will actually have the money on board all the time. While the small wagon, with you in it, will be the decoy?"

"That's right," Gilan said cheerfully. "Sometimes I'm so devious I confuse myself."

"I wouldn't like to be in your shoes when Foldar catches up with you and realizes you've tricked him," Douglas said.

"That's part of the plan. I want him to catch up with me. It'll save me tracking him down."

Douglas shook his head at the words. "Better you than me. I wouldn't care to face him when he's angry. Those eyes of his are enough to send shivers down your spine. They're cold and lifeless, like a snake's."

"I've killed a few snakes in my time," Gilan said, dropping his insouciant manner. Douglas rubbed his chin nervously as he saw the sudden steel in the young Ranger's eyes. He let his own gaze slide away and quickly changed the subject.

"Of course, the men who load the wagons will know which one has the money inside. We'll have to make sure they don't talk."

"Keep them locked up for a day," Gilan said, and Douglas's brows came together in a frown.

"Isn't that a little drastic?" he asked.

Gilan shrugged the protest aside. "You don't have to chain them up in a dungeon. Just keep them incommunicado for a day. We can't risk word of the double bluff getting to Foldar. And we know there's an informer somewhere in the castle. This way, you and I will be the only ones who know the real story."

"And Philip, of course," Douglas said. "He has to count the money and certify the tax forms. Do you want me to lock him up too?"

Gilan hesitated for just a moment, then said easily, "No. I'm sure we can trust Philip."

• • •

"How many men in your troop?" Gilan asked the red-bearded plow-man. His name was Bran Richards and he was the commander of the local troop of archers. Every fief in the kingdom was charged with maintaining a ready force of archers. The men trained year-round, in addition to their normal tasks of plowing, harvesting or milling. In the event of a war, they could be called up into the royal army and be ready to fight immediately.

"Fifteen," the man replied. "It should be eighteen, but we lost three men in the war. I'll have to recruit three new men and start training them soon."

"Hmm. Well, six should be enough for my purposes. Pick your six best archers and wait for me the day after tomorrow three kilometers past the point where the coast road and the high road diverge. There's a small copse of trees there where you can hide. Stay out of sight. In fact, it might be best if you moved into position before first light."

Bran nodded. "Whatever you say."

A new thought struck Gilan. "One thing," he said. "Tell your men this is just a routine field exercise. Don't mention that I'm involved, all right? In fact, don't mention it to anybody."

Bran nodded his understanding. He gestured to the flagon on the table between them. They were sitting in the comfortable parlor of his home. "More cider?" he offered. But Gilan shook his head.

"I need to keep a clear head," he said. "I've got a lot of arrangements to make."

6

THE OBSERVER ON THE HILL WATCHED AS THE PORTCULLIS SLOWLY
rumbled open to emit a small covered cart drawn by a single horse.
Trotting behind it, tethered by a lead rope to the rear of the cart, was
a bay horse. Seated beside the driver was a tall figure wearing the
unmistakable cloak of a Ranger. The observer watched as the cart
slowly trundled to the point where the road forked. It bore to the left
at the fork, following the coastal road.

Some ten minutes later, a second cart—larger than the first
and drawn by a pair of horses—emerged from the gate. An escort
of six mounted men-at-arms clattered out after it. This cart veered
to the right at the fork, following the high road that led toward the
forest.

"Just as Lord Foldar said," the man on the hill muttered to himself. He hurried to where his horse was tethered, mounted and rode
off at a gallop. He stayed off the road until he was far enough ahead
of the slow-moving cart to be unobserved. Then he spurred up onto
the road and increased his speed. At a point where a fallen tree lay
by the roadside, he reined in. Foldar emerged from the trees, unmistakable in his high-collared black velvet cloak. Underneath his black
surcoat, he wore a shirt of chain mail, also black. On his left arm, he

bore a triangular shield. His long sword was in a scabbard attached to his saddle bow.

Foldar trotted his horse closer. "Report," he said.

The rider hesitated. He was never particularly comfortable when he was under his leader's direct gaze. The man rarely, if ever, seemed to blink.

"The small cart left twenty minutes ago," he said. "The Ranger was with it."

"That's the same Ranger that you assured me you killed, is it?" Foldar asked quietly. His henchman shifted uncomfortably in his saddle.

"Yes, Lord Foldar. My apologies. I thought—"

But the bandit leader made a curt gesture with his right hand. "Stop babbling. Did the second cart leave?"

"Ten minutes later, Lord. It's coming along the high road, through the forest, just as you expected," he said.

Foldar sneered dismissively at the man's feeble effort to ingratiate himself. "And the decoy?" he asked.

"The small cart took the coastal road, lord."

Foldar paused a moment. It was a clumsy attempt to deceive him, he thought, although he gave the Ranger credit for traveling with the decoy cart himself. That, at least, showed a degree of originality. But it would be all the more galling for the Ranger when he realized his stratagem had failed. He would be miles away from the point of the real attack, and helpless to intervene.

"Very well," he said. "Now get off the road and out of sight."

"Yes, Lord," the observer said submissively. They rode back into the trees, where a group of a dozen heavily armed mounted men waited for Foldar's orders.

"You, you and you," he said, jerking a thumb at the messenger and two other men. "Take up a position on the far side of the road.

When you hear my horn, attack immediately, making all the noise you can."

The three men muttered their acknowledgment. As they were about to move off, he stopped them.

"Stay out of sight," he said. It was a warning as much as a command. Then, as he dismissed them with a gesture, they rode to their positions. He glanced around the other men. "Once the escort is distracted, we'll attack. But not before my order."

Several of the riders nodded. They were grateful they hadn't been selected for the first attack. They knew Foldar would hold back the main attack until the soldiers in the escort were fully engaged. The three men he had selected would be outnumbered two to one and it was unlikely that they'd all survive. They had all earned Foldar's displeasure over the preceding days.

They heard the convoy coming before they saw it. The hooves of the escort's horses clattered on the hard, compacted surface of the high road and the cart's axle squeaked loudly in a teeth-grating rhythm. Then the cart and its escort came into sight around a bend. Two of the escort's soldiers rode ahead of the car, two more to either side, with the remaining two men bringing up the rear. As well as the driver, there was another armed man on the cart's seat.

The members of the escort were all alert, their eyes scanning the forest on either side of the road. The rear guard twisted in their saddles every thirty seconds or so to scan the road behind them. This early in the journey, Foldar had expected them to be on their guard, which was why he had dispatched the three men to the far side of the road to distract their attention from the main attack. He waited now as the cart drew level with the spot where he and his men waited, unseen, in the trees. The horse nearest him surged forward a pace or two before its rider could check it.

"Be still, blast you," Foldar said, noting the man's identity. The bandit paled. He knew his leader would remember him and punish him at a later date. It might be best to desert the band after this raid, he thought.

Foldar had a small ivory-and-brass hunting horn hanging from his belt. He raised it to his lips and hesitated, judging distances and the speed of the cart's progress. When the moment was right, he blew a short blast from the horn.

The men of the escort heard it, of course, and they heard where it came from. As one, they swung around to face the trees on the left side of the road, hands dropping to sword hilts. Then they heard shouting and a sudden thunder of hoofbeats from their right and swung back in that direction. For a moment there was confusion and they milled around uncertainly. Then the senior man shouted orders and formed them up on the right side of the road, in time to face the onrushing riders.

In the first exchange, the attackers had the advantage, with the impetus of their charge behind them, and the element of surprise. The escort barely had time to form into a defensive line before the three bandits were upon them. One of the escort's horses was hurled from his feet as a bandit drove his galloping horse into it at full speed. Another defender wheeled away, dropping his sword and clutching at his wounded upper arm, trying to stop the sudden flow of blood from a sword thrust.

But once the initial energy of the charge was dissipated, the bandits were in trouble. One fell quickly to a sword thrust as he stood in his stirrups to strike at the escort leader. Then there were two men facing five, and the members of the escort quickly encircled them.

In the trees on the left side of the road, Foldar watched, eyes slitted, waiting until the escort was fully engaged. He could have attacked earlier and possibly saved the remaining two men in the diversionary attack. But he cared little for their well-being and he knew his own chances of success would be greater if he waited. Now, seeing only one of his men left in the saddle, he judged the moment was right. He raised his sword, then swept it forward, leading his men out of the trees and charging toward the convoy.

As he had ordered beforehand, they made no sound. There were no battle cries, no shouted challenges, just the muted thud of the horses' hooves on the soft grass.

Foldar saw the last of the three men from the initial attack slump suddenly in his saddle as a soldier from the escort drove a sword into his side. Then, as he had expected, the escort relaxed, thinking the fight was over. Several were in the act of sheathing their swords when one looked up and saw the group of galloping men barely twenty meters away. The man shouted a warning and the others turned in confusion once more, wondering where this new attack had come from.

Then, above their cries of alarm, Foldar heard another sound— a whirring, hissing sound as a flight of arrows arced down around him. Barely seconds later, he heard the dull thuds of contact as the arrows struck home. Four of his men tumbled from their saddles and lay still. Their horses continued to charge for a few more meters, then, with nobody to urge them on, they slowed and trotted aimlessly.

Another multiple whirring sound surrounded him, and two more of his men went down. The remainder hauled on their reins and swung away from the wagon and its escort. Foldar brought his own battlehorse to a sliding stop, searching for the source of those two deadly volleys.

And saw it. Sixty meters away, half a dozen archers had emerged from the trees. A tall figure on a bay horse was beside them, directing their shooting. Even without the distinctive mottled cloak, Foldar recognized the young Ranger. He cursed bitterly, wondering how the man had gotten here so quickly and how he had mustered the troop of archers.

But there was no time to think about it. His own force, initially nine men, was now reduced to three, and the members of the escort, heartened by this unexpected turn of fortune, were rallying to charge them.

"Run!" he yelled to the survivors. "Scatter! Rendezvous at the camp tomorrow!"

He didn't wait to see if they heard him or acted on his orders. He wheeled the battlehorse and set his spurs to its flanks, sending it thundering away, building to a gallop as he continued to spur it and flail at it with the flat of his sword.

He swept into the trees at a full gallop, the massive horse smashing its way through the lighter undergrowth, swerving to avoid the larger trunks. The branches whizzed by his head and shoulders, occasionally slapping painfully at him as he was too slow to duck. Tears sprang into his eyes from the impact and he could barely see where he was going. But he trusted the horse to avoid any major obstacles and crouched low over its neck to avoid the whipping, slapping branches, tucking his head forward so that his helmet took the brunt of the continuous impacts. Blindly, he continued to rake the horse with his spurs each time he sensed it beginning to slow its mad, headlong rush through the trees.

Then they burst out of the shadows under the trees into the sunlight and he looked up to see clear farmland stretching for several kilometers ahead of him. A low stone wall was rushing to meet him and he forced the horse at it, sensing that it was about to balk at the obstacle. The massive animal gathered itself, then launched itself over the low wall. As they soared clear of the ground, the thud of its hoofbeats ceased for a few seconds. In that time, Foldar heard another set of rapid hoofbeats behind him.

The horse crashed back to earth and the impact threw him forward, over the horse's neck. He clutched wildly at its mane to retain his balance, nearly losing his hold on his sword as he did so. When he had regained his seat, he twisted in the saddle, searching for the source of those other, pursuing hoofbeats.

As he looked, he saw the bay horse clear the wall he had just jumped, the Ranger on its back sitting easily in the saddle. The bay barely broke its stride, but was back at a gallop almost instantly, gaining on the lumbering battlehorse with ease.

Foldar glanced around. There was open ground all around him. The nearest trees were at least two kilometers away. He would never reach them in time. He glanced back at his pursuer. The Ranger was alone and armed with only a sword. There was no sign of the longbow that Rangers habitually carried. Foldar's lips curled back from his teeth in an expression that was half smile, half snarl. He knew that the sword was not a primary weapon for Rangers. And Foldar himself was a well-trained, experienced swordsman who had fought in a score of combats over the years. His shield was hanging from a retaining strap, banging uncomfortably against the horse's flanks as it galloped. He had relinquished his grip on it when he turned to escape. Now, he hauled it back into position, slipping his left arm through the straps and seizing the handgrip.

Then he checked his battlehorse, dragged it around in a half circle and clapped his spurs to its flanks again as he charged back to attack his pursuer.

Gilan nodded to himself as he saw the bandit leader's change of direction. He had tossed his bow to Bran, the archer troop leader, when he set out in pursuit of Foldar. He could see that the black-cloaked figure was heading for the thick trees and the bow would have been an encumbrance as Blaze weaved her way between the massive trunks and under low, overhanging branches. In addition, Crowley's instructions had been to capture Foldar if possible and bring him back for trial. That meant he would have to face him in close combat, not shoot him down from a distance. As the thundering battlehorse drew closer, Gilan slid his own sword from its scabbard. He felt Blaze tense under him.

"Not yet," he muttered, and the horse flicked her ears in acknowledgment.

Foldar was angling at him so that they would meet right side to right side. He had his kite-shaped shield held horizontally across the saddle bow to protect his body, and his long sword was raised, ready to strike. It was a matter of seconds . . .

"Now!" shouted Gilan, although the shout was unnecessary. The sudden pressure of his knees and the twitch of the reins told Blaze exactly what he wanted her to do.

The bay mare leapt sideways to the right, crossing quickly in front of the battlehorse before Foldar had a chance to react. Foldar tried to twist in the saddle but the shield, held at an angle, impeded the movement; and Gilan and Blaze slipped by on his left. Foldar wrenched at the reins, held in his left hand, but once more the shield was an impediment. The battlehorse lurched awkwardly and began a clumsy turn to the left.

There was nothing clumsy or slow about Blaze's movements. Under Gilan's direction, she had risen to her hind legs, pirouetting like a dancer to reverse her direction with barely a pause. As her foreleg hooves hit the ground again, she was already galloping full tilt after the battlehorse.

They came in at an angle from behind Foldar and to his left. His horse was still trying to swing around in a circle to the left, as he dragged at the reins and raked cruelly with his right spur. As a result, the big horse was unsteady and off balance as Blaze, at full speed, drove her shoulder into the battlehorse's side, between the saddle and its front left shoulder.

Blaze was ready and braced for the thundering impact. Foldar's horse wasn't. Already unbalanced, it was hurled sideways, then lost its footing and crashed over on its side. Foldar had an instant to decide whether the horse could recover or whether he would be trapped under it. He kicked his feet from the stirrups and leapt clear, landing on the shield and rolling to absorb the impact. The horse slid several meters on the damp ground, its hooves thrashing the air dangerously. Then, with a startled grunt, it rolled clumsily to its feet and cantered away.

As Foldar slowly regained his feet, Gilan slipped from Blaze's saddle. He stood several meters from the bandit leader, his sword held lightly, tip angled slightly down.

"I suggest you surrender now," Gilan said quietly. "Just lay your sword down."

Foldar laughed harshly. "You suggest that, do you?" he said. "Well, I suggest that you turn around and walk away. If you do that, I might spare your life. You're out of your league here, Ranger. You don't have your bow to hide behind now."

Foldar was making a serious mistake. He had a limited knowledge of Rangers, and limited knowledge can be a dangerous thing. He knew that Rangers were master bowmen. He'd never heard of any that were trained with the sword. As far as he was concerned, the odds were stacked in his favor in this encounter. He decided that he would enjoy killing this interfering young man who had spoiled his plans. He waited to see if Gilan would respond. But the tall Ranger remained silent.

"What are you doing here, anyway?" Foldar asked suddenly. "You were seen on the decoy cart. Your horse was tied behind it. So how did you get here so quickly?"

Now Gilan smiled. "The decoy cart?" he said. "Oh, you mean the small cart that left earlier? That's no decoy. That's the real tax cart. It's miles away by now. And I was never on it. That's just a young soldier wearing my cloak."

"But your horse—"

"Funny, isn't it. I left Blaze outside the castle last night. There was a bay horse in the stables. I borrowed him and tethered him behind the cart. They're very similar, although you probably should have noticed that he's a gelding, while my horse is a mare. But then, you probably never got that close."

Foldar hesitated as he realized that he'd been tricked. "I was told . . ." He cut the statement off abruptly. But Gilan had heard it.

"Yes, I'm sure you were. You were told the money was loaded on the larger wagon. And it was. But last night, I switched it all around again. Made for quite a late night, I can tell you. But nobody else knew about it. Certainly not your informant. Who is that, by the way?"

"You'll never know," Foldar told him. "And even if you did, it'd do you no good . . ."

He was still talking as he launched his attack. It was an old trick, designed to catch an opponent off guard. But Gilan was an experienced fighter. He parried Foldar's three quick sword strokes easily as the man charged, giving ground before him. After the first violent, high-speed attack, they circled warily, each taking stock of the other. Gilan could see that Foldar was a capable swordsman. And he had the advantage of the tall shield on his left arm. As he blocked Gilan's strokes with it, and forced Gilan's sword away to the right, he could follow through with his own sword, forcing the Ranger to recover hastily in order to parry the stroke. And if he parried Gilan's stroke with his sword, he could then use his shield as an offensive weapon, driving it forward into the young Ranger, buffeting him and sending him off balance. The shield gave the bandit an advantage and Gilan decided he should do something about that.

He switched hands.

He saw the momentary look of surprise on Foldar's face. Then the black-clad swordsman drove forward again, swinging his sword at Gilan's head. But now the situation had changed. Now that Gilan was wielding his sword in his left hand, Foldar was forced to parry mainly with his own sword. To use his shield, he would have to bring it right around his body, taking his sword arm away from his opponent. In addition, Gilan's attack now came from Foldar's right—the side unprotected by the large shield.

Foldar retreated hastily, trying to adjust to this new situation, and not managing to do so very well. Gilan now slipped his saxe knife from its scabbard, holding it in his right hand. As he blocked Foldar's sword away to his own left, he could follow through and move in close, stabbing with the heavy saxe.

The second time he did this, he opened a wide cut across Foldar's ribs, the saxe slicing easily through the chain mail beneath Foldar's surcoat. Foldar gasped in pain and immediately covered up, with his shield protecting his body.

This was Gilan's opportunity to launch an overhead attack, aimed at Foldar's helmet. He gave the bandit no time to bring his own sword into play but hammered a lightning-fast series of overhead strikes, forcing Foldar to raise his shield to protect himself.

One of the blows broke through, glancing from the rim of the shield and catching the bandit full on the helmet. He stumbled backward and dropped to one knee, his breath coming in ragged gasps.

"I'll give you one chance to surrender," Gilan said quietly. "One only."

Gilan had been trained in a hard school. He knew he was more skillful than Foldar, even with his left hand. But he also knew that a duel like this was a chancy affair. One slip, one missed step on the damp grass, could spell disaster for him. He had been trained to offer an opponent one chance to surrender. But only one.

"Surrender yourself!" Foldar snarled. He thrust forward from his semi-kneeling position, using his rear leg to propel himself at Gilan, his sword seeking for the tall figure. Gilan had sensed the move coming, a fraction of a second before Foldar moved. He saw it in the man's eyes. He caught the sword with his saxe knife, flicking his wrist and deflecting it to his right, so that Foldar spun awkwardly, exposing his unprotected back to Gilan's sword.

Foldar, trying to recover, felt a terrible impact between his shoulder blades. Then a burning pain.

"Aaah . . . aaah," he cried, his voice weak, his mind still wondering what had just happened to him. He felt his sword drop from his fingers, which were suddenly lacking the strength to support it. Then he saw the grass rushing up to meet him.

Gilan withdrew his sword and stepped back. Foldar was face-down on the grass, blood staining the black surcoat. Gilan shrugged. Crowley had asked him to capture the man if possible. As far as Gilan was concerned, "if possible" didn't involve risking his own life.

"Perhaps it's better this way," he told the dead bandit. "Snakes have a way of escaping."

7

"So Foldar's dead. That's a relief." Douglas was pacing the floor of his office as he listened to Gilan's account of the attack on the convoy. "Mind you, you took a big risk, swapping the money back to the smaller cart and sending it unprotected."

Gilan made a dismissive gesture. "Not really. I was confident that Foldar's informant would tell him the money was in the large wagon."

Baron Douglas's eyes narrowed for a moment as he met Gilan's steady gaze. Then, as always, they slid away from direct contact.

"Hmm. Yes. The informer. Any idea who that might be?"

"Well," said Gilan deliberately, "aside from you and me, only one other person knew that the money was supposed to be in the large wagon."

"Philip?"

Gilan nodded. "Exactly."

Now the Baron shook his head sadly. "I never would have thought it! The man's been with me for years. Still, I suppose if the temptation is great enough, anyone can go bad." He sighed deeply, obviously finding the whole matter distasteful. "I suppose we'd better have him in here, then."

"If you would," Gilan said.

They waited in silence for the few minutes it took for Philip to be summoned. The seneschal entered the Baron's office warily. He looked at the Ranger and at the Baron. Of course, he knew about the events that had taken place earlier in the day. He was intelligent enough to sense that he was under suspicion, as one of the few people who had known the intended whereabouts of the tax money.

"Why did you do it, Philip?" the Baron began, his voice heavy with disappointment.

"My lord?" Philip replied uncertainly. Thus far, he had been accused of nothing, although he knew that couldn't be too far off.

Gilan held up a hand to stop the Baron from saying more. "If I may, Baron Douglas?" he said, and the Baron signaled his acquiescence for Gilan to handle the questioning. He turned away, his hands clasped behind his back, a picture of betrayed trust.

"Philip," Gilan said quietly, "what were you doing at Ambrose's house?"

The Baron swung quickly back to face them, a puzzled expression on his face. Philip's face showed surprise too. But there was no puzzlement there. He knew what Gilan was referring to.

"Ambrose?" said Douglas. "Who the devil is Ambrose?"

"Ambrose is a wealthy merchant in the village," Gilan told him. "Philip owed him money."

The seneschal hung his head. "You know about that?" he said, his voice barely audible.

The Baron now stepped forward, stopping only a meter or so from Philip, dominating the smaller man as he sat slumped, head down, unable to meet his Baron's gaze. "So you took money from Foldar to betray your fief?" he said. "To betray me?"

Philip looked up now, anguish and bewilderment on his face. "Foldar?" he said. "I never took money from Foldar, my lord. I swear it."

"Then how did you pay your debts?" the Baron demanded angrily, and again Philip's head sank. He opened his mouth to reply, but Gilan beat him to it.

"He stole it from the tax money already collected," he said, and both men looked at him in surprise.

"He what?" the Baron asked, a second before Philip managed to reply.

"I never meant to keep it. I always intended to repay it! I swear. And I did repay it."

"I know," Gilan said. He looked now at the Baron. "For the past few months, Philip has spent his nights working for Ambrose and some of the other merchants in the village. I watched him the other night when he came back from Ambrose's with a large sack of money. He put it in the treasury. It was in a rather distinctive white sack, and I saw it when I loaded the money onto the cart the other night. I wondered, then: If a man was planning to help Foldar steal the tax money, why would he bother to replace the money he'd already stolen?"

"But . . . what did he do for these merchants?" the Baron asked, mystified.

Again, Philip looked shamefaced. "I was helping them with their accounts. Their record keeping was very sloppy and they were all paying far more tax than they were obliged to. I showed them how to reduce their taxes. They paid me for my services, and when I had earned enough, I replaced the money I'd borrowed from the treasury." He looked pleadingly at Gilan. "It was all perfectly legal, I swear."

Gilan hid a smile. "Perhaps. Whether it was ethical is another matter. You could be said to have a conflict of interest, being the person responsible for collecting the tax in the first place." He turned back to the Baron. "The fact is, my lord, Philip isn't our traitor."

"Then who is?" Douglas asked.

Gilan fixed him with an unblinking stare. After a few seconds, the Baron's eyes dropped. Then Gilan spoke quietly. "You are, my lord."

"Me? Don't be ridiculous!" All the bluster was back in the Baron's voice now. "Why would I betray the fief, and the kingdom, to Foldar?"

"The usual reasons, I suppose. Money probably figures among them. And I suspect that you were secretly in league with Foldar, and Morgarath, during the rebellion. Perhaps Foldar was threatening to expose that fact if you didn't help him. I'm sure it'll all come out at your trial."

"Ridiculous!" Baron Douglas shouted, as if volume somehow equated with innocence. "How could I be in league with Foldar? I've never met the man!"

"So you told me when I first arrived," Gilan said. "And then, the other day, you said to me: 'Those eyes of his are enough to send shivers down your spine. They're cold and lifeless, like a snake's.' A strange thing to say if you'd never met him."

The Baron glanced desperately around the room, looking for a way to escape. His eyes fell on his dagger, lying on the desk, and he lunged for it.

But Philip was quicker. He lunged forward as well, scooping up the heavy inkwell and throwing it, and its contents, into the Baron's face. Douglas staggered back, clawing at his eyes, trying to rub the heavy black ink out of them.

"You would have seen me hang for your crime!" Philip shouted. The Baron finally cleared his eyes so that he had partial vision. He found himself staring down the length of Gilan's sword. The Ranger smiled at him, but there was no real humor in the smile.

"We'll leave for Castle Araluen this afternoon," he said. "I rather hope you try to escape on the way."

This time, Douglas managed to hold Gilan's eyes. What he saw there made him quail. He decided then and there that there would be no escape attempt. Gilan took a pair of leather-and-wood thumb cuffs from an inner pocket and tossed them to Philip.

"Put these on him, would you?" he asked. The seneschal nodded, then hesitated.

"Who'll be in charge here when he's gone?"

Gilan raised one eyebrow. "For the moment, I suppose you will be. After that, we'll have to see. Just try to make sure the King gets some tax from this fief, would you?"

Philip nodded several times as he busied himself securing the Baron's hands behind his back with the cuffs. "Of course. Everything he's entitled to." Then he couldn't resist a slight smile. "But no more."

"That's fair enough," Gilan resheathed his sword and took Douglas by the elbow, shoving him toward the door. As they went to exit, he looked back at the seneschal, who was kneeling to mop up the spilled ink on the office floor.

"I've heard that the pen is mightier than the sword," Gilan said. "But I never knew the inkwell could be mightier than the dagger."

THE ROAMERS

1

THE TRADING BOAT WAS ESSENTIALLY A GIANT RAFT—A FLAT
deck built across half a dozen large logs that provided flotation.
Bundles of hides, wool, grain sacks, flour and cloth were stacked in
the middle of the deck, covered by tarpaulins. Behind them, a
deckhouse provided shelter for the small crew. The skipper stood
on a steering platform at the stern, equipped with a long sweep oar
that served as a rudder. There were four other oars—although at
the moment only two of them were manned, keeping the boat
moving slightly faster than the slow current of the Tarbus River. In
addition, if the wind was favorable, a stumpy mast and a square
mainsail could be hoisted.

It was an efficient way to get the goods to the market at the
river mouth. The alternative was a three-week overland journey
by ox cart. Even allowing for the twists and turns in the river,
the trading boat would make the trip within five days. The farmers and millers of Wensley, and half a dozen other villages along
the river, found it a more convenient way of selling their produce. The riverboat captain would pay them for their goods,
then sell them at a profit down the river. The producers might
receive less than the market price, but they were also saved a

lengthy, arduous trip, during which their goods might be stolen from them.

Theft was one of the dangers faced by the riverboat traders as well. Recently, there had been a sharp increase in the activity of river pirates preying on the traders. As Halt had commented to Will, "It seems whenever someone has a good idea like this, other people simply can't wait to rob them."

The riverboat was coming to a sweeping bend in the river. The skipper and the oarsmen heaved mightily to keep the ponderous craft out in the middle of the flow, avoiding the protruding sandbar of the left bank. Clumsily, the raft swept around the bend, at an angle to the flow. The helmsman worked his long steering oar to straighten his craft, calling on the oarsmen to pull in opposing directions—one forward and one backward—for half a dozen strokes, until he was satisfied that they were aligned with the flow once more. Let her get out of alignment, he knew, and before too long they'd be slowly spinning in the current, out of control. Then it would take an even greater effort to get the boat back in the correct position for the next bend.

Once the boat was traveling straight again, he called to the oarsmen—his two sons—that they could relax. They resumed their earlier gentle stroke. Then he tensed as he saw movement in the reeds along the right bank.

"Oswald! Ryan!" he shouted. "Oars! Look lively now!"

He had barely completed his warning when a long, narrow boat emerged from the reeds and headed toward them. She was packed with men—he estimated fifteen at least—and pulled eight oars. He leaned on the tiller, angling the boat back toward the left shore, while his sons heaved on the oars again.

There was no chance that they could outrun the other boat. His only chance was to beach the raft before they could board it, then escape into the trees. They might lose their cargo that way, but not their lives. The crew of the other boat were all heavily armed and all yelling threats and abuse at him.

Their leader stood in the prow of the boat, brandishing a long sword. "Heave to!" he yelled. "If you keep running, we'll kill you all!"

The skipper of the riverboat shook his head at the threat. The pirates would kill them anyway, he knew. In the past months, the bodies of a dozen riverboat traders had washed ashore along the river. Their boats and their cargoes had never been seen again.

"They're cutting us off!" he called, although his sons could see what was happening as well as he could. The fast pirate craft was angling toward their bow.

Then a voice from under the tarpaulin covering the cargo replied quietly, "Get your boys back astern then. Tell us when the pirates come aboard."

The skipper nodded. "Oswald! Ryan! Leave it now and get back here!"

The two muscular oarsmen needed no second bidding. They left their oars swinging in the rowlocks and scrambled back to the steering platform, arming themselves with heavy studded cudgels that were lying handy. Without the oars to propel her, the boat began to rotate slowly again and the skipper wigwagged on his oar, pulling left, feathering it and pulling it left again, to straighten her.

The pirates were only a few meters away, the boat coming on fast. The pirate leader crouched, ready to spring up onto the raft. The boat struck them at an angle, grating against the rough timber of the riverboat and swinging around to lie parallel to her. As they touched, the pirate leader leapt onto the decking, shouting to his men to follow. Half a dozen of them surged behind him, waiting their turn to leap onto the raft.

"They're boarding," the skipper shouted. As he did so, a section of the tarpaulin covering the cargo was thrown aside and two green-and-gray-clad figures emerged from their hiding place beneath it.

Each of them had a massive longbow, with an arrow nocked and ready to draw.

"King's Rangers!" shouted the one on the left. "Throw down your weapons and surrender!"

For a moment, the pirate leader was stunned. The sudden appearance of the two Rangers stopped him in his tracks. Then his mind worked rapidly. He and his men had been caught in an act of piracy. The penalty was hanging—certainly for him as their leader. There was only one possible course he could follow. He snarled incoherently in rage, then turned to yell at his men.

"Come on! Kill them! Kill them all!" He started down the raft at the two cloaked figures.

"Not the answer I wanted," Halt said quietly. He drew, sighted and shot before the pirate could take a second step.

The heavy, black-shafted arrow struck the man in the center of his chest, hurling him backward. He crashed off the edge of the raft into the mass of men trying to follow him aboard. The narrow pirate boat rocked dangerously as men scattered and fell. One of them went overboard. Others crashed backward into the rowers. The result was pandemonium.

Then one of them took charge. The idea of facing two Rangers, with their fabled skill for fast, accurate shooting, was a different matter from killing helpless riverboat men.

"Let's get out of here!" he yelled at the helmsman. Then he screamed at the oarsmen, who were trying to extricate themselves from under the fallen bodies of their companions, "Row, blast you! Row! Get us out of here!"

Slowly, order began to prevail in the pirates' boat. Halt turned to the two riverboat oarsmen and jerked his thumb toward the pirate craft.

"Grapple her! Quickly!"

The two boats were beginning to drift apart, as the pirate helmsman worked his tiller back and forth to swing his boat away. Oswald and Ryan dropped their cudgels, seeing no further need for them, and raced forward. Oswald grabbed up a three-pronged grappling iron that had been left ready, whirled it around his head and released it.

It soared across the widening gap, trailing a stout hemp line behind it. It clattered into the stern bulwark of the pirate boat and immediately Oswald hauled back on it, setting the sharp barbs into the timber. He began to haul the pirate boat back toward the raft.

In the meantime, Ryan had snatched one of the long oars from its rowlock. As his brother heaved the pirate boat in, he set the oar against it, pushing it out so that the pirates were trapped, three meters from the raft.

Halt and Will had made their way to the prow of the riverboat. Now they stood, their longbows threatening the pirates.

"Cut that rope!" screamed the pirate helmsman. Seeing none of his men willing to move under the threat of those bows, he drew a heavy dirk from his belt and let go of the tiller, moving toward the grapnel.

Will's bow thrummed. There was the familiar whip of the limbs and the scraping sound of the arrow passing across the bow, then the helmsman reared up, an arrow in his side. Will had shot to wound him in the arm. But at the last moment, the man had moved, exposing his ribs.

He looked up at the young Ranger in horror as he realized what had just happened to him. The dirk clattered onto the floorboards of the boat, then the helmsman fell sideways. His legs were trapped as his body went over the bulwark and the boat took on a sudden, dangerous list. Then one of his crewmen freed the dead man's legs and tossed them overboard. The boat came back upright and the body of the helmsman drifted away with the current. The water around him was slowly turning red.

"Throw your weapons overboard!" Halt ordered. For a second, nobody responded. Then he raised his bow and suddenly knives, clubs, hand axes and swords all splashed over into the brown river water.

"Oswald, tie off that rope," Halt ordered, and the river trader quickly looped the grapnel rope around a bollard. Halt's attention had never wavered from the pirates. Now he gestured toward the sand spit on the left bank of the river.

"Get on those oars!" he ordered. "And tow us ashore on that sandbank!"

Under the force of six of the oars the pirate boat began to swing toward the shore. As the strain came onto the rope, she moved more slowly, dragging the heavily laden raft in her wake. At a signal from Halt, Oswald and Ryan resumed their place at their own oars and helped propel the raft toward the sand.

When Halt felt the raft grate against the sandbar, he leapt down in knee-deep water, Will beside him. The two longbows continued to threaten the pirates.

"Out of the boat," Halt ordered. "Facedown on the sand. First man to make a move I don't like, I'll shoot."

For a moment, the boat's crew hesitated. After all, there were only two archers facing them. Then common sense reasserted itself. They were unarmed and those two archers were Rangers. In the space of ten seconds, they could unleash four or five arrows each. With two of their members already dead, none of them liked those odds. Slowly, reluctantly, they stepped ashore, then lay facedown in the sand.

"Put your hands behind your backs," Halt ordered, and when the pirates did so, he called to the riverboat crew. "Ryan, Oswald, tie them up, please."

The two brothers were happy to oblige. They moved quickly among the prone figures, carrying short lengths of cord that they had prepared earlier in the day. They tied them firmly and, being boatmen, they knew how to tie a knot that wouldn't loosen.

"Now tie them all to one long rope," Halt said. "We wouldn't want any of them to make a run for it."

The riverboat skipper tossed them a long, heavy cable and the brothers quickly attached the bound men to it. Then they hauled them on board the riverboat and deposited them, none too gently, on the planking.

"There's a garrison town about three kilometers down the river," Halt said. "We'll deposit these beauties there for trial. In the meantime, we can all relax and enjoy a leisurely boating trip down the Tarbus."

"Except for us," Ryan said as he returned to his place at the oar. But he was smiling. He was delighted to see these pirates out of action. The riverboat community was a small one and he'd lost several friends to pirates in recent days.

"Yes," said Halt, smiling in return. "Except for you."

2

"I WISH ALL OUR MISSIONS WERE OVER AS QUICKLY AS THAT ONE," Halt said.

It was the following day. They had deposited the pirates with the garrison of Claradon, then hired rowers to bring them back upriver in the pirates' boat. They had reclaimed Tug and Abelard where they had left them stabled at the start of their river journey and were riding home.

"I have to say, I expected we'd be going up and down the river for weeks before the pirates took the bait," Will said. "Not just four days. What a stroke of luck."

"Yes. I didn't fancy the idea of hiding under that stuffy tarpaulin for the next few weeks," Halt said. "But I guess sometimes the luck falls our way."

They rode slowly up the main street of Wensley, nodding to the people who greeted them as they passed. Most of the greetings were friendly. But Will noticed several townsfolk who reacted with surprise at the sight of the two Rangers, then hurried away. He grinned.

"Looks like some people are surprised to see us back so soon," he said. "I wonder what they've been up to."

Halt raised an eyebrow. "I'm sure we'll find out in the next few days. There are always people waiting to take advantage of our being absent."

As the affair with the pirates was an internal Redmont Fief matter, they hadn't bothered to ask Gilan to fill in for them. But Halt had been a Ranger long enough to know that even a peaceful village like Wensley had its share of petty thieves, gamblers and confidence tricksters who would be ever ready to take advantage of his and Will's absence.

They reached the turnoff to the little cabin in the trees and Will nodded toward the castle, dominating the landscape on the hill above them.

"Are you heading up to the castle straightaway?"

Halt hesitated, looked at the sun and saw there were still several hours of daylight left. "No. I'll come to the cabin. I can get started on my report for Crowley."

"Better you than me," Will said cheerfully. There were some advantages to being the junior Ranger, he thought. Halt turned an unsmiling gaze on him for several seconds. Will shifted uncomfortably in the saddle. It was never a good sign when Halt looked at him like that.

"On second thought," the older Ranger said, "I might sit in the sun on the porch and let you write the report. I'll sign it—after I've made numerous corrections."

"It might not need any corrections," Will suggested tentatively, and Halt smiled at him.

"Oh, I'm sure I'll find lots of them."

Will was about to answer when they heard the sound of galloping hoofbeats behind them. They both turned to see Alyss about a hundred meters away, coming from the village and closing on them fast.

"Someone's glad you're home early," Halt observed, a slight

smile touching the corner of his mouth. He liked Alyss and he was delighted with the relationship that had grown between her and Will.

Will smiled too at the sight of her. She sat on a horse beautifully, he thought, and her long blond hair streamed out behind her in a most attractive way. Then, as she grew closer, he could see no sign of a welcoming wave or smile, and the smile on his own face faded.

"Something's wrong," he said. Halt had come to the same conclusion. They stopped and turned their horses back to face her as she slid her white mare to a stop.

"Will!" she cried, her voice anguished. "I'm so sorry! Ebony's missing!"

3

"Missing? What do you mean missing?" Will asked. Even as he said the words, he realized how ridiculous they were. There could only be one meaning to Alyss's statement.

"She's gone. Three days ago. I left her by the cabin while I went to a meeting in the castle. I'm so sorry, Will. I should have taken her with me! But I thought . . ."

Will reached out and touched her hand to calm her. She was on the verge of tears, he could see.

"No reason why you should have," he said. "I often leave her on her own at the cabin."

When he and Halt had left to pursue the pirates, Alyss had moved to the cabin temporarily to keep the young dog company and to feed and water her each day. But of course, Will had known Alyss would have duties that would take her to the castle. Ebony wasn't a puppy. She would have appreciated Alyss's company, but she could be trusted to stay close to the cabin if Alyss was called away for an hour or two.

"Maybe she wandered off into the forest," Halt suggested. But Will shook his head.

"She wouldn't do that. She's trained to stay where she's told."
He looked at Alyss again. "When did you last see her?"

"Three days ago, as I said. I'd given her her morning feed and
walked her down to the village. Then I had a message that I was
needed at the castle. I left her on the porch and told her to stay. I
came back two hours later and she was gone. I thought at first that
she might have chased something into the forest, so I went looking
for her, calling her. But there was no sign of her."

"What about the village?" Will asked. "Did anyone there see
her?" If there was any chance that Ebony had wandered, she
would have gone no farther than Wensley. She was a popular dog
with the villagers and on a few occasions she had sought out their
company.

Alyss shook her head. "I asked, but nobody had seen her. I'm so
sorry!"

Now an insidious worm of concern began gnawing at Will. Initially, he had thought there would be some simple explanation for
the dog's absence. But Alyss's agitated state was contagious. Alyss
was usually calm and in control, even in the worst crisis. He was
beginning to think there was more to this matter than he had heard
so far—that there was something Alyss was yet to tell him.

Unless some accident had befallen Ebony, there was really only
one reason for her continued absence.

"Someone must have taken her," he said. One look at Alyss's
face told him that this was what she feared. "What is it?"

Tears began to flow down her cheeks as she answered. "There
was a band of travelers who came through the district—"

"Travelers?" Will interrupted. "What sort of travelers?" Although he had a suspicion that he already knew. Alyss's next words
confirmed it.

"Roamers. They camped outside Wensley for a night, then

moved on. I didn't even know they were there until I started asking about Ebony. They were here the day she disappeared."

Roamers were itinerant travelers who made their way about the country in horse-drawn caravans. They had no permanent home but would camp for a day or two near villages, until such time as the village people moved them on. Roamers usually traveled in extended family groups—mothers, fathers, uncles, aunts and children roaming together. They were musicians and performers and would entertain villagers and farmers to earn their money. Usually, they seemed to be charming and romantic folk. And usually, when they were in an area for more than a day or two, things began to go missing—clothing, small valuables, the occasional chicken or duck.

Roamers originated on the continent, to the southeast of Toscana. But over the centuries, they had spread across the western-world and developed a cyclical pattern of travel. They would appear, stay a few days, move on and not be seen for several years. Then, one day, they would return. They were a close-knit, mysterious group. Black-haired and swarthy of skin, their younger women were often remarkably beautiful and their men were hotheaded and argumentative—among themselves and with outsiders.

There was another thing Will remembered about Roamers. They were known to have a strong bond with their animals—horses, mules and dogs—although, paradoxically, they often mistreated them. If Ebony had been taken by a band of Roamers, it would be best if he got her back as soon as possible.

"I'm going after them," Will said decisively. "They won't move fast and I should be able to catch them in a day or so."

He began to swing Tug's head around, but Halt reached out and took hold of his bridle.

"Just hold on a moment," he said. "If she has been taken by

Roamers, the last thing you'll want to do is go charging in demanding that they hand her over."

"What are you talking about, Halt? I want her back and I want her back now."

But Halt was shaking his head. "Roamers are difficult people to deal with," he said. "They resent outsiders and they're very clever at covering their tracks. They're nearly as good at staying concealed as we are. If they decide to keep her hidden, you'll be hard-pressed to find her. And if they realize they've stolen a Ranger's dog, she'll be in danger."

"Danger? What sort of danger?" Will asked.

"Chances are they'll kill her to get rid of the evidence," Halt told him.

Will sat back in his saddle, openmouthed. "Kill her?" he repeated.

Halt nodded. "Rightly or wrongly, Roamers have been badly treated for many centuries. They've developed a highly defensive frame of mind. If they realize they have a stolen dog, and she's the property of a Ranger, they'll assume that the law will come down heavily on them—"

"And I will!" Will said hotly. But Halt put up a hand to calm him down.

"If you can find her. And the safest way for them will be to get rid of her. Kill her and bury her. Or drop her in the river. Anything to make sure you don't find her in their possession. You simply can't risk that."

"You're saying I should just let them get away with it?" Will asked uncertainly.

"Not at all. Go after her. But do it carefully. Be subtle. Don't let them know you're a Ranger, and don't let them know you're looking for a lost dog."

Will sat, thinking over Halt's words, a troubled look on his face. After a little while, Alyss spoke up.

"I'll go with you."

Automatically, Will shook his head. "No, you won't."

Her mouth tightened into a thin line. "Will, I feel responsible for this. I want to help."

"I think it might be a good idea," Halt said, and they both looked at him, Will in surprise and Alyss with gratitude. He continued. "They might be less suspicious of a young girl than they would of a fit young man of military age. They may be cunning, but they do have one weakness, which is that they regard women as second-class citizens, and they don't have any idea of how capable and how dangerous a Courier can be. I think Alyss might stand a better chance of finding out where the dog is."

"Won't she be in their camp?" Alyss asked.

Halt pursed his lips. "Possibly. But they've got a stolen dog. She's valuable and they may well expect her owner to turn up, looking for her. My bet is they'll keep her hidden somewhere close by their camp until they're well and truly away from the district. If you try to track them, Will, and find out where they're keeping her, there's a very good chance they'll spot you. They'll be on the alert while they're still close to Redmont. On the other hand, I doubt they'd be concerned about Alyss. As I said, they have little regard for women."

There was another point that Halt was reluctant to raise. Will was already sufficiently concerned. But the more Halt thought about it, the surer he was that he had to mention it.

"There's something else you should know about Roamers," he said. "They often train dogs for fighting."

"Fighting?" Will said, his voice almost a whisper. "What do you mean?"

"They train them to fight other dogs—then they stage fights and people bet on them. Or they meet up with other Roamer bands and pit their champions against each other. It's vicious and cruel and it's highly illegal, of course, which is another reason why they'll be keeping the dogs out of sight."

"That's horrible," Alyss said. Her face was white.

Halt nodded. "I know. It's hard to understand, given their reputation for loving animals. But it's a fact."

Will had been thinking over what Halt said and now he shook his head.

"There's no point in them taking Ebony, Halt. She's not very big and she's definitely not aggressive. They'd never manage to turn her into a fighting dog."

Halt took a deep breath. But he thought Will should know the worst. "Even the best dog can turn savage if it's treated badly, Will. That's why it's important that you find her as quickly as possible."

4

It was a grim-faced pair who set out two hours later.

On Halt's advice, Will had taken off the green-and-gray cloak that marked him as a Ranger. It was concealed inside his blanket roll. He kept his longbow and arrows in a canvas bow case slung from Tug's saddle.

Similarly, Alyss had changed from her distinctive white Courier's robe. Instead, she wore a plain green dress of homespun fabric and a brown woolen cloak. The choice of colors was intentional. They would help her blend in to the woodland background in which they'd be traveling.

Inquiries at the village and some of the outlying farms told them that the Roamers had moved off to the south. They were traveling in a convoy of five caravans, with an accompanying assortment of horses, dogs and goats. None of the locals who had seen them on the road had noticed a black-and-white border shepherd among the dogs. Nor had they noticed anything that might pass for a fighting dog, but that was hardly surprising.

"Dogfighting being illegal," Will said to Alyss, "they'd keep any fighting dogs hidden from view. And of course, Ebony was stolen. They'd keep her hidden too."

Even though the Roamers had a three-day lead—and the best part of a fourth day as well—he had expected to catch up to them quickly. After all, whenever he'd seen Roamers on the move, they had traveled at little more than walking pace. However, by the end of the second day, he inquired at a farm and found that the caravans had passed through two days prior. He was puzzled by this and mentioned the fact to Alyss.

"I asked Lady Pauline about Roamers when I went to the castle to fetch my traveling gear," she said. "She's had a bit to do with them over the years. She told me it's normal practice for them when they move on to really push the pace for the first few days, particularly if they've stolen something. That way, they're well out of the district by the time the theft is discovered."

"Makes sense," Will said. He looked up at the sky. The sun was almost setting and there was only half an hour of daylight left.

"Do you mind if we push on after dark for a few hours? We'll try to find a farm to put us up for the night, rather than set up camp in the dark."

"Fine by me," Alyss said. She shared Will's anxiousness to catch up with the band. The fear that Ebony could be pitted against a vicious fighting dog any day was now uppermost in both their minds.

The moon rose shortly after dark, bathing the countryside around them in a pale blue light. They rode on in silence until, around nine that evening, they saw a lighted window in a small farmhouse.

"Better stop here," Alyss advised. "Farmers go to bed early. If we wait any longer, we'll be waking them up. Chances are, they won't like that."

She proved to be right. When they approached the farmhouse, to the accompaniment of the furious barking of a pair of farm dogs, they were greeted by a farmer who appeared at the door, a lantern in his hand. He was already dressed in a nightshirt and it was clear that he was about to retire for the night.

"What do you want?" he called suspiciously. Mindful of the dogs, which seemed eager to get at them, Will and Alyss had stayed outside the fenced-off farmhouse yard.

"We're travelers," Will called in reply. "My sister and I are looking for lodging for the night. We're happy to pay you for your trouble."

The farmer paused. The idea of payment was obviously attractive to him.

"Dismount and come here. Let's have a look at you," he said.

Will dismounted, Alyss following him. He stopped with his hand on the gate latch, nodding to the two dogs.

"Are those dogs all right?" he asked.

The man nodded. "They are, unless I tell 'em otherwise. Down, you two! Shut your noise!" he shouted suddenly at the dogs, and they sat instantly. The barking ceased, but they continued to whine softly, as if seeking permission to tear these interlopers apart.

Will and Alyss advanced slowly into the farmyard. Will noted with some slight amusement that Alyss managed to keep him between her and the dogs. The dogs shifted, their bodies quivering with tension as the two strangers came closer. But the farmer's control over them was total.

The farmer held the lantern higher as they approached. When they were three meters away, he called for them to stop.

"Far enough," he said. He studied them for several minutes. Will noticed that he held the lantern in his left hand. His right, which he kept by his side, held a heavy, spiked club. Behind him, Will saw someone else moving inside the farm, heard a male voice ask a question. A brother, perhaps, or an older son.

"They look all right," the farmer replied over his shoulder. "Just a pair of youngsters. They look harmless enough."

Alyss smiled at the words. Will did have a youthful, innocent-looking face. But to describe him as harmless was so far off the mark as to be laughable. He could well be the most dangerous person this farmer had ever laid eyes on.

"We can't fit you in the house," the farmer said. "There's six of us here."

"The barn would be fine," Will replied. "We just want a roof over our heads. It looks like rain."

The farmer glanced up at the sky and sniffed the air experimentally. "Aye," he said, "there'll be rain before sunrise, sure enough. I'll want seven coppers from you for the lodging. And we've no food for you," he added quickly. "We've already eaten and the fire's banked for the night."

"That's fine. We have our own food." Will undid his belt purse and fumbled in it. "I'm short of coppers. I've give you one silver crown instead."

The crown was worth ten coppers, but he was happy to pay the extra if it meant he and Alyss could spend the night under shelter. The farmer set the lantern on the ground and held out his hand, snapping his thumb and forefinger together.

"A silver crown it is then," he said.

Will stepped forward. One of the dogs, a heavyset brindle, quivered and whined as he came closer. He noticed that even though it was supposedly sitting, its muscles were tensed so that its backside hovered several centimeters from the ground. It peeled back its lips in a snarl as he handed the coin over. The farmer inspected the coin and nodded, satisfied.

"All right then. My wife will give you breakfast in the morning—cover the three extra coppers. And no fire in the barn. No candle and no fire. There's a lantern inside the door, but leave it where it is. That'll be enough light."

"Thanks," Will said. Then one of his constant needs asserted itself. "All right if I light a fire in the yard there? I'd like to make coffee."

The farmer grunted assent. "Keep it well away from the barn. And remember, the dogs will be inside this yard all night. Try to approach the house and they'll have you."

"We'll remember," Will said.

The farmer grunted again. "I bid you good night then. Rest well." He made a shooing motion for them to leave the farmhouse yard.

"Same to you," Will said. He and Alyss stepped back to the gate, let themselves out and closed it carefully behind them. Satisfied that they were outside the fence, the farmer closed the door. They heard a heavy lock shooting home on the inside. The two dogs remained on the doorstep. They dropped to the ground, lying with their noses on their paws as they watched the two strangers lead their horses to the barn.

Tired by hours of hard traveling, they slept soundly. Will woke once after midnight, hearing the steady patter of rain on the roof. He pulled his blankets higher around his chin, glad they were sheltered from the weather, and went back to sleep. There was something very soothing about listening to rain when you were warm and dry in your blankets.

It was daylight when he woke again, hearing a rooster crowing and hens clucking in the barnyard. The rain had stopped but there was a fresh, wet smell to the air.

By daylight, the farmer showed a more friendly face. His wife gave them a substantial breakfast. Will looked at the pile of eggs, bacon, potatoes and toasted bread with a smile.

"Farmers eat well," he commented.

Alyss raised an eyebrow. "That's because they work harder than you."

Before they left, they asked if the family had seen any sign of Roamers in the area.

"Two days ago," the farmer answered promptly. "They wanted to camp on our property but I moved them on. Things have a habit of going missing when Roamers are around."

"I know," Will said. "I'm missing a dog."

The farmer scratched his nose thoughtfully. "Aye, I can imagine. Well, I'd waste no time catching up with them. A Roamer camp is no healthy place for a dog."

He didn't elaborate, but Will had no doubt what he was referring to. They said their farewells and were on the road two hours after sunrise. This time, they pushed the pace up, trotting the horses for twenty minutes, then walking them, dismounted, then trotting again. Each hour, they took a ten-minute rest, then pushed on again. They didn't stop for a midday meal but ate dried beef and fruit, and hard bread, while they rode.

Their efforts paid off. When they stopped at sunset in a small hamlet, they discovered that the Roamers were now only a day ahead of them. They paid to sleep in the kitchen of one of the larger houses, as the hamlet had no inn. They ate and turned in early, and then, before sunrise the following morning, they were back on the road again, keeping the same fast pace.

As the sun came up and tendrils of steam began to rise from the damp grass, Tug shook his mane violently.

We'll catch up to them today. I feel it in my bones.

Will hesitated, glancing sidelong at Alyss. He wasn't sure how she'd react if he began talking to his horse.

"Go ahead and answer him if you want to," she said, her gaze fixed on the road straight ahead.

He regarded her in surprise. "Can you hear him?"

She shook her head, smiling. "No. But Pauline has told me you Rangers all speak to your horses—and you get that furtive look about you if anyone is within earshot."

"Oh." He wasn't sure if he should continue now and answer Tug. Their communication was a very private matter between them.

No need to answer me.

"That's all right then," he said. The reply was one that both Tug and Alyss could take as being addressed to themselves. They rode on in silence for several kilometers, Alyss suppressing a smile.

5

⟨⟨⟨⟨⟨⟨⟨⟨⟨⟨⟨⟨⟨⟩⟩⟩⟩⟩⟩⟩⟩⟩⟩⟩⟩⟩

THE ROAMERS CONTINUED TO HEAD SOUTH. WILL AND ALYSS found the signs of their previous day's encampment off to the side of the road in an open field. The soft ground showed signs of wheel marks left by the caravans, and there were several blackened circles in the grass where the Roamers had lit their fires. Will dismounted and felt the ashes.

"Cold," he said. "They're still a good way ahead of us."

But it was obvious that they were catching up. Perhaps, as Alyss suggested, the Roamers were slowing down, having left the immediate scene of their theft behind. Will nodded. It was a possibility.

Midway through the afternoon of the third day, they caught up with the caravan. Alyss and Will were on a long, flat stretch of road when they rounded a bend and saw the encampment only a few hundred meters ahead. Five of the strange, curved-top caravans were parked in a flat, open space to form a rough square that delineated the camp. People were moving from one to another and several fires were sending slow spirals of gray smoke into the air. Somewhere, someone was playing a zither. The music was in a haunting minor key and the rhythm had a stirring, strangely foreign feeling to it.

Alyss's first instinct when she saw the camp was to curb her horse, but Will saw the movement of her hand on the reins and stopped her in time.

"Keep riding," he said. "We don't want them to think we were looking for them. We'll head for that village on the hill."

They could see the roofs of a small village above the trees. More wood smoke rose from their chimneys. Will studied the camp as they rode slowly past. There were several dogs visible, but none of them showed Ebony's distinctive black-and-white coloring. One of them barked halfheartedly at them and was rewarded with a kick from a Roamer passing close to it. It whined and scuttled under a caravan.

"Should you be looking at them?" Alyss asked. "Won't it give us away?"

Will shook his head. "It'd be more unnatural to ignore them," he said. "They're used to strangers staring at them. If we looked straight ahead, they might suspect something."

He could make out more detail now. The horses that had pulled the caravans were enclosed in a small pen, surrounded by a hastily erected wooden fence—long beams placed over X-shaped supports. To one side, three women were bent over a large tub, working busily. As he watched, one of them stood, wrung out a brightly colored shirt and pegged it onto a rope line strung between two trees. Then she went back to washing another item. Already, several shirts and items of underclothing hung damply on the line.

"Washing day," Alyss remarked.

"Looks like they may be settling here for a few days," Will said. "Not surprising. They've been moving fast since they left Wensley. They're probably ready for a rest."

Four men sat around a fire on low stools, passing a flagon from hand to hand. They stared at the two travelers as they rode slowly past. Even at a distance, the two young riders could sense the un-friendliness in the stares.

"Looks like visitors aren't welcome," Will said.

They were past the camp now and it would be showing too much interest if they were to turn in the saddle and stare back at it. But Will now had a good idea of the layout.

"I would have thought they might have camped closer to the trees," Alyss said. The camp was surrounded by several hundred meters of open ground on all sides. "They'd get more shelter then."

Will shook his head. "Staying out there on open ground makes it that much harder to get close to the camp without being seen," he pointed out. "Halt was right about these people. They're not going to be easy to fool."

He had already decided that he would come back to the camp that night to reconnoiter. But now he had some misgivings. If the Roamers were as cunning as Halt had said, it might be difficult to get close enough to hear anything useful—even for a skilled Ranger. And there were those blasted dogs as well. They'd be prowling the campsite at night, on the alert for strange sounds or smells. Dogs could make things very difficult for an honest intruder, he thought wryly.

The village on the hill had a small tavern, but no inn. However, the tavern keeper let out space in his stables for travelers, and Will and Alyss were happy to settle for another night rolled in their blankets on beds of straw. The fact that they weren't in the main build-ing also meant it would be easier for Will to slip away that night and study the Roamers' camp.

They ate first, then retired to the stable, ostensibly to sleep. As Will readied his equipment, he was surprised by Alyss's stepping into the stall he was using as a bedroom. She was wearing dark tights and a black thigh-length jacket, belted at the waist. Her heavy Courier's dagger was sheathed at her side and she also wore the dark brown cloak.

It was obvious that she intended to accompany him and he opened his mouth to voice his refusal, but Alyss held up a hand to stop him.

"I'm coming," she said. "Think about what Halt said. I'm logically going to be the one to make contact with the Roamers. It makes sense if I know what I'm getting into."

"Yes," said Will, "but—"

"I won't try to get close," she said. "I'll leave that to you. I'll stay in the cover of the trees, seeing as much as I can. Then you can fill me in on the details."

Will hesitated. What she said made sense, he realized. And he could rely on Alyss not to do anything rash. He nodded briskly.

"All right. Let's get moving."

They avoided the main street, slipping down a side alley to a service road that ran parallel and led out of the village. Once they were away from the small cluster of buildings, the road petered out and they were walking in an open, recently harvested field. The edge of the trees was a bare fifty meters away.

Their boots crunched softly on the brittle, newly mown stubble of the field as they hurried toward the Roamer camp. For the last half kilometer, they kept to the shelter and concealing darkness of the woods, until they came to a point where they could see the camp.

The fires were burning in two of the fireplaces, and two of the caravans had windows lit by yellow lantern light. The other three were dark. There were still several figures seated in the open space around one of the fires—two of them were men and the third was a woman.

"Stay here," Will breathed in Alyss's ear. "I'm going to try to get closer."

She nodded and he slid away from the tree that they were sheltering behind, crawling on his belly through the long, damp grass. There were few bushes or trees that he could use for shelter, so he moved slowly, sometimes waiting in a spot for several minutes until a cloud scudded across the sky, bringing a patch of moving darkness with it.

He was fifty meters from the camp when one of the dogs raised its head and yapped tentatively. He froze where he was. He heard a Roamer man call to the dog, then a grunt of exertion as he rose from his low seat to peer out into the darkness.

"See anything?" the woman asked him.

"The fire's too bright."

"The dog heard something, else he wouldn't have yapped," she said.

He snorted dismissively at her. "The dog's a fool. Probably heard a badger or a weasel."

"Maybe you should go look," she suggested, and he reacted angrily to the words.

"Maybe you should! You have a good idea like that, you should be the one who does it."

"I'm not a man," she said. There was a defensive tone in her voice and Will recalled Halt's words about how Roamer men were dismissive of their women. "It's not my job."

"That's right, woman. Your job is to clean and cook and mend my clothes and keep your mouth shut. So I suggest you get on with that last part now!"

"I'm going to bed," she said, anger in her voice.

Her husband watched her go. "Women!" he said disgustedly. "You're lucky you're not married, Jerome."

"Don't I know it," the man called Jerome answered heavily. He shook the jug experimentally, decided it was empty and tossed it aside.

His companion yawned and stretched. "Well, I'm for bed too," he said after a few moments. He rose and walked unsteadily toward the caravan his wife had entered, stumbling on the stairs, then slamming the door behind him as he entered. Obviously, Will thought, that hadn't been the only jug they'd drunk that night.

With only Jerome left staring into the fire, there was no chance of overhearing any more. Slowly, Will backed away from the camp and slid silently back to the trees where Alyss waited.

"Well?" she said expectantly. He shrugged.

"Didn't hear much that was useful to us," he said. "Except Halt's right about their attitude to women. It seems Roamer women aren't expected to have an opinion on anything."

"So what will we do?" Alyss asked.

Will hesitated for a few minutes. "We need to know more about them," he said finally. "What they do. How they behave. What their routines are." He chewed thoughtfully on the inside of his lip. He was very conscious of Halt's warning that the Roamers would be a difficult target. He couldn't afford to make a mistake that might tip them off to the fact that they were being pursued.

"We'll come back tomorrow and just watch them for a few hours, see if there's any weakness we can exploit. For now, let's go back to the tavern. I could use a cup of coffee to warm me up."

Staying low, they crept quietly away, heading back into the trees. When they could no longer see the lights of the camp through the thick screen of tree trunks, they straightened and picked up the pace.

Back at the village, they slipped unnoticed into the tavern. It was late but there were still a dozen customers drinking and talking loudly—as people tend to do when alcohol is involved. Three men sat at a table near the bar, playing dice. As Will and Alyss waited for their coffee, Alyss watched the progress of the game with mild interest.

One of the players had just won a large hand and was raking in his winnings when he became aware of her scrutiny. He looked up and smiled at her. After all, he was in a good mood—and Alyss was a remarkably beautiful girl.

"Evening, gorgeous," he said to her. "Looks like you brought me luck. Care to sit with us?"

Alyss smiled at him. His tone was friendly, and she could hardly expect courtly manners from a simple farm worker. "Afraid not," she said. "My boyfriend might get lonely."

"He can join us too," said one of the other players. "We always welcome strangers—and their money."

They all laughed and Will smiled at them as well. "I think not, gentlemen. My purse is too thin already."

"Not fond of gambling?" the third man at the table asked and Will shook his head, smiling sadly.

"Too fond of it, I'm afraid. That's why my purse is so thin."

That elicited a sympathetic laugh from the gamblers. They knew that condition all too well.

"Pity about that," said the first man to have spoken. "You'd have a chance to win some big money on Sevenday. There's a d—"

But before he could complete the statement, one of the others seized his wrist.

"That's enough now, Randell!" the other man said hastily. "No need to go blabbing about it to the world!"

"What? Oh . . . no! Sorry!" The man seemed taken aback by the warning. He dropped his eyes from Will's gaze. "Forget I spoke," he mumbled.

His friend smiled apologetically. "Ah, Randell here runs on a bit at times, young feller. Pay him no heed. No heed at all."

"Of course." Will spread his hands to indicate that he understood. Their coffee had arrived and he took that as an opportunity to finish the conversation. "Good night, gentlemen," he said, and he and Alyss turned toward a table at the back of the room. As they made their way through the chairs and tables, he overheard a few more words of conversation from the dice players.

"Are you mad, Randell?" asked the third man. He was obviously trying to keep his voice low but the intensity of his words made them carry to Will's attentive ears. "You don't go telling strangers about the . . ." He stopped himself, then finished, "The you-know-what."

"Sorry! Sorry!" It was Randell now, upset at his carelessness. "Still, no damage done and they look harmless enough. Not as if . . ."

The rest of his words were lost in the low hubbub of voices in the tavern. As they sat, Will and Alyss exchanged meaningful looks. Then she smiled at him.

"Laugh," she said. "Laugh out loud. Now."

Puzzled, he threw back his head and laughed. She joined in, then touched his hand fondly and took a sip of her coffee. Still smiling, she said quietly, "Don't want them to think we're talking about what just happened."

He nodded, smiling broadly. It seemed strange to be talking seriously while keeping a happy smile fixed on his face. But Alyss was experienced in this sort of deception and he allowed himself to be guided by her.

She leaned toward him and ran her hand fondly down his cheek. "Let's try to look as if we're having a romantic chat," she said.

He nodded, smiling still, and took her hand gently, touching his lips to it.

"What did you make of all that?" she asked, then looked shyly around the room, as if embarrassed that people might be watching this show of affection. "Keep smiling," she admonished as she saw his brow furrowing thoughtfully. Hastily, he adjusted his expression.

"Something's happening on Sevenday. Something that involves gambling and the chance to win big money."

"So," she said, brushing her hair to one side in a coquettish gesture, "it's something out of the ordinary. What does that suggest?"

He could tell they were thinking along the same lines. "Dogfighting," he said. "That's why the Roamers have settled in for a while. They'll be running a dogfight somewhere in the forest on Sevenday."

"Tomorrow is Twainday," Alyss said thoughtfully. "That gives us a little time."

"Not much," Will said. All pretense of smiling and romance was gone now. "We still don't know how to find Ebony. We need to get busy tomorrow."

6

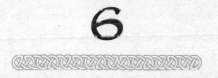

SHORTLY AFTER SUNRISE, THEY WERE BACK IN THEIR OBSERVA-
tion post of the previous night, watching the Roamers' camp. For
some hours, nothing out of the ordinary seemed to occur. The
Roamers went about mundane day-to-day tasks, like lighting fires,
preparing breakfast, cleaning, and mending items of equipment and
clothing.

Then, around midmorning, Jerome, the heavyset man from the
night before, emerged from one of the caravans. He was dressed in
a brightly patterned shirt that came down below his hips and had
wide, voluminous sleeves, gathered by a leather cuff at each wrist. A
heavy leather belt was around his waist and Will could see the hilt
of a long knife in a scabbard worn on his left-hand side. He wore
black trousers and knee-high brown leather boots. Of more immediate interest to Will, he carried a large canvas sack in his hand. As
he climbed down the steps from his caravan, two of the camp dogs
ran low-bellied toward him and tried to sniff at it. He cursed at
them and they slunk away.

"What do you suppose is in the sack?" Will asked quietly.

Alyss, lying beside him, wrapped in her brown cloak, glanced at
him. "From the interest those dogs showed, I'd say it's meat."

"My guess too," Will said. He had also noticed the brown stains on the sack—dried blood in all probability.

Jerome walked toward the far side of the camp, then turned and called to the caravans.

"Petulengo! Where the blazes are you, boy?"

"Coming, Jerome!" called a high-pitched voice. The door of one of the caravans slammed open and a young boy, no more than twelve or thirteen by the look of him, hurried down the set of steps, tucking his shirt in as he went. He was olive-skinned and had long dark hair, held back from his face by a yellow headband.

"Next time be ready when I tell you," Jerome said. He was obviously not the forgiving type. "Now keep watch behind me." He strode toward the trees on the far side of the clearing. The boy had to half run to keep up with Jerome's long strides, and he stayed a few paces behind him.

"Wait here and keep an eye on things," Will said. "I'm going to see where our friend Jerome is off to."

It was easier said than done. He had to skirt in a wide arc to stay clear of the campsite, then move along the road to the edge of the far tree line. Despite losing time doing so, once he entered the trees he was confident he'd pick up Jerome's trail soon enough.

He was mistaken. He found the boy's trail easily enough. But Petulengo hadn't stayed with his older companion. He was following some distance behind him, obliterating the tracks Jerome made as he twisted and turned his way through the forest. Jerome zigzagged so much that there was no way of establishing his base course and there was a distinct danger that Will would be spotted by Petulengo.

The boy was dangerously alert too. Several times, when Will made a slight noise—and it was impossible to move in total silence—the dark head would snap up and around and Will would have to freeze in place, concealed from view by his cloak and his own ability to stand stock-still.

Petulengo stayed so far behind Jerome that Will never sighted the burly Roamer. He had to be content to shadow the boy. After a short while, he realized how effective the Roamers' system was. The boy obviously knew where Jerome was heading, so he could stay a long way behind him and effectively frustrate any stranger who might be trying to track him — as Will was doing.

After ten minutes, Will had to admit defeat. He simply couldn't take the risk that he might be spotted—it might cost Ebony her life. Seething with frustration, he made his roundabout way back to the spot where Alyss was watching the camp. She saw by the look on his face that he had had no luck. She pointed to the campsite.

"I think I might have found our way in," she said.

Will followed her pointing finger and saw a figure he hadn't noticed before. It was an old woman dressed in filthy rags, her hair long and gray and unkempt. She moved around the camp, bent almost double, collecting firewood from the central wood stack and distributing it to the individual cooking fires as ready fuel.

With that task done, she filled a bucket from a large water barrel attached to one of the caravans and proceeded to distribute that as well.

It became obvious that she was nothing more than a drudge, a beast of burden in the camp. If any of the Roamers came close to her, they ignored her at best, or spat a curse at her as they passed. One of the men cuffed her around the back of the head. She shied away from him, dropping her bucket and spilling the water. Her shrill cry of protest was met by uncaring laughter from the man. As she stooped to retrieve her bucket, he kicked it, sending it rolling away from her. She scuttled after it, one hand instinctively raised to ward off another blow, sniveling and whining.

At the same time, a door in one of the caravans banged open and a Roamer woman, at least twenty years younger than the gray-haired woman, shouted at her, "Hilde! Get that water in here at once! What are you doing, you layabout!"

Hilde whined something unintelligible and the man who had caused her to spill the water snarled at her as well. She hobbled back to the rain barrel to refill her bucket, pursued by the Roamer woman's sharp insults and orders.

In the Roamer camp, Hilde was the lowest of the low.

Will frowned at Alyss. "I don't see how that will help us."

She smiled back at him. "While you were gone, I heard one of the Roamers telling her to get more firewood. We wait till she leaves camp. Then we follow her and I take her place."

"You have to be joking!" Will said. He looked from the bent figure of the crone, now hobbling back to the caravan with a full water bucket, to Alyss—slim and beautiful and young. "You don't think they might notice a slight difference in her appearance?"

"I don't think they notice her at all," Alyss said seriously. "They don't see her as a person, just as a piece of equipment or something to kick or cuff or curse when they're in the mood. Don't forget, I've been trained to disguise myself when necessary. If I put ash and dirt through my hair and hobble around like her, I doubt they'll see the difference. Particularly if I swap clothes with her." She shuddered slightly. "That's the one part I'm not looking forward to."

Will studied the hobbling, mumbling figure again. "You really think you can pass yourself off as her?"

Alyss nodded. "If she were one of them, I'd never get away with it. But they take no notice of her. And people see what they expect to see. You've told me that often enough."

He was silent for a few seconds and she pressed home her argument.

"This way, I'll be inside their camp. I'll be able to listen to their conversations, and with any luck I'll find out where they're keeping Ebony. Or if Jerome and the boy go off into the forest, I'll follow them. Odds are they won't take any notice of Hilde collecting firewood. And you can follow me, at a distance. That way, you can stay well back out of sight until we find where they've got Ebony hidden."

"I'm not sure," Will said. "It might work. But it's a big chance . . ."

"I'm willing to take it. What can they do to me? After all, you'll be watching here in the forest if I am found out. And I honestly think it's our only chance to find Ebony."

"Let me think," Will said. He knew that if he were in Alyss's place, he wouldn't hesitate to put the plan into operation. But he'd be risking Alyss, as well as Ebony, and he simply couldn't make that decision.

"Better think fast," Alyss said. "She's leaving the camp."

He looked up. Hilde was trudging toward the forest, a small ax in her hand and a large wicker wood carrier slung over her shoulder. She was heading for a point fifty meters to the north of where they lay concealed.

"All right," he said, coming to a decision. "Let's do it."

It was easy to find Hilde. The sound of the small ax rang through the forest as she cut pieces of deadfall into manageable lengths. Will and Alyss ghosted through the trees as she slowly moved farther and farther away from the encampment. When they felt they were a safe distance away, Will stepped quietly from the trees in front of her. To Hilde, it seemed that the young man in the green-and-gray cloak had suddenly materialized out of thin air. She gasped in fright and staggered back, one hand raised in front of her face. Will recognized the gesture. It was one that older people used to ward off what they called "the evil eye" from strangers.

He also noted that, although she had the ax in her other hand, she made no movement to defend herself with it, nor to threaten him. Hilde's instincts for self-protection seemed to have been dulled by her time with the Roamers.

"Relax, Hilde," he said softly. "I'm not going to hurt you."

"Who are you? How do you know my name? I've done nothing wrong!" she babbled, still averting her gaze from his. He looked to Alyss, standing concealed in the trees, and made a gesture: *help needed here.*

Alyss moved into sight now and Hilde backed away as she saw her.

"It's all right, Hilde," Alyss said in a soothing voice. "We're not going to hurt you. We're here to help you."

Perhaps the sight of another woman gave Hilde greater confidence. Slowly, she lowered the arm she had thrown up to shield her face. She leaned forward to peer more closely at Alyss. Alyss smiled encouragingly at her. It had often been said that Alyss's smile was a sight worth seeing, and it seemed to have a calming effect on the old woman.

"Who are you?" Hilde asked.

"My name is Alyss, and this is my friend Will," she said, indicating the young Ranger. Hilde glanced at him, all the suspicion and fear returning to her face as she did so. Alyss continued quickly. "Tell us, Hilde, why are the Roamers so cruel to you?"

It was the right approach to take, Will realized. It immediately placed Alyss on Hilde's side. The old woman sniffed, wiping her nose with the ragged end of her sleeve.

"Cruel? Ay, that they are. Beat me, they do. And curse me and kick me. And I try to do my best for them, but I'm old now. I can't move as fast as I used to. I try, but I'm too slow and they beat me."

"But aren't you one of them?" Alyss asked. She took the old woman's hand gently in her own and Hilde looked up at her through teary eyes, eyes whose color seemed washed away by age.

"One of them? No. I'm Gallican. Least I was. When my man died, the village had no further use for me. Wanted the farm, you see. They threw me out with nothing. Left me to die. The Roamers took me in. I was grateful at first, but after a while, I wished they hadn't. Might have been easier to die. Been with them now for . . ." She paused and a vague look came into her eyes. "I don't know how long."

"Why do you stay with them?" Will asked, and she looked at him. By now she seemed to accept that if he was a friend of Alyss's, she had nothing to fear from him.

"Where else could I go?" she said. "Nobody wants an old woman. It was stay with the Roamers or starve." She laughed suddenly, a harsh cackle that had no humor in it. "Not that they feed me well. It's scraps for me—anything that's not good enough for the dogs."

Alyss and Will exchanged a quick glance.

"The dogs," Alyss said. "The dogs in the camp?"

"Aye. Those too. And the oth—" She stopped, a fearful gleam in her eyes. "Yes, the dogs in the camp," she amended quickly. With an enormous effort, Will prevented himself from looking at Alyss again. He looked away casually, as if he hadn't noticed Hilde's stumble.

"Why don't you run away?" Alyss asked.

Hilde looked at her as if the question was insane. "How? Where would I go? I've got nothing. If I tried to run away, they'd come after me and drag me back. Old woman like me can't run fast. Nothing I can do. I'm stuck with the Roamers and I'll have to make the best of it." Her voice was heavy with the inevitability of her predicament.

"Hilde," Alyss said slowly, "if you could get away from the Roamers, would you want to?"

"Well, of course!" Hilde replied eagerly. Then reality claimed her once more. "But how? I can't run. And what would I do if I did get away? No, it's foolishness to even think of that."

"We'd help you," Will said, and she looked at him suspiciously.

"Why would you do that?"

"Let's just say we have a score to settle with these Roamers," Will told her.

She wavered. The idea of escaping her current life was an attractive one. "But what would I do?" she asked.

Alyss answered this time. "We have a friend who owns a restaurant. I'm sure you could work for her. It'll be a lot easier than what you're doing and nobody would kick you or curse you."

"But you'd have to work," Will warned her, and she turned her gaze to him.

"I'm not afraid of work," she said. "I don't expect handouts. But pay me a little, let me have a little to eat and give me somewhere warm to sleep . . . that'd be like heaven."

"I'm sure Jenny would give you plenty to eat," Will said. "And she's an excellent cook."

"We'll give you some money for now," Alyss said. "And Will can take you to another village to wait for us. We have horses, so he'll take you far enough to be safe from the Roamers."

Hilde wavered still. "You're sure this friend of yours will give me a job?"

Alyss nodded emphatically. "If we ask her. Yes. It'll be light work and you'll have a good life, Hilde. And, to seal the bargain, you can have this fine dress of mine."

Hilde's eyes opened wide at her words. The dress was a simple enough one, but it was made of good quality wool, soft and warm to the touch. And it was unpatched and clean and in infinitely better shape than the rags she was wearing.

"But what will you wear?" she asked.

Alyss gestured to Hilde's ragged skirt, blouse and shawl. "I'll trade for your clothes."

Hilde frowned, puzzled by the idea. "Why would you want to wear these?"

Alyss allowed herself the ghost of a smile.

"Believe me, I don't want to. But it's sort of necessary for what we have in mind."

7

EVEN THOUGH HE HAD SEEN ALYSS'S SKILL WITH DISGUISES before, Will was startled by the transformation. She had cut her hair shorter to match the length of Hilde's. Then she'd rubbed earth and ash into it so that it was matted and gray and tangled. Her face was darker and it was lined and worn, seemingly with age. It was only when he looked closely that Will could see it was the result of skillful makeup. Alyss, like all Couriers, never traveled without a makeup and disguise kit. It was one of a Courier's most valuable tools of trade.

But the most telling part of the deception was her perfect adoption of the older woman's body language. Alyss had observed her closely throughout the morning and she had copied Hilde's crouched, subservient body position exactly. She moved the same way, hobbling bent over, eyes down and with a sideways, shuffling skip. It was in their favor that Hilde rarely made eye contact with any of the Roamers. But even if Alyss did, Will was almost certain they would never notice the substitution.

In addition, she was wearing Hilde's stained and tattered clothes and that completed the picture. She smiled at Will as she emerged from behind the screen of bushes where she had changed. She held the ragged clothing out, keeping it away from her body as long as possible.

"This is the part I like least of all," she said.

Hilde, for her part, was delighted with her new green dress. She paraded around the small clearing in the forest, muttering admiring phrases to herself. Will guessed she'd probably never owned such a fine piece of clothing in her life.

"Now," said Alyss, "I suggest you take Hilde to that village we passed through yesterday morning. Put her in the inn and come back here. In the meantime, I'll take her place in the camp."

But Will shook his head. "I'll do that tonight," he said. "First I want to be sure that your disguise holds up. Hilde and I will be watching from the trees, just to make sure you're all right."

"I'll be fine, Will," she reassured him.

"Then there's no rush to get Hilde away. If they fall for your disguise, they won't go looking for her, will they?"

She smiled. She liked that he was concerned for her safety, even though she was totally confident in her ability to carry off the impersonation. She reached out a dirt-stained hand and touched his.

"You're right. And I'll feel safer knowing you're watching."

Alyss's confidence turned out to be well founded. When she hobbled back into the camp a few minutes later, laden with the firewood that Will had collected while she changed and disguised herself, none of the Roamers showed the slightest interest in her.

As the day wore on, they would shout at her from time to time, setting her to some menial, difficult or unpleasant task that they didn't want to do. On several occasions, when she was intentionally tardy in carrying out their orders, she was punished with kicks or cuffs to the head. She reacted exactly as she'd seen Hilde do—

cowering away, whimpering in pain and fear and trying to cover her head with her bent arms.

It was a masterful performance. Watching it, with Hilde dozing contentedly some meters farther back in the forest, Will felt his lips compress into a tight line each time Alyss was struck. He marked down the Roamers responsible. Once this was all over, he thought grimly, he would be carrying out a little retribution for those careless blows.

As the afternoon passed, he realized that Alyss had carried off the deception and he began to relax. He woke Hilde as dusk drew in. The old woman had not had such a long, uninterrupted rest in years and she woke reluctantly.

"How's the lady managing?" she asked, and he smiled reassuringly at her.

"Perfectly. The Roamers have no idea you're gone. Want to see?"

He led her carefully forward through the trees and she crouched in the shadows watching as Alyss hobbled around the camp, dumping stacks of firewood by each fireplace, then lighting the fires for the evening meal's preparation. Hilde was fascinated to observe her alter ego at work. On one occasion, when one of the Roamers threw a piece of firewood at Alyss, hitting her on the leg, she winced in sympathy. Eventually, Will touched her arm and they withdrew into the trees, heading to the spot where the horses were tethered. She hopped along beside him, bent-backed and awkward. But after a while, she looked up at him, a hint of a smile on her lined face.

"Lucky they haven't noticed how she's not as pretty as me," she said, then cackled.

Will stopped to look at her, eyebrows raised. "You think you're prettier than her?" he said incredulously.

She cackled again. "Of course I am. After all, I've got a fine new green dress!"

There was no answer to that, he thought.

• • •

Alyss spent an uncomfortable night, shivering under one of the caravans, wrapped in Hilde's threadbare blanket. She tried not to think of the small creatures that undoubtedly shared the blanket with her, but by morning she was covered in red bites and scratching miserably.

"All part of the disguise," she told herself.

She had quizzed Hilde as to what duties she would have to carry out. She lugged water and wood, fed the goats and chickens from the swill bucket and scoured the cooking pans clean with sand and water. If Roamer women were reluctant cooks, they were even more reluctant cleaners.

From time to time, the men or women would summon her to carry out some other menial task—cleaning boots that had been soiled with cow or dog droppings, beating the dust from a rug taken from a caravan.

Around eleven o'clock, she saw the boy Petulengo approach Jerome's caravan and wait expectantly outside it. This was the opportunity she had been waiting for. She hurried to the caravan she slept under and fetched the big firewood basket. As she did so, she heard Jerome's caravan door bang open and his heavy footsteps clumping down the steps. She glanced furtively in his direction. Once again, he was carrying the heavy, bloodstained sack. Once again, he had to shoo the camp dogs away from it.

He nodded when he saw Petulengo already waiting for him.

"Just as well for you," he said. "I don't like to be kept waiting."

The boy said nothing but fell into step behind the heavily built Roamer. They headed off in the same direction they had taken the previous day. Alyss, the firewood basket slung over her shoulder, hobbled slowly after them. She knew that while Petulengo was there to prevent any strangers from following Jerome, Hilde would be a familiar and unthreatening figure. Chances were, the boy would ignore her and she could discover where Jerome had Ebony hidden. And while she was following the two Roamers, Will would follow her, keeping well back. That was the plan they had agreed to on the previous day.

She had left the caravan compound, heading in the same general direction as Jerome and the boy, when a shrill voice stopped her.

"Hilde! Where are you going, you worthless crone?" It was one of the younger women from the camp. She was leaning over the railing at the rear platform of her caravan, beckoning urgently to Alyss.

Cursing under her breath, Alyss stopped and held up the basket for the woman to see. With a crack in her voice, she called back, "Fetching firewood, mistress! We're getting low!"

The woman considered the answer. For a moment, Alyss thought she was going to call her back to the camp. But eventually, she merely nodded. "Collect some redberries while you're there!" she called. "Lots of them. Camlo wants me to make redberry wine and I'm out of them!"

Alyss heaved a sigh of relief. This would actually work to her advantage. She could wander all over the forest searching for the berries. If her path happened to cross that of Petulengo and Jerome, all the better.

"Yes, mistress! I'll fetch a good batch!" she shouted. Then she turned and scuttled toward the trees before the woman could think of another task for her.

She bent and picked up some of the lighter branches as she went, keeping an eye out for Petulengo. She followed a random zig-zag path through the trees, allowing the concentrations of deadfalls to determine her movements. But she managed to stay in touch with the two Roamers. Occasionally, she saw flashes of Petulengo's yellow shirt among the trees. If he was even half awake, she decided, he must have noticed her. She decided to put her theory to the test and changed her path, heading more directly toward where the boy was seated on a tree stump. By pure fortune, there was a redberry bush a few meters past him. She shuffled up to it, eyes down, pretending not to notice the boy. With an exclamation of pleasure, she began to strip the berries from the tree, dropping them into the wood basket.

"What are you doing, Hag Hilde?" His young voice had an unpleasant note to it.

She feigned surprise and jerked around to face him, keeping her eyes lowered, as Hilde would have done. She guessed that a display of subservience would feed his young ego, and she was right. "Fetching redberries, master," she said, showing him the wood basket. "Mistress Drina wants to make wine from them."

"Bring them here," he demanded, and she shuffled toward him, holding out the basket. He grabbed a large handful and began to eat them, the red juice flowing down his chin.

"Not bad," he said, grinning unpleasantly. "But if you want to pass by me, you'll have to give me more. There's a toll, you know."

A narrow track ran away through the trees behind him. She guessed that this was the path Jerome had taken, and Petulengo was keeping watch at this junction to make sure nobody could follow him without being seen.

As she'd hoped, Petulengo didn't see her as any threat. He was obviously willing to let her pass down the track for the sake of a handful of berries. She nodded subserviently, hiding the sense of exultation that rose within her.

"I'll fetch you some more," she said, and hobbled back to the tree. She stripped a sizable quantity of the sweet berries from the tree, reaching as high as she could to get to them. Petulengo watched her incuriously, then leaned forward as she returned with the basket held out to him.

He scooped the lot out of the basket and she whined a protest.

"But that's all I've got, young master! And there's no more on that bush!" she said.

He smiled at her and spat a stream of juice past her. "Too bad. You'll have to find more."

She crouched, bobbing her head and whining. Then she pointed down the track.

"There's a clump of redberry bushes down there, I know," she said.

He shrugged at her. "Then go get more. And make sure you've got plenty for me on the way back."

Interesting, she thought. He wasn't planning on moving from this spot, which meant Jerome must be somewhere within easy distance. Jerome and the dogs. She hoped that Will was somewhere nearby, waiting for her to discover the location of the dogs' holding pen.

She hobbled past the sarcastic young boy and headed down the track. She hadn't gone ten meters when she heard his call.

"Hilde!"

At the same time, she heard the swish of his stick spinning end over end through the air. She had the sense not to turn and the thick piece of wood caught her on the back of her head. She stumbled and fell, spilling her firewood onto the ground. Petulengo laughed.

"Mind your step, Hilde! The track's a little rough there!"

Cursing under her breath, trying not to let him see the murderous look in her eyes, she clambered to her feet and began laboriously replacing the sticks in her basket.

"Petulengo!"

They were both startled by the shout from a little way down the track. Petulengo stood up from the tree stump, looking puzzled and slightly nervous.

"Yes, Jerome?" he called.

"Is everything clear?" Jerome replied. This time, Alyss, seemingly engrossed in gathering the firewood again, could have sworn she heard a quick yelp, hastily cut off.

"All clear, Jerome."

Alyss smiled to herself. Obviously, she counted as nobody. Well, they'd learn, she thought.

"Then come here! I need you."

"Coming, Jerome!" Petulengo started down the narrow trail. As he passed Alyss, he managed to kick her basket over, scattering the wood once more. She heard his laughter as he ran lightly down the track.

"Little swine," she muttered.

8

LEADING THE BENT OLD CRONE BEHIND HIM, PETULENGO hurried down the narrow track to where another track ran off at right angles. This was narrow and overgrown and difficult to make out. Had Petulengo not known it was there, he would possibly have hurried past. He bent under the low-lying branches that grew over the track and, after a few meters, emerged into a small clearing.

Instinctively, he shied to one side as he realized that Jerome was only a few meters away, holding the collar of a massive black dog.

Petulengo knew its name. Demon Tooth. Its coat was black, but not a healthy, glossy black. This coat was matted and wiry. The skin underneath the short hair was scarred in a dozen places—mementos of the fights Demon Tooth had contested—and these scars formed ridges and corrugations in the fur.

Its head was large and the shoulders and body powerful. The eyes were wild and yellow and the lips were drawn back in a furious snarl, the dog's mouth white with slobber as it struggled in Jerome's grip.

Normally, Demon Tooth would be held by a heavy chain. But Jerome had unfastened it and now gripped the dog between his knees to restrain it. He had both hands on a thick leather collar around its neck, holding its head straight so that it couldn't savage him. Demon Tooth, sensing that the chain no longer restrained him, fought to free himself completely. Jerome was a powerful man but the strength of the dog's struggling was almost beyond him. He glared at Petulengo now.

"Bring the shepherd," he said. "I'm moving the dogs to a new spot."

Every few days, he would move the dogs to a new hiding place, to make sure that they remained undiscovered. Petulengo looked across the clearing. On the far side, chained to a tree, was the black-and-white border shepherd Jerome had stolen. Petulengo eyed the dog warily. Under Jerome's instructions, he had spent the past few days teasing it and provoking it, trying to overcome its natural good temper. Yesterday, he had succeeded and the border shepherd had snapped at him. She was not a big dog, but she was fast, and Petulengo had only just escaped being bitten. She eyed him now and her ears flattened as she recognized him. She showed her teeth in a snarl and he decided that he didn't want to risk getting close to her again.

"No," he said. "She'll bite me."

"Curse you!" Jerome snarled. "Who cares if you're bitten! Get that dog now!"

Normally, Petulengo wouldn't dare to disobey Jerome. But the big man had his hands full and there was little he could do. Later on, he might remember Petulengo's disobedience. But later on could take care of itself. Jerome cursed him but the boy continued to shake his head.

"Hilde can do it," he said. "I'll get Hilde."

"Hilde? What's Hilde doing here?" Jerome was puzzled by the suggestion. But he was tiring rapidly and wasn't sure how much longer he could control Demon Tooth.

"She's collecting redberries for Drina. She's just out there!"

Jerome gave up the argument. He needed someone to bring the shepherd along and he had no more time for discussion. Hilde would serve as well as anyone. He could deal with Petulengo later, when they were back in camp.

"All right! Get her. But hurry!"

The boy ran back down the path to the right-angle fork. Looking around desperately, he uttered a low cry of relief as he saw the old woman stripping redberries from a bush some ten meters back along the track.

"Hilde!" he shouted. "Come here!"

She looked up, then, as he gestured urgently to her, she began to hobble down the track. As she reached him, he impatiently dashed the basket from her hands and grabbed her sleeve, dragging her along.

"Come on! Hurry up, blast you!"

She stumbled into the clearing and saw Jerome struggling with a terrible, huge dog. Then she caught her breath as she saw a black-and-white form cowering on the far side of the clearing.

Ebony. Chained, tail between her legs, ears flattened to her head, her coat matted with dirt and mud. It was all Alyss could do to stop from calling out her name.

"Unchain the shepherd and bring her along!" Jerome ordered. His voice was tight as he struggled with the surging, twisting black monster held between his knees.

Alyss ran to the dog. As she approached, Ebony's ears came up as she recognized a familiar and beloved scent. With senses far more acute than any human's, she penetrated Alyss's disguise immediately.

Alyss fumbled with the chain to loosen it.

"Get a move on! I can't hold this one all day!" Jerome yelled at her.

Demon Tooth, sensing that Jerome's attention was distracted, made a sudden violent lunge, sending the Roamer off balance and breaking his grip on the collar. As Jerome sprawled on the damp grass, Demon Tooth, trained to attack other dogs without hesitation, launched himself across the clearing at Ebony.

As the massive, black killer bore down on her, Ebony, finally free of the chain, crouched with her head low, hindquarters high. She was a sheepdog and she was bred to move fast and change direction in an instant. Demon Tooth was less than a meter away when Ebony sprang to one side. The killer's jaws clopped shut on empty air.

Demon Tooth spun, skidding on his haunches, to renew the attack. But now Alyss interposed herself between the two dogs. She had scooped up a fallen tree limb from the ground and she thrust it at the charging dog, catching Demon Tooth's neck in the forked branches at its end. For a moment, it checked Demon Tooth's momentum, although Alyss was driven back. But then the branch snapped and Demon Tooth snarled as he focused on the two-legged target who had attacked him. He gathered the muscles of his hind legs, ready to spring at Alyss's throat.

Alyss heard a *whizz-thunk!* and a long, gray-shafted arrow suddenly appeared in the center of Demon Tooth's chest. The huge dog staggered under the impact. He gave one brief howl of agony, then his legs collapsed and he fell on his side.

Jerome looked in horror at the sight of his dog lying lifeless on the ground. In the confusion of the moment, he hadn't seen the arrow. But he had seen the old woman, Hilde, attack his dog with a tree limb. Now Demon Tooth lay unmoving.

"You old witch!" he screamed, and sprang at her.

He fastened his hands around her throat, shaking her and choking her. Alyss fought against him, but he was too strong. Her head snapped back and forth and her vision began to fade.

Then a black-and-white shape flew at Jerome, leaping high to fasten her teeth on his arm.

Jerome yelled. Ebony hung grimly from his forearm, her teeth sunk deep in the flesh. Her weight threw him off balance. He staggered, caught his foot on a tree root and fell, crashing across the still body of Demon Tooth.

"Let go, Eb! Come here, girl!" Alyss gasped. Obediently, Ebony released her grip on Jerome's arm and trotted to her friend, tail sweeping heavily from side to side. Jerome tried to rise as well. Nursing the arm Ebony had bitten against his side, he put his other hand on Demon Tooth's prone body to give him purchase to rise.

And realized, too late, that the dog was still alive.

Maddened by rage and pain, Demon Tooth snarled at the touch and attacked blindly. Jerome's shout of terror was cut off as the dog's teeth snapped closed. Jerome thrashed wildly, trying to break that dreadful grip, gurgling horribly.

Then he was still.

Now Demon Tooth turned those terrible yellow eyes on the girl and the dog a few meters away. Rising shakily to his feet, he snarled a challenge.

Ebony, ears flattened back against her head, the white ruff of fur around her throat standing erect until it was twice its normal size, leapt to place herself between Alyss and the slowly approaching monster.

Whizz-thunk!

The second arrow hit Demon Tooth in the side, just behind the left foreleg. Without a further sound, the killer dog fell, dead before he hit the ground.

Will stepped out of the trees, his bow in his hand. He ran to Alyss and Ebony and didn't know which one to hug first. So he went down on his knees beside them and threw his arms around both of them.

Both seemed quite happy with that arrangement. One of them even licked his hand. He couldn't see through the tears in his eyes, but he hoped it was Ebony.

9

THE ROAMERS WATCHED APPREHENSIVELY AS THE GRAY-CLOAKED Ranger and the tall girl wearing Hilde's tattered rags came out of the trees and headed for the camp. Trotting beside them was the black-and-white border shepherd Jerome had stolen outside Wensley village.

Petulengo had spread the word of what had happened in the forest. He had watched in horror as Demon Tooth was struck down by an arrow, then the horror mounted as the terrible killing machine turned on Jerome. The appearance of the Ranger had been the final straw. Petulengo had turned and run back to the camp, babbling a confused account of what had happened in the clearing.

Now the members of the extended family stood in a silent half circle, watching the two grim figures and the dog as they made their way into the compound formed by the caravans. Petulengo stood nervously at the back of the group, trying to hide himself behind the older Roamers, peering around them to see if he had been noticed. He was amazed at the transformation that had overcome Hilde. She still wore the same shabby, tattered rags. But she stood tall now, slim and graceful. She had managed to dash some of the ash and dirt from her hair and he could see blond patches peeping through the gray.

Will stopped a few meters from the Roamers. Their hostility was all too obvious. But they were experienced in the ways of the world and they knew a Ranger when they saw one. They knew too of the Rangers' legendary skill with weapons and their total authority in matters of the law. They weren't about to oppose him in any way. Roamers lived on a knife's edge of reluctant tolerance as it was. They avoided direct confrontation with the authorities whenever they could.

"Jerome is dead," Will told them. A buzz of interest swept through them. Petulengo had told them as much, but the boy had been panicky and almost incoherent. Now the fact was confirmed. Their leader was gone. To be truthful, not all of them were sorry to hear it.

"He was killed by that vile dog that he was keeping in the forest," Will went on. "I suppose that's a fitting end for him. The dog is dead too. I killed it."

He paused. The Roamers fixed blank expressions on their faces as he gazed around them, and he gave a small snort of annoyance.

"I know you'll all claim that you knew nothing of what he was doing," he said. "And I know you'll all be lying. I should arrest you all here and now. But then we'd have to disinfect our jail after you were released, and it's all too much trouble. But you will move on. You have eight hours to be clear of Redmont Fief and I will be following to see that you go. You won't see me. But I'll be there."

He paused to let those words sink in. "Another thing. I'll make sure you're not welcome in any of the adjoining fiefs. You'll find no place willing to welcome you or let you stay even a day. You'll be hounded out and moved on wherever you go." He could see a surly acceptance in their faces. They expected no better than this. They had taken a chance with the stolen dog and they'd been caught out. It was always the way for Roamers.

"In fact," he continued, "you might find life altogether easier if you simply get out of the country."

He scanned the line of sullen faces in front of him. He was confident they'd be gone from Araluen within a week. Of course, they'd be back again some time in the future, but he'd face that problem when it came.

"Now start packing and get on the road."

He made a contemptuous gesture with his thumb, jerking it toward the road. The line of Roamers broke up, slowly at first, then moving with more speed as they began to break camp and pack their belongings away. He leaned down and ruffled the fur around Ebony's ears. She looked up at him and her tail swept in a long, slow back-and-forth movement.

"Nice to have you back, girl," he said softly. Then he turned to Alyss. "Ready to go?"

She held up a hand. "One thing I have to take care of," she said. She looked around the camp and spotted Petulengo, lurking guiltily by the goat pen. "Petulengo!" she called. Her voice was high and penetrating and he started, realizing he had been spotted. He looked around, seeking an escape route. But as he did so, Will unslung the massive longbow from his shoulder and casually plucked an arrow from his quiver. Suddenly, escaping didn't seem like such a good idea.

Then Alyss favored Petulengo with her most winning smile.

"Don't be frightened, dear," she said soothingly. "I just want to say good-bye."

She beckoned to him, smiling encouragingly, and he stepped forward, gradually gaining in confidence as he realized that, somehow, he had won the favor of this young woman. Some of his old swagger returned as he approached and stood before her, urged a little closer by that smile. Underneath the ash and the dirt, he thought, she was definitely a looker. He gave her a smile in return. Petulengo, it has to be said, fancied himself with the ladies.

Treat 'em rough and they'll eat out of your hand, he thought.

Then the smile disappeared like a candle being blown out. He felt a sudden jolt of agony in his right foot. Alyss's heavy boot, part of Hilde's wardrobe, had stamped down on his instep, just below the ankle. He doubled over instinctively, gasping with pain.

Then Alyss pivoted and drove the heel of her open left hand hard into his nose, snapping his head back and sending him reeling. His arms windmilled and he crashed over onto the hard-packed dirt of the compound.

He lay groggily, propped up on his elbows, coughing as blood coursed down the back of his throat.

"Next time you throw firewood at an old lady," Alyss told him, all traces of the winning smile gone, "make sure she can't do that."

She turned to Will and dusted her hands together in a satisfied gesture.

"*Now* I'm ready to go," she said.

PURPLE PROSE

1

WILL PUSHED HIS EMPTY PLATE AWAY AND LEANED BACK IN HIS chair, feeling that delightfully uncomfortable sensation that comes when you eat just a little too much of something really delicious.

Lady Pauline smiled fondly at the young man. "Would you like extras, Will? There's plenty left."

He patted his stomach, surprised to find that it seemed to actually feel tighter than normal, as if it were straining at his clothes from the inside.

"Thank you, no, Pauline," he said. "I've already had seconds."

"You've already had fourths," Halt commented. Will frowned at him, then turned back to Pauline, smiling at her. At least she didn't make disparaging comments the way her husband did.

"That really was a delicious meal," he said. "The beef was so tender and so beautifully rare. And the potatoes! Why, they were a symphony of flavor and texture!"

"Funny," Halt said in a lowered tone. "I didn't hear any trumpets and flutes."

"It's kind of you to say so, Will," Pauline said. "But I'm a professional woman and I don't actually do the cooking. Our meals here are provided by the castle kitchen. If you want to compliment any-one, it should be Master Chubb."

"Oh . . . of course," Will said, feeling foolish. Halt and Pauline had invited him for dinner in the comfortable apartment provided for them by Baron Arald. As two of Arald's senior, and most valued, advisers, they were entitled to a suite of rooms and the use of all the castle's services. Now that Will thought about it, he couldn't picture the tall, elegant diplomat working over a hot oven, with an apron protecting her white gown.

"Getting a little flowery with your language, aren't you?" Halt said. "*A symphony of flavor* indeed!"

Will shrugged diffidently. "I'm trying to make my language more poetic," he admitted. Halt frowned, but Pauline allowed herself the faintest vestige of a smile. Sometimes young men could be so serious about the strangest things, she thought.

"Is there any reason for this sudden interest in things poetic, Will?" she asked.

"Well," he said, "it's about my speech for the wedding."

"Horace and Evanlyn's wedding, you mean?" Halt said.

Will nodded. "As the best man, I have to propose a toast to the bride and groom."

"As you did at our wedding," Pauline said, smiling at the memory.

"Exactly. And I want it to be special. Because they're both such good friends of mine."

"The speech you made at our wedding was definitely special," Halt said. He too could recall the event clearly. He had been im-pressed and touched by Will's simple affirmation of love and affec-tion for them both. The fact that he mentioned it now was clear proof of that. Halt had spent his life concealing his feelings from the world at large. He rarely allowed his emotional side—which he called his mawkish side—to show.

"I've been working on the speech," Will said. His hand went unconsciously toward an inner pocket in his jacket. "I wonder if you'd mind having a listen to what I've got so far . . . ?" He left the question hanging, looking from Pauline to Halt and then back again.

"How could we refuse?" Pauline asked. So young and so serious, she thought to herself.

Halt glanced quickly at her. Too late, he had tried to signal her to find a graceful way of refusing to listen to the speech. She was a diplomat after all, he thought. Graceful refusals were her daily stock-in-trade. He sighed softly. Will was already smoothing out several sheets of paper from his pocket. He looked up at them to see if they were ready. Pauline leaned forward in her seat and nodded encouragingly. Halt raised his eyes to the ceiling.

Will took that as a signal to proceed. He cleared his throat several times, smoothed the paper a few more times and frowned as he read ahead, committing the first few lines to memory.

"You'll understand," he said, "this is just a first draft. It's by no means the final wording that I'll be using on the day. I'll probably go through it and change it here and there. I mean, I'll definitely go through it, and when I do, I'll probably change it here and there . . ."

"Of course," Pauline said, and gestured for him to proceed. He cleared his throat again.

"Getting a cold?" Halt asked innocently, then winced as Pauline kicked him under the table. Even wearing light evening slippers, she packed a wallop, he thought, leaning down to rub his calf muscle.

Will looked up from the speech, his cheeks flushing. "No," he said. "Why do you ask?"

"Ignore him, Will, dear," Pauline said. There was an underlying steely note in her voice that Will didn't notice. Halt did, however.

He had known this woman for many years and decided that silence would be his best option for the next few minutes.

"Very well . . . ," Will said. He cleared his throat again. Finally, he began.

"It is with the greatest fulsomeness of heart that I—"

"Whoa! Whoa! Bring the ship back to the shore there! It is with the greatest *whatsomeness* of *what?*" Halt asked incredulously, his plan to remain silent suddenly forgotten. Will looked up at him, flustered.

"Fulsomeness of heart," he repeated. Then he checked the text in front of him once more. "Yes. That's right. Fulsomeness of heart."

"And what on earth does 'fulsomeness of heart' mean?" Halt asked. He glanced at his wife and noticed that she was concealing a smile.

Will made an uncertain gesture with his right hand. "Well, it means . . . you know . . . a lot of . . . um . . . *fulsomeness* . . . in the heart."

Halt continued to stare at him, uncomprehending. He shook his head, so Will tried again. Now he was more than flushed, Pauline noticed. His cheeks were aflame.

"It means I'm happy. Very happy," Will said eventually.

"Then why don't you say 'I am happy, very happy'?" Halt asked.

Will shifted uncomfortably in his chair. "Well, that would be a little"—he searched for a word, then found it—"prosaic, wouldn't it?"

Halt's eyebrows shot up. "Prosaic? First it's funsomeness . . ."

"Fulsomeness," Will said, through slightly gritted teeth. Halt ignored him.

"Now it's prosaic. I'll be butted by a billy goat if I know what that means!"

"Don't be colorful, dear," said Pauline. "It means 'ordinary.'"

"Oh, so I'm ordinary, am I?" he challenged Will. "And when did it become a crime to use words that people could understand?"

"I said before, I'm trying to make this speech memorable," Will said.

Halt slumped back into his seat. "It'll be memorable, all right," he muttered. "For years, people will say, *Remember that speech Will gave that nobody could understand?*" Then he waved a hand for Will to continue. "Let's hear some more of it."

Will shuffled his sheets of paper and began over again. "It is with the greatest fulsomeness of heart—"

"Heard that already."

"Halt . . . ," Pauline said warningly.

"That I stand in your illustrious presences on this most auspicious of felicitous occasions to render praise and adulation to two of the most revered and cherished companions of my youthful years."

"Good grief," Halt muttered, earning himself another sharp kick in the calf.

"It would be contumelious of me not to recognize the—"

"No! No! No!" Halt said, waving his arms across in front of his body. "That's enough! No more!"

"Is there a problem?" Will asked haughtily.

Halt rolled his eyes. "Yes, there's a problem! You sound as if you swallowed a dictionary and then threw it up!"

"Don't be coarse, Halt," Pauline said, and the gray-bearded Ranger subsided, muttering to himself. Will appealed to Pauline.

"What do you think of it, Pauline? You're good with words."

Pauline hesitated. She loved this young man as if he were her own son and she would never willingly hurt his feelings. But she couldn't let him continue with this overblown nonsense.

"Do you think the language might be a little . . . florid?" she asked tentatively.

Halt snorted, looking away, out the window.

"Florid? It's positively purple in the face!" he said. "It sounds like something Baron Arald would say!"

Will looked at him, a stricken expression on his face. "Oh, surely it's not as bad as all that," he said.

Halt merely turned to him, raised an eyebrow, then looked away again.

"Will, you spoke so beautifully at our wedding. Just do the same again," Pauline told him.

But he shook his head. "Everybody says that. But the thing was, nobody was expecting much from me then. Everybody will be expecting so much more this time. Besides, this is a royal wedding, so the speech will be recorded in the annals. It has to be special."

"Gorlog save us!" Halt said.

Pauline turned to him curiously. "Who exactly is Gorlog, dear?" she asked.

"He's a northern god. I borrowed him from the Skandians. He's very useful if you want to blaspheme without offending people."

"Other than Skandians?" she suggested, but he shook his head, grinning.

"No. They don't mind. They don't like him very much."

Pauline nodded, filing that piece of information away, then turned back to Will.

"I have a suspicion that you might be trying too hard, Will," she said. She pointed to the sheets of paper on the table before him. "Why don't you take another look at it and simplify it a little?"

Will pursed his lips doubtfully. He could ignore Halt's criticism, he thought. Halt had no sense of poetry in him. But Pauline was a different matter. Still, he had spent hours laboring over these words and he was reluctant to abandon them.

"I'll think about it," he said finally.

Halt snorted yet again. He seemed to be doing a lot of that this evening.

"Just ignore him," Pauline said to Will. "You know what he's like."

"Yes," Halt said. "I'm sorry I've been so contumentulous."

"That's contumelious," Will told him.

Halt smiled a wolfish smile. "Yes. That too."

Pauline patted Will's hand gently. "As I say, just ignore him. I'll speak to him later," she added ominously. Will glanced in his old mentor's direction and saw something that surprised him. Something he had never seen before.

The smile was gone. Halt was afraid.

2

WILL HAD SPENT AN UNSUCCESSFUL AFTERNOON HUNTING.

Jenny had expressed a need for fresh venison in her restaurant, and he had been happy to try to oblige her. But as he knew, sometimes even the most skillful hunter can come home empty-handed. In a way, that was part of the fascination of hunting. The only deer he had seen in a long afternoon had been a young doe and her fawn, obviously still dependent on its mother.

He had smiled at the pair and shooed them on their way, laughing quietly as they bounded off into the trees.

"Go away and grow up a little," he had said, adding as an afterthought, "both of you."

Because he hunted to provide food and not from any sense of pleasure in the kill, he wasn't disappointed with his lack of success, but accepted it philosophically. Jenny had other meat she could offer on her menu. It wasn't as if people were going to go short. So he was in a relatively good mood as he rode back to Redmont.

Relatively. There was one matter that was nagging away at him. The more he thought about it on the return journey, the more bothered he became.

As he was unsaddling Tug and putting the tack away, the little horse looked curiously at him.

Why the long face? Tug had never really understood the principle behind that old joke, Will thought.

"That's supposed to be my line to you. After all, you're the horse. The joke is, a horse walks into a tavern and the innkeeper says, 'Why the long face?'" he said. Tug shifted from one foreleg to the other, his equivalent of a careless shrug.

So what? What's on your mind?

"It's this speech I'm giving at the wedding," Will told him, rubbing him down with a dry piece of old blanket, then looking around for the brush to curry him with—Tug's coat had picked up a lot of burrs as they had pushed through the undergrowth in their fruitless search for game. "It's got me worried."

That's why horses don't give speeches.

"Horses don't have weddings either, so far as I know," Will told him.

True. But we do have bridles.

Tug's ears pricked forward with appreciation of his own wit. He emitted the horse equivalent of a snigger. Will sighed.

"You don't get any better, do you?" he said, and continued plying the brush. Tug stood still for a few minutes, enjoying the contact and the pleasantly abrasive feeling of the stiff bristles working through his coat.

"Halt wasn't very impressed with it," Will said after a few minutes' silence.

Halt is rarely impressed by anything.

Halt and Tug had a history of disagreement, which stemmed from Halt's beliefs about how many apples were good for a horse.

"That's true. But I asked Pauline, and even though she didn't say so directly, I don't think she liked it either."

He waited, pausing between brushstrokes. But there was no response. He wasn't sure if that was a good thing or not. Maybe Tug was trying to find a tactful way of saying that if Pauline didn't like it, he might have a problem. Then, when he thought about it, he realized that Tug was rarely tactful about anything. He leaned to one side to get a look at the horse's face. Maybe he'd fallen asleep standing up. Horses could do that, he knew. But the big brown eyes blinked and looked back at him.

An idea struck Will. A possible way to settle the question in his own mind. He finished the last of his brushstrokes, stepping back a pace to admire how neat the horse's normally shaggy coat looked.

"Maybe I could read a bit of it to you," he suggested. Tug shifted from one foot to another again. But now the movement was more wary than before.

I told you. Horses don't make speeches.

"No. But you'll know something good if you hear it," Will told him. He set down the brush and reached for his inner pocket.

Tug rolled an eye doubtfully. *What if I don't?*

"What if you don't know something good?" Will asked.

No. What if I don't hear something good?

Will was taken aback by this lack of faith.

"Oh, you will," he said stiffly. "Just listen to this."

I haven't had my apple yet.

"You can have it when you've heard my speech."

Is it a long speech?

"It's several pages now. But it's so good, it won't seem long. You'll be begging for more at the end."

He looked at the horse and was surprised to see a skeptical expression on his face. Will had no idea that horses could show such an emotion. It was unsettling. He unfolded the sheets on which he had written the speech, smoothed it out and cleared his throat.

Bless you.

"What?"

You sneezed.

"I didn't sneeze. I cleared my throat. Like this." He did it again. Tug blinked several times.

Sounded like a sneeze to me. Could be the plague.

"It was not a sneeze and it's not the plague. You're going to hear this speech whether you like it or not," he said firmly. Then he hastened to add, "Although I'm sure you will like it. It's really good."

Tug emitted a deep abdominal rumble. Will looked sidelong at him. It had sounded like criticism, he thought. Then he realized it couldn't have been, as he hadn't begun the speech yet.

He smoothed the pages once more and began reading.

" . . . It would be contumelious of me not to pay tribute at this juncture in time to a multifarious assemblage of persons who, by the assiduous attention to the needs of . . ."

Will paused. He had been reading for several minutes and Tug hadn't stirred. Now he wasn't sure, but he thought Tug had made a noise—a deep, droning noise.

"What was that?" he asked. But there was no immediate reply. Shrugging, he looked back to the sheet of paper in his hand. "Where was I? Oh yes . . . to a multifarious assemblage . . ."

The noise came again. This time he was sure it came from Tug. It seemed to be centered in his throat and chest. Then the horse's entire body shuddered. Will looked at him curiously. Perhaps his beautiful words had reduced his old friend to tears, he thought. He stepped around to face Tug as the droning noise came once more. The horse's eyes were tight shut and his knees were locked. He was fast asleep. Will realized, as the droning noise came again, that he was snoring.

"You faithless wretch," he said. Tug snored again.

Disgusted, Will folded the sheet of paper and returned it to his inner pocket. He turned on his heel and strode from the stable. As he reached the door, the regular droning sound stopped. He glanced back at Tug.

Where's my apple?

He glared at the horse. "I'm sorry. I don't have one. Perhaps you could dream one up."

He walked out of the stable, his back stiff, every line of his body showing how affronted he was by his horse's behavior. He reached the front of the cabin, where Ebony lay sprawled on her side in the sun. As he mounted the steps to the cabin, one eye opened and her heavy tail thumped once on the boards of the verandah.

He regarded her for a moment. Dogs were never judgmental, he thought. A dog would stick by you, right or wrong. In a dog's eyes, you could do no wrong. A dog would always give you an honest opinion.

"Good girl, Eb," he said, and the tail thumped again. He sat down on a bench set against the wall of the cabin. Ebony watched him, craning her head back to see him without moving her body. He clicked his fingers at her.

"Come here, Ebony. Come here, girl."

With a grunt, she rolled onto her belly, then stood and shook herself. Then she came to him, head lowered, tail sweeping slowly.

"Down." He gestured and she sank onto her belly at his feet, her eyes fixed on him. He took the paper from his pocket once more and looked at those big beautiful eyes. One deep brown, the other a slightly manic blue.

"I'm going to read you a speech, Ebony," he said.

The tail thumped once.

"And I want your honest opinion."

The eyes never wavered from his. He unfolded the paper and began to read. After a few paragraphs, Ebony sighed and dropped her nose onto her outstretched forepaws, but she continued to watch him, seemingly without blinking, as he read the beautiful phrases of his speech. Finally, he reached the ending, a part he was particularly proud of. He read it out, then read it again for emphasis.

"Well," he said, "what do you think?"

The eyes continued to stare at him. The nose remained resting on the forepaws. There was no movement. But at least, he thought, she was awake.

"Did you like it, Ebony?" he asked, and the tail thumped once on the floorboards. He smiled at her, reached down and ruffled her ears. A good dog would never let you down.

"It's pretty good, isn't it?" he asked. There was no reaction from the dog.

"Is it good, Ebony?" The tail thumped on the floorboards again and Will was assailed by a terrible doubt. He stared at the dog, their gazes locked.

"Is it good?" he repeated. There was no reaction.

"Is it good, Ebony?" *Thump* went the tail.

"Is it the biggest load of rubbish you've ever heard?" No reaction.

"Is it the biggest load of rubbish you've ever heard . . . Ebony?" *Thump* went the tail. He glared at her.

"You're just reacting when I say your name, aren't you?" No reaction.

"You're just reacting to your name, aren't you . . . Ebony?" *Thump.*

Will stood, shaking his head in annoyance.

"I just can't trust anyone to give me an honest answer. Well, blast Tug. And blast you too, Ebony."

Thump went the tail.

In high dudgeon, Will went into the cabin and shut the door firmly behind him. On the verandah, Ebony lay watching the door for a few seconds. Then, when Will didn't come out again, she rose, shook herself and walked to a patch of warm sunlight. With a groan of pleasure, she flopped onto her side, legs outstretched, head tilted back, and went to sleep.

3

How would you rate the Battleschool's state of readiness?
Excellent. Good. Average. Below average. Bad.

Will shrugged and made a check mark beside *Excellent.*

Part of any Ranger's job was to periodically assess the fief's Battlesschool and report to Castle Araluen on the quality of training, the proficiency of Battleschool members and the overall state of readiness in the event of an attack. Redmont's Battleschool was one of the best in the country and Will's assessments were almost always in the *Excellent* range. He sometimes wondered why he couldn't just write "see last assessment," but the King's Battlemaster demanded detailed answers each time. He sighed as he saw the next question.

On what do you base this rating?

He couldn't answer this with a simple check mark. He'd have to write something justifying the rating. He tried to remember the wording of his previous report. As he did so, the door flew open suddenly and Halt entered the cabin.

"Hullo. Didn't hear you coming," Will said.

Halt gave him a satisfied nod. "Good. Every now and then I try not to blunder around like a blind man in a pottery shop. I'm surprised Tug didn't hear me."

"Tug's sulking. I didn't give him an apple yesterday."

Of course, they both knew that if it had been anyone other than Halt approaching, Tug would have given a warning signal, sulking or not.

"Good. He eats too many apples anyway." Halt looked at the papers on the desk before Will and a wary expression came over his face. "You're not working on that speech, are you?"

Will sighed. "No. Doing my Battleschool assessment for the Royal Battlemaster. I don't know why I have to spell it all out. They should know by now that there are no problems at Redmont Battleschool."

Halt shrugged. "An army runs on paperwork," he said. "Anyway, you can forget about it for now. We've got a job."

Will sat up and took notice at that. "A job?" he said. "Where are we going?"

There was a large-scale map of Araluen on the wall of the cabin and Halt moved to it, tapping his forefinger on a spot in the southwest coast, a little above the border with Celtica.

"Hambley," he said. "We've had reports that there are moondarkers working their way down the coast. Hambley is their next logical target."

"Moondarkers?" Will hadn't heard the term before. Halt wasn't surprised. It had been many years since any organized gangs of moondarkers had operated in Araluen.

"Wreckers," he explained. "Ship wreckers. They work in the dark of the moon and light false beacons on dangerous stretches of the coast. Ships passing by see the beacon fires and think they've reached port. So in they sail, and before they know it, they're on the rocks. The ship breaks up and the moondarkers help themselves to the cargo."

"What happens to the crews?" Will asked.

"If they survive the wreck, they come ashore. Usually, they don't survive that."

"These moondarkers sound like nasty people," Will commented.

Halt nodded. "Exactly. And they're hard to track down because the locals are usually frightened of them." A frown crossed his face. "Or in some cases, they're in league with them."

"They share in the spoils," Will said.

"That's right. There's a lot of stuff the wreckers don't want—timber and cordage, for example. Casks of dried food. Canvas, metal fittings. All the sorts of things that a poor village would find invaluable. Now let's get a move on. The dark of the moon is only a week away, and that's when they'll come out of hiding. I want to be on the road this afternoon. I've sent a message to Gilan and he'll keep an eye on things here while we're away."

"I'll get my travel gear," Will said. He hesitated, looking at the unfinished assessment form. "I suppose I could do this while we're on the road," he said.

Halt picked up the form and tore it in half, before Will's cry of protest could stop him. "Better idea. Leave Gilan a note saying the assessment is due but you haven't got around to it yet. Then he can do an assessment of his own and fill out the form for you."

Will hesitated, looking at the torn piece of paper in Halt's hands.

"Isn't that a little sneaky?" he said. Halt grinned happily.

"It certainly is. And isn't that what Rangers are supposed to be?"

An hour later, they were on the road to the southwest. Mindful of Ebony's recent abduction by Roamers, Will had left her at the castle, in Pauline's care. Intelligent and loyal as she was, Ebony was still young and excitable. They couldn't risk taking her along on what would probably turn out to be a dangerous assignment. Pauline was delighted to have the dog for company, and Ebony was devoted to her.

As they rode, Will chuckled quietly to himself. Halt turned in his saddle to look at him.

"Something funny?"

"I keep thinking about Gilan doing that Battleschool report," Will said. "You're right. It's so sneaky."

Halt beamed. "It serves him right for all the times he tried to ambush me on the way to Gatherings," he said. "Sometimes former apprentices lose all their respect for their former masters." He glanced meaningfully at Will, who hastened to reply.

"Not me!" he said. "I still have enormous respect for you, Halt!"

Halt looked searchingly at him for several moments, then, seemingly satisfied, he nodded to himself. "Just bear it in mind."

They continued without speaking any further for a few hundred meters, then Will broke the silence again.

"The good thing about this is that I can work on my speech in the evenings," Will said.

"You brought it with you?" Halt asked him, a little apprehensively.

Will nodded. "I thought it would be a good opportunity to work on it without distractions."

There was a long silence, then Halt said, "I certainly won't interrupt you. I mean, I wouldn't want to impede the creative flow or anything like that. In fact, you can just consider me not there at all if you want to work on it." He wondered if Will would detect the sarcasm behind that statement, but his former apprentice nodded gratefully.

"Thanks, Halt. I appreciate that. Now, what's our course of action going to be?"

Halt considered for a few moments as he marshaled his thoughts.

"As I said this morning, we can't expect any help from the locals. We can't take the chance that they'll betray us to the moondarkers."

"The moondarkers aren't locals, then?" Will asked.

Halt shook his head. "No. They travel up and down the coast. If they work one area for too long, word gets out and people like us turn up to stop them. Also, ships quickly learn to avoid that part of the coast."

"You said you had word from an informer. Can we expect any help from him?" Will asked. But again, the answer was in the negative.

"If he's wise, he'll have nothing to do with us. After all, he's got to live in the area after we've gone."

"That makes sense. So what's our plan?"

"We'll make camp and scout around—hopefully without being seen ourselves. Usually the moondarkers don't stay in the villages, so they'll have a camp somewhere in the area as well. That'll be hard to conceal because there will be fifteen to twenty of them. So we scout around for that—and we look for signs that they're getting ready."

"Like what?"

"Like a beacon fire being prepared on the wrong headland. They'll have to build that a day or two in advance. Plus we'll need to post a lookout to the north for ships making their way down the coast. And we need to keep an eye out for other people who are looking for the same thing."

"And if we see any of these things happening?" Will asked. Halt smiled at him. The smile reminded Will of a wolf showing its teeth.

"Then I'll ask them to stop. I can be very persuasive when I put my mind to it."

"I've noticed that in the past," Will said.

They made good time for the rest of the day, setting the horses into the Ranger forced march pattern, alternating between cantering and walking. Dusk was falling when Halt indicated a cleared spot under a group of trees.

"That looks like a decent campsite," he said. "We may as well get set up before it's too dark."

"Do you want me to cook?" Will asked. He knew Halt was capable of doing it. But Will actually enjoyed the work of preparing meals and he was an excellent camp cook, always carrying a traveling kit of spices and ingredients to improve the flavor of the meals he prepared. Since Rangers were often forced to exist on dried meat and fruit and flat bread, he always felt they should enjoy good meals when they had the chance.

Halt agreed with him in this matter.

"I'll look forward to it," he said. "Once we're near Hambley, it'll be cold camps and hard rations, so we might as well enjoy some hot food and coffee while we can. I'll clean up later."

In spite of their former master-apprentice relationship, Halt nowadays considered Will an equal and was always willing to share campsite chores with him.

"Excellent," Will said. Like a lot of cooks, he liked the process of preparation but was less enthusiastic about the cleaning up that followed. "That'll give me time to work on my speech."

"I'll look forward to that, too," Halt said, straight-faced.

4

A RIDGE OF HILLS RAN BEHIND THE TOWN OF HAMBLEY, ABOUT half a kilometer inland. The town itself was built around a small but well-protected harbor. On the northern breakwater, Will could see a large metal framework some six meters in height.

"That's the real beacon," Halt told him, noticing his interested gaze. "It's lit every night and it shows any approaching ship where the north breakwater is and gives them a steering point. But as you can see, the tall headland behind it hides it from the view of any ship coming down the coast until the ship is only half a kilometer away."

They were lying on their bellies at the top of the ridge of hills overlooking the town. The horses were back on the reverse side of the ridge, out of sight. The two Rangers, lying prone and concealed by their cloaks, would be invisible to anyone within fifty meters, let alone half a kilometer.

"Now look farther north," Halt said, and Will obediently shifted his point of view. Beyond the headland, a curving strip of beach swept north, ending in another, slightly lower headland. "My guess is, that's where they'll build the false beacon. You can see how the water is shallow for several hundred meters out from the beach. Any ship turning in there, thinking they've found the harbor, will be on the sand before they know it. I imagine the wreckers will set up spot fires and lanterns on the low ground behind the beach so it'll look like the town. The ship's captain will see what he expects to see. A beacon and a township. But it'll be a kilometer farther north than the real one. This ridge of hills we're on will create a dark backdrop. Someone looking from out to sea will see the lights against the darkness. They won't see details."

He rubbed his jaw thoughtfully, brushing away an ant that had ventured to explore his beard.

"That shallow sandy bottom will suit them admirably. The ship will be stuck on it, but unless there's really bad weather, she won't break up. That means the moondarkers can wade out at low tide and unload her at their leisure. And they'll get all the cargo instead of losing some as it's washed away."

Will glanced sideways at the gray-bearded Ranger. "You seem to know a lot about how they work, Halt."

Halt nodded grimly. "Moondarking was a blight on this nation during the first war with Morgarath," he said. "The King's troops were too preoccupied with the rebellion to attend to other matters. And you know how quickly criminals will take advantage of a situation like that."

Will nodded. "So how did you stamp them out?"

"Oh, after the war, Crowley and I mounted a bit of a campaign against them. After a while, they seemed to decide that Araluen wasn't the best place to go moondarking. Most of them moved on to Gallica, where conditions were more conducive to their trade."

"Most of them?" Will asked. "What about the others?"

"They stayed here," Halt said grimly. "You'll find their graves up and down the west coast if you look closely."

"You and Crowley were quite a team in the early days, weren't you?" Will asked. A ghost of a smile touched Halt's mouth.

"We had our moments," he said. Then he began to slither back from the top of the ridge, staying low until he could stand without being skylined to any observer below them. Will followed and looked expectantly to his old teacher for orders.

"We'll head north toward that beach," Halt said. "We'll camp on the ridge and keep watch for any activity on the headland or on the low ground inland from the beach."

"You're sure that's where they'll set up?" Will said.

Halt shrugged. "You can never be sure of anything. But it's the most logical place. Any farther north and they'd be too far away from Hambley itself. Besides, the coastline curves in to the east up there, so the whole topography is different. This spot is close enough to the real town to confuse any skipper who's not on his toes. We'll scout through the woods as well, to see if we can find their camp. If they're in the area, they shouldn't be too hard to find. They won't be trying to remain hidden the way we will be and it'll be a big camp."

"You said there could be fifteen to twenty of them . . . ," Will began.

"That's right. And they'll need carts and horses to carry away the cargo, so the camp will be a big one."

"Can we handle that many?" Will asked tentatively.

Halt looked steadily at him. "These men are cold-blooded murderers," he said. "But they're not warriors. They'll get one warning to surrender, then we start shooting. Crowley and I handled this many. It shouldn't be a problem."

"That was Crowley and you," Will said. He was surprised by Halt's answer.

"You're better than Crowley."

Will would have been even more surprised if Halt had added what was in his mind: *You're probably better than me, too.*

. . .

They struck north and set up a small, well-concealed camp in a thicket of trees on the inland slope of the ridge. Abelard and Tug were unsaddled and left to graze close to the camp. If by chance they were discovered, their shaggy coats and lack of saddles or bridles would probably lead their discoverers to assume they were wild ponies. There were numbers of those roaming the hills in small groups.

There would be no campfire, and the two Rangers sighed as they resigned themselves to a diet of cold water and hard rations for the duration of the mission. They set up an observation post on the ridge, digging a shallow pit, then roofing it over with dirt, branches and leaves so that they could watch the beach and the headland unobserved. It was not unlike the sort of hide that hunters built, Will thought. Then he smiled grimly as he realized they *were* hunters. But they were hunting men.

There were still a few hours of daylight left when they finished. Halt gestured to the pit.

"Keep an eye on things," he said. "I'm going to scout around and see if I can find any sign of a camp."

Will nodded. A camp would confirm that they were on the right track. After all, they were still working off information received from the anonymous informant. It could well be a wild-goose chase. But one of the first things a Ranger learned was to watch and listen patiently for hours or days on end.

Will moved in a crouch to the observation post, which was on the slope of the ridge overlooking the beach, and crept inside. He settled down, made himself comfortable and leaned back against the dirt wall. They had left an observation slit that ran the entire width of the hide, and as he sat back in the deep shadows, he had an uninterrupted view of the headland and beach.

He reached into the satchel he had slung over one shoulder and took out paper, pen and a small traveling inkwell. The draft of his speech was in there too, but for the moment he would content himself with noting down impressive phrases to include in it. He could do that while keeping a keen eye on the beach below him. Reading or rewriting the speech would be too much of a distraction. But jotting down the odd descriptive phrase would only take a second or two at a time.

One such came to mind—a description of Horace and Evanlyn—and he quickly unscrewed the inkwell, dipped in his pen and jotted it down.

The much beloved boon companions of my tender youthful years, he wrote. And muttered to himself, "Oh, that's good. Very good."

He scanned the beach and the headland again, but nothing was moving. Then he jotted down another phrase.

It is with prideful joy that I have the temerity to add my unstinting adulation to what has already been avowed before this eminent assemblage . . .

"I do like that. Very much," he said to himself. He sighed happily and leaned back against the earth wall of the pit, waiting for further inspiration to strike.

It took Halt less than two hours to find the camp.

Not surprisingly, it was the smell of wood smoke that first alerted him to the presence of people in the woods. It was faint at first, but as he followed in the direction from which the light breeze was blowing, it became stronger. Then he began to notice other signs. A dog barked. Then he heard the ring of an ax on wood. The sounds and smells took him back over the ridgeline, into the woods on the seaward side. Eventually, he found himself looking down into a cleared hollow in the trees.

There were half a dozen tents pitched in a neat group, and several cooking fires were already lit. Off to one side, four solid-wheeled carts were parked. Beyond them, he could make out horses tethered among the trees. People moved about the campsite, talking and calling to one another. There was no real attempt at concealment, as there was nobody to remain concealed from—so far as the moondarkers were concerned.

He counted the people he could see. Sixteen of them, and all men, he noted. And that last fact was further confirmation that this was a moondarkers' camp.

He watched for a few minutes as several of them began to prepare the evening meal. His stomach complained quietly as the delicious aroma of meat roasting over the fires wafted around him. He silently withdrew from his vantage point.

"Nothing to do here but get hungry," he murmured to himself, and headed back to the smoke-free, roasted-meat-free camp hidden on the reverse slope. He thought about what his dinner would be: cold water, dried meat and fruit, and hard bread.

The thought didn't make him more kindly disposed toward the moondarkers.

5

As Will had observed, a great deal of a Ranger's time was spent sitting, watching and waiting. This could go on for days, then there would be brief periods of heart-stopping action.

He and Halt alternated in the observation post, each spending three hours at a time watching the sand flats and the headland below them.

In the hours when they weren't on watch, they exercised the horses and hunted for small game. One welcome change was that Halt had decided they no longer needed to maintain a cold camp. The moondarkers were a good distance away from their campsite, with the ridge between them. Plus the Rangers had chosen a site at one of the highest points on the ridge. The chance that one of the moondarkers would walk uphill and stumble upon them was slight.

All the same, the older Ranger insisted that they could not light the fire if the wind was blowing from the north, as it might carry the smell of their wood smoke back to the enemy. It was a slim chance that they would notice it even then, as their own camp had three or four large cook fires and the smell of pine smoke was everywhere. But a slim chance was a chance, and Halt was unwilling to take it.

As he said, being careful had helped him stay alive all these years and he was looking forward to maintaining that record.

This meant that Will could prepare more interesting meals for them, and that at least gave him something to do in his off-duty time. It also gave the pair of them something to look forward to in the boring schedule of watch keeping.

The schedule they had adopted meant that Halt had the last watch—when the sun had dropped behind the ridge. They'd get plenty of warning when the moondarkers were preparing to act. To avoid the risk of discovery, the moondarkers would wait till the last minute to set out their false fires and beacons. They'd do that by daylight, and until they did, there was no need to keep watch through the night.

Will took to bringing both their evening meals to the observation post. They would eat together and discuss their tactics for such time as the moondarkers might strike.

"I've been thinking," Halt said on the third night. "We might have to look at getting some help."

Will grinned at him. "I thought you said we could handle sixteen people easily," he said.

Halt nodded in acknowledgment of the point. "I did say that. But it occurs to me that I'm going to need you on the headland while I'm on the beach. That might make things awkward."

"How's that? What will I be doing on the headland?"

"You'll be attending to the beacon fire. We'll have to let them light it before we act. Until they do that, we have no proof that they're actually trying to bring a ship ashore. We need to see the ship and we need them to light the fire to lure it onto the beach."

"The fact that they've prepared a signal won't be enough?" Will asked.

Halt shook his head, frowning. "It's not concrete proof. They could always claim they were planning a bonfire to celebrate some-one's birthday. Or that they were planning to roast a pig or a sheep. We need actual proof. Unfortunately, Duncan is a bit of a stickler for that. At the same time, we have to make sure that they don't actually cause the ship to run aground."

"So you want me to wait till they light the beacon, then I'll put it out while you arrest everyone else?" Will said.

Halt raised an eyebrow at him. "Do you have any idea how big this fire is going to be? It's not a campfire you can kick some sand over. It'll be a great stack of logs and oil and combustibles and it'll be at least two meters high. Once it's going, you won't be able to simply 'put it out,' as you say. You'd need a bucket chain to do that—and in any case, there's no water source for half a kilometer."

Will hadn't thought of that. "So what do I do?" he asked. In answer, Halt reached inside his jerkin and produced a small packet wrapped in oilskin, about six centimeters by three.

"You throw this in the fire," he said.

Will took the packet and examined it. It was tightly packed, but he could feel the grainy nature of the contents as he squeezed the oilskin. It felt as if the packet was full of coarse sand.

"What is it?" he asked. Halt tapped it with his finger.

"It's a colored dye and it's highly flammable," he said. "When you throw that in the fire, it will flare up and change the flames to some bright color—I'm not sure what it will be. They're usually yellow or red. Whatever it is, once the ship's captain sees the flames change color, he'll realize that this isn't the real beacon and he'll head back out to sea. But we'll have the proof we need."

"All right. That makes sense. But how are you going to cope with the sixteen moondarkers on the beach while I'm doing this?" Will asked.

"I'm going to need help," Halt said. "I'll wait till we know they're planning to strike—when they have their beacon and their lanterns and spot fires prepared—then I'm going into Hambley to confront the head of the village watch."

"I thought you said they're probably in league with the moondarkers?"

"Not actively. They'll turn a blind eye and pick over whatever the moondarkers leave behind. On top of that, if they know we're in the area, they'd probably warn them off. But I've been keeping an eye on the village when I've been off watch, and there's been no traffic in there from the moondarkers' camp."

"So if you go into the village at the last minute and give them no time to send a warning to the moondarkers, they can hardly refuse to help you," Will said.

"Exactly. They might be reluctant. But they'll have to provide men from the village watch to help us. They can hardly admit to a King's Ranger that they think it might be a good idea for a ship to be wrecked on their coast."

Will chewed his lip doubtfully. "You're putting a lot of faith in the respect people have for Rangers," he said.

Halt inclined his head, conceding the point. "True. But I've done it before and it's never let me down in the past. These people aren't really criminals. They're desperately poor and they lead a hard life. But if they understand they can be punished for not lending us a hand, they'll come on board."

"Of course, they could just knock you on the head and drop you off the end of the harbor mole," Will said. Halt considered the idea.

"They could. But it's not likely. After all, I'll be prepared for them to try something like that—as unlikely as it might be. Plus they'll know there's another Ranger in the area. I'll make sure I tell them. I doubt they'll take the risk then."

"So I throw the dye in the fire and you arrest the moondarkers on the beach. It seems we have every contingency covered," Will said. In spite of his questioning Halt's plan, he knew how strong the aura of power and authority that surrounded a King's Ranger could be in these out-of-the-way villages.

"You never have every contingency covered," Halt said somberly. "There's always something that can go wrong."

He finished the last spoonful of the savory rabbit stew that Will had prepared, scraping the last vestiges out of his bowl.

"Any more?" he asked hopefully.

But Will shook his head. "Sorry. You finished the last of it."

Halt grunted moodily. "Thought so." He glanced at the lengthening shadows. Already, the land below them was in deep shade and the sea had taken on a silver-gray sheen. "Well, I doubt they'll be starting anything now. We might as well have coffee back at the camp."

"That's why I stick with you," Will said. "You're full of good ideas."

The following day, the moondarkers went to work.

Will noticed the first sign that something was happening halfway through his morning watch. A horseman came pelting down the coast road below the ridge. Then, when he was level with the spot where the moondarkers' camp was situated, he turned off the road and urged his horse up a narrow, steep trail through the trees. Will quickly lost sight of him, but there was no doubt as to where his destination lay.

He scrambled out of the hide and, staying low, ran back over the ridge to tell Halt.

"Odds are there's a ship making its way toward Hambley," Halt said. "It's standard practice for them to leave a lookout up the coast to spot any ships approaching. If that's the case, they'll be setting up their fires today."

"What do we do?" Will asked.

Halt jerked a thumb in the direction of the moondarkers' camp. "Let's see what they're up to."

They left the camp together, moving like wraiths through the trees, blending into the shadows and the gray-green undergrowth so that they were barely visible. An observer would have had great trouble seeing them at any distance greater than twenty meters. But such was their training and the constant practice they carried out that they moved instinctively, without thinking about what they were doing.

As they stepped through the undergrowth, their feet in their soft-soled boots sought out twigs and branches underfoot before they set weight on them. If they felt an impediment, it was quietly nudged aside with a toe, then they proceeded, letting the weight settle gently onto the extended foot so that they moved with barely a sound.

It looked simple—the way anything looks when it's the result of years of meticulous practice.

It took them half an hour to reach the vantage point from which Halt had originally observed the moondarker camp.

Will pointed to a lathered horse tied up outside one of the tents. Obviously, it belonged to the messenger who had arrived earlier. He was about to comment on their lack of care for their horses when three men emerged suddenly from the tent. One of them, a tall, black-bearded man in a leather vest and breeches, began shouting orders. The camp came alive as other tents disgorged their occupants.

They began to load the carts Halt had observed on his previous visit, stacking them with ready-cut firewood and lanterns and long willow poles. The horses were gathered in from the spot where they were tethered and harnessed between the carts' shafts. The men gathered tools and sacks of provisions. Ominously, they also buckled on swords or shoved clubs through their belts.

"We've seen enough," Halt said. "Let's get out of here before we're noticed."

They headed back to the concealment of their observation post. Some time after, they saw the moondarkers emerge from the forest at the bottom of the hills and move out onto the flatland adjacent to the beach.

Three of the carts were unloaded there, the men thronging around them and carrying piles of cut firewood and lengths of iron, setting them up in positions determined by their leader—the tall man in the leather vest. Will watched curiously as the man moved away from his companions, his back to the ocean, and began directing them where to build fires and set up the lengths of iron—which fitted together to form tripods. From time to time, he referred to a sheet of paper in his hands, indicating that a pile of firewood should be moved slightly in one direction, and one of the tripods be brought forward or back a little.

"What's he up to?" Will asked. Even though they were over a kilometer away, he kept his voice to a whisper.

"I'd say he's got a plan of Hambley there—how it looks from the seaward side. He probably put that together sometime in the past few days. Now he's setting up fires and lanterns on the tripods so that they'll form the same general pattern as the town itself."

Will shook his head in reluctant admiration. "They're thorough, I'll say that for them."

Halt nodded. "Yes. They know what they're doing, all right. They're not beginners, more's the pity. Hullo," he said, "that last cart's on the move. My guess is it's bound for the headland."

Four of the men, having completed setting up a section of the town of lights, had clambered aboard the final cart, which was still laden with timber. One of them took the reins and slapped them on the horse's back. Reluctantly, the animal threw its weight against the collar holding the traces and began to move toward the headland. It was a heavy load for one small horse and they moved slowly. As they reached the slope leading to the headland, the horse made harder work of it and the urging increased.

"They'd move faster if a few of them walked," Will commented.

Halt shook his head. "They're thieves and criminals. They always tend to look for the easy way—not the most efficient way."

Slowly, the cart lumbered up the grassy slope to the end of the headland, until the man at the reins hauled on them to stop. The horse needed no second urging. It stopped virtually in mid-stride and stood, head hanging, turning back to stare vindictively at the men who were putting it to such hard work.

"If I were them," Halt said, "I'd stay well out of kicking distance with that horse."

The men dismounted from the cart and began unloading it. Most of the load was in the form of cut timber—firewood, Will guessed, judging by the regular length of the pieces. But there were several small casks and more iron rods. Finally, three of them lifted down a heavy metal basket, almost a meter across and a meter and a half high.

"That'll hold the fire for the false beacon," Halt told him. "They'll make another tripod with those rods, then sit the fire basket on top. Load it with firewood and they're almost ready."

"What are the casks?" Will asked, although he thought he already knew.

"Oil," Halt told him. "When the time gets closer, they'll pour that over the firewood to make sure it lights quickly. If they do it too soon, it might dry out or evaporate. They'll probably soak the wood thoroughly sometime around sundown."

Instinctively, Will glanced up to see where the sun lay. It was just past its zenith.

"When do you think they'll light the beacon and the fires?" he asked.

"They've missed the full dark of the moon," Halt replied. "Although there's only a small sickle moon due tonight. My guess is they'll wait till it sets over the hills. That'll be sometime around ten o'clock. I'll head into Hambley and rouse the watch around nine thirty. There'll be no time for them to get a message to the moondarkers, even if they were so inclined."

"More waiting and watching," Will commented.

"That's what we do," Halt agreed. "But don't wait for me to get back with reinforcements. If they light the beacon and you see a ship out there, get down immediately and throw that dye in the fire. I'd rather lose a chance to catch this bunch than have a ship driven ashore and its crew put in danger."

As the afternoon passed, they watched the moondarkers make their final adjustments to the pattern of fires and lanterns that they had set up. The four men on the headland stacked their firewood into the metal basket, which was suspended some two meters above ground level on the tripod they had assembled. Then they boarded the cart once more and headed back down to the beach. This time, heading downhill with a reduced load, the horse made better time. Will noted that the two small casks were left on the ground by the tripod.

Finally, the tall, bearded leader of the group seemed satisfied with their arrangements. He called a rest break and they lit a small cook fire and prepared a meal. The men lounged around on the long grass inland from the beach. They ate their meal, then sat talking. Some of them stretched out and slept.

"Going to be a busy night," Halt noted. The fact that they hadn't bothered to return to their camp was proof that this was going to be the night when they struck. Will felt the familiar tightening in his stomach that always came when he was awaiting action. Halt smiled at him, noting that Will's replies to any comments that he made were becoming shorter and more clipped.

"Nervous?" he asked.

"No," Will said promptly. Then he reconsidered. "Well, maybe a little. I'm a bit keyed up, and just sitting around waiting doesn't help."

"It's a good thing to be on edge," Halt told him. "Only fools don't feel that way. Feeling like this will keep you on your toes, and that means you won't get overconfident."

Will looked at his old teacher curiously. He seemed calm and unperturbed. But then, he always seemed that way when something important was due to happen.

"What about you, Halt? Are you nervous?"

The gray beard was split by a slow smile. "I feel like there's a stone in my stomach and I'm trying to digest it," he said.

Will was amazed. Halt had just described his own feeling perfectly. "I'd never have guessed," he said, shaking his head slowly.

"I've learned to hide it," Halt told him.

6

"THEY'RE ON THE MOVE," HALT SAID.

Flashes of light were beginning to show on the flat plain below them—specks that quickly flared up as the moondarkers lit their fires and the flames took hold. Will and Halt could see dark shadows moving among the pools of light as more and more fires added their glow to the night.

Will glanced up. The thin sickle moon was directly overhead and was beginning its descent. In fifteen minutes' time, it would be hidden behind the tall ridge.

Halt moved forward to a spot where he had a clear view to the north. He gazed steadily out to sea in that direction, searching the darkness. Then he gave a small grunt and pointed.

"There's a ship," he said.

Will moved to join him, screwing up his eyes to search for the light that would tell them a ship was approaching. He shook his head. "Can't see it," he muttered.

Halt held his right hand up at arm's length, palm out, his fingers pointing upward. Slowly, he folded down his little finger. "See that long, low headland—the second-to-last one? Go three fingers out from that and you'll see it."

Will held up his own arm and hand. With one eye closed, he extended three fingers, setting his ring finger against the headland Halt had indicated. Then he looked to the left of his index finger and, sure enough, saw a dim pinpoint of light on the dark ocean.

"Got it," he said. The finger system was a piece of Ranger field craft. Given a reference point, like the end of the headland, one person could tell another how far to look to the left or right simply by extending or retracting his fingers. As a young apprentice, Will had been surprised at how effective the system was, in spite of the difference in hand size and finger width.

Halt was assessing the wind strength and direction. "He's going to have to sail against the wind to get here," he said. "It's blowing from the south. I figure he'll take at least two hours to get level with the beacon."

"Time for you to get going then," Will said.

His old teacher nodded. "Yes. I'd better not leave it any longer. We might as well head down together. Get yourself set up at the landward end of the headland. Then, once you see the ship is offshore, sling that dye into the fire."

"Hullo," Will said, pointing the headland. "They're lighting the beacon."

There was a small glow visible beside the tripod. Then long tongues of yellow flame began to stream up into the night. The southerly wind blew the flames sideways. As the fire grew, it dragged more oxygen in, creating its own draft of air.

"Makes sense," Halt said. "If we can see the ship's masthead light from up here, they'll soon be able to see the beacon. You wouldn't want it suddenly flaring up out of nowhere. Might make them suspicious."

They slipped back over the ridge to where the horses were waiting. Knowing that this was going to be the night, they had saddled the horses shortly after dark. They led them over the ridge and down the first, steep part of the slope. Then, as the slope became less precipitous, they mounted and rode down a winding, switchback track.

They were almost at the bottom when Halt found a trail branching off to the south. He reined in and Will drew up beside him.

"I'll leave you here," he said. "I should be back within an hour. If not, remember what you have to do."

"Toss the dye into the fire," Will said.

"That's right. Don't do it too soon. I'd like a chance to round up these moondarkers. But don't leave it too late either. We don't want a ship aground on those sandbanks out there. Sure you've got the dye?"

Will touched the lid of the satchel slung over his shoulder. "It's here," he said. "Don't worry."

"All right then. I'll be off. See you in an hour or so."

With that, he wheeled Abelard away to the south and trotted slowly down the narrow trail. After several seconds, a bend in the trail hid him from sight. Will twitched the reins on Tug's neck.

"Come on, boy," he said. "We've got work to do."

He followed the trail to the bottom of the ridge, emerging onto the flat ground beyond the trees. Slightly to his left and further toward the sea, he could see the glow and flare of the fires that marked the fake town. To his right, the fake beacon blazed fiercely. A strange, fuzzy halo circled the flame, formed by the sea salt that saturated the air. Staying close to the dark background of the tree line, he urged Tug toward the headland at a slow trot.

They reached the point where the headland jutted out, rising in a gradual slope from the edge of the trees to the cliff, where it dropped away into the sea. Will checked Tug and eased down from the saddle. He stroked the shaggy horse's muzzle fondly.

"You stay here, boy," he said. The deep, almost inaudible rumble from Tug's sturdy frame told him that his horse wasn't happy with that idea.

"I know. I know," he said. "You'd rather come along and protect me. But we'll be a bit obvious if I ride out there. It's two hundred meters of open ground and I can't risk being seen by the moondarkers on the beach."

I can be very unobtrusive when I choose.

"I admit that. But just humor me, all right?"

I always do.

Tug sounded huffy, he thought. But he usually sounded that way when Will went off without him. Tug was convinced that Will was unable to look after himself unless he, Tug, was around to keep an eye open for him.

As he was talking softly to his horse, Will had been scanning the open ground of the headland. There were rock outcrops, clumps of bushes and two or three trees. Not a lot of cover, he thought. But enough for him.

He scanned the headland more carefully, searching for any sign of the moondarker who had lit the beacon. He assumed the man had gone back to join his companions. There was no sign of him, and there was no need for him to remain on the headland. Will had seen the amount of firewood that had been piled into the iron fire basket. There was fuel there to keep the beacon burning for at least two hours, he reckoned. And by that time, it would be all over.

One way or the other.

"Stay here," he told Tug. "I need to move up so I can see the ship when it arrives."

I'll be here. Yell if you need me.

"I'll do that." Will grinned, then he slipped away across the windswept grass of the headland, crouched low and moving smoothly from shadow to shadow. A normal observer would have lost sight of him within ten meters. Tug, with his heightened senses and knowledge of his master's movement skills, kept track of him easily. But he nodded his head approvingly.

I can see you. But I doubt if anyone else could.

There was a stunted tree some seventy meters from the beacon. It had become gnarled and twisted by the constant sea winds over the past twenty years of its life. Will slid quietly into its shadow and sat at its base, his back against the weathered old trunk. He sat without movement, his cowl pulled up, and willed himself to meld into the background of the dark wood.

"Trust the cloak," he muttered to himself. From this point, he could see the beach and the pattern of fires and lanterns there, the flaring yellow beacon and the dark sea beyond. Earlier in the night, with the sickle moon behind it, the sea had taken on a silvery sheen. Now that the moon was long gone, it was a featureless black mass. When he strained his ears, he could hear the gentle sound of waves breaking on the shore.

Even the conditions were playing into the moondarkers' hands, he thought. If there had been a big sea running, there would have been breakers and telltale flashes of white foam to mark the position of the beach. As it was, these small rollers barely raised a ripple on the shore.

He stood quietly and set his gaze to the north, scanning slowly, dividing the ocean into segments and searching each one thoroughly, as he tried to catch sight of the ship once more.

Finally, he spotted it. It was farther down the coast than he had expected, but also farther out to sea. It was obviously near the end of a long tack. The skipper was probably trying to make as much distance down the coast as he could before turning into the wind and swinging back toward the shore—and the false beacon that he could probably see by now.

Will watched the dim point of light moving southwest for a further ten minutes. Then it appeared to stop where it was and he frowned, wondering what was going on. Then he perceived motion again, although this time the light was moving back toward him, at a shallow angle. It was the angle that had made it appear to have stopped.

He looked anxiously toward the beach. The fires and lanterns that marked the false town were still burning clearly. But there was no sign of the moondarkers. Or of Halt.

He looked out to sea once more and was startled by the distance the ship had covered since he looked away. It seemed to be awfully close to the shore—close enough that Will could now see the fuzzy halo of salt air around the masthead light. He shifted anxiously from one foot to another. It was nearly time for him to act. Once more he looked toward the beach. But there was no sign of Halt, no sound of any conflict there.

Maybe the people of Hambley had refused to help Halt. Maybe they had overpowered him and were holding him prisoner. If that were the case, Will realized, Halt's life was in grave danger. The townsfolk, if they had refused to help him, couldn't allow him to live and report them. For a moment, he wanted to run back to where Tug waited and ride desperately to the village, intent on rescuing his old mentor.

But he had a duty to perform, and time was running out.

Hitching his longbow into a secure position over his shoulder, he set out toward the beacon.

He moved in a crouch, keeping close to the ground. But now he moved with deceptive speed, gliding silently up the shallow slope toward the beacon. As he came closer, he could hear the crack and snap of the wood burning, overlaid with the wind-fanned roar of the flames themselves. Out on the open ground of the headland, exposed to the brisk sea breeze, the flames streamed sideways like long, flickering ribbons of fire, and showers of orange sparks flew away, disappearing into the dark night sky. Even though he was still some meters away, he could feel the heat on his cheeks.

Now that he was closer to the beacon, all he could see was the circle of flaring light that surrounded it. Outside of that there was only blackness. He shielded his eyes from the direct glare of the flames and peered out to sea. The ship was there, even closer now. His hand went to the cover of his satchel, where the oilskin-wrapped block of dye was ready. He began to unbuckle the retaining strap when he became conscious of movement in the darkness to his right.

"What the blazes are you up to?"

Instinctively, he threw himself sideways. He felt the wind of the battleax as it whipped past him, missing him by centimeters.

7

He regained his balance and the saxe knife seemed to leap from its scabbard into his hand. He circled so that his back was to the fire and took stock of his attacker.

Big, powerful, and unexpectedly light on his feet. The man matched Will's shuffling movements quickly, never getting off balance. And between them, its head wavering from side to side, was a long-handled, single-bladed battleax.

Without warning, the man swung the ax in a whistling, deadly arc. Will leapt backward, only just avoiding the massive blade. Then, as he tried to close in and get inside the ax's reach, his attacker reversed the blow with incredible speed, swinging the blunt back of the ax at him like a heavy metal club or war hammer, causing him to leap out of the way once more.

The second leap had taken him away from the beacon fire. He contemplated throwing the saxe knife, but he'd seen how fast his assailant was. Chances were he might deflect the knife and Will would be left without a weapon, other than his small throwing knife. Throwing the saxe was very much a last option, he decided.

He backed away, eyes on the ax head as it caught the light of the flames, glittering yellow. He had to get back to the beacon and drop the dye in it. But their constant circling meant that the man was now between him and the fire.

He thought about drawing his throwing knife and using the two knives together. Then he had a sudden memory of a time in Celtica, many years before, when Horace had queried Gilan over the right tactics to use against a man armed with an ax.

"I wouldn't advise anyone to face a battleax with just two knives," Gilan had told him. As Will recalled, that particular training session had ended with Gilan suggesting that the best tactic might be to jump off a cliff.

At least there's one of them close by, he thought.

The man suddenly swung again and, instinctively, Will threw the saxe up to parry the blow. But the swing was a feint and the man, with incredibly strong wrist work, twisted the ax back again and caught the saxe knife squarely in the middle of the blade. There was a ringing clang and the force of the blow tore the big knife from Will's grip, sending it flying across the headland, the firelight flashing on its pinwheeling blade as it went. At the last moment, Will managed to avoid the follow-up stroke with another desperate leap.

He was farther than ever from the beacon now. He had no time to look and see how close the ship might be. This man was too good, too fast. Somehow, he had to neutralize that ax, with its enormous reach. For a moment, he thought of calling Tug. Then he stopped. The long-handled ax was designed as a weapon for foot soldiers to use against mounted warriors and, more specifically, their horses. Tug would come charging in to save him and the odds were he would be killed or maimed by a stroke from that ax.

An idea came. He slipped the longbow off his shoulder, holding it upright in his right hand, below the grip.

"Planning on shooting me, then, are you?" The man grinned at him. The minute Will reached for an arrow, the ax would split him from shoulder to waist, and they both knew it.

Will shuffled to his left, working his way back to the beacon. The man feinted several times and Will danced out of reach each time. But on each occasion, he managed to get closer to the beacon.

He slipped the satchel from his other shoulder, holding it by the strap, swinging back and forward, threatening the axeman with it. The man's eyes narrowed warily as he watched.

Then Will flipped it overhand so that the strap caught on the edge of the iron firebox and the satchel swung into the fire. It was a totally unexpected move, and the man, expecting Will to swing the satchel at his head or face like a weapon, couldn't stop his eyes from following it. He was distracted for no more than a fraction of a second, but it was enough. Will stepped in and slipped the end of the bow over the head of the ax, snagging the weapon in the narrow gap between the bow and the taut bowstring.

The bowstring was a string in name only. It was a stout cord designed to handle the eighty-pound draw weight of the longbow. Will heaved back on the bow, dragging the ax head down. His opponent tried to pull his weapon clear, and for a moment they struggled. Will had the bow in his right hand, which made it awkward to draw his throwing knife. He scrabbled in his pocket and found a striker, bringing it out and closing his left fist around its heavy brass shape.

The man was still jerking and tugging at the ax, twisting it in an attempt to break it free from the tenuous hold of the bow and the string. Will knew he had only seconds to act. Any moment now, the bow or the string would break.

WHOOOOFFFF!

An immense explosion erupted in the firebox. A blinding pillar of flame, vivid purple in color, shot seven meters into the air.

"What . . . ?" The axeman threw his disengaged left hand up in an instinctive movement to shield himself from the sudden explosion. As he turned toward the firebox in shock, his right jaw was exposed and Will swung the striker as hard as he could, an unsophisticated full round-arm swing that slammed his reinforced fist into the man's jaw—at a point where nerve centers connected to the brain.

Will felt the grip on the ax suddenly loosen as it fell from the man's hands to the grass, its weight dragging the bow tip down with it. A second later, his opponent hit the ground himself, his eyes rolled up in his head, his limbs slack and his body folding up like a rag doll.

Will staggered away from the flaring beacon. Fine grains of purple ash drifted down from the dark night sky and covered him. Shielding his eyes from the blaze, he looked out to sea. The ship had gone about and was clawing away from the beach, heading out to safe waters once more.

And now, for the first time, he became conscious of voices shouting on the beach and the ringing clash of weapons. He turned and looked. There was a large crowd of men visible in the light of the fires and lanterns—many more than the original number of moondarkers. They were fighting and struggling with each other, but as he watched, the fighting died down and it was obvious that one group had gained the upper hand in the struggle. The others were being compelled to sit down on the beach, their hands held behind their heads, under heavy guard. Will wasn't surprised to see a familiar cloaked figure striding among the victorious group, pointing and issuing orders.

He moved over to the prone figure of the axeman, who was beginning to stir now. He rolled him onto his stomach and fastened his hands behind his back with a pair of leather thong thumb cuffs. Then he sank wearily onto the grass to wait for Halt.

• • •

As they rode home a few days later, Halt allowed himself one of his rare smiles. The majority of the moondarkers had been captured, with the aid of the Hambley town watch. Two of the wreckers had managed to escape in the confusion on the beach, but the other fourteen had been secured. Most important, the tall bearded man, their leader, was one of the prisoners.

Halt and Will had escorted them, secured together with chains and with their hands shackled, to the nearest garrison castle, where the local lord had been delighted to find room for them in his dungeon. They would be tried at the next District Assizes. With Will's and Halt's sworn testimony noted down by the castle lord's secretary, there was no doubt that they would be convicted. All in all, it was a good result. Although Halt noticed that his young friend didn't seem to share in his sense of satisfaction.

"Why the long face?" he asked.

Will turned to him moodily. "Don't you start. I get enough of that from Tug."

I tell it better than he does.

"Still," said Halt, seemingly unaware of Tug's interjection, "it's been a good operation. We've shut down the moondarkers, captured their ringleader and saved a ship and its crew. You should be feeling happy."

"I ruined my bow in the fight," Will said. "The upper limb is hopelessly twisted. It'll never shoot straight again."

Halt shrugged. "You can always replace a bow," he said. "Can't say the same for your head."

"It was my favorite bow," Will said.

Halt raised an eyebrow. "Well, that makes it much more valuable than your head, I suppose."

Will sighed. "I suppose you're right," he said. "I can always make another bow. But there was something else . . ."

He paused and Halt turned toward him, frowning, wondering what was on his mind. He'd noticed that his usually exuberant young friend had been somewhat withdrawn since his struggle with the axe-man on the headland. Will had said little about the encounter and Halt wondered if, in fact, it had been a closer call than he was letting on. Perhaps that fight had shaken his confidence, he thought.

"Something else?" he prompted. If Will was having a reaction to the struggle with the moondarker, it would be better for him to get it out in the open and not bottle it up inside.

"I forgot . . . ," Will said miserably. "When I threw my satchel in the fire, I forgot that my speech was in there."

Halt took a few seconds to recognize the full import of the tragedy. Then he spoke very deliberately.

"You threw your speech in the fire?" he said.

Will gave a very dejected nod. "Yes."

"And . . . would I be right in assuming that this was your only copy of the speech?"

"Yes."

A long pause. Then: "You didn't make any notes, did you?"

"Well, yes. I did. Quite a lot of them, in fact."

"Ah. I see."

"But . . . they were in the satchel too." Will shook his head and turned to Halt. "Halt, it was such a great speech! I'd been working on it for weeks, you know."

"I know," Halt said. He was working very hard to keep his voice noncommittal.

They rode on in silence for several minutes. Then, tentatively, Halt opened the subject once more.

"Can you by any chance remember any of it?" he asked.

Will shook his head. "Not a word. I've been trying ever since. But I can't think of a single word."

"You know, Will, a great speech is usually a pretty memorable one," Halt said carefully. He was treading on delicate ground here. The previous time he'd discussed the speech with Will, Pauline had berated him for his lack of sensitivity.

"I suppose so," Will agreed.

"So, doesn't the fact that you can't remember a single word of that speech tell you anything?"

Will frowned. That thought hadn't occurred to him and he didn't know if he cared to consider it.

"Are you saying that maybe it wasn't such a great speech?"

"No. You're saying that. Let me put it another way. Who is this speech for?" It wasn't grammatical, but Halt had a habit of ignoring good grammar for the sake of brevity and clarity.

"Who? Well, it's for—"

But before he could answer, Halt interrupted. "Is it for the King, or the Baron, or the hundreds of guests who will undoubtedly be present?"

"No."

"Is it for some future historian, leafing through the records and finding an account of the wedding?"

"No."

"Then who?"

Will shifted in his saddle uncomfortably. He could see where Halt was going. "I suppose it's for Horace and Evanlyn."

"You suppose?"

"I know. It's for Horace and Evanlyn." There was a note of certainty in his voice now.

Halt nodded several times. "And what do you want to say to them?"

"I don't know . . . I suppose I want to say that . . . I love them both. They're two of my very dearest, very oldest friends. That I can't imagine a more perfect match than the two of them."

"Why not?"

"Because they're both brave and loyal and totally honest. They're just perfectly suited to each other. She's bright and vivacious and funny. He's steadfast and utterly dependable. And just as funny in his own quiet way. I would trust my life to either one of them without hesitation. I have done so in the past."

He paused, thinking, hearing his own words and his true thoughts for the first time, devoid of any false embellishments and overblown phrasing.

"Anything else?"

"I don't know . . . Yes. One more thing. I want them to know that if they ever need me, if they ever need to call on me, I will be there, no matter what."

"That's what you want to say?" Halt asked.

Will paused, then nodded. "Yes," he said. There was a definite sense of purpose about him now. Halt was pleased to see it.

"And do you think that's what they want to hear?"

"Yes. Yes, I do."

Halt reined in and Will checked Tug to stop beside him. They half turned in the saddle, facing each other, and Halt spread his hands and raised his eyebrows.

"Well then, Will, that's all you need to say."

Slowly, a rueful smile spread over Will's face. "That speech I wrote," he said. "It was pretty awful, wasn't it?"

"It was appalling," Halt said, then couldn't resist adding, "and I say that with the greatest fulsomeness of my heart."

Will winced as the memory of that phrase came back to him.

"Did I really write that?" he said.

Halt nodded. "Oh yes. You really wrote that."

"Just as well I threw it in the fire, then," Will said. He clicked his tongue and Tug started trotting down the highway again. Halt urged Abelard to follow them. He caught up and they rode side by side for several hundred meters in silence once more.

Then Halt said quizzically, "I didn't realize your speech was in the satchel. Mind you, it does explain one thing I've been wondering about . . ." He let the sentence hang, unfinished, so that Will had to ask the question.

"What was that?"

"Why the flames turned purple. It wasn't the dye. It was the speech."

"And I suppose you'll tell everyone about that, won't you?" Will asked.

Halt turned a beatific smile upon him.

"Of course I will," he said.

DINNER FOR FIVE

1

FOR WHAT MUST HAVE BEEN THE TENTH TIME IN AS MANY
minutes, Jenny glanced around the interior of her restaurant.
Everything seemed to be in order. The tables were neatly positioned,
the chairs arranged around them in perfect symmetry. Each table
was laid with a red-and-white-checked cloth, and the eating utensils
glistened in their places. She walked quickly between the tables,
checking that knives and forks were on the correct side of the settings. Her headwaiter, Rafe, hovered anxiously behind her.

Rafe was a good worker and a loyal employee. He was well in-
tentioned, cheerful and honest. In fact, he was everything Jenny
could hope for in a head waiter. Except for one failing. Rafe had an
unfortunate tendency to confuse his left hand with his right. This
meant that, from time to time, his cutlery settings became reversed,
and for a perfectionist like Jenny, that was a source of extreme
annoyance.

Some time back, Will had more or less solved the problem. He
had pointed out to Rafe that a knife was like a small sword, and
so it should be used in the right, or sword, hand. This simple
mnemonic had been remarkably effective. For some weeks after,
Rafe could be seen setting tables, from time to time making a mock

sword stroke to establish which hand was which and which side the knives went on.

But occasionally, Jenny noticed, he became overconfident and placed the knives and forks where instinct told him they should go. When that happened, they mysteriously reversed their positions on the tables and Jenny's temper, always close to boiling point, would explode.

Her friend Alyss, with a diplomat's eye for compromise, had suggested that she could solve the problem by simply folding the knife and fork together in the napkin and placing the rolled bundle in the center of the setting. But Jenny was stubborn.

"Right is right and left is left," she said. "Why can't he learn that?"

She sensed Rafe behind her as she checked the restaurant. Out of the corner of her eye, she could see that his right hand was describing small, jerking motions as he made incipient sword strokes to test the positioning of each setting. As she checked the last table, she turned to him and nodded.

"That's all fine, Rafe. Good work." She saw his shoulders sag in relief and a beaming smile break out across his open, honest face.

"Thank 'ee, Mistress Jenny. I do try my best for 'ee."

"I know, Rafe," she said. She patted his hand and for a moment regretted the number of times she had cracked him across the head with a ladle when he had failed to live up to her high standards.

But only for a moment.

He followed her now to the kitchen, where her assistant chef was hard at work cutting and chopping in preparation for the evening meal. Scullery assistants hurried to and fro, bringing more food from the larder for the cook to prepare and polishing serving platters and cooking pans till they gleamed. At Jenny's appearance, the pace in the kitchen increased noticeably.

Rafe could afford to be more sanguine about this part of the inspection. If something was wrong in the kitchen, he couldn't be blamed for it. Jenny cast a professional eye around the room. Somewhat to Rafe's disappointment, there seemed to be nothing wrong. He would have enjoyed seeing someone else suffer the cracking impact of Jenny's ladle on the back of their head. She gestured to a row of ducks spitted on a long metal rod, their skins glistening with the spiced and flavored oil that had been rubbed over them.

"Those ducks will have to go over the fire no later than four o'clock," she told the assistant chef.

The woman looked up, blew a stray strand of hair away from her eyes and nodded. "Aye, Mistress Jenny."

"And make sure Norman turns them regularly. They must cook evenly."

"Aye, mistress. Norman? You hear the mistress there?" she called to a young scullery assistant, who was currently bringing a basket of potatoes from the vegetable locker.

"Aye, Miss Ailsa. Aye, Mistress Jenny. I'll turn them regular like. Never fear."

Jenny nodded. The ducks would be placed on their spit over the large open fire in the dining room. They would be turned regularly so that the skin roasted evenly and crisped to a golden brown. The fat dripping onto the coals would sizzle and hiss and fill the room with its delicious odor, creating a truly mouthwatering atmosphere. Jenny had learned from Master Chubb, her mentor, that there was a certain amount of show business necessary in a good restaurant. There were only six ducks, but their effect on the atmosphere would far outweigh their relatively small number.

"Very well." Jenny cast one more look around, trying to find something out of place, something that needed correction, and failed. Her staff watched her anxiously. This would be the first time in many months that Jenny had not overseen operations in the restaurant herself. She was something like a new mother leaving her baby in the care of others for the first time.

It would take a very special circumstance for Jenny to trust her restaurant to them in this way. Both Rafe and Ailsa knew that. And this was a special occasion. Tonight, she was cooking a romantic dinner for two in her cottage for a special guest.

A very special guest.

Tonight, the handsome, young Ranger Gilan was coming to dinner.

Resolutely, Jenny turned her back on the restaurant and strode up the high street of Wensley Village. It felt unnatural for her not to be in the kitchen at this time of day, preparing for the evening dinner service. But she had left Ailsa and Rafe in charge and she had to trust that she had trained them well.

"After all, I have to have some time off occasionally," she muttered, resisting the almost overwhelming temptation to rush back and see what disasters had occurred in the two and a half minutes since she had left.

She entered the butcher's stall, halfway down the high street. Edward, the butcher, looked up and smiled as he saw her. Jenny was an excellent customer, of course, buying large amounts of his product for her restaurant. And on top of that, she was extremely pretty. Just the sort of young lady that butchers the world over enjoyed flirting with.

"Ah, Mistress Jenny. Looking more beautiful than ever!" he boomed. "You've brought a light of rare beauty into my dim little shop."

Jenny rolled her eyes at him. "I see you have a surplus of tripe available today, Edward."

He laughed, unabashed. "Ah, bear with me, Jenny. There's few as pretty as you come in here in a day and you should know it. You're a rare treat for these poor old eyes."

Edward was barely thirty-five. But it's an unfailing trait of butchers to behave as if each customer is far, far younger than they. With the more mature housewives, it was probably a good tactic, Jenny thought.

"Do you have my order?" she asked. She enjoyed the hearty, good-natured atmosphere of the butcher's shop, but today she was in a hurry. Edward turned to his apprentice, who had been watching their exchange with a grin on his face.

"Dilbert, fetch Miss Jenny's order," Edward said, then added, "*d-na yrruh tuoba ti.*"

Jenny smiled to herself. It was another peculiarity of the butcher's trade that they learned to talk in butcher speak, in which words were pronounced backward. This allowed butchers to have private conversations even when their shop was full of customers. Often, the remarks passed were about the customers themselves, although the customers never had the faintest idea what was being said. Edward was obviously letting Dilbert get some practice in this strange language and had just said, "And hurry about it."

Jenny had discovered this strange phenomenon some time ago and had secretly practiced backward speak herself. Now she smiled as Dilbert moved toward the cool room.

"*I epoh s'ti a ecin gel fo b-mal,*" she said sweetly, and both the butcher and his apprentice let their jaws drop as she told them that she hoped it was a nice leg of lamb. Edward hurriedly searched his memory, trying to recall if he had ever said anything disparaging about Jenny in butcher speak. He thought not, but he couldn't be sure. Sensing his concern, she smiled at him.

"You'll never know," she said, and he hurriedly looked away from her and went back to slicing a rump of beef into thick steaks.

Dilbert returned, carrying a leg of lamb, and placed it on the counter for Jenny's inspection. It was a prime piece of meat, its freshness confirmed by the whiteness of the fat glistening around the edges. Jenny eyed it critically, a slight frown on her face. It would never do to let Edward know that she was too pleased with his produce. She poked the leg, feeling the slight resilience in the flesh, then slapped it with the flat of her hand, creating a resounding smack. She nodded, satisfied at the sound. If asked, she would have been at a loss to explain why she invariably tested a piece of meat by slapping it. It was merely part of a ritual that she had developed over the years.

"That's fine, Edward. Wrap it for me, please."

Edward nodded to Dilbert and the boy produced a length of clean muslin and proceeded to wrap it around the leg of lamb. As he did so, Edward glanced slyly at Jenny.

"Not too much for just two people, is it?" he asked.

Jenny shook her head. She had thought her dinner with Gilan was a private affair, although she should have known that it was impossible to keep a secret in this village. But Edward was right. The leg was a little large for just her and Gilan.

She estimated that it was close to three kilos in weight. But whatever was left over would go to good use.

"Whatever we don't eat, I'll give to the orphans in the Ward," she told him.

Edward raised his eyebrows. "Lucky orphans," he said. He knew Jenny's reputation as a cook.

Jenny placed the wrapped leg in her basket.

"Thanks, Edward," she said. "It's a nice piece of meat. I'll try to do it justice."

She smiled, including Dilbert in her thanks, and left the shop.

2

THE THREE MEN HAD BEEN WATCHING THE VILLAGE, AND particularly the silversmith's home and workshop, for the past week. Now, Tomas decided, it was time to act. He jerked his thumb toward the heavy, iron-reinforced front door of the house and spoke out of the corner of his mouth to Nuttal.

"Right. Get going."

Nuttal was the smallest of the three of them. He was a thin man, a little reminiscent of a ferret in his features and his tendency to make sudden nervous movements. It was his small stature that had made Tomas select him for the task. Of the three of them, he was the least threatening.

Nuttal strode across the high street toward Ambrose's house, glancing nervously from side to side as he went. Tomas let him get halfway, then nudged Mound in the ribs.

"Right. Come on!"

They walked hurriedly across the street, angling toward the side of the house. They saw Nuttal arrive at the front door and reach inside his jerkin for a small leather-wrapped pouch. Then they hurried down the narrow side passage to the small window they had noticed several days before.

• • •

Ambrose, the silversmith and jeweler for Wensley Village, was preparing for his afternoon's work. He was a creature of habit and he had certain routines he followed every day.

In the mornings, he would work at his desk, checking bills from suppliers and accounts to customers. Then he would work on designs for his jewelry, sketching new ideas onto fine vellum with a sharpened graphite stylus.

At midday, he would set the paperwork in order on the crowded worktable that served as a desk. He would rise, leave the house— carefully making sure that both the front and rear doors were secured—and walk to the tavern in the village. There he would have his luncheon.

As with everything else, this was a matter of habit. Pickles, tasty cheese and fresh bread, washed down with a half pint of ale. Then, after a brief conversation with any other customers who might be in the taproom, he would return home, ready to begin his real work— the making and repairing of silver jewelry.

Today, as he did every day, he took care to lock the front door behind him, and made his way to the kitchen, where he went down on one knee in front of the hearth. He selected one particular paving stone. It was marked with two seemingly random scratches—many of the flagstones were scratched and these particular marks were ones that nobody else would have found significant. But when Ambrose inserted a blunt-ended knife into the gap between this stone and its neighbor, he was able to lift it easily from its position, revealing a small cavity below. He reached in and withdrew a large iron key, then he rose to his feet and went into his office. He would replace the stone when he returned the key to its hiding place.

Beside the worktable was a large and formidable-looking strongbox. It was a meter and a half high and a meter wide. Inside it, he kept his supply of raw materials—silver ingots and precious stones. At times when he was particularly busy and had a backlog of pieces to make, there could be a small fortune in silver and jewelry in the strongbox. Today was not one of those times, but there was still a considerable amount of precious metal in the box.

He was in the act of placing the key in the strongbox lock when he heard someone knocking on his front door.

He withdrew the key and hesitated for a second or two, wondering if he should replace it in its hiding place. The knocking was repeated and he came to a decision. Leaving the strongbox where it was, he slipped the key into the side pocket of the long leather work vest that he wore and made his way through the house to the front door.

Whoever was there began to knock once more—this time louder and more insistently.

"All right! I'm coming! I'm coming!"

He reached the door, but instead of simply opening it, he unlatched the cover of a small spy hole in the top of the door. This hinged inward to allow him to look out through a rectangular aperture, which was itself barred by two heavy iron rods set into the wood.

There was a small and rather grubby-looking man standing outside his door, shifting nervously from one foot to another. He held a small leather sack in his hands.

"What do you want?" Ambrose said grumpily. Tact and charm were not his long suits. The small man looked up and saw Ambrose glaring out at him, his eyes framed in the barred aperture. He held the leather sack up to the aperture.

"It's my mother's necklace. See?"

Ambrose frowned. "I don't see anything that looks like a necklace."

"Oh, yes." The man hastily untied the neck of the sack and tipped its contents into the palm of his left hand. Then he held it up to the spy hole for Ambrose to inspect. "See? The clasp and one of the links are broken. I have to get it fixed."

Ambrose squinted at the piece.

"Hold it closer," he demanded, and Nuttal complied. It was a good piece, Ambrose saw. An excellent piece, in fact. It was made from heavy links of silver, with a silver filigree pendant, and he could see where the silver chain and the clasp were both broken. He had no idea that they had been broken when Tomas had snatched the chain from the neck of a noble lady in the southern part of the fief the previous week.

The fact that it *was* an expensive piece made him relax his guard a little. He was normally a cautious man. That was only to be expected, considering his trade. Thieves weren't in the habit of bringing expensive jewelry to him, but still, the man at the door was a stranger.

"Who are you? I don't know you," he challenged.

The small man shrugged apologetically, as if that were somehow his fault.

"I work at the castle," he said. "In the armory. Master Gilbert said for me to bring the necklace to you. Said you'd be able to fix it."

That made sense. There were over a hundred people employed at the castle and Ambrose certainly didn't know all of them. He did know Master Gilbert, however. On several occasions they'd worked together when Ambrose had added silver decoration and chasing to pieces of armor and sword hilts. He unlatched the locking bar across the inside of the door.

"You'd better come in," he said. "I'll take a look—"

He spun around as he heard a splintering crash of breaking wood from the rear of the house. As he did so, Nuttal put his shoulder to the unlatched door and slammed it inward, sending the gray-haired silversmith sprawling onto the hallway floor. Nuttal followed him quickly, closing the door behind him.

Ambrose managed to regain his feet, his eyes fixed on a heavy wooden club in a rack inside the front door. Nuttal shoved him back again, sending him reeling away from the weapon and into the arms of Mound, who had just emerged from the back of the house with Tomas.

Mound was a big, muscular man, and he wrapped the silversmith up in a bear hug, pinning his arms. Ambrose opened his mouth to call for assistance.

"Help!" he yelled. "I'm being—"

He got no further. Tomas stepped forward and shoved a grubby, crumpled-up ball of cloth into the craftsman's mouth, gagging any further cries and reducing his voice to an almost inaudible mumble.

"Shut up!" Tomas ordered, although the instruction was hardly necessary. He clamped a hand over the cloth in Ambrose's mouth to make sure the silversmith couldn't expel it. Ambrose's eyes swiveled above the hand to look at him. They were wide with alarm.

"Hold that in place," Tomas ordered Mound, and the big man quickly changed his grip on Ambrose, holding him now with his left arm around his neck, while his right held the gag in place.

Tomas stepped back. He was breathing heavily with the tension of the moment. He glanced sidelong at Nuttal. The small man's eyes were wide too, as if he were the one about to be robbed. He was a nervous rat of a man, Tomas thought. Still, it was good policy not to let his disdain show.

"Good work, Nuttal," he said.

Nuttal bobbed his head several times. "He fell for it!" he said delightedly. "Fell for it good and proper, he did!" He held the chain up to Ambrose, dangling it before his staring, angry eyes. "Fix my chain, will you, please? My mam will be so happy," he sneered, then cackled with laughter.

"Leave off," Tomas told him angrily. Then he looked back at Ambrose. "Right, you, let's take a look at this strongbox of yours."

He saw a flash of alarm in the man's eyes, quickly masked. He gestured to Mound and they dragged the silversmith through to the workroom. They stopped short when they saw that the strongbox door was closed fast.

"Blast it!" Tomas said. "You knocked too soon! You should have waited till he opened it." He swung angrily on Nuttal, but the little man shrank away.

"How was I to know? I couldn't see him. I didn't know. I tell you—"

"Shut up!" Mound told him. Then he turned to Tomas. "Chances are he would have relocked it anyway before he answered the door."

Tomas paused, then nodded, reluctantly agreeing that his comrade was making sense.

"Then there'll be a key," he said. "Where is it, you?"

This last was addressed to Ambrose, although the man could hardly reply with the balled-up linen still blocking his mouth. But once again, Tomas saw that flash of alarm in the man's eyes. There was a key, he realized. And it must be somewhere close to hand. He looked around the workroom, then strode to the table, brushing the piles of paper off the scarred wooden surface and onto the floor.

He shot a glance at Nuttal. "Check the kitchen," he said. "See if it's with his other keys."

The little man moved into the kitchen, looking to see if there were keys hanging anywhere. Usually people would hang their keys by the fireplace and hearth, but there was nothing there. Then he saw the displaced hearthstone on the floor, and the small black cavity beside it.

"Here!" he called. "Here's where he hides it!"

He went down on his knees as the others entered, dragging the reluctant Ambrose with them. He scrabbled around in the hole in the floor but looked up, crestfallen, as he found only empty space.

"Nothing here," he said. "It's gone."

Tomas grabbed the lapels of Ambrose's leather vest and pulled him forward so their faces were only centimeters apart.

"Where is it?" he demanded, shaking the jeweler so that his head snapped back and forth. "Where have you hidden it?"

Mound reached over his shoulder and snatched the gag from Ambrose's mouth. The silversmith drew a deep breath in, then tried to shout for help.

"Help!" he began. "I'm being—"

Tomas's fist drove into his stomach, driving the breath from him in an explosive gasp. The silversmith doubled over, gasping for breath, groaning in pain.

"Shut up your yelling!" he ordered roughly. "Or I'll cut your blasted tongue out. Now where's that key?"

But Ambrose clamped his mouth shut and shook his head doggedly. Tomas slapped him several times, sending his head snapping from side to side with the force of the blows. But Ambrose remained resolutely silent.

"Maybe he's got it on him," Mound suggested. He sometimes felt that Tomas was too prone to giving way to his vile temper. His anger often clouded his sense of reason.

Tomas looked up at him, considered the statement and nodded briefly. He shoved the silversmith toward Mound, releasing his grip on the vest.

"Search him," he said briefly. As he said the words, Ambrose, momentarily unsecured, tried to dart away into the forge. Mound caught his arm and dragged him back. The sudden attempt only served to convince him that he was right. The key was on Ambrose's person.

He found it almost immediately. The large side pockets of the leather vest were the first two obvious places to search and the key was a large and heavy one. He withdrew it from the vest pocket and held it up triumphantly.

"Well, what do you think this is?" he asked, grinning. Ambrose's frantic attempts to break free from his grip only served to confirm what he already suspected. This was the key.

Tomas snatched it from him and inserted it into the keyhole of the strongbox. Seconds later, the heavy door swung open on well-oiled hinges. Inside, silver ingots and precious gems caught the light and glittered a welcome. The three robbers sighed with satisfaction. The strongbox wasn't as full as it might have been—Ambrose had made and sold a lot of jewelry in recent days—but there was still plenty there to keep them in comfort for several months.

Ambrose groaned. Silently, he cursed his own stupidity and laziness. He should have returned the key to its hiding place under the hearthstone. Now he would lose hundreds, if not thousands, of royals' worth of silver and gemstones. And he had nobody to blame but himself.

Nuttal came forward with a large canvas sack and the robbers proceeded to scoop silver and gems from the safe, dumping it into the sack willy-nilly. Mound hesitated as he took out a wooden tray of finished pieces—necklaces, rings and brooches that Ambrose had been making to order.

"What about these?" he asked.

But Tomas shook his head.

"Too recognizable. He'll have drawings of them somewhere

around here. If we get caught with one of those pieces, we'll see the inside of Castle Redmont jail before we can blink. Just take the ingots and the loose stones. They can't be traced."

Their attention was fastened on the treasure inside the strongbox—treasure that was rapidly being transferred to their sack. Ambrose took a stealthy step toward the door to the hallway. None of the three noticed. He stepped again, and this time, Tomas's head jerked around.

"Hold it, you!" he said angrily.

Mound strode to the silversmith and grabbed his arm.

"Tie him up!" Tomas ordered. Nuttal hurriedly complied, producing a length of rope from under his jerkin. Ambrose, his arms fastened behind him, was pushed onto a wooden settle.

"Don't know why we don't knock him on the head and be done with him," Mound muttered under his breath as he returned to the strongbox.

Tomas leaned toward him and spoke in an undertone, inaudible to the silversmith. "We need him to send the constable and the posse in the wrong direction, remember?" He saw comprehension flood into Mound's face as he remembered that detail of the plan and they nodded meaningfully to each other. Then Tomas stood up from his kneeling position beside the strongbox and continued in a louder voice, "Right! We're done here, lads. Let's be on the road to Stiller's Ford! With luck we should make it before dark."

They paused only to replace the gag in Ambrose's mouth and to tie his ankles together as well. Under the strain of the moment, the silversmith didn't register the fact that his ankles were tied only loosely—far more loosely than his arms. Laughing to themselves, the trio left through the back door of the forge, then crept down the side passage once more to the road.

They paused, checking to make sure there was nobody in the

immediate vicinity to notice them emerge from the side alley onto the high road. They crossed to the far side and hurried away to the south, passing through the outskirts of the village. En route, they encountered several villagers, who looked at them with scant curiosity. They were strangers, but that was not an uncommon thing in Wensley. The village was situated close to Castle Redmont, and as a result, visitors were often seen coming and going.

They left the village limits and headed down the high road into the woods. But once out of sight, they hurriedly moved off the road and into the trees, then half ran in a large semicircle, back to the northern end of the village.

"You're sure the house will be empty?" Nuttal panted as they ran through the trees. Tomas gave him a withering glance. Nuttal was an incurable worrywart, always assuming the worst, he thought.

"It has been every day for the past week. Why should today be any different?" he asked.

3

THE AROMA OF BAKING TART FILLED THE HOUSE. JENNY STOOPED to the oven door, unlatched it and opened it, allowing even more of the delicious smell to waft around the house. Protecting her hands from the fierce heat with an oven cloth, she reached in and removed the plum tart from the oven.

The rich plum filling glistened temptingly and the pastry strips crisscrossed on top were a perfect golden brown. She placed the hot tart on a windowsill to cool. Plum tart was one of Gilan's favorites, she knew. She'd serve it cold, with cool, thick cream poured over the top. Her mouth watered at the thought. Jenny was a chef, but unlike some members of her profession, she also enjoyed the food she created. Satisfied that the dessert was in good shape, she turned her attention back to the leg of lamb.

She had prepared it by rubbing the outer surface with oil and lemon juice. Then she had made thirty or forty small incisions in the flesh. Into these, she pushed sprigs of rosemary and slightly crushed garlic cloves. The trick with food, she believed, was not to use too many herbs or spices or flavors. Rather, use a few and pick the ones best suited to the dish you were preparing. She smiled at the leg, closed the damper on the oven firebox a little to reduce the heat, then slid the lamb into the oven on a baking tray. Later, she would add chopped and oiled potatoes and pumpkin. Blanched leafy green vegetables, prepared at the last minute, would complete a simple but delightful meal.

Smiling to herself, she noticed Gilan's note on the kitchen dresser and picked it up to read it once more. The oakleaf crest marked it as official Ranger Corps notepaper. But the contents were anything but official.

Dear Jenny, she read, *I'd be delighted to have dinner with you this Thursday. I'll come by your house around six in the evening. Looking forward to it already.*

Love, Gilan.

Her smile broadened as she took in the opening "Dear Jenny" and the closing "Love, Gilan."

"Oh yes indeed," she muttered to herself. A warm tingle ran through her at the prospect of not only seeing Gilan once more, but of spending several delightful hours in his company—a perfect dinner for two.

She replaced the sheet of paper on the kitchen dresser, propping it up so that her eye would fall on it any time she glanced in that direction. Then she returned to the more mundane task of preparing her potatoes—peeling them and cutting them into quarters. She placed the peeled and chopped vegetables in a bowl of water to prevent them from blackening in the air. Later, she would drain them and rub them with seasoned oil to ensure a perfect, crisp finish when they were baked.

She was setting the bowl on a lower shelf, out of the direct sunlight, when she heard her back door open and close, and footsteps in the living room. Jenny's home, unlike most in the village, had the kitchen situated toward the front of the house, facing onto the village high street. She spent a lot of her time cooking and baking and she liked to see the goings-on in the street while she did so. Her kitchen window was large and commanded a view of the road leading up to the bridge over the Tarbus and on to the castle set on a hill above the village.

Curious now at the sound, she wiped her wet hands on a kitchen towel and hurried toward the parlor. Perhaps it had been the wind opening the unlatched door and slamming it shut, she thought. But it paid to make sure. She opened the door to the parlor and went through.

Three men, roughly dressed and strangers to her, stood transfixed for several seconds at her sudden appearance.

"What the blazes are you doing here?" the middle one asked finally. He was flanked by the others, one smaller and one larger than he, and his face was heavily bearded, framed by long, unkempt hair. The eyes were set under heavy, dark brows and they appeared angry.

"I might ask you the same question!" Jenny replied with considerable spirit. Her immediate reaction was one of indignation. How dare these rough-looking strangers barge into her home and then have the arrogance to ask what she was doing there? She turned back to the door. Perhaps there was a member of the village watch patrolling the high street. In any event, she thought there would be someone there. Her neighbor was a woodcutter, tall and powerfully built. He'd send these three packing in no time.

But she made her move too late.

"Stop her!" Tomas ordered, and Mound leapt forward, seizing her arm and swinging her back into the parlor. Then he released his grip so that she spun across the room and fetched up against a settle, falling awkwardly across it. Jenny was furious.

"How dare you!" she said, her voice rising in tone and volume as she scrambled back to her feet. But the bearded man had moved quickly to face her and he shoved her roughly back against the settle.

It caught against the back of her knees and she stumbled again, sitting down heavily on the cushioned bench.

"Shut it!" the man snarled at her. His hand dropped to a heavy dagger sheathed at his waist and her eyes narrowed as she saw the movement. This was not a time to argue, she realized. She was in grave danger here. She stopped the shouted protest that had been on the tip of her tongue and watched him carefully, taking stock of him.

He was confused, she saw. Confused and angry, and that could be a very dangerous combination for her. She held up a placating hand in surrender and sat back on the settle, making no further movement to rise to her feet.

"All right," she said, lowering her voice. "Let's just calm down, shall we?"

"You said she wouldn't be here!" the smallest of the three men said to the bearded one—obviously the leader, Jenny thought.

The leader, satisfied for the moment that she would make no further attempt to escape or call for help, turned angrily on his companion. "How was I to know?" he said. "We've watched her for five days and every day she's spent all her time at the restaurant!"

Interesting, thought Jenny, her mind racing. They've been watching me. Why? What do I have that they want?

The bearded man looked back at her. "Why do you have to be here today?" he demanded angrily. "Today of all days?"

She sensed that it would be best to make no reply. The bearded man let go a string of curses. The largest of the three stepped forward and placed a hand on his shoulder to calm him.

"Nothing we can do about that," he said. "She's here and we'll just have to make the best of it."

"I say we make a run for it!" the smallest man said. He was peering around nervously, as if expecting more villagers to materialize in the room at any moment.

"Don't be stupid," the large man told him. "If we try to leave now, we'll be seen, and the posse will be on our heels within minutes. That silversmith has probably freed himself by now and raised the alarm. Tomas's original plan is still good. The silversmith thinks we're heading for Stiller's Ford. We stay here till after dark, then head off to the north while they're searching for us in the south."

"Mound's right," the bearded man said. He seemed to be back in control of himself, Jenny noted. "We stick to the original plan. We'll wait here till it's good and dark, then slip away as we planned. Nothing's really changed."

Jenny's mind was racing and a small frown furrowed her brow as she tried to piece together the string of events prior to their arrival at her house. They had robbed Ambrose, the village silversmith. That would explain the sack that she now noticed on the floor of the parlor, just inside the doorway. They had left Ambrose loosely bound so that he would be able to free himself after a short delay, and they'd given him the impression that they were heading south. In the meantime, assuming that her home would be empty till the restaurant closed for the night, they had sought to hide out here until darkness would conceal their movements. Then they would escape in the direction opposite the one where the pursuit was concentrating.

Outside in the street, they could hear shouting and the sound of running feet. Obviously, the alarm had been raised and the constable was summoning the village watch to organize a posse.

She realized that the three robbers were studying her closely and she tried to assume an innocent, thoughtless expression.

"What about her?" the small man said, jerking a thumb in her direction.

"Well," said Tomas, with an unpleasant smile, "at least she can make sure we have a good meal while we're waiting." He sniffed the air, noticing for the first time the scent of the roasting lamb that was wafting through from the kitchen.

But the small man shook his head angrily at the answer and the larger man, Mound, took up the question with deliberate, ponderous logic. "What about when we leave?" he asked. "What happens to her then?"

"We'll gag her and tie her up. Or take her with us," Tomas said. But he had paused too long before answering. Instinctively, Jenny knew that they would do neither of those things. After taking so much trouble to lay a false trail, they couldn't afford to leave her behind unharmed. And she was sure they wouldn't take her with them.

They needed her silenced, and there was only one way they could be sure of that.

4

GILAN ENTERED REDMONT KEEP, HEADING FOR BARON ARALD'S
office on one of the higher floors.

He was taking the stairs two at a time when he heard a soft tread
on the stairs above him. He paused so as not to run into the person
coming down, and stepped to one side to make room. By the sound
of the light footsteps, he thought it was a woman.

He was right, and his face lit up in a smile as he recognized Alyss,
beautiful and graceful as ever in her white Courier's gown. She
smiled in return as she saw him, hiding a flash of disappointment.
For one hopeful moment, seeing the green-and-gray cloak and cowl,
she had thought that perhaps Will might have returned.

"Hello, stranger," she said. "We weren't expecting you till next
week. Will and Halt have only just left."

Will and Halt had been formed into a Special Task Group by
Crowley. In times when they were absent from Redmont for an extended period, Gilan would travel from the neighboring fief to take
over their duties.

"I know," he said. "Originally I wasn't coming till Monday, but
I had an offer I couldn't turn down." The offer, of course, had been

Jenny's invitation to dinner. His gaze wandered up the stairway. "I'm just reporting to the Baron," he added.

Alyss took the hint. They could gossip later. Gilan would be here for some days, she knew. But she smiled more widely. "And then you'll be reporting to young Jenny, I imagine?" she said meaningfully, and he grinned.

"Well, yes, as a matter of fact. I'm having dinner with her."

Alyss's perfect eyebrows raised and her lips formed an O shape. "Sounds romantic," she said.

But Gilan ignored the implied invitation to tell her more and took a different tangent. "Speaking of which, how are the preparations for the royal wedding?"

Horace and Evanlyn—or, as she was more widely known, Princess Cassandra—were to be married later in the year. Alyss was the Princess's bridesmaid.

"Very well indeed," she told him. "There's even a rumor that Shigeru may be attending."

It was Gilan's turn to raise his eyebrows. "The emperor himself?" he said. "That's impressive."

"He grew very fond of Horace while we were in Nihon-Ja," Alyss said.

"He must have," Gilan said. Then he gathered himself together. "I should be going. We can chat later."

Alyss stepped aside and gestured for him to proceed up the stairs. He nodded his thanks and resumed his rapid climb. Alyss watched him go, smiling to herself.

"They're always in such a hurry," she mused.

In the office, Baron Arald wasted no time in bringing Gilan up to date on matters within the fief. There were no important items to discuss. Halt and Will had recently foiled and arrested a gang of highwaymen preying on travelers through the woods. Since then, the fief had been peaceful. Still, thought Gilan, one never knew. Trouble could crop up at any time in a large territory like Redmont.

He had no sooner had the thought when there was a loud and prolonged knocking at the door to Baron Arald's office.

"Come in," the Baron called, frowning slightly. The knocking had been somewhat overvigorous. Gilan hid a smile as he thought that whoever it was had better have a good reason to cause such a ruckus.

As things transpired, they did.

The door swung open immediately to reveal a member of the Wensley village watch—the half-dozen volunteers who served under a full-time constable to keep the peace in the village. Gilan didn't know the man by sight, but he recognized the watch uniform—a metal-studded leather vest and a round hardened-leather helmet. In addition, the man had a heavy club and a large dagger hanging from a weapons belt. Behind him, Arald's clerk, scandalized by this rude interruption to the Baron's meeting, was making urgent, fluttering gestures over his shoulder.

"I'm sorry, my lord!" he began. "This man just barged in before—"

The Baron waved a hand at him. "Never mind," he said. "It's obviously an emergency. What's the trouble, Richard?"

This last was addressed to the watchman and Gilan smiled once more, impressed by the Baron's use of the man's name. Many barons, he knew, would have no idea of the individual names of their village watchmen. It was one of the qualities that made Arald an effective, as well as popular, leader.

"Your pardon, my lord," Richard replied. He was breathing heavily and Gilan guessed he had run all the way from the village. "There's been a robbery."

He noticed Gilan in the room for the first time and nodded deferentially to him. Gilan inclined his own head in reply.

"Who's been robbed?" the Baron asked. "And by who?" Sometimes, in the excitement of the moment, his grasp of good grammar deserted him.

"It's Ambrose Shining, my lord," Richard replied, and the Baron sat straighter in his chair.

"The silversmith?" he asked. This sounded like more than mere petty theft. "How much did the thief take?"

"Thieves, my lord. There were three of them. And Ambrose says they've taken several hundred royals worth of silver and gemstones."

"He's all right?" Gilan put in. "They didn't harm him?"

Richard shook his head. "They left him tied up and gagged. It took him half an hour to free himself and then he raised the alarm."

"So he didn't see which direction they took when they left?" Gilan asked.

"No, sir. But he heard them talking. They were planning to head for Stiller's Ford."

Gilan fingered his chin thoughtfully. That made sense. Beyond Stiller's Ford there was wild country, an area of thick woods, high, rugged cliffs and deep rivers. It had long been a favored hiding place for criminals. Years ago, when he had been Halt's apprentice here in Redmont, the two of them had cleaned out the area, capturing many of the outlaws who were hiding there and scattering the rest.

"So what action has the constable taken so far?" Arald asked.

The watchman turned his attention back to the burly nobleman. "He's sent a galloper on to Stiller's Ford to rouse the constable there, my lord. And he's following with a posse of ten men."

Arald relaxed a little and exchanged a glance with Gilan.

"Hmm," he said. "Sounds as if the constable has things pretty well in hand. These men will be caught between two forces—and presumably they have no idea that the constable knows where they're heading. Does Walter need anything from me? Half a dozen men-at-arms? A few cavalrymen? Anything like that?"

Walter was the village constable and he was a capable official, but Arald thought he should make the offer. Richard was shaking his head.

"He simply wanted me to inform you, my lord. He said he'll have these three rounded up by morning. One of the posse men is a po—" He paused. He had been about to say "poacher," but he realized that might not be a politic thing to say in front of the Baron. "A hunter," he amended. "He knows a back trail through the woods that will get them to Stiller's Ford well before morning. They should be there ahead of the thieves."

Again, Arald let his glance wander to Gilan. "Looks as if we won't need your skills for this one, Gilan," he said comfortably.

Gilan nodded assent. He had been glancing out the window. He couldn't see the sun, but the length of the shadows outside told him it must be hovering near the brink of the horizon. "Be too late for me to track them anyway," he said. "It'll be dark soon. And as you say, the constable seems to have things in hand."

The matter seemed straightforward, he thought. If the constable and his posse failed to apprehend the thieves at Stiller's Ford, then Gilan might need to join the pursuit. But that seemed unlikely.

Arald smiled at the watchman standing to attention before his desk. "Thanks, Richard. I imagine you'll want to join the posse and get after these men?"

Richard allowed himself a faint smile in return. "I would, my lord. I've known old Ambrose all my life. But I don't know the turn-off to the back trail they'll be taking. I'll stay behind in case I'm needed in the village."

Arald pursed his lips thoughtfully. "Not a bad idea at that," he said. With the other members of the watch absent, along with a further five able-bodied villagers in the posse, an opportunist might well take the chance to cause mischief in the village. "Very well, Richard. We won't keep you any longer."

The watchman gave a short bow of his head in salute, turned and left the room, accompanied by the still-annoyed clerk. As the door closed behind them, Arald looked once more at a sheet of notes on the desk in front of him.

"Well, I think that just about finishes our business, Gilan," he said. "You'll join us for dinner? My wife would be delighted to hear the latest gossip from Whitby Fief."

Gilan hesitated. Strictly speaking, he should have expected to dine with the Baron on his first night at Redmont. But Jenny's invitation had driven any thought of protocol from his mind. He realized that Arald was grinning at him.

"Got a better offer, perhaps?" the Baron said slyly.

Gilan felt himself flushing. "Um . . . well, sir . . . as a matter of fact, Jenny had asked me to—"

The Baron held up a hand to silence him. He knew Jenny, of course. She had been a ward in his castle and had been an apprentice to Master Chubb, his chef. She was every bit as good at her craft as Chubb was. And in addition, she was blond and vivacious and pretty. In the Baron's eyes, that constituted a much better offer than dinner with himself and his wife. For a moment, he felt a little old.

"Say no more," he said magnanimously. "We'll have plenty of opportunities to dine together while you're here."

"Thank you, my lord," said Gilan. "We'll definitely do it another night. In fact, perhaps I could invite you and Lady Sandra to be my guests at Jenny's restaurant later in the week?"

Arald beamed with pleasure at the thought. Chubb was a

master chef, without doubt, but Jenny brought an array of imaginative and adventurous new ideas to her cooking and the prospect of a meal cooked by her was too tempting to refuse. Besides, Lady Sandra would enjoy an opportunity to get out of the castle for an evening. Gilan, for his part, knew the presence of such exalted guests in her restaurant would do Jenny's business no harm.

"Later in the week then," Arald said. Then he couldn't help smiling. "And enjoy your evening."

"Thank you, my lord," said Gilan, rising to leave.

As he turned toward the door, Arald added in an undertone, "And the dinner as well."

5

Tomas leaned around the doorjamb into the kitchen. The large window facing onto the village high road would allow any passerby to see him and his men if they went farther into the room. He gestured to Jenny. "Pull that curtain."

She eased past him and pulled the curtain across, cutting off the view of the street. Satisfied that he couldn't be seen, Tomas moved into the kitchen and prowled around, looking in containers, opening and shutting drawers. Nuttal and Mound entered with him, but they contented themselves by sitting on the straight-backed chairs at the kitchen table.

Tomas's eye fell on the plum tart, which Jenny had set to cool on the sill of the side window. "What's this then?"

"It's a plum tart," she told him.

There was a dangerous tone in her voice that should have told him to keep his hands off, but Tomas was used to ignoring such warnings. He seized the pie dish and brought it to the kitchen table. Setting it down, he drew his dagger, cut a large, uneven chunk out of the pie and crammed it in his mouth. He chewed for a few seconds, then a look of distaste came over his face and he allowed a large, half-chewed mouthful to spill out of his mouth onto the kitchen table. He tossed the rest of the slice beside it.

"Not sweet enough," he exclaimed angrily. "Should be sweeter than that."

Jenny's eyes narrowed. It was one thing to break into her home and hold her captive. But such oafish criticism of her cooking took things to a new level of enmity. "The filling is made from plums," she said. "They're supposed to be tart. That's what plums taste like."

Tomas shook his head vehemently. "It's a tart. It should be sweet," he said. "What would you know about it?"

"It is a tart, and that's what it should be . . . tart!" She searched for another word, realizing how ridiculous the repetition sounded, but couldn't find one. "Just the way it is!" she added, her cheeks beginning to burn with anger. Gilan loved her plum tart, she knew. And he particularly loved that she didn't make it too sweet, but let the natural flavor of the plums come through. What would this buffoon know? How *dare* he criticize her cooking!

Tomas eyed the angry young woman before him. Pretty girls shouldn't argue with their betters, he thought. And he was convinced that he was her better, for the simple reason that he was male. She needed to be taught a lesson. Needed to be brought down a peg or two. He swept the tray and the tart off the table with the back of his hand, sending it rattling to the floor. The tart broke into several pieces and he stamped his foot on the two larger ones, mashing them into the floorboards.

"Oy!" said Mound, half rising from his chair, and angry at his leader's self-centered behavior. "I wouldn't have minded a piece of that!"

Tomas included him in his glare. "It was no good," he said. "Needed sugar."

Nuttal, ever anxious in the face of any sort of altercation, rose and moved away from the table.

"You numbskull!" Jenny flared at Tomas, her eyes flashing from the ruined tart—Gilan's tart, she thought—to his face. This . . . *thing* . . . had ruined Gilan's tart. Suddenly, she hated him with all the passion she could muster. "When Gil—"

She was about to say "When Gilan gets here, he'll make you pay for that!" but stopped herself in time. She mustn't give them any warning that the young Ranger was due to arrive in less than an hour.

Tomas leaned forward, his brow creased with a thoughtful frown. She had been about to say something and then she had stopped herself, he thought. In his experience, when people did that, they knew something that they didn't want him to know. "Go on," he said. "When . . . what?"

Jenny shook her head, dropping her eyes from his gaze. "Nothing," she said, trying to sound casual. "It's nothing important."

"Then you can tell me what it is," he said in a silky voice, moving closer to her.

"It was nothing," she insisted. But before she could back away, he reached out and grabbed her forearm in both his hands. He gripped hard, then, with a sudden movement, he twisted one hand to the right and the other to the left, still maintaining his hold. The effect on her flesh where his two hands met, suddenly twisted hard in opposing directions, was agonizing. A burning pain shot up her arm and she screamed. Tomas released the pressure and the pain eased.

"Leave her be," Mound said. He had resumed his seat, but now he stood again, confronting Tomas across the table. He wasn't totally against torture if it could provide useful information. But he felt Tomas enjoyed it too much. The bearded thief glared at him, his hands still loosely circled around Jenny's arm.

"Back off, Mound! Don't be soft! There's something she isn't telling us and I plan to know what it is."

"All the same . . . ," Mound said, and made an ineffectual gesture toward Tomas's hands, still gripping her forearm, ready to inflict more pain at any second. But he couldn't find a valid argument to stop Tomas, and his voice trailed off. A cruel smile twisted Tomas's lips and he tightened his hold on Jenny's arm again.

"Now, miss, you were going to tell me . . ."

Jenny set her teeth, glaring in fury at him, determined that, no matter how bad the pain might be, she would tell him nothing. She felt his hands tighten again, then Nuttal interrupted.

"What's this then?"

They all looked at him. He had been prowling the kitchen, examining implements and her pots and pans, when his gaze fell on the note she had propped up on the dresser. He picked it up and peered at it more closely. He couldn't read, but he recognized the oakleaf letterhead at the top of the page.

He tapped it now with his forefinger. "That's a Ranger's mark, that is," he said. He proffered the sheet to Mound, who was the only one among them who could read. "What's it say?"

Tomas released Jenny's arm and moved to look over Mound's shoulder as the big man slowly read the note, his lips moving as he silently sounded out the words. Then he read aloud.

"Dear Jenny, I'd be delighted to have dinner with you this Thursday. I'll come by your house around six in the evening. Looking forward to it already." He looked up. "It's signed 'Gilan,'" he said.

Tomas allowed a string of curses to spill from his mouth. "Gilan!" he said. "He's the one who comes here when the local Rangers are called away."

Nuttal was frowning, not understanding. "But you said he wasn't coming till next week."

Tomas sneered as if he were talking to a simple child. "And that's what I was told. That's why we robbed the silversmith today!" He looked angrily at Jenny. "This Gilan, he's a friend of yours, is he?"

She tried to look as if the whole subject of Gilan was totally unimportant. She shrugged. "I just know him, that's all. Sometimes he drops by."

"And he's 'just dropping by,' as you put it, tonight? At six o'clock!" Tomas shouted at her. "Were you going to mention this at all?"

Jenny said nothing. There was no answer she could make to that, other than *Why should I?* And if she said that, it would only serve to infuriate Tomas even further.

"We've got to get out of here!" Nuttal interrupted. His eyes were flicking around the kitchen as if he expected Gilan to walk in the door at any moment. "We'd better make a run for it!"

"Don't be an idiot!" Tomas turned his anger on the smaller man, much to Jenny's relief. "We can't leave now! It's still broad daylight outside. We'll be seen!" He turned back to Jenny. "I won't forget this," he told her ominously. He spat out a string of curses again, and Jenny flinched with the intensity of it all. "Let me think . . . ," he muttered to himself. But it was Mound who came up with the answer.

"We do as we planned to do all along," he said. "We wait till a few hours after dark and then we leave."

"And wave good-bye to the Ranger as we go?" Tomas demanded sarcastically.

Mound met his gaze evenly, allowing the other man to see that he wasn't cowed. Then he replied deliberately. "There are three of us. One of him."

"But he's a Ranger!" Nuttal's voice rose to a near shriek and Mound shot him a disparaging look.

"'That's right. And he's not expecting us to be here. He's expecting to walk in and have dinner with his girlfriend here."

Tomas was starting to nod as he saw where the big man was heading. "And when he does?"

"When he does, we'll simply knock him on the head before he realizes what's happening. Then everything's back to normal," Mound continued.

Knock him on the head. It sounded relatively harmless, Jenny thought. But she knew it was anything but. Mound confirmed it a few seconds later as Nuttal continued his whining protest.

"But he's a *Ranger!*" he repeated frantically. The big man placed a hand on his shoulder and turned him so that their eyes met.

"Yes," he agreed. "And two seconds after he walks in that door, he'll be a dead Ranger."

6

TIME DRAGGED. EACH MINUTE THAT PASSED SEEMED LIKE HALF an hour. Jenny had a water clock in her kitchen and she glanced at it constantly. The level seemed to remain unchanged for minutes at a time, and once, she rose to make sure that the water was dripping freely from the upper vessel into the lower.

It was barely a quarter past five and Gilan wasn't due until six. Somehow, she thought, she had to prevent him from walking into the trap that Tomas and Mound would set for him. Skilled as Gilan was, he would have little chance of avoiding their ambush. She glanced at the door. The robbers had discussed their plan. Ten minutes before Gilan was due to arrive, they would place Jenny, bound and gagged, in a chair facing the door. Mound would stand beside the doorway while Tomas and Nuttal hid in the adjoining room. When Gilan opened the door, he would immediately see Jenny. His first instinct would be to rush forward to free her, and when he did, Mound would strike from his hiding place behind the open door. He had a heavy cudgel—hard wood studded with blunt iron spikes. One blow would crush Gilan's skull, Jenny knew. Then Tomas and Nuttal would finish the job with their daggers.

In her mind's eye, she could see Gilan facedown on the floor, blood seeping from his head, still and lifeless. Her eyes misted with tears and she shook her head to dispel the vision.

Then she was seized with anger as she looked at the three men. Mound and Tomas were playing a game of dice on the kitchen table, bickering from time to time over the scores. Tomas was a particu larly bad loser, she thought. Then anger slowly gave way to hatred as she watched the bearded man, listening to his boasting when he won a hand and his complaints and whining when he lost.

Mound was silent. He was actually the real danger man of the three, she thought. He was big and muscular. And he seemed a type who would remain calm in a crisis. Tomas was a self-centered bully and Nuttal was a sniveling coward. But Mound was the one to watch. If she could find a way to stop him, she would be well on the way to saving Gilan's life.

And her own. She realized the fact with a jolt. Her own life was in just as much danger as Gilan's. She had realized earlier that the three men would not leave her behind to tell where they had gone. Yet, somehow, she could face the thought of her own fate far more easily than Gilan's.

Her gaze went back to Mound. Powerful. Brooding. Unflustered. How could she stop him? She knew she couldn't wait much longer. Soon they would tie her up and place her in the chair opposite the door. She glanced at the clock, heard a minute *plop!* as a drop fell, spreading ripples across the surface of the water in the bottom cylinder, and glanced at the scale. It was nearly half past five.

She looked back at Mound. He was sitting closest to the oven, where the leg of lamb was sizzling quietly inside. For the first time in an hour, she became conscious of the mouthwatering smell of the roasting lamb. She looked at the kitchen bench beside the oven. Her heavy rolling pin, the one she had used to roll out the pastry for the ruined plum tart, was standing in its rack on the bench. A few centimeters beyond that was her array of knives, every one of them razor sharp. If she could get her hands on one of them, she thought, she could show these ruffians a thing or two. But she knew they would never let her get close to the knives. The rolling pin was another matter. That and the heavy iron skillet hanging from a hook on the wall. If she could just find some way to distract the robbers' attention for a few seconds ...

She thought nothing of the fact that she was prepared to take on three armed criminals with nothing more than a couple of kitchen utensils. Jenny's protective instincts had been aroused. If she didn't do something, Gilan would die.

She realized she could never live with that. Then, with another shock, she realized that she *wouldn't* live with that.

Plop! Another drop of water. Another thirty seconds gone.

"Any sign of him?" Tomas asked, looking up from the desultory dice game. Nuttal moved to the kitchen window, pulled the curtain back a crack and peered out at the darkening street.

"Nothing," he said, letting the curtain fall again. Jenny held her breath, willing him to move away from the window over the kitchen bench. An idea had formed in her mind, but if they were all grouped close to the oven and the bench, her task would be more difficult. She let the breath go as Nuttal returned to his seat across the kitchen, sitting down and staring aimlessly into space.

Time to act, she thought.

"The lamb's done," she said. All three of them looked at her. She'd been silent for the past twenty minutes, and for a moment, none of them knew what she was talking about. She gestured to the oven.

"There's a leg of lamb roasting. I should take it out or it'll be burned and dried out."

"What do we care about that?" said Nuttal in his whining voice.

Mound glared at him. "I care about it. I'm hungry and we'll need food for the road. A roast leg of lamb would go very nicely, I reckon."

"Oh," said Nuttal, looking somewhat crestfallen. "Yeah. I suppose so."

Jenny glanced at Tomas. "What do you say?" she asked. "If it doesn't come out now, it'll be ruined." In fact, she knew the lamb could easily take another thirty minutes or so of slow roasting. But these three wouldn't know that.

Tomas sneered at her. "Ruined like you ruined the plum tart?" he said. Then he waved a hand toward the oven. "Yeah. Go ahead if you want to."

She rose, picked up a cloth and opened the oven door. The rich aroma of the lamb filled the room. There was a set of wooden tongs on the bench and she casually picked them up, holding them ready under her arm as she reached in, her hands protected from the heat by the kitchen cloth, and seized the iron roasting pan with the brown, sizzling leg of lamb in it.

Mound had turned to watch as she took the lamb from the oven. Fat sizzled and jumped off the leg and he unconsciously ran his tongue over his lips. He hadn't eaten all day, he realized.

Tomas, across the table, watched with equal interest and appetite.

As Jenny straightened, holding the heavy iron roasting pan, she contrived to let the wooden tongs fall from under her arm. They clattered on the floor and she feigned a moment of confusion.

"Oh! Blast!" she said. She started to stoop as if to retrieve them, then seemed to realize she was still encumbered by the roasting pan. She hesitated uncertainly. As she had hoped, Mound rose from his chair and moved toward her. He began to stoop to pick up the tongs, but she stopped him, stepping toward him.

"I'll get them," she said. "Hold this for a second."

She thrust the iron pan toward him, and unthinkingly, he took it in both hands. It was a natural reaction. There was a second's pause before he registered the fact that the pan was hot and the blazing iron seared the flesh of both his hands. He screamed in agony and recoiled, dropping the pan and thrusting his hands into his armpits to try to ease the breathtaking agony of the burns. He crashed into the table, sending it sliding into Tomas, who was just coming to his feet.

Ignoring the pan on the floor, Jenny reached back and seized the heavy rolling pin from the bench. Mound, with both his hands cradled in his armpits, was completely vulnerable as she stepped forward and swung the heavy piece of hardwood into the side of his head.

Crack!

Mound looked up at her, his eyes glazing from the blow. "You—" he began, but she swung the pin again, slamming it against the other side of his head this time.

Crack!

His eyes rolled up and he crashed to the floor, unconscious.

But she felt a shaft of panic strike her as the handle of the rolling pin snapped at the second impact, sending the heavy cylinder of wood spinning away across the room and leaving her unarmed. Tomas came around the table, his dagger drawn, held at waist height. She saw the fury in his eyes and realized he would kill her if she didn't act. The bench, with its knives and the heavy skillet, was out of reach. But there was another potential weapon at her feet.

She bent quickly, just as Tomas lunged. The dagger passed just over her as she stooped unexpectedly. Then Tomas, stepping over Mound's unconscious body, put his foot in a patch of grease from the lamb and his feet skidded apart. As he struggled to regain his balance, Jenny had time to grab the shank end of the heavy leg of lamb. She swung it up from the floor blindly, with all her strength.

Tomas was caught with his legs spread wide apart and the leg of lamb thudded between them. His eyes opened wide with surprise at the sudden jolt of pain, and the breath was driven from his body in an explosive *whoof*.

The dagger dropped from his hand. Jenny, still holding the unwieldy leg of lamb in both hands, straightened and spun in a full circle to gain momentum, then slammed the thick end of the roast into Tomas's jaw. It made a solid, meaty thud and the bearded robber, his face smeared with hot fat and grease, was sent sprawling across the kitchen table. He rolled off the far side, knocked over a chair and hit the floor, out cold.

It had all happened in the space of a few seconds. Nuttal, with his customary inability to react quickly to a situation, stood goggle-eyed across the kitchen, staring at Jenny and his two unconscious companions. Then his hand dropped to his own dagger and he started toward her, mouthing a curse.

Only to stop and duck hurriedly as she sent the leg of lamb whirling across the room at him. He felt it pass just above his head, then came upright again and saw that his delay had given the young woman time to reach her knife rack. He stepped backward as the first knife, a heavy-bladed carver, followed the leg of lamb, catching the light as it spun end over end toward him.

With a shrill neigh of fright, he ducked again, only to realize that a smaller but equally sharp vegetable knife was following the first. This one bounced off the wall behind him and, as it spun back, nicked his ear. Blood ran down his neck.

A two-tined carving fork followed in rapid succession. This one hit the wall point first and stuck there, vibrating fiercely. Nuttal looked at it, his resolve weakening by the second. He looked back at Jenny, saw that she had a heavy cleaver in her hand and was drawing it back to throw. And there were still another four knives in the knife rack.

He ran for the door—and just in time. The cleaver whirred end over end and thudded into the wall beside the carving fork, right where he had been standing. It vibrated with a much more ominous tone. Mewling with fear once more, he wrenched open the front door and ran outside.

Straight into Gilan, who was walking up the path from the front gate. Nuttal rebounded, then threw himself at the Ranger, his dagger sweeping up for a killing stroke.

Like all Rangers, Gilan had superb reflexes. He had no idea who his attacker might be, but he reacted instantly. He swept his right arm across his body to deflect the hand holding the dagger and, in the same movement, pivoted on his right foot and brought the heel of his open left hand up to smash into Nuttal's jaw. Nuttal's head jerked backward. His heels left the ground by several centimeters and he crashed backward onto the front steps of the house, out cold. Gilan paid him no further attention. He sprang up the three low stairs to Jenny's house. He sensed that the pretty blond girl who had come to mean so much to him was in danger. The door was open a few inches and he shouldered it aside and sprang through into the kitchen, his heavy saxe knife appearing in his hand as if by magic. He crouched, his eyes darting from side to side, searching for danger.

And saw Jenny by the kitchen table, her face in her hands, weeping. At her feet were the still forms of two men. One large and heavyset, the other slightly smaller and heavily bearded. Both were either dead or unconscious, Gilan saw. In any case, neither one offered any threat to him or Jenny. He resheathed the saxe.

"Jenny?"

She looked up and saw him, then dashed across the room into his arms. He held her close to him, enjoying the sensation, noting the fresh scent of her hair and skin. She sobbed uncontrollably, great racking sobs that set her whole body shuddering.

"There, there," he said, stroking her hair gently as he held her. "Everything's all right now."

She leaned back in his embrace to look at him. Her face was streaked with tears, her blue eyes red-rimmed. He thought she had never looked so beautiful.

"You weren't supposed to be here till six," she said.

"I finished early at the castle and came straight down. And I'm glad I did."

"So am I," she said, and buried her face against his neck once more. Again, he stroked her hair tenderly.

"Come on, my sweet," he said. "There's no need to be afraid anymore."

Once more, she leaned back in his embrace. "I'm not afraid," she said. "I'm furious."

"What's been going on here?" he said, then put two and two together. "Are these the men who robbed the silversmith? You caught them?"

She nodded, sniffing. "I'd planned a lovely dinner for two and then these three barged in," she said. "They ruined your plum tart." She indicated the sorry remnants of pastry and plum filling, which had now been smashed and trampled into the floorboards several times. "And then they got your leg of lamb as well."

Gilan looked down quizzically at the two unconscious men. The bearded one was lying doubled over, knees up to his chest, moaning weakly. Smears of lamb fat had congealed in his beard and his nose had been smashed sideways, out of line.

"So they had our dinner?" Gilan asked.

Jenny sniffed, wiping her nose with the back of her hand. "That's right."

"Well," he said, "I don't think they enjoyed it."

THE BRIDAL DANCE

1

WILL WAS PORING OVER A PILE OF DOCUMENTS SPREAD ON THE table when Halt entered the little cabin in the trees.

"Morning," said the younger man, without looking up. "Coffee's ready."

He wasn't surprised by Halt's arrival. He'd heard Abelard's hoofbeats on the soft ground several minutes ago, followed by Tug's whinnied greeting to his friend. Halt checked Will's coffee cup; it was three-quarters full and needed no replenishment. He poured himself a cup and moved to sit opposite Will at the table.

The bearded Ranger looked quizzically at the papers in front of his former apprentice. He tilted his head slightly to make it easier to read them upside down. Then he nodded to himself as he made out the contents of the top sheet.

"Working on that series of accidents at the castle, I see," he said.

Will looked up at him and nodded. "Yes. Desmond asked me to look into them. He's worried that they're not really accidents. He thinks they might have been intentional."

"He may be right. There have been too many to be just coincidence. There was another one last night, in the dining hall."

Will raised an eyebrow at that. "What happened this time?"

In the past six days, there had been a series of potentially dangerous events around the castle. A pile of masonry had somehow managed to fall from the upper battlements into the courtyard below. The stone had been cut and piled, ready to repair some damage to the wall, but the stonemason swore it had been set well back from the edge. Then the Battleschool's quintain—a pivoting arm with a sandbag counterweight, where students practiced their jousting skills—had inexplicably failed. The pivoting arm, struck by a student's lance, had suddenly come adrift from its support pole and gone whirling across the jousting field, narrowly missing two second-year apprentices as it came to earth. Then a heavy curtain, used to divide part of the Great Hall during cold weather, had somehow fallen from its support rail and collapsed to the floor, pinning a servant underneath it. The curtain was several meters high and four meters long. It was woven from thick material and it was a considerable weight. Fortunately, the servant had come out of the affair with no serious injury, although she did wrench her right knee painfully and had been confined to the infirmary for two days.

As Desmond, the Baron's head steward, said, it was all too much to be brushed aside as mere coincidence. Now, according to Halt, there had been another event.

"It was in the dining room," he said. "Apparently, when the servants brought a heavy vat of soup to the front table, the table collapsed under its weight as they set it down. One of the knights was scalded and a servant burned his hand on the vat as he tried to stop it from falling."

"Could have been worse, of course," Will remarked, and Halt agreed.

"Yes. All of these 'accidents' could have been. We've been lucky so far. But I think there's someone behind it all and he or she has to be stopped."

Will shuffled the reports in front of him into a neat pile, then placed a granite paperweight on them to hold them in place.

"I'll go up and nose around the castle," he said. "See what I can pick up. Do you want to join me?"

Halt shook his head. "I'm going out with the mail coach," he said. "These robberies are becoming a nuisance."

The two Rangers had been having a busy time. In addition to the mishaps at the castle that Will was investigating, there had been a series of robberies, with a bandit gang stopping the mail coach and stripping it of any valuables it carried. Halt was planning to trail that morning's coach and see if there was any attempt to stop it.

"Are you expecting trouble?" Will said.

"Not really. There are no valuables in today's load. I'm pretty sure the bandits are getting inside information on the shipments and striking only when it's worth their while."

"So if nothing happens today, that'll confirm it?" Will asked.

His old mentor shrugged. "It won't be absolute proof, but it'll be a fair indication."

Will rose and headed for the door. "Well, better get to it. I'll go and call on Desmond, then take a look at this dining room table."

"How's your speech going?" Halt asked, hiding a smile. As best man at the upcoming wedding between Horace and Princess Cassandra, Will would be giving a speech. His first draft had been burned in a battle with moondarkers.

"I haven't had a chance to look at it yet. I'll get on to it in the next few days," Will said.

Halt waved farewell, tilting his chair onto its back legs as he drained his coffee.

Will frowned at him. "When I was your apprentice, you used to tell me not to do that. Said it'd loosen the chair legs."

"And so it will," Halt said, smiling contentedly. "But it's your chair now, so why should I care?"

"This has been cut halfway through," Will said, crouched beside the ruined table from the dining room. He was studying the trestle legs that had supported one end. One of them had given way. It was splintered and jagged for half its width where it had broken. But the other half had been cut through. There was a clean, straight saw line in the wood.

Desmond, bending to peer past him, nodded. "So it has. And whoever did it doesn't seem to care if we know about it. There's no attempt to make it look accidental."

Will stood, nodding to a servant nearby who was waiting to remove the ruined trestle and replace it with a new one. He and Desmond drew away to continue their conversation in private. "So now," he said, "I suppose you'll have to inspect all the trestles before each meal serving—just to make sure another one doesn't give way at an awkward moment."

Desmond shook his head in exasperation. "What a blasted nuisance that'll be! And we're shorthanded at the moment. Half the castle staff are helping with the harvest—and we've got the wedding coming up as well."

Will glanced back thoughtfully at the ruined trestle, lying to one side as the dining hall servants replaced it.

"It's almost as if someone is trying to make your life more difficult," he said. "I mean, these accidents are fairly trivial. They could have caused injury, of course. But the major problem so far is that they're forcing you to be more vigilant and inspect the furniture and the battlements regularly."

"And as I say, I'm short of staff," Desmond agreed.

"Had any trouble with any staff members lately?" Will asked.

"Anyone been disciplined or dismissed? Could be someone with a grudge against you—or against Redmont as a whole."

Desmond scratched his chin thoughtfully. "Nobody springs to mind," he said, then added as a thought struck him, "There's Robard, of course, but I'm sure he wouldn't "

"Robard?" Will interrupted him. "Who's he?"

"He's an assistant steward I'm training. Or rather, he was. I had to demote him. He's back working as a dining hall waiter for a few months to teach him a lesson. Actually," he continued, "I was going to sack him, but the Baron intervened on his behalf. Said anyone can make a mistake. He suggested I give him a few months of hard work, then reinstate him."

"What did he do wrong?" Will asked.

Desmond shrugged. "Well, we suspected he'd been stealing. Nothing serious, mind you. Nothing too valuable. Just little items that seemed to go astray when he was the last person seen with them. I couldn't prove anything, which was why the Baron suggested I should give Robard the benefit of the doubt. Also, he had been treating the junior staff in the castle very badly—hectoring them, always criticizing their work, never showing them any sign of encouragement. We felt he needed to be taught a lesson."

"And was he aware of the plan to reinstate him after a few months?"

"Aaah . . . well, no. He wasn't, actually." Desmond looked crestfallen. "Perhaps I should have told him the demotion was only temporary, but I thought it would be better if reinstating him appeared to be a reward for improved behavior. A spontaneous gesture, as it were."

"So he may well be feeling aggrieved. After all, even if he was guilty, you couldn't prove anything, so he might think he's been hard done by."

"That's true, I suppose." Desmond was obviously troubled by the idea. He'd always had a soft spot for Robard, even if the youngster did have a bit of a wild streak. The head steward had hoped that as the young man matured, he'd outgrow the bad behavior. Now, the thought that his trainee was possibly behind the potentially dangerous events happening around the castle caused him to doubt his own judgment.

"It looks as if I'd better have a talk with him," he said reluctantly.

Will eyed him shrewdly for a moment or two. He guessed what was going through the older man's mind. "Would you like me to do that?" he asked. "After all, I have no previous history with him." And, he added silently, I'll be less likely to go easy on him.

Desmond looked at him gratefully. "Could you?" he said. "I'd really appreciate it if you could, Will."

Will smiled. He remembered from his time as a ward in Castle Redmont that Desmond was a kindly person who disliked conflict of any kind. The need to punish a favored apprentice would be highly unpleasant for him.

"I'll be pleased to help out," Will told him. "Have him report to me at two o'clock this afternoon. I'll be using one of the offices in the Baron's suite."

Robard looked around uneasily as he entered the office. Will sat at a table with his back to the large window, so that he was silhouetted against the glare of the exterior sunlight. This was why he had chosen early afternoon as the time for their meeting. He wore his cloak with the cowl up so that his face was obscured in shadow, and his head was bent over a small pile of papers on the desk before him.

"Sit down," he said, keeping his voice neutral, neither friendly nor accusing. There was a straight-backed chair in front of the desk and Robard made his way to it and sat. Will, watching him from under lowered eyebrows, saw that he was sitting nervously to attention. He had to admit, however, that this was no real indication of guilt on the part of the trainee steward. A summons to an interview with a Ranger would be enough to make any castle servant nervous.

He'd seen Robard before on several occasions—usually formal dinners at the castle. He was a stocky young man, a little below average height. In a few years, he would probably go from stocky to overweight. There were already signs of it in the heaviness of his jowls and the beginnings of a soft extra fold of flesh under his chin. A trainee steward didn't have too many arduous physical duties to perform, and the job presented an ever-present opportunity to indulge in fine food and drink.

On previous occasions, Will remembered, Robard's manner had been one of extreme self-confidence, bordering on arrogance or bumptiousness. Those traits weren't in evidence today, however. After letting the young man sit before him in silence for several minutes, Will finally set down the pen he had been using to make totally meaningless notes on the sheet of paper before him. The sheet was one of several he had borrowed from Arald's secretary and it detailed the contents of the castle granary in the first quarter of the previous year. Robard wasn't to know that, of course, and now Will covered the sheet with a leather folder to obscure its real contents. He looked up and threw back the hood of his cloak.

"You're Robard," he said. He kept his voice quiet, below the volume of normal conversation. He had found that this technique often caused discomfort among guilty people under questioning. They had to strain to hear what was being said and often became fearful that they might miss something important. Shouting and blustering right from the outset, on the other hand, often served to put a person on the defensive.

Robard leaned forward slightly. "Um . . . yes, sir. That's right."

"And you know why you're here." It was a statement, not a question. But now a trace of a frown formed on Robard's smooth, closely shaved face. That and a flicker of uncertainty.

"No. No, I don't."

"Don't waste my time, Robard." The voice was still low pitched and quiet. But the lack of volume somehow made it seem more ominous, more threatening. Robard shook his head and raised his hands in a defensive gesture.

"No. Really. I—"

Will suddenly slammed the flat of his hand onto the surface of the desk. Several of the items there jumped in the air, then rattled back into place again. The unexpected, sharp CRACK! made Robard flinch, and now Will's voice was no longer quiet.

"DON'T . . . WASTE . . . MY . . . TIME!" he shouted.

Robard shook his head helplessly. "But I . . ."

Will stood, leaning forward over the desk and thrusting a finger at the hapless trainee. Framed against the full glare of light from the window, he was a black silhouette, faceless and expressionless. He shot out a series of rapid accusations.

"The battlements. The quintain. The curtain," he said, stabbing his forefinger on the desk to emphasize each point. "You might have gotten away with them. But you made a big mistake with the trestle. You were seen."

Robard began to protest, but Will allowed him no chance to answer and, more importantly, no time to think. "Two members of the kitchen staff *saw* you! They have identified you and they will swear it was you who weakened the trestle. Big mistake, Robard. They saw you! And they'll testify against you! You're looking at ten to fifteen years hard labor in the fields."

"No! I swear I don't know what you're talking about!"

"Are you stupid? Are you not listening to me? YOU WERE

SEEN! We have witnesses who saw you cutting through the trestle! We won't even need a trial. There are two of them. We have their sworn statements!" He rapped his knuckles on the leather folder that contained the documents he had been pretending to study.

"You'll be sent to the fields. In chains! Baron Arald is furious. He's ready to pass sentence right now! Your only hope is to confess and beg for mercy."

Having taken in Robard's slightly overweight physique and soft, unmarked hands, Will had shrewdly guessed that the prospect of unremitting hard physical labor would be the greatest threat he could make against him. He was right. He could see the panic in the other man's eyes.

"But they couldn't have . . ."

"They did! I told you! They saw you! You were careless! You should have checked there was nobody in the kitchen!"

"But I did! I—"

Driven by panic and Will's relentless badgering, the words had left Robard's mouth before he had time to consider them. Too late, he realized what he had said as Will sat back in his chair, his head tilted to one side as he studied the trainee steward.

"You did?" he repeated. "You did what?"

"I . . . I . . . mean . . . I didn't. I didn't do it." Robard tried to recover, but he knew it was too late. He seemed to collapse, to shrink in the chair as he slumped down.

Will continued, in a calmer, more reasoning tone, "Just admit it, Robard. Things will go easier on you if you come clean. Why did you do it?"

"I tell you I didn't . . . ," Robard began, trying to recapture his former appearance of indignation. But it was a sorry attempt and Will dismissed it with a short movement of his hand.

"It's a strange way to repay the people who cared about you," he said quietly.

Robard raised his eyes to meet the Ranger's steady gaze. "Cared about me? They humiliated me. The Baron demoted me so that I was being ordered about by people who'd been junior to me. And didn't they enjoy that!" he added.

Watching him, Will suddenly had an insight into his bitterness. As assistant steward, Robard had undoubtedly thrown his weight around. His sense of self-importance would have seen to that. Then, in a flash, he was answerable to the very people he'd been bossing around. It couldn't have been easy.

"Why couldn't they have just fired me and been done with it?" he said now, and Will shook his head sadly.

"They didn't want to fire you. They planned to punish you, then reinstate you when they thought you had learned a lesson."

Robard's jaw dropped. "Reinstate me?" he said, his voice just above a whisper. "You mean I could have . . . ?" He paused, not sure what to say next.

Will nodded. "If you'd just waited a month or two, you would have been back in your old position. And you might have learned a little about how to treat those under you."

"I didn't know. They should have told me!" There was a flash of the old indignation and anger once more—a sign of Robard's arrogance. Everything that happened to Robard would always be somebody else's fault, never his own, Will realized. He was that type of person.

"So you decided to teach Baron Arald a lesson," Will said. "You arranged for a series of 'accidents' to occur around the castle, just to get revenge?"

Robard opened his mouth instantly for an immediate denial. Then he seemed to grasp the hopelessness of his situation. He closed his mouth, paused, then answered in a small voice, "Yes."

His eyes dropped. He couldn't meet Will's steady, accusing gaze. There was a long silence in the room.

Will let it continue. Then, when he judged the silence had gone on long enough to be uncomfortable, he asked, "Was there anything else?"

"Anything else? How do you mean?"

"Besides the quintain and the curtain and the other things. Have you done anything else we ought to know about?"

Just for a second, Will saw a flash of something in the servant's eyes. It looked suspiciously like guilt, but before he could be sure, Robard dropped his gaze.

"No," he muttered. "There was nothing else."

"You're sure?" Will pressed.

But Robard continued to stare at his hands in his lap as he said in a barely audible voice, "I'm sure. There was nothing."

"Hmm," Will said. Very deliberately, he reopened the leather folder and scratched a note on the file inside. The noncommittal sound and the action were intended to convey his disbelief concerning Robard's last answer. He closed the folder with a snap. "We'll talk more about that tomorrow. Remember, things will go better for you if you tell me the entire truth. And I don't believe we've reached that point yet."

Let him sweat on it overnight, Will thought. Tomorrow, he'd question him further. He had no doubt there was something else and he was determined to discover it. Tomorrow's session, he promised himself, would make today's interview seem like a friendly chat. Finally, Robard was disconcerted by the Ranger's steady, unblinking stare.

"What will happen to me?" he asked miserably.

For a second or two, Will didn't answer. "That's not for me to say," he replied. "I'll report to Desmond and the Baron and they'll decide. Possibly a term in the dungeons. Perhaps hard labor in the fields for five to ten years. Who knows?" He was exaggerating, of course, but he wanted these dire possibilities to weigh on Robard's mind overnight.

"But at best," he concluded, "I imagine you'll get your wish."

Robard's eyes came up then. "My wish?" he said. "What wish is that?"

"You said they should have fired you. I'm guessing they will."

2

Six o'clock in the morning. Feet pounding on the soft earth under the trees.

Tug's muted nicker of warning sounded from the stable behind the cabin and Will was instantly awake. Someone was running through the trees, toward the cabin.

He rolled out of bed and slung the belted double scabbard over his left shoulder so that his two knives were easily to hand. The running feet were closer now. One person, he thought. A man, probably, judging by the weight of the footsteps. He glanced at the cloak hanging by the door and rejected the idea of donning it. Dressed in the loose trousers and overshirt he wore as sleeping clothes, he padded barefoot to the door of the cabin. Ebony was already there. She'd risen from her blanket by the fireplace and was sniffing the gap under the door for some sense of the person outside. She looked up at him, her ears pricked and alert, heavy tail sweeping slowly. He put a finger to his lips, signaling her to remain silent.

Tug's call had not carried any sense of danger. It was merely an alert that someone was coming. Will put his eye to the peephole in the door—so tiny that it was virtually invisible to anyone on the other side. He saw a servant in castle livery mounting the steps to the verandah. The man paused, holding his sides and breathing heavily for several seconds, then moved to the door and raised his clenched fist to knock on the hard wood.

He stepped back, startled, as Will opened the door.

"Oh! Ranger Will! You're awake!" he said, nonplussed.

"Apparently," Will replied. It was the sort of dry reply that Halt had made to him over the years when he stated the obvious. Unconsciously, he had grown to mimic his former teacher's manner. "What can I do for you?" he asked.

The servant—Will could tell by his uniform that he was one of the dining hall servants, answerable to Desmond—pointed urgently through the trees in the direction of the castle. "You're to come to the castle," he said. He was still flustered. First he had run all the way from Castle Redmont to the cabin, and then had the door snatched open just as he was about to knock. And now he had forgotten the right form for passing on a message.

Will raised an eyebrow. "I am?"

The man shook his head and made an apologetic motion with his hand. "My apologies, Ranger Will. Master Desmond has asked if you will please, please come to the castle just as soon as you can."

"And is there a reason for all this haste?" Will asked mildly.

The servant nodded several times before replying, "It's Robard, sir, the former trainee. He's dead!"

Robard's body was lying faceup by the window in his small room. As he had fallen, it seemed that he had clutched desperately at the heavy drape masking the window. The thick material lay over his midriff and upper legs. Shattered wooden curtain rings littered the floor around him.

His eyes were wide-open, giving his face a look of startled surprise.

"Has the body been moved?" Will asked, on one knee beside the still form.

"This is how he was found," Desmond told him. He was craning to look over Will's shoulder. The thought struck him that they had adopted similar positions the day before when they'd examined the trestle.

Will leaned closer to Robard's slightly open mouth and sniffed experimentally. He thought he could catch a faint trace of something—something sickly sweet. He glanced around the room. There was a water jug on the small bedside table, but no glass. He looked further. No sign of a glass or beaker anywhere. Unless . . .

Carefully, he lifted an edge of the tangled curtain and heard something rattle briefly on the floor. He raised the curtain farther and saw the beaker where it had fallen from Robard's hand. The drape had hidden it. There was a small damp patch on the floor. Gingerly, Will retrieved the horn beaker and sniffed it. The same sickly sweet smell greeted his nostrils.

"Poison," he said briefly, and there was a stir among the servants who had crowded into the doorway of the room. He glanced at Desmond. "Do you think you could clear these people away?" he asked.

Desmond complied, stepping toward them and making shooing gestures with both hands. "Come along now. There's nothing for you here. You've all got work to do, so be about it!"

Reluctantly they dispersed, and Desmond closed the door behind them. He turned back to Will, who was weighing the beaker in his hand.

"Is it suicide, do you think?" he asked.

Will shrugged. "Could be. Was there any note? Suicides usually leave a note. Who found him, by the way?"

"One of the dishwashers. Robard was rostered on for early

duty and hadn't turned up. The chef sent a junior staff member to wake him. He found him like this and called me. He didn't touch anything—I asked. And he said nothing about a note."

Will looked around the room. There was no sign of a note. In one corner was a plain wooden desk with a straight-backed pine chair placed in front of it. Will checked the desk and found several sheets of paper scattered haphazardly on the top. One was a list of ingredients for a soup recipe. Another was a note of Robard's on-duty hours for the next four days. There were several other sheets, all crumpled, and each one containing variations on the beginnings of a letter of apology to Baron Arald and Desmond. He was about to turn away when he caught sight of another scrap of paper—just the corner torn off a larger sheet, in one of the pigeonholes at the back of the desktop. He retrieved it and studied it. There were two words on it, apparently names: Serafino and Mordini. Toscan names, he thought. Very exotic. He handed the scrap of paper to Desmond. "These names mean anything to you?"

The head steward shook his head, his face blank. "Never heard of them. We use some Toscan *providores* from time to time, but I don't recognize these names."

Will took the paper back and slipped it into an inner jacket pocket. He looked around the room and sighed. "It's sad, isn't it? I'll never understand suicide. I suppose you can let your people back in here to take him to the infirmary. There's nothing more to see."

"So you think it was suicide?" Desmond asked him.

Will pursed his lips thoughtfully. "I think it looks like suicide. But I don't like the fact that there was no note. I think I'll ask around the village and see if anyone's heard of these two Toscans." He tapped the breast of his jacket where the small piece of paper lay.

·   ·   ·

"I remember them," Jenny said. "They had dinner here twice while they were in the village. They had a room at the inn but said they preferred my cooking."

"Most people do," Will said, and she smiled at the compliment.

"A girl does what she can."

"Any idea what they were doing in the village?" Will asked.

Jenny shook her head. "I don't ask people their business. Just what they want to eat. They might know at the inn, of course," she added.

Will nodded. "That's the next place I'll ask."

Making a small farewell gesture to his old friend, Will trudged up the main street of Wensley Village to the inn—one of the few two-story structures in the high street. It was late morning and the innkeeper, Joel, was resting in a back room before the lunchtime rush started. His assistant scurried off to fetch him at Will's request. Will suppressed a smile. Even after all these years, he was still surprised at the way ordinary folk—people he had known all his life—leapt to do his bidding. He assumed it was a result of the aura of mystery and power that surrounded the Ranger Corps. He was unaware that in his case, and with his reputation, that aura was intensified many times over.

Joel emerged from the back room. His hair was disheveled and he was buckling a wide belt around his equally wide waist. Will guessed he had been snoozing. He shrugged mentally. Why not, he thought. Innkeepers kept late hours, often tending to the needs of their clientele till the wee hours of the morning. It was good sense to catch up on sleep whenever a chance offered itself.

Joel snapped his fingers at the taproom servant and ordered fresh coffee. He knew how fond the young Ranger was of the beverage. They sat at one of the pine tables in the taproom. Its planks had been rough sawn originally, but years of service in the inn, with elbows, tankards, plates and sometimes heads rubbing on it, had rendered the wood smooth and slick.

"What can I do for you, Ranger Will?" he asked after they had exchanged pleasantries. Will glanced up as the servant placed a mug of coffee in front of him. He spooned honey into it and sipped. Then he leaned back with a sigh of satisfaction.

"Your coffee is still the best in the village, Joel," he said. "I know Jenny would love to find out where you source your beans."

Joel smiled. "I'm sure she would. But I keep my supplier secret. There aren't too many ways I can best Jenny's restaurant, but my coffee is one of them."

Will knew that Joel traveled some distance from the village each month to meet the trader who supplied his coffee beans. The man's identity, and the blend of beans, was a strictly guarded trade secret. Once, years earlier, Will had toyed with the idea of trailing him and revealing the coffee merchant's identity to Jenny. But he decided that it wouldn't be fair to use his skills against the innkeeper. If Jenny wanted to track him, well and good. He realized that Joel was still waiting for an answer to his question.

"You had two guests here a few days ago," he said. "Toscans, I believe."

Joel nodded immediately. "That's right. Wool buyers, they were. Signore Mordon and Seraf-something-or-other."

"Mordini and Serafino," Will corrected him, and Joel continued his nodding.

"Yes. That'd be them. I can never remember foreign names too well."

"And they were Toscans?"

"They certainly sounded like it. It's a pretty obvious accent, after all."

Will's eyes narrowed. The Toscan accent was a broad one, and easily recognized. Which made it all the easier for a non-Toscan to mimic, he thought.

"And you say they were wool buyers," he queried.

Joel allowed himself a smile. "Actually, they said it. I was just repeating it. Why do you ask? Have they been up to no good?"

Will ignored the question as he stood, deep in thought. "Did they do any trading?" he asked finally.

Joel shrugged, his face blank. "I wouldn't know. I suppose Barret would be the one to answer that."

Barret was the largest wool broker in the village. Most of the farmers from the surrounding area sent their wool to him for sale. He did the trading and kept a commission on each sale.

"So he would. I'll ask him," Will said.

But when he asked the wool broker, he met another blank.

"They never approached me, Ranger," Barret said. "I met them in the tavern once, and Joel told me they were in the wool business. But I never heard from them. Don't know why. Maybe my stock's not good enough." He sounded miffed by the fact that he'd been ignored. He half suspected that the Toscan buyers had found a better price from one of the smaller brokers in an outlying hamlet. If that were the case, he would have liked the chance to haggle a little. Barret disliked losing business.

Frowning, Will made his way back to the inn. The lunch trade was now in full swing and the taproom was three-quarters full. He caught Joel's eye and beckoned him over.

"About those Toscans," he said. "Have you re-let their room since they left?"

Joel shook his head. "No. Business has been slow this past week. We changed the linen and made the beds. And Anna would have swept it out, of course. Did you want to look around in there?"

"If you don't mind," Will said.

Joel crossed to the bar and unhooked a key from the rack on the wall.

"Up the stairs and second room on the right," he said. "But I'm pretty sure they left nothing behind."

He was right. The room was tidy and empty. There was no sign that it had been occupied by two men a few days previously. Or was there? Will sniffed the air experimentally. The window had been kept closed and there was a faint trace of . . . something in the room. Something familiar. A slightly sweet smell. Not unpleasant. It was only the barest vestige of a scent and it was difficult to place it. He moved around the room, testing the air in different spots. In some spots, he couldn't pick it up at all. It was most obvious by the beds.

"So," he said to himself, a little vexed, "we have two Toscan wool buyers who don't buy wool and leave a faint perfume behind in their room. How curious."

He walked slowly downstairs, deep in thought, and returned the key to the rack. He waved farewell to Joel and stepped out into the afternoon sunlight. If only he could identify that smell, he thought. He was sure it was a familiar one. But the more he tried to place it, the farther the answer seemed to slip from his grasp.

It wasn't until that evening that he realized what it was.

He was braiding a new bowstring. He'd noticed some slight fraying on the one currently on his bow and thought it better to replace it before it deteriorated further.

He finished forming the loops at either end, securing them with wound thread. Then he reached into his tool kit for a lump of beeswax to finish the job and bind the individual threads that made the string into one cohesive whole. As he began to rub the wax along the string, and small flakes of wax fell off onto the floor, the pleasantly sweet smell struck his nostrils.

Beeswax! That's what he'd noticed in the room. It was used by archers to strengthen and waterproof their bowstrings. And used on crossbow strings as well.

His mind had been probing a suspicion that the Toscans were not Toscans at all, but were from a neighboring city-state where the inhabitants spoke with a similar accent. It was a difficult accent to conceal, and so the best way for the two strangers to hide their identities might have been to assume a similar accent and pose as Toscans.

Instead of Genovesans.

He couldn't have said why he had been thinking about Genovesans since he'd heard of the presence of two foreigners in the village—and found their names scrawled on Robard's sketch. Serafino and Mordini could just as easily be Genovesan names as Toscan, and the average Araluen wouldn't know the difference between the two.

Robard had died suspiciously. Perhaps his death had been suicide, but Will wasn't convinced. And it seemed that his death was due to poisoning—a skill the Genovesan assassins were expert in. Years of training with Halt had led Will not to simply accept what seemed to be the obvious when there were circumstances out of the ordinary. As Halt had drummed into him on many occasions: *Better to suspect something and find nothing than suspect nothing and find something.*

"So," he said aloud, "if they are Genovesans, what are they doing here?" Ebony raised her head at the sound of his voice. Then, realizing he wasn't talking to her, she let her head fall again with a sigh of contentment.

The most likely answer was that they were in Wensley to plan an assassination. That was what Genovesans did, more often than not. They were professional assassins whose weapons included the crossbow, a multiplicity of razor-sharp daggers and—last but by no means least—poisons in a variety of forms.

"Maybe they're after me and Halt," he mused to Ebony.

The dog looked at him, moving only her eyes. Then she thumped her tail once on the floor.

"Who's after me now?" asked a voice behind him, and he turned to see Halt grinning at him. Rangers loved to surprise each other with their silent movement and concealment skills. Usually, Will was hard to catch off guard, but tonight he was preoccupied with thoughts of the mysterious foreigners.

Halt was muddy and tired after a long day in the saddle, trailing the mail coach—to no avail, as it turned out. He had stopped by the cabin to draft a report of the day's activities while they were still fresh in his mind. Then he was heading for a hot bath, followed by dinner with Pauline.

Quickly, Will laid out his suspicions. Halt listened, frowning.

"It's quite a leap to have two Toscan wool merchants turn into two Genovesan assassins—all on the strength of a little beeswax," he said when his former apprentice had finished.

"Except they didn't buy any wool, and their names were in Robard's room. And he died by poisoning," Will added.

"That's true," Halt conceded. "Any idea where they are now?"

Will shook his head. "Nobody knew where they were heading. Mind you, they could be camped in the forest somewhere close by."

"What makes you think that you and I might be their targets?" Halt asked.

"I don't really," Will said. "It was just conjecture. Who else here do they have reason to hate?"

Some time previously, in Hibernia, and then in the north of Araluen, the two Rangers had clashed with three Genovesan mercenaries. The result had been three dead assassins, although Halt had nearly lost his life in the process. But Halt waved the idea of revenge away.

"It's not a matter of who *they* hate," he said, with his usual dis-

regard for grammar. "That's not their style. They kill for m
for revenge. You have to find a target someone else hates—
who's paid them."

There was a short silence as they mulled over the situation.
Then, seeing that no answer seemed likely to spring to mind, Will
asked about Halt's activities.

"Nothing," the gray-bearded Ranger said in disgust. "I trailed
that coach for miles, through rivers, through valleys. It poured rain
for two hours and I got soaked. And never a sign of bandits."

"Maybe they saw you," Will said, and was rewarded with an icy
glare from his mentor. When a Ranger didn't wish to be seen, he
wasn't. "Sorry," Will added meekly. "When's the next trip?"

"Ten days," Halt said. "And it's a long one. I might not make it
back for the wedding."

"Pauline won't like that." Will grinned and Halt glared at him.

"She has already made that abundantly clear," he said. "Made
any progress on that speech?"

Will scowled. "I've been a bit tied up lately. I'll get to it."

Halt raised an eyebrow. "Time's passing every day," he said
mildly.

The wedding would happen within the month. Already, dignitaries were beginning to arrive at Redmont.

"Why isn't the wedding being held at Castle Araluen?" Will
asked. He'd been wondering about that for some time.

"Officially, the dining hall there is being refurbished and won't
be ready in time. Also, Evanlyn feels that the whole affair will be
more informal and friendly here. *A little less magnificent* was the term
she used. Unofficially, Duncan liked the idea of having Jenny and
Master Chubb do the catering."

"Still, he could have drafted them to do the catering at Araluen,"
Will said, but Halt shook his head gravely.

"That would have put his own chef's nose out of joint. It's never a wise thing for a king to annoy his chef. Too easy for him to slip something unpleasant into his food and . . ."

In the same instant, they both realized the significance of what they were saying. The King would be here in Redmont at the end of the month—along with other nobles and rulers of several overseas countries.

"What do you think?" Will asked. There was no need for him to spell out his meaning. Their thoughts were attuned.

"I think it's all circumstantial and vague," said Halt. "But I think you should check it out thoroughly."

3

During the next few days, Will crisscrossed the surrounding countryside, searching for traces of the two foreign wool traders. He asked in nearby hamlets and villages, but the men had not been seen anywhere. He also combed the woods and the forests, in case the two men were camped somewhere in the vicinity. But he found nothing.

After several days, the urgency went out of his search and he began to think that he had overreacted. When he pressed himself to think about it, he could come up with half a dozen plausible explanations for the evidence he had uncovered, none of which involved assassination.

In addition, things at Redmont were becoming increasingly hectic with the arrival of local and overseas dignitaries.

First of these was Erak, Oberjarl of the Skandians. In typical fashion, Erak eschewed traveling overland on horseback but sailed up the Tarbus River in his old wolfship, *Wolfwind*. As he approached the small quay at the outskirts of Wensley Village, his men hoisted a long pennant to the masthead. Will couldn't suppress a grin as he recognized it. It was Evanlyn's—or, more correctly, Princess Cassandra's—personal pennant of a stooping hawk. Erak had flown the banner many years previously, when he had returned Cassandra, with Will, Halt and Horace, to Castle Araluen. Then, he had done it to still any fears in the hearts of Araluens who saw a wolfship so far inland. Now, with a treaty in place for many years, those fears were unlikely.

"We're going to have to get him to return that one of these days," Halt said to Will as they watched the ship approach.

Will grinned. "Have you ever convinced a Skandian to give any-thing back?"

Halt shook his head gloomily. Then they stepped down the quay to welcome their old friend and ally, philosophically resigning themselves to the bruised ribs that would result from Erak's enthu-siastic greeting.

When he recovered his breath, Will commented on the fact that Erak was yet to adopt the new Heron-class sail plan for his vener-able ship. Erak smiled.

"We're both too old to change our ways," he said cheerfully. "Besides, it does my crew good to have to do some extra rowing. They're getting fat and complacent."

A few days later, the greeting ceremony was repeated as Seley el'then, Wakir of the Arridi province of Al Shabah, arrived in his turn. Will searched through his entourage for sight of a familiar face.

"Umar isn't coming?" he said, with some disappointment.

Selethen shook his head. "Unfortunately, he's too fond of his desert sands. The prospect of setting foot on a ship was too much for him."

"I'm sorry to hear it," Will said. Umar and his Bedullin tribe had rescued him from death in the burning desert wastes when he had gone in search of Tug, lost in a sandstorm.

Selethen smiled mischievously. "So was his wife. She was look-ing forward to a wedding. I fear Umar will suffer for this."

In all the bustle of settling the Skandians and Arridi into their quarters, the matter of the Toscan wool traders slipped from Will's consciousness until, by chance, he ran into Desmond one afternoon. The head steward beckoned to him as he was making his way through the keep courtyard to attend to a matter of the stabling of the Arridi troops' horses.

"Will!" Desmond said. "I've been meaning to show you something."

He handed over a piece of paper that had obviously been crumpled into a ball, then unfolded and smoothed out. Will studied it with mild interest. It appeared to be a table plan for a banquet.

Down one side was a series of notes. Will read them, frowning. *Entry. Meal service and speeches. Dance. Departure.* The sight of the word *Speeches* gave him a guilty start. He was really going to have to do something about his own speech, he thought. He looked more closely. There was a small mark beside the word *Dance*, and he studied it for a second or two. He noticed the left-hand side of the plan had been heavily scratched out. He pointed to it.

"What's this?" he asked.

Desmond nodded. "Yes. I wondered about that too. Then I checked and realized we'd changed the plan for that part of the hall when we heard there'd be two shiploads of Skandians. We had to put the Gallican delegation there—they're not fond of our Skandian friends."

Realization dawned on Will. "This is the seating plan for the wedding feast?" he said, and when Desmond nodded, he added, "Where did it come from?" Even as he asked, he had a sense that he already knew.

"We found it in Robard's room. He had a small bin he used for rubbish. It was under the fallen drape, which was why we didn't notice it. One of the maids found it a day or so later when she was tidying up. She put it aside but forgot to give it to me until yesterday."

"Why would he have this?" Will asked.

Desmond shrugged casually. "It's not unusual. Even though we'd demoted him, I still used him to help with table planning and seating arrangements."

Will fingered his chin thoughtfully. In spite of Desmond's reassurance, his suspicions were aroused. He studied the drawing and noticed another small mark, this time between two buttresses on the east wall.

"What's this?" he asked, and Desmond leaned over to look.

He shrugged, his face blank. "No idea," he said. "Could be just a mark on the paper—a blot or a stain of some kind. It's pretty faint."

"It's right opposite the bridal table," Will pointed out. A large rectangle marked the position where the bridal party would be seated on a raised dais. Desmond simply shrugged again. He didn't seem to think that was any cause for alarm. Will tapped the sheet of paper with the back of his hand.

"Let's go and take a look at this spot," he said, and he strode away toward the keep, Desmond hurrying behind him.

Servants were already at work in the Great Hall, building the raised platform where Cassandra, Horace, Duncan, Will and Alyss would be seated. The scent of fresh-sawn pine filled the air.

Will positioned himself between the two buttresses. They were four meters apart, and as he had noticed, standing there put him directly opposite the platform.

Desmond stood beside him, more than a little curious. "What are you worried about?" he said.

Will gestured toward the half-built platform. "I'm thinking this would be an ideal vantage point if someone wanted to harm the

King. Those buttresses would pretty much conceal an attacker from view," Will replied.

But before he finished the sentence, Desmond was shaking his head. "Not on the day," he said, pointing to the sketch. "On the day, this area will be packed with people and tables. There'll be at least thirty people who will have a clear view of this point. I think you're imagining things, Will."

But Will wasn't convinced. "Maybe," he said. Then he added, "I'll hold on to this sketch if you don't mind."

Desmond made an expansive gesture with his hands. "Be my guest. Now, if you don't need me any further, I have one or two things to attend to."

"Just one or two?" Will grinned. He knew the head steward was run off his feet with preparations for the wedding. Desmond rolled his eyes dolefully.

"Make that one or two hundred," he said.

Later that night, Will sat for some time, a mug of coffee gradually going cold beside him, as he studied the rough drawing, trying to make sense of the cryptic marks. A small cross beside the word *Dance*. And another mark, perhaps nothing more than a blemish, against the wall between the buttresses. Desmond was right, he realized. A crossbowman would have no chance of remaining unseen there, with the area packed with happy, noisy guests. Further, even if there was a way he could remain unseen, his view of the platform would be constantly obscured by people coming and going, greeting each other, moving from one table to another, and by a constant procession of servants bringing food and wine.

He checked the copy of the table assignments Desmond had given him and was further reassured. The table set between the buttresses had been reserved for Gundar Hardstriker's crew of sea wolves. With a score of big, excitable Skandians close by, it would be no place to suddenly produce a weapon of any kind.

Feeling a little better about things, he set the seating plan aside and reached for his pen and a clean sheet of paper. Perhaps he should make a start on his speech, he thought.

"Your Majesty, Your Excellency, Your . . ." He paused, not sure what honorific he should use for Erak, Oberjarl of the Skandians. In all the years he'd known Erak, he'd never had to address a formal speech to him. His pen hovered uncertainly and a drop of ink fell onto the paper. He studied it. It was like the mark against the word *Dance*, he thought. Easy enough for a mark like that to happen. He glanced at the seating plan, then back at the embryonic speech. For the life of him, he couldn't remember how he had started the last one. Perhaps that was a good thing, he thought morosely. It couldn't have been too memorable.

He clicked the inkwell top shut and set down the pen. "I'll get on to it tomorrow," he said aloud. Ebony raised her head and looked at him skeptically. "I will," he insisted.

Then he rose from the table and went to bed. But there was still the tiniest worm of doubt eating away at his mind and it took him some time to fall asleep.

4

Two days later, the matter was driven from his mind by the arrival of *Wolfwill*.

The elegant ship, with its curving triangular sail hauled in hard against a beam wind, fairly flew up the last stretch of the Tarbus. Word had come ahead of its imminent arrival and there was a large crowd gathered to greet it. Erak, standing next to Will, sighed as he watched the graceful ship approach, a bow wave of white at her forefoot.

"Changing times, young Will," he said in a lowered tone.

Will glanced up at the massive Oberjarl and saw a look of regret in his eyes. Erak missed the old days of freedom, when he and his crew roamed the world, raiding and stealing and fighting. Will sensed that Erak would love to go back to those times, and to do so in a ship like *Wolfwill*. Much as he professed to love his old square-sailed wolfship, the newer design, with all its speed and grace, was something no true sailor could look upon without envy.

When the ship was less than forty meters from the quay, the onlookers heard a sharp order from the burly figure at the steering oar—Gundar. Sailors moved quickly to obey him and the long, curving boom came quickly down, the wind spilling from the sail as the sail handlers gathered it in and folded it.

At the same time, a banner was unfurled from the mast top: three stylized cherries on a light blue background. The fast-sailing *Wolfwill* had been assigned the longest trip of all, bringing the guest with the greatest distance to travel.

Shigeru, Emperor of Nihon-Ja, had arrived for his friend's wedding.

Although his arrival had been expected for some days, the sight of the banner was concrete proof and the large crowd broke into a chorus of cheering. Then the slight figure of the Emperor himself strode quickly down the main deck of the ship to take a position in the bow, watching as *Wolfwill* ran smoothly up to the quay, the last way falling off her as she reached the timber pilings.

The ship kissed gently against the quay, and the cheering redoubled as Shigeru leapt nimbly over the bulwark and strode up the rough planks, flanked by the commander of his personal bodyguard. The dozen Senshi warriors who made up that bodyguard were caught unawares by the Emperor's impulsive action. They scrambled ashore to follow him, hurriedly forming into two ranks, marching behind him with the peculiar stiff-legged gait of the Senshi.

King Duncan reacted more quickly than they did. Seeing Shigeru leap ashore, he strode quickly forward to meet him. Stopping a few meters short of the Nihon-Jan ruler, Duncan bowed deeply from the waist. A mutter of surprise ran around the assembled Araluens. Most of them had never seen their King bow to any man. Shigeru's eyes twinkled and he bowed in his turn. Being more accustomed to the action, he took his bow even lower than Duncan's. The two rulers stood thus, bent at the waist, eyes down, for several seconds. Then Shigeru spoke.

"I'm not sure about you, Your Majesty, but my back is killing me."

Duncan smothered a short bark of laughter, then answered in

a low tone. "Perhaps we should straighten up, Your Excellency. If we leave it too long, we may never manage it."

The two leaders stood erect and eyed each other. Duncan, tall and broad shouldered, his rust-colored hair beginning to show gray at the temples and in his beard. Shigeru, clean shaven and much smaller, but with a wiry strength and an irrepressible energy and curiosity.

"Welcome to Araluen," Duncan said.

Shigeru nodded an acknowledgment. "It's a pleasure I have looked forward to for some time." Then he looked beyond Duncan and his face lit up with genuine pleasure as he saw a tall figure approaching from the crowd.

"*Kurokuma!*" he said, and Horace almost ran the last few paces, narrowly avoiding the near-sacrilege of shouldering the King aside as he greeted his friend. The two embraced, the slight figure of the Emperor dwarfed by the young warrior.

"I was worried you might not make it," Horace said. There were traces of tears in his eyes as he stepped back and, rather belatedly, bowed to the Emperor. Shigeru smiled and returned the formal greeting.

"There was nothing to stop me from coming," he said as they straightened. "My empire is safe in the stewardship of Lord Nimatsu and his Hasanu warriors."

Horace grinned. "It'd take a brave man to argue with them," he said. Then, remembering his manners, he stepped aside to usher Selethen forward. The tall Arridi made his usual graceful salute and greeted the Emperor as an old friend. Then it was time to introduce another honored guest. A little uncertainly, not sure of the possible outcome, Horace made the introductions.

"Lord Shigeru, Emperor of Nihon-Ja, please meet Erak, Oberjarl of Skandia."

Erak stepped forward, feet wide apart, thumbs thrust into his belt. The position of Oberjarl was an elected one and Skandians did not believe in any hereditary right to rule. For this reason, and to demonstrate his independent nature, Erak never referred to Duncan as "Your Majesty," addressing him instead by his position—King. He was determined not to show any greater deference to this squirrel-size ruler from the east. He gave a perfunctory nod of his head in lieu of a bow and said gruffly, "How do, Emperor?"

Shigeru's lips twisted as he tried to suppress a smile. He had learned a lot about Skandians on his journey aboard *Wolfwill*. He mimicked Erak's nod and gruff tone perfectly. "I do quite well, Erak-san. How do yourself?"

Prepared for a scandalized reaction, Erak was somewhat taken aback by the Emperor's rapid adjustment of manner. Then he laughed delightedly, and turned to Horace. "By Gorlog's braided beard! He'll do, young Horace, he'll definitely do!"

Just in time, Horace realized that Erak was about to slap the Emperor heartily on the back and he caught Erak's massive hand. "Not a good idea, Erak," he said.

Erak was puzzled for a moment, then realized that six of the Emperor's Senshi had fallen into a crouch, their curved swords half drawn from their scabbards. "Oh . . . yes. I see. Wouldn't want to antagonize these bantam roosters." He turned the gesture into a vague wave in the Emperor's direction.

Will stepped forward and greeted the Emperor in his turn.

"It's good to see you again, *Chocho-san*," the Emperor said warmly. "Is Arris-san here as well?"

"She's helping the Princess with her preparations, Lord Shigeru. We'll see them tonight. Baron Arald has arranged a private dinner to welcome you."

Shigeru smiled. "I look forward to seeing them both, *Chocho*."

Behind him, Will heard Erak asking nobody in particular, "*Cho-cho?* What's this *Chocho* business?"

His tone left no doubt that he knew exactly what *Chocho* meant. Will guessed that Gundar must have told him at some stage. Will's nickname among the Nihon-Jan people was *Chocho*, or Butterfly, and it had made him the butt of continuing jokes in the past. Now, he guessed, seeing a mischievous light in Erak's eye, it was all going to start again.

The dinner that evening was a happy affair, bringing together old friends who had not seen one another for many months. Master Chubb had decided to assert his dominance and had ruled that he would cater, without the assistance of Jenny. Much as he admired his former apprentice's skill and ingenuity, every so often he liked to remind the world about who had taught her her craft.

As Baron Arald observed at the end of the meal, surreptitiously letting his belt out another notch, "This spirit of competition between Jenny and Chubb is one of the best things that ever happened to me."

The group broke up early, with most of the guests happy to seek their beds. Duncan was the official host of the dinner and so was the last to leave. As he and Cassandra made their way to the door of the Baron's informal dining room, Will caught up with them.

"Your Majesty. Could I have a word?" Then, seeing that the Princess was about to leave them alone, he added, "Please stay, Evanlyn. This concerns you too."

Many years ago, he had given up the effort to think of his old friend as Cassandra. She had been Evanlyn when they met and she would always be so to him. They sat at a side table, in comfortable chairs. One of the servants asked if they required wine. Duncan nodded but Will asked for coffee.

"Couldn't drink coffee now," Duncan muttered. "I'd be awake all night."

"I don't have that problem, Your Majesty," Will said. Then he added, with a hint of a grin, "My clear conscience lets me sleep peacefully."

Evanlyn snorted in derision. "If there was ever a Ranger with a clear conscience, it certainly wasn't you, you schemer. How's your speech coming?" It seemed everyone had heard about his original speech and its destruction in the moondarkers' fire.

Will shrugged. "I'll get to it tomorrow," he said. "I've been a bit distracted."

"So, Will," the King said, "what did you want to tell us?"

Quickly, Will laid out his investigation into the death of Robard, the Toscan wool merchants and his suspicions that they might, in fact, be Genovesans. When he finished, Will sensed that neither Duncan nor Evanlyn shared his concern.

"It's circumstantial, Will, and the chances are, all these things could be coincidence. Robard may well have killed himself rather than face years of hard labor. And the Toscans could well be Toscans." He was about to ask Will if he had shared his suspicions with Halt, and if Halt had any opinion on the matter. Then he realized that to do so would be a disservice to the young Ranger. Will's opinion was as valid as Halt's, Duncan realized.

Will shook his head doggedly. "I don't like coincidences, Your Majesty."

Duncan nodded gravely. "Still, they do happen—and more often than we might expect."

"Do you have any suggestions as to what we might do, Will?" Evanlyn asked.

He went to answer, then hesitated. "Well, I did think we might . . ."

Evanlyn cocked her head at him and frowned. "You're not going to say 'postpone the wedding,' are you?" she said, and he shrugged helplessly.

"We-ell . . . ," he began, but she cut him off instantly.

"Because that is definitely not an option. We are not postponing. We are not shifting to another location. That's not the way we do things."

"Will," Duncan said, in a more reasoning tone, "we really appreciate how much you care about our safety. But do you have any idea how many false alarms, how many so-called threats to our lives, we receive each year?"

"No. I—"

"There must be dozens!" Evanlyn told him. She looked to her father. "When was the most recent, Dad?"

Duncan thought for a few seconds. "As I recall, less than three weeks ago. We had reports that some of Morgarath's former cronies were planning to kidnap me while I was out hunting. It all came to nothing, of course."

"It's part and parcel of being the royal family," Evanlyn told Will. "There are always these rumors and suspicions. Most of them are far more concrete and detailed than this set of circumstances you've uncovered. And the vast majority of them—ninety-nine out of one hundred—come to nothing."

"As Cassandra says, it's all part of being King," Duncan added. "We have to live with it. We take precautions, of course, but we can't let vague rumors or coincidences like this rule our lives. If we bow to them, we'll never have any life worth speaking of."

"We'll stay locked in our castle all day and night like hothouse blossoms." Evanlyn smiled at him. "And you know that's not my style."

At that, Will was forced to smile in return. It was a wan little smile, but a smile nonetheless. The idea of Evanlyn, or Cassandra, remaining locked up in Castle Araluen like a fragile flower in a hothouse was so totally foreign to her nature that he couldn't begin to consider it.

Duncan placed a hand on his shoulder. "We're not discounting this, Will. We never ignore these things completely. But, as threats to our well-being go, this is way down on the scale of credibility. Keep an eye on things by all means, and if there's any change, any further information, let us know."

"And we still won't postpone the wedding," Evanlyn said firmly. Her father smiled at her, then included Will in the smile.

"As she says," he affirmed.

5

THE DAYS BECAME MORE FRANTIC, AND BEFORE WILL KNEW IT, the day of the wedding had arrived. He dressed in his ceremonial uniform, designed by Crowley some years prior for Halt and Pauline's wedding, and checked himself in the mirror before leaving the cabin. He patted his jacket pockets to make sure he had everything, and realized with a start that he had never got around to rewriting his speech. He rolled his eyes at his image in the mirror.

"Ah, well," he said. "Everyone tells me I should just speak from the heart."

It was a beautiful sunny day and the wedding was held in the open—in the courtyard of Castle Redmont, where hundreds of spectators could watch. The battlements were lined with staff from the castle and people from the village, and a section of the courtyard had been set aside by Arald for the villagers and staff to celebrate later. Already, several bullocks and boars were turning on spits over fire pits. The smoky aroma of roasted meat drifted through the courtyard.

Arald performed the ceremony. The King, of course, was giving his daughter away. Shigeru had been granted the honored position of Patron-Sponsor of the wedding. When he had inquired politely about the nature of his duties, Duncan had grinned and directed him to Lady Pauline.

"Ask Pauline," he told the Nihon-Jan monarch. "She invented the position for me at her wedding."

Evanlyn, scorning fashionable practice, appeared right on time for the wedding, to the second. As she emerged from the keep, escorted by King Duncan and attended by Alyss, her bridesmaid, there was a concerted gasp of admiration from the assembled crowd.

"Oooooohhhhhhhh!"

Duncan smiled proudly. His daughter did look beautiful. Again, typically, she had ignored current fashion, which called for brides to wear voluminous dresses with long trains and layer after layer of lace.

She wore a simple but elegant dress of white satin, a narrow dress that accentuated her slim figure. There was a minimal veil in her light hair and she appeared tiny and petite alongside her tall, broad-shouldered father.

Will, standing beside Horace at the dais where the ceremony would take place, glanced at Evanlyn, nodded approvingly, and then had eyes only for the blond girl walking gracefully behind her.

Alyss wore a formalized version of her Courier's uniform, a style that left one shoulder bare. In deference to the bride, the Courier's normal color of white had been changed on this occasion to pale blue. She was beautiful, Will thought, and his heart swelled in his chest.

Beside him, his best friend had his gaze fixed on his bride-to-be. Horace, as befitted his station as a knight, wore ceremonial armor for the occasion—glistening silver mail and a white surcoat bearing his green oakleaf insignia. At his side he wore the sword of Nihon-Jan steel that had been presented to him by the Emperor months before. His left hand tightened on the hilt as he watched the wedding procession approach.

"My god, she's beautiful," he whispered to Will.

"Indeed she is," the young Ranger responded.

Neither of them was aware that they were talking about two different people.

Arald performed the ceremony with the correct mix of solemnity and friendliness. Fortunately, Lady Sandra had cautioned him against his propensity to crack jokes. Ruefully, he had agreed.

"I'm afraid my humor is too witty for most folk," he had said. "It seems to go over their heads."

"I'm sure that's exactly what it does, dear," his wife had replied, patting his hand.

It was a short ceremony and it seemed only minutes before he delivered the final words: "I now pronounce you man and wife. You may . . ."

Horace, without waiting for further invitation or permission, swept Cassandra into his arms and kissed her long and thoroughly. She responded quite eagerly. The crowd cheered with delight, startling the swallows that nested in nooks and crannies along the battlements so that they soared into the air in an apparent avian tribute to the newlyweds.

Duncan beamed with pride and at the same time surreptitiously wiped away a tear. Alyss and Will exchanged knowing smiles.

" . . . kiss the bride—I suppose," Arald concluded, feeling the words were superfluous in light of the events.

Then there was a clamor of congratulations. Sir Rodney led the Battleschool staff and students and the other spectators in three rousing cheers for the couple, then three more for the King. Warming to the task, he then led cheers for Shigeru, Selethen and Erak, until his fiancée laid a gentle hand on his arm.

"I think that's enough cheering, dear," she said.

He looked a little startled. He had been quite carried away, he realized. "Oh yes, of course. Quite so, my dear."

All in all, it was a good thing that the ladies of Redmont were present that day.

Finally, the wedding party processed to the Great Hall, where tables were set for the banquet. Arald eyed the glistening table settings and decorations. "This is the best part of any wedding day for me!" he said enthusiastically to Lady Sandra. She rolled her eyes.

"This is the best part of any day for you," she replied drolly. He considered the statement, then nodded emphatically.

"I can't deny it," he said, and she smiled, knowing why she loved him.

Horace and Evanlyn led the way onto the raised dais where the official table was placed. As Will followed in his turn, he looked up admiringly. The dais was surmounted by a magnificent canopy of tasseled white silk, supported on poles and a light framework, and standing three meters above the platform. It was a beautiful finishing touch, he thought.

Everyone was seated, with a prolonged clattering as benches and chairs were dragged into position on the flagstone floor of the hall. Then Shigeru, who had remained standing, stepped to the front of the dais and spoke. Not the first time, Will was surprised by the depth and timbre of the voice that came from his slight frame.

"My friends," he said as silence fell about the room and people craned to see this exotic character from another kingdom, "I am told it is my pleasant duty as Patron-Sponsor to open these festivities. I am also told"—he turned and smiled at King Duncan—"that it is my equally pleasant duty to convey an expensive present upon these young people."

Duncan nodded gravely, then couldn't help a grin breaking through. The role of Patron-Sponsor had been created by Lady Pauline and his own secretary at Halt's wedding, to avoid an embarrassing situation in which the King had no role to play at the wedding.

"Accordingly, I have decided to grant them the castle of Hashan-Ji, in the Koto province of my country, with income from its surrounding farmlands, timber forests and hunting rights." He turned and smiled at Horace and Evanlyn. "By strange coincidence, it's quite close to my summer palace."

There was an audible gasp of surprise from the audience, then a subdued murmur of conversation ran around the large room. This was a magnificent gift indeed.

Shigeru held up his hands for silence and, gradually, the muttering ceased.

"I have appointed a steward to administer the castle in your absence. But I hope there will be times when you will be able to visit. You will be known as Lord and Lady *Kurokuma*, of course."

He turned to the wedding table and bowed deeply. After a moment, as the full realization of what he had given the couple sank in, the people in the hall began to applaud. Then some stood, and others followed, until the entire group was on its feet, clapping and cheering as the slight figure resumed his seat.

Horace leaned over to Cassandra and murmured something. She nodded enthusiastically and then the tall knight stood, holding his hands up for silence. As the noise slowly died away, he turned to Shigeru, bowed, then spoke. "This is a great honor, Lord Shigeru. My wife and I—"

For a moment, he got no further. It was a time-honored tradition that the first time a groom used the phrase "my wife and I," the entire gathering should cheer. He waited for silence again while they did, grinning sheepishly, then continued.

" . . . would like to request that all future income from the castle and its estate be shared among the families of those Kikori who gave their lives for you in the war against the traitor Arisaka."

A moment of silence greeted this announcement. Then Sir Rodney's voice boomed around the hall.

"Oh, well done, Horace! Well done indeed!"

And the clapping and cheering started once more.

Duncan rose to speak as a long line of servants emerged from the kitchen, snaking between the tables to serve the first course of the banquet. He welcomed Horace to his family and, with a wry grin, wished him well in his future life with Cassandra. Looking meaningfully at the grinning young man beside him, he offered one piece of advice.

"Never try to change her mind when she has it set on something," he said, shaking his head in mock despair. There was laughter at that. Most people knew that their Princess was a headstrong and determined young lady.

Then the crowd was applauding the King's speech and he resumed his seat. As the first course was cleared and the servants brought the second course, Selethen rose to his feet and delivered a charming speech of congratulations from the ruler of his country, and his own personal best wishes. Again, the crowd applauded, but not as enthusiastically as they had for Duncan. Selethen, after all, was not a well-known figure in Araluen.

The enthusiasm returned with the next course and Erak, the next speaker. The huge Oberjarl took his place at the front of the platform and delivered his own best wishes and congratulations to the couple. There had been a time when a Skandian ruler would not have been a welcome guest at an Araluen ceremony. But that was

long past. The assembly knew of the debt they owed to the Skandians. Gundar Hardstriker and his crew, present today in the hall,
had helped save the Kingdom from an invasion by the fierce Scotti
tribes.

Erak spoke of an earlier battle, when a small group of Araluens
had helped his men turn back an invasion by the fierce riders from the
east—the Temujai. He singled out Cassandra for particular praise,
recounting her cool courage in the battle as she continued to direct
the shooting of a small group of archers, even when they were under
direct attack. Many of those present knew the overall story, but they
hadn't heard the specific details of Cassandra's courage on that day.

Diplomatically, he neglected to mention the fact that, at the time
of the battle, she had been under sentence of death from his prede-
cessor, Ragnak.

There was more cheering as he sat down, then more servants
arriving with more food.

Will, who was thoroughly enjoying himself, realized that Erak
was the last of the distinguished overseas speakers and now it was
his turn. He rose hurriedly.

Alyss, seated beside him, put a hand over his and squeezed gently. "Take your time," she said. "And speak from the heart."

He paused, took a deep breath and stepped forward to the front
of the platform. His hand fluttered for a moment at the breast of his
jacket, unconsciously seeking speech that wasn't there. He stood,
looking out at the assembled people, and his mind went utterly
blank. Then it cleared and he knew what he was going to say.

"I had written a speech for this moment, but as it happened, it
was burned in a fire some weeks ago. That may well turn out to be
a good thing."

"Hear, hear!" came a gruff voice from the crowd. A voice he
recognized all too well.

"Thank you for that, Halt," he said, nodding to the table where Halt, Pauline and Crowley were seated. He was glad that his old mentor had made it back in time for the wedding. He knew that his absence would have lessened the day for Horace and Cassandra. Another ripple of laughter ran around the room and he relaxed. These were friends, he realized. There was no cause for nervousness.

"Since then, people have been advising me to simply speak from my heart." He turned and smiled briefly at Alyss.

"So here's what's in my heart. I came to Redmont as an orphan, with no family, no brothers or sisters. That has changed. Over the years, Horace has become closer than a brother to me, and Evanl . . . Cassandra," he corrected himself, "has become the most beloved of sisters. I would trust my life in their hands. Horace has saved my life on too many occasions to recount. And Cassandra saved my sanity some years back. I owe them so much. It's a debt I can never repay. All I can say is, I can imagine no better husband for Cassandra than Horace and no better wife for Horace than Cassandra. I love them both. Please stand and drink to their future happiness. Cassandra and Horace!"

There was an echoing crash of benches and chairs being pushed back as everyone came to their feet, then hundreds of voices repeated his toast:

"Cassandra and Horace!"

The sudden noise rang through the vast hall and startled a swallow that had nested high in the rafters. The little bird darted out in sudden fright, the movement catching Will's eye. Then, as the noise subsided, it perched on a massive support beam. But his eye, drawn upward, had registered something else. It was a detail he had forgotten—something so familiar that he had overlooked it completely.

High above the floor of the hall, a narrow, stone-balustraded gallery ran around the inside of the walls.

His heart pounding, Will returned to the table.

Alyss smiled at him. "Well said," she began, then, seeing his face, "What's wrong?"

"Maybe nothing," he said. "I have to check something." He glanced along the table. Horace and Evanlyn were deep in discussion with Shigeru. Erak and Duncan were similarly engaged.

He made a decision. He'd handle this alone.

Alyss squeezed his hand. "Just be back before the bridal dance," she said. Horace would be the next to speak, when the final course arrived. Then the dancing would begin.

He nodded, a little distractedly. "I will."

As unobtrusively as he could manage—and Rangers could be very unobtrusive when they chose—he made his way down from the dais and headed for the opposite wall. Halt and Crowley were seated some distance away, out to his right. As ever, Halt had chosen to take as inconspicuous a position as possible. It would take time for Will to make his way through the crowded hall, and the thronging servants, to alert them. He saw a quicker alternative.

Gundar's crew were seated at a table between the two buttresses that Will had noted on the map. They were only a few meters away and he hurried toward them. Nils Ropehander saw him coming.

"Good speech, boy!" he began. Will made a decision. Nils was big, and powerful, even for a Skandian. And he didn't ask questions.

"Come with me! I need you," Will said urgently.

Nils shrugged. "Then I'm your man." He shoved back his chair and stood.

As they made their way out to the wall, Will said to him, "Are you armed?"

Nils shook his head, grinning. "They wouldn't let us bring weapons."

Will realized the truth of that statement. Skandians, weapons and strong drink were not a good combination for a wedding. He, of course, had his two knives. They were part of the formal Ranger uniform that he wore. He searched the wall between the buttresses. There was a door here that led to a stairway, he remembered now. And that stairway would lead to the gallery above.

One of the wedding marshals was standing nearby. There were six marshals, stationed at the exits throughout the hall. Their role was purely ceremonial these days, but it was a reminder of the times when order had to be kept at public assemblies like this. To that end, the man carried an official rod of office—a two-meter heavy blackwood staff surmounted by a solid brass knob. Will snatched it from the startled man's grasp and handed it to Nils.

"Here. Use this."

Nils hefted it experimentally. "Not bad," he said.

The marshal finally recovered from his surprise. "What the blazes do you think you're doing, Ranger Will?" he began indignantly, but Will cut him off.

"You'll get it back. No time to explain!"

Then he plunged through the small doorway that led into the narrow, ascending circular stairway, with Nils close behind him. They wound their way up the dark stairs. Will's boots were soft-soled and they made virtually no sound on the bare stone steps. Nils, like most Skandians, wore sealskin boots and these were nearly as quiet. His breathing was less so and it became more and more noisy as they ascended the steep stairs.

From the hall, Will heard a burst of applause and realized that Horace had finished his speech. The groom had been commendably brief. The next item on the agenda would be the bridal dance.

Already, Will could hear the faint squeaking and twanging noises of the orchestra tuning their instruments.

Then realization hit him like a thunderbolt. This was why the mark had been placed against the word *Dance*.

This would be the time when Duncan would be most exposed to an assassin's arrow. Previously, when he was seated at the wedding table, the silken canopy covering the dais had screened him from a high vantage point such as the gallery. But now, he and Cassandra would move down to the dance floor and circle the room on their own before the other guests joined them. For at least thirty seconds, he would be a perfect, unobstructed target.

"Blast you, Horace," he said through gritted teeth. "Just this once, couldn't you have rambled on a bit?"

"What say?" Nils wheezed. But Will just gestured for him to redouble the pace.

"Come on!"

He heard Desmond's voice dimly through the stone walls as the head steward announced the moment when the King and the bride would take the floor. There was a long round of applause. Will pounded up the stairs, taking them two at a time. Behind him, he heard Nils stumble. In his mind's eye, he could see Duncan holding out his hand to help his daughter rise from the table. They would turn and bow to the audience, then walk slowly to the stairs that led down to the main floor.

He had only seconds.

He reached the wood-and-brass door that led to the balustrade and, with an enormous effort, stopped himself from flinging it crashing back on its hinges. Quietly, slowly, he eased the heavy door open, a few centimeters at a time, then peered around the edge.

He felt his heart jolt with panic as he saw them. Two figures, clad in those familiar dull purple cloaks, crouched some eight meters away. One of them raised his crossbow. He stayed back from the balustrade itself, lessening the chance that he might be seen by those in the hall below. The second Genovesan crouched a meter or so beyond him. He had a crossbow as well. But his wasn't leveled at the King. He would be the reserve shooter, in case something went wrong.

Everything seemed to be happening in slow motion as Will slid the heavy saxe from its ceremonial scabbard. Behind him, he could hear Nils huffing and puffing up the last few meters. The stone walls enclosing the stairwell seemed to screen the sound from the assassins' hearing.

He had time to notice that the Genovesans weren't using their standard crossbows. The ones they held were smaller, like the bows used by Arridi cavalry. He wondered about that, then dismissed the thought. The range was far from extreme. The smaller bows would be more than capable of hitting their mark. And besides, if the Genovesans ran true to form, the bolts would probably be poisoned—even a slight wound would be fatal.

He saw the shooter's knuckles whiten as he tightened his grip on the crossbow's stock, saw him take in half a breath.

Then his own arm went back and forward in one action and sent the saxe knife spinning across the space between them. It was a blur of brilliant light as it crossed the intervening space.

At the last moment, Will had realized that the shooter, if struck by the knife, might involuntarily trigger the release of the bow. He'd aimed for a different target.

The heavy saxe's blade, spinning as it went, sliced through the thick cord of the crossbow, severing it instantly.

As the tension was suddenly released, the limbs of the bow sprang forward with an ugly crack. The bolt fell from the bow, bouncing and clattering across the stone floor of the gallery. The shooter recoiled in surprise as he tried to understand what had just happened. His companion was quicker to comprehend. Escape was now his first priority and he swung his bow on the figure who had suddenly appeared in the stairway door. Will's throwing knife was already on its way as the bow swung toward him. He had drawn and thrown at the second Genovesan before he even saw the result of his first throw.

He would have hit him if the first assassin hadn't chosen that moment to rise from his crouching position, straight into the path of the spinning knife. It took him in the chest, killing him instantly, and he sagged back against his companion, jolting his aim so that the crossbow bolt went off line, thudding into the wooden door, close by Will's head.

The shooter dropped the bow and drew a long-bladed dagger from inside his cloak. He shoved his dead accomplice to one side and advanced quickly on Will, who was now unarmed. He was only a meter or so away when Will felt a rush of movement behind him and Nils's voice said, "Get down!"

Instantly, he dropped to his hands and knees and saw the startled expression on the Genovesan's face at the sight of the huge Skandian sea wolf who had just appeared in the doorway. Then Nils, holding the blackwood stave like a spear over his shoulder, shot it forward in an overhand thrust, slamming the heavy brass knob into the Genovesan's forehead, right between his eyes.

The force of the blow, with Nils' shoulder, arm and body weight all behind it, was sickening. The Genovesan flew backward two or three meters before he crashed to the stone floor of the gallery. His dagger fell from his hand and he lay unconscious. Nils looked at the staff in his hand once more and nodded approvingly.

"Not bad at all," he said.

Will rose and glanced hurriedly over the balustrade to the hall below. Nobody seemed to have noticed the commotion above them. The music probably drowned out the slight noise they had made, he thought. He saw that Duncan and Evanlyn were already halfway around their circuit of the floor. He looked at Nils, who was smiling contentedly, then jerked his thumb at the unconscious Genovesan.

"Hold on to him," he said. "I've got to get back down there."

"I'll make sure he doesn't go anywhere." Nils nodded cheerfully. Then, before Will could leave, he put a huge hand on his shoulder.

"You know, Ranger, this couldn't be a better wedding. A beautiful bride. A handsome groom. Good food, good ale. And to cap it all off, a fight. It's just like being back home."

Then Will was fairly flying back down the stairs. He estimated that he had less than thirty seconds to get back to the dais and lead Alyss onto the dance floor.

He may have saved Duncan's life, but if he missed another wedding dance with Alyss, his own wouldn't be worth living.

6

THE GROUP ASSEMBLED IN BARON ARALD'S OFFICE LOOKED UP AS
Halt entered the room.

"So, did our Genovesan friend tell you anything?" Duncan
asked.

Halt had been assigned the task of interrogating the surviving
assassin. Will, for all his experience and prowess in battle, was still
somewhat hampered in such matters by his young face and relatively
ingenuous looks. Halt's face, on the other hand, was anything but
young and definitely not ingenuous. Halt had the ability to make a
threat and appear as if he had every intention of carrying it through.

Possibly because he usually did.

He nodded now in answer to the King's question. "Not at first.
Genovesans are notoriously closemouthed and they're not afraid of
death threats. He fully expects to be executed. He accepted that risk
when he took the job."

"So how did you persuade him to talk?" Erak asked.

"Genovesans aren't afraid to die. But they are afraid of the sort
of suffering their own weapons can cause," Halt told him. He
nodded to Horace, sitting on the edge of the Baron's desk, close to
Cassandra. "I took a leaf out of your book, Horace. I threatened to

infect him with one of his own poisoned arrows. He went a little green about the gills when I told him that the only man in Araluen who could produce an antidote lived eight days away in the north. Then he seemed quite willing to talk."

"He really believed you'd do it?" Cassandra asked, and Halt turned to her.

"I have a very honest face," he said with great dignity.

"Of course you do," Cassandra replied.

Before Halt could continue, Will interposed a question that had been bothering him. "I've been wondering," he said, "why did they wait till the bridal dance? After all, I noticed the gallery when I was standing at the front of the dais, making my speech. That means the front of the dais could be seen from the gallery. So they could have chosen to shoot when the King was making his speech."

"Two reasons," Halt told him, with a faint smile. "The target was exposed for a much longer period during the dance. And the target wasn't the King. It was Cassandra."

That caused a definite stir in the people listening to him. Duncan was the first to recover.

"Cassandra? Cassandra was the target? Who wanted her killed?"

"Apparently, a man named Iqbal," Halt said. He looked at Selethen, who was frowning at the name.

"Iqbal?" he said. "He's Yusal's brother." He turned to the rest of the group. Some of them weren't familiar with the name. "Yusal was the Tualaghi chief who organized Erak's kidnapping some years ago," he explained. "But Iqbal is being held prisoner in the mountain village of Maashava. He was one of the men sentenced to hard labor there."

Halt shook his head. "Apparently not anymore. It seems Iqbal made his escape from Maashava some months ago. The Maashavites haven't got around to telling you about it yet."

Selethen's brow darkened and he muttered a soft curse. "That's typical of them!" he said bitterly. "They're so blasted insular up there in their mountains! They've always distrusted the central government. I suppose they were trying to find a way to make themselves look blameless for letting him escape."

"Of course," Halt replied, "they may have sent word by now. You have been out of the country for several weeks." He looked at Cassandra. "This Iqbal fellow is quite angry with you, Cassandra," he said. "After all, you did foil all their plans and reduce his brother to a drooling wreck. He wanted revenge. He hired the Genovesans to kill you. And he suggested that they should use Arridi crossbows when they did it. The plan was to leave one behind."

"Which would have caused a lot of distrust between our two countries," Selethen said thoughtfully.

"Just so," Halt agreed. "I gather that our friend Iqbal would enjoy seeing bad blood between Araluen and Arrida. It would distract you from the task of hunting him down. And on top of that, killing Cassandra would leave Duncan with no heir to the throne. That could well destabilize the succession, and the country."

"And the plan would have worked if Will hadn't been so alert," Horace said. He looked at his friend gratefully. "How many times have I said 'thank you' since we've known each other?"

Will shrugged, embarrassed by the sudden attention of everyone in the room. "Friends don't have to thank each other," he said. But Cassandra rose and moved toward him.

"We don't have to," she said, "but we want to." She placed both hands on his shoulders and leaned toward him, then paused and smiled at Alyss.

"With your permission, of course?"

Alyss smiled. "Of course," she said, as the Princess kissed Will on both cheeks. She reflected that there had been a time when she would have torn Cassandra's hair out by the roots for such an action. We've come a long way, she thought.

Duncan rose and approached Will, reaching out to shake his hand. "My gratitude as well, Will. I have only one daughter and I'm rather fond of having her around. Particularly now that she has Horace to keep her in order."

Cassandra responded with a most unroyal poking out of her tongue. Duncan chose to ignore it.

"I wonder," he continued, "if there will ever come a time when I don't have to thank my Rangers for their service to me and my family."

"I doubt it, My Lord," Halt said, and there was a murmur of laughter in the room. They could laugh now, Halt thought, but if Will hadn't been so alert, the atmosphere in the room would be vastly different. He caught the eye of his young protégé and mouthed the words *Well done*. He saw Will's face flush with pleasure. Two unspoken words of praise from Halt meant more to Will than any amount of gratitude from the King.

"Rest assured, Your Majesty, that Iqbal won't be enjoying his freedom for too much longer," Selethen said. "As soon as I'm back in Arrida, I'll make it a priority to hunt him down."

"I'd appreciate that, Selethen," Duncan told him. "I might even send a Ranger or two along to help you find him. I can't say I like the idea of someone trying to kill my daughter and getting away with it."

The two men exchanged a long glance. Then Selethen nodded. Watching them, it occurred to Cassandra that she wouldn't care to be in Iqbal's shoes over the next few months.

The meeting broke up soon after and they all headed back to their quarters. As they approached the stairway, Alyss took Will's hand and led him into an unoccupied office to one side. He smiled at her, uncertain what she had in mind.

"Alyss . . . ," he began, but she inclined her head in warning and laid a forefinger on his lips to silence him.

"This makes two weddings where our dance has been interrupted," she said. "At Halt's you had to go racing off, and at this one, you nearly didn't make it back in time."

She paused to let the message sink in, then finished:

"You'd better be there at ours."

THE HIBERNIAN

Author's note: I'm often asked who was Halt's mentor, and how and where he served his apprenticeship. This story provides the answer to those questions. It's set in the time shortly after Halt's departure from his family home at Dun Kilty, in Hibernia.

1

CROWLEY RODE WITH A HEAVY HEART, IGNORING THE BRIGHT sunshine and the singing of birds in the trees. It was a beautiful summer day in Gorlan Fief, but the young Ranger had no eyes for the rich sweep of green fields and wildflowers that surrounded him.

His horse seemed to sense his malaise. He clopped heavily, head drooping, moving with increasing lethargy as he felt no urge from his rider to maintain the pace at which they had started.

For as long as he could remember, Crowley had harbored one aim in life: to become a King's Ranger. It was the pinnacle of achievement as far as he was concerned. As a young teenager, he could see no better way to serve his King and country, no more honorable career for an adventurous and loyal citizen.

Others might, and did, strive to become knights and warriors. But Crowley had always believed that the Ranger Corps was the real center of power and influence in the Kingdom—the place where an ambitious, intelligent and, above all, skilled young man could really make his mark and play an important part in the path of history.

His mentor, Pritchard, had reinforced that dedicated sense of purpose throughout Crowley's training. As the young boy had devel-oped his ability in tracking, unseen movement and archery, Pritchard had been at pains to remind him of the real reason why he should perfect such skills.

"We don't do it for ourselves. We don't do it for the glory. We train and we practice against the day when the King and the people of Araluen have need of these skills. As Rangers, it's our duty to be able to provide them."

Pritchard was gone now, of course. He had been driven out of the Kingdom on a trumped-up charge of treason three years prior—shortly after he had presented Crowley with his silver oakleaf, the symbol of a graduate Ranger. Crowley had been assigned to a small, remote fief on the northwest coast and word had reached him of Pritchard's fate months after his mentor had been forced to flee. Rumor had it that he had gone across the western sea to Hibernia.

Crowley found himself isolated in more ways than one. Hogarth Fief was remote and difficult to reach, and news of what was happening in the country as a whole was intermittent at best. But he felt emotionally isolated as well. The Ranger Corps as he knew it, and as Pritchard had known it, had been subverted and weakened until it had become little more than a dissolute social club for sons of noble families—usually those too lazy or without the skill to become knights or warriors. Whereas once Rangers had selected apprentices to join the Corps, and submitted them to five years' rigorous training, these days, a new Ranger simply had to buy a commission to be granted the silver oakleaf.

Many of the older Rangers had quit in disgust. Some of the more vocal, like Pritchard, were forced to leave the Kingdom. Although the Corps had a theoretical strength of fifty members, training and appointment of new Rangers under the old system had fallen off in recent years. There had barely been thirty properly trained Rangers when Crowley received his appointment. He estimated that there might be ten or twelve of these still serving, but they were scattered in remote parts of the Kingdom.

The key to the problem was King Oswald. He had been a good king in his younger days, energetic and fair-minded. But now he was old and weak and his mind was going. He had accepted a group of ambitious barons as his ruling council. Initially, they were appointed to take care of the day-to-day matters of ruling the Kingdom and to relieve him of the repetitive, annoying minutiae that came across his desk every day. But as time went on, they encroached more and more into the important decisions, until Oswald was little more than a rubber stamp to their rulings.

Prince Duncan might have prevented this by taking over as Regent in the King's place. But the council, led by a charismatic and scheming baron named Morgarath, had undermined his position with his father. Oswald became convinced that his son was unready to rule. His council told him that the Prince was too impulsive and too inexperienced for the job. Believing them, Oswald had posted his son to a fief in the far northeast of the Kingdom. There, isolated from the seat of power in Castle Araluen, and without any organized support, Duncan languished, frustrated and ineffectual, unable to resist the changes that were being imposed on what would be his Kingdom.

All in all, thought Crowley, it wasn't the life he had imagined himself leading. He leaned forward and patted Cropper's neck.

"Still, it could be worse," he said, trying to raise his own spirits. Cropper's ears pricked up and his head rose as he heard the more positive note in his master's voice—a note that had been missing for some days now.

Good to see you're feeling better.

"Well, no sense in moping," Crowley said, forcing the dark thoughts aside.

Taken you three days to figure that out, has it?

"Give credit where it's due. I may have been moping for three days, but I'm over it now."

You say.

In spite of his recent gloom, Crowley found himself smiling. He wondered if he'd ever get the last word with his horse.

Probably not.

"I didn't say that out loud!" he said, a little surprised. Cropper shook his mane.

You don't have to.

They crested a rise and Crowley could see a building beside the road, a few hundred meters ahead. It was small, but larger than the general run of farmhouses in the area. And there was a signboard swinging from a beam in front of the porticoed doorway.

"That's what we need!" he said brightly. "An inn. And it's just about lunchtime."

I just hope there are apples.

"You always hope there are apples."

As they rode closer, a slight frown returned to Crowley's forehead. He could hear raised voices from the inn, and loud laughter. Usually, that sort of sound indicated that someone had taken too much liquor. And these days, with no firm hand ruling the Kingdom, drunkenness was all too often accompanied by meaningless violence. Unconsciously, he loosened the big saxe knife in its scabbard.

Another burst of raucous laughter greeted him as he swung down from the saddle and led Cropper into the fenced-off yard beside the inn. There were feed bins and water troughs set along the fence at intervals. He found a full feed bin and left Cropper before it, filling a bucket with fresh water from a pump and pouring it into the water trough. He glanced around. There were four other horses in the yard. Three of them were long-legged cavalry mounts and their saddle cloths and tack were military pattern. The fourth was a nondescript gray, tethered a little apart from the others. All four of them turned their heads curiously to view the newcomer, then, seeing nothing to hold their interest, they returned to the feed bins in front of them, their jaws moving in that strange rolling, grinding motion that horses use. Crowley made a hand signal to Cropper.

"Wait here."

What about my apple?

Sighing, Crowley reached into his jacket packet and produced an apple, holding it out on his flattened palm for the horse. Cropper took it gently and crunched happily, his eyes closing as the juices spurted inside his mouth. Crowley loosened the saddle girth a few notches and turned toward the inn.

After the bright sunshine outside, it took his eyes some time to adjust to the dimness inside. But as he opened the door and entered, a loud male voice stopped in midsentence and, for a moment, silence hung over the room.

"And what do we have here?" the male voice began again. Now that Crowley's eyes had adjusted, he could see it belonged to a beefy soldier lounging against the bar. He wore a surcoat and mail shirt and was armed with a sword and a heavy-bladed dagger.

He had two companions, similarly dressed and equipped. One sat at a long bench by a table close to the bar. He was turned around away from the table, facing the bar. The other was sitting on the table itself, his feet perched on the bench. Behind the bar, Crowley saw the innkeeper, a smallish man in his fifties, and a young serving girl who looked to be around twenty. Both of them cast nervous glances at the three soldiers.

As the speaker turned slightly to face Crowley, the Ranger made out the blazon on his surcoat—a sword with a lightning bolt for a blade. They were members of Morgarath's Gorlan garrison, he thought.

He glanced around the room. There was one other occupant. A man sat at the rear of the room, dressed in a dark green cloak. His hair and beard were black and he was spooning food from a bowl on the table in front of him, seemingly ignoring the other customers.

"I said, *what do we have here?*" the man at the bar repeated. There was an unpleasant edge in his voice now. As Crowley moved closer, he could see that the man was flushed and his heavy-jowled face was damp with perspiration. Too much to drink, he thought. The man's two companions chuckled quietly as he pushed himself up from the bar and stood straight, glaring at Crowley. There was an air of expectation about them. Crowley stopped about two meters away from him. The man was taller than Crowley, and heavily built. He was carrying a lot of fat, Crowley thought.

He spoke evenly in return, allowing no sense of the wariness he felt to enter his voice.

"Name of Crowley," he said. "King's Ranger to Hogarth Fief."

Out of the corner of his eye, he sensed a movement at the back of the room. The solitary diner had raised his head at the words *King's Ranger*.

The heavily built soldier reacted to it as well. His eyes widened in mock admiration. "A *King's Ranger!*" he said. "Ooooooooooooh my! How very impressive!"

More laughter from his friends. He turned his head and grinned at them, then turned back to Crowley, resuming the expression of fake admiration.

"So tell me, *King's Ranger*, what are you doing here in Gorlan Fief? Don't you have important things to do at Ranger headquarters—like getting drunk and gambling?"

Crowley ignored the jibe, reflecting sadly that it was a fairly accurate picture of how the newer members of the Ranger Corps spent their time. The other soldiers laughed again. Their laughter was becoming louder, he noticed.

"I've been at Castle Araluen for an assembly," he said, maintaining a pleasant tone. "Now I'm heading back to my home fief. Just passing through Gorlan."

"And we're honored to have you with us," the soldier said with heavy sarcasm. "Perhaps we could buy you a drink?"

Crowley smiled. "I'll just have coffee," he said, but the soldier shook his head vehemently.

"Coffee's no drink for such an honored guest. After all, you're a . . . *King's Ranger.*" He managed to make the words sound like an epithet. "I insist that we buy you a glass of wine. Or a brandy. Or a drink worthy of such an exalted person as yourself."

One of the other soldiers snorted and chuckled drunkenly at his friend's wit. Crowley held his smile. There was nothing to be gained by causing a scene, he thought. Just suffer through the heavy-handed sarcasm, have a drink and leave.

"Well, perhaps a tankard of ale," he said.

The soldier nodded approval. "Much better choice!" he said. He jerked a thumb at a small ale cask set on the bar. It would have been filled from a larger cask in the cellar. "We're drinking ale too. But sadly, this cask is empty!"

His face darkened with anger as he said the last word and he swept the small cask off the bar and onto the floor. It rolled under a table. The violent movement was unexpected and the girl behind the bar flinched and uttered a small cry of fright. She instinctively moved closer to her employer, as if seeking safety in numbers. The soldier ignored her. His eyes were fixed on Crowley, but he spoke to the innkeeper. "We're out of ale here, innkeeper. And my friend the King's Ranger would like a glass."

"Forget it," Crowley said. "I'll have a coffee."

"No. You'll have an ale. Innkeeper?"

The small man behind the bar reached nervously for a large bunch of iron keys hanging on a peg behind him. "I'll fetch another cask from the cellar," he said.

But the soldier, his eyes still fixed on Crowley, held up a hand to stop him. "Stay where you are. The girl can fetch it."

The innkeeper nodded nervously. "Very well." He handed the key ring to the girl. "Get another cask, Glyniss," he said. She looked at him for a moment, unwilling to move from behind the meager shelter of the bar. He nodded at her.

"Go on. Do as I say," he said curtly. "You'll need the bung starter."

She picked up the bung starter, a heavy wooden mallet used to loosen the wooden plug in large casks. Reluctantly, she made her way out from behind the bar and edged past the two soldiers at the table. The one sitting on the bench laughed and pretended to lunge at her. She flinched away from him, with a cry of fright. Then, hurriedly, she went to move past the soldier who had been doing all the talking so far. But as she got within reach, his hand shot out and he grabbed the key ring from her. She hesitated and put her hand out for the keys.

"Please?" she said. But he laughed and held them at arm's length, to the side and out of her reach.

"What? You want these?" he said, and she nodded, biting her lip with fear. He smiled at her and held the keys out, dangling them in front of her face. "Then take them."

As she reached for them, he flipped them quickly over her head to the soldier sitting backward on the bench. He caught them, laughed and stood up, swaying slightly as the girl moved to him.

"Please. I need the keys."

"Of course." He grinned and flipped them back to the soldier in front of Crowley. As she turned, her face showing her anguish, the soldier shoved her with his boot so that she stumbled forward, fetching up against his beefy companion.

"Oho! Think you can throw yourself at me and charm them from me, do you?" He tried to plant a kiss on her cheek, but she twisted her head away from him. He laughed again.

In the five years of Crowley's apprenticeship, his biggest struggle had been to overcome and control his too-quick temper. "It's that red hair of yours," Pritchard used to say. "Never knew a redhead who didn't have a temper."

Now, after listening to and accepting the mockery from the oafish soldier, he felt the familiar boiling-over sensation in his chest. He grabbed the man's arm and twisted it painfully, forcing his grip loose from the girl, who moved quickly to stand behind Crowley. The soldier's face blazed with rage now.

"Why, you pipsqueak! I'll break you in half!"

He swung a wild roundhouse blow at Crowley, who ducked easily under it. Then, putting all the force of his shoulder behind it, Crowley planted a short, power-laden jab into the man's soft belly.

There was an agonized grunt of escaping breath as the soldier doubled over. He clawed at the front of Crowley's jacket, trying to support himself, but the Ranger stepped back out of reach. Unfortunately, he had forgotten that one of the heavy timber columns that supported the ceiling beams was close behind him. He backed into it and stumbled, his concentration broken for a few seconds.

Before he could recover, the other two soldiers were upon him. One of them forced him back against the pillar with a heavy dagger at his throat. The other stripped the longbow from his shoulder and threw it across the room. It clattered off one of the tables onto the floor.

The first man had staggered to his feet again, still clutching his belly and wheezing painfully.

"You little sewer rat!" he spat at the Ranger. Then he nodded to the man who had thrown Crowley's longbow away. "Tie his hands!"

Crowley, the dagger still at his throat, could offer no resistance as his arms were dragged backward and his hands were tied behind the rough wooden pillar. He stood unmoving as the heavily built soldier stepped forward and took the dagger from his companion's hand. He moved it from its position against his throat until it was touching his nose.

"Now, what shall we do with you, King's Ranger?" he said. "I think we might just cut your nose off. That'll teach you not to stick it in our business."

The girl gave another cry of fear at his words and his cruel smile widened slightly.

"Yes. I think that's what we'll do. What do you think, boys?"

Before either of them could reply, another voice responded.

"I think you should turn him loose."

2

THE VOICE WAS DEEP AND CONFIDENT, WITH A DISTINCTIVE Hibernian accent. Crowley swiveled his eyes in the speaker's direction. The stranger from the back of the room had risen from his table and moved toward them. In his hands was an enormous longbow, similar to the one that had been stripped from Crowley. There was an arrow on the string. So far, the stranger hadn't drawn it back, but he held the weapon with such easy familiarity that Crowley guessed he could draw, sight and shoot in the space of a heartbeat.

The knife was withdrawn from Crowley's face and the soldier turned in a crouch toward the Hibernian. Instantly, the bow came up and there was a slight rasp of wood on wood as the arrow went back to full draw. The soldier found himself staring at instant, razor-edged death.

"You don't want to shoot me," he said. All his former sarcasm and anger had gone and now his voice had a telltale quaver in it. The bowman raised an eyebrow quizzically. The other two soldiers were spread out to either side of their leader. Their swords were drawn. Crowley could tell they were trying to gauge their chances of reaching the man and cutting him down before he could shoot.

"And why's that, would you tell me?" The words were delivered with that Hibernian lilt. There was a sense of amused mockery behind it.

"I'm one of Baron Morgarath's men-at-arms, on official duty . . ."

"You mean it's your official duty to get drunk and annoy people in taverns?" the stranger asked sardonically.

The soldier frowned, not sure how to answer that question. After a brief moment's hesitation, he blustered on. "If you kill me, you'll be flogged and flayed and hung."

The stranger pursed his lips thoughtfully. Crowley had been assessing the bow as the two men talked. Its draw weight had to be at least eighty pounds, he thought. Yet the dark-haired Hibernian had been holding it at full draw for some moments now, with never a sign of wavering or shaking. Crowley wondered how long he could sustain this stalemate.

"And what's the penalty if I just hurt you a great deal?" the stranger asked.

The soldier's eyes came together in a puzzled frown. "What—?" he began. But at that instant, the stranger lowered his point of aim and shot him through the left calf.

The man let out a high-pitched scream of shock and pain as agony lanced through his leg. He looked down in horror to see that the arrow had gone clean through the muscle and the leaf-shaped broadhead was protruding out the other side. His leg gave out under him and he collapsed to the floor.

His companions stood in stunned surprise for a moment. Then they surged forward. The stranger tossed his bow behind him and drew what appeared to be a short, heavy-bladed sword from beneath his cloak. With a start of surprise, Crowley recognized it as a saxe knife—identical to the one he wore at his waist. The first soldier slashed at the stranger, but with the low ceiling of the inn, it was a cramped, ineffectual blow, with little power behind it. The stranger flicked it aside easily, and as the soldier met no solid resistance and stumbled forward, he slammed a left hook into his jaw, sending him reeling back into his companion, the sword dropping from his grasp.

The second man cursed and shoved his comrade aside, then moved forward, swinging a horizontal stroke at the Hibernian.

Steel rang on steel as the Hibernian blocked the stroke. At the same time, Crowley felt his own saxe knife sliding from its scabbard. He looked around to see that the girl had drawn it and was cutting through the rope that bound his hands.

Again, the two blades rang and screeched together. Crowley nodded his thanks to the girl and took the bung starter from her unresisting hand.

"Thanks," he said. He stepped up behind the soldier who was preparing another stroke at the Hibernian. The dark-haired man watched his opponent with a look of amused disdain. Seeing the soldier's clumsy sword work, Crowley realized that the Hibernian could have simply moved in and driven his saxe into the man's body as he deflected the blade.

He wasted no further time thinking about it but swung the bung starter overhand and slammed it against the back of the soldier's skull. The soldier gave a faint cry and his knees sagged. He crashed, senseless, facedown into the sawdust that was spread on the floor.

Crowley looked up and met the stranger's dark eyes.

"Thank you," the Hibernian said, returning the saxe knife to its scabbard. He nodded at the unconscious man on the floor between them. "I wasn't sure what I was going to do with him."

Crowley smiled. "I'm sure you'd have thought of something," he said. "But the bung starter was conveniently at hand."

The Hibernian looked at the heavy wooden mallet.

"A bung starter, eh? It certainly stopped our friend here." He said it without any hint of a smile. Then he glanced to where his first attacker was slowly recovering, dragging himself on hands and knees to where his sword had fallen by one of the tables. He held out his hand. "May I?"

Crowley handed him the mallet and the stranger stepped over the unconscious man to where the second soldier had just taken hold of his sword. The stranger put his foot on the blade, jamming the soldier's fingers between the hilt and the floor. As the man yelped with pain, the Hibernian thumped him on the head with the bung starter. Crowley winced at the impact as the man crashed unconscious to the floor.

"Was that really necessary?" he asked. The Hibernian looked up at him. Again, there was no hint of a smile in those dark eyes.

"No. But it was really satisfying." The Hibernian held the bung starter out to the startled serving girl, who had watched proceedings in wide-eyed disbelief.

"I think we could use that ale now, Glyniss," he said. She nodded wordlessly, then turned away and headed for the cellar, looking back over her shoulder at him as she went. He made a gentle shooing motion to hurry her along.

Crowley held out his right hand. "Thanks for lending a hand," he said. "I'm rather fond of this nose."

"There's a lot to be fond of," the stranger replied, still deadpan. Crowley squinted down the feature in question. He liked to think of his nose as noble and hawk-shaped. Aquiline, someone had once suggested. In more honest moments, he admitted that it was a little on the large side. He realized that he was standing, cross-eyed, inspecting his nose while the other man watched him with a steady gaze. He recovered his composure and held out his hand.

"Anyway, thanks," he said. "I'm Crowley Meratyn, Ranger of Hogarth Fief."

The stranger took his hand and shook it.

"Halt O'Ca . . . ," he began, then corrected himself. "Halt. My name is Halt. I'm traveling through."

Crowley gave no sign that he had noticed the hesitation. He smiled. "I take it you're from Hibernia?" he asked, and the stranger nodded.

"Clonmel," he said. "I decided it was time to widen my horizons."

A weak voice from the floor interrupted them. "Please, Ranger, this leg is hurting awful bad."

It was the overweight soldier who had started all the trouble. He had drawn himself into a sitting position against one of the table legs and was trying to staunch the flow of blood from the arrow wound in his leg.

"I imagine it is," Crowley said. He knelt beside the man, examining the wound, then looked up at Halt. "Did you want to reuse this arrow?"

"Not the shaft. Break it off. I'll reuse the head and the fletching."

The easiest way to remove a through-and-through shot like this was to break the arrow off close to the entry wound and pull the shortened shaft through. The barb on the broadhead meant that it couldn't be withdrawn backward, of course.

Quickly, Crowley snapped off the shaft and pulled it free. He ignored the man's whimpering as he did so. Once the arrow was out, blood flowed steadily from both entry and exit wounds and he hurriedly dressed them, cleaning them with hot water the innkeeper brought from a kettle hanging over the fire. He bandaged the leg firmly, then washed his hands in the bowl of hot water and stood up.

"That should hold him for a while," he said. He glanced at the man's two unconscious companions, then busied himself fastening their hands behind their backs with thumb cuffs. Halt looked on with interest.

"They're a handy idea," he said. He helped Crowley drag the two men into a sitting position, leaning against one of the long benches.

"I've been wondering . . . ," Crowley said as they worked. "I watched the way you handled yourself. You could have killed these two without a lot of trouble. And Weeping Beauty over there as well." He gestured to the injured soldier, sitting hunched and whimpering with pain over his bandaged leg.

Halt shrugged. "I'm new in the country," he said. "Thought it might be awkward to explain two or three dead bodies to their baron. Barons can be very short-tempered about that sort of thing, I've found."

"That's true. Still, I'll see what he has to say when I take these three back to him with my report."

Halt raised an eyebrow. "You're going to take them back to this Baron, Morg . . ." He hesitated over the name.

"Morgarath," Crowley corrected him. "Yes. He's arrogant and overbearing, but I think even he will have to take notice of an official report and complaint by a King's Ranger."

"Well, if you don't mind, I might come along and help you keep an eye on these three. I'd be interested to see what sort of man this Morgarath is."

"I could tell you," Crowley said heavily, "but it's probably better you see for yourself. Come along by all means. Castle Gorlan is a day and half's ride from here and there are a few things I want to talk to you about."

Halt nodded. "I'll look forward to it," he said. Then he turned as he heard the cellar door scrape open on stiff hinges. "And here's Glyniss with our ale, right on time."

3

THEY RODE ON LATER THAT AFTERNOON, AFTER CROWLEY HAD eaten. He removed the thumb cuffs from the two men and instead tied all three men's hands firmly in front of them so they could ride more easily. He roped their horses together and tethered a lead rope to one of them as well, just in case the men were tempted to try to escape.

His dark mood of the morning had left him now and he felt positively cheerful as they rode. Halt glanced up at him as he began to whistle a jaunty folk tune.

"What are you doing?" he asked, a dark frown forming on his brow.

Crowley shrugged and grinned at him. "I'm in a good mood," he explained.

Halt's eyebrow went up. Crowley had noticed that the Hibernian seemed to use that facial reaction quite often. "So you're in a good mood. Why are you making that shrieking sound?"

"I'm whistling. I'm whistling a jaunty tune."

"That's not whistling. It's shrieking. At best, it's shrilling," Halt replied.

Crowley turned in the saddle to regard him with some dignity.

"I'll have you know, my whistling has been widely praised in Hogarth Fief."

"A dour place it must be if people consider that shrill noise to be musical."

The overweight soldier with the leg wound began whining with pain, interrupting their discussion of what was and what was not considered good music. The three soldiers were riding in front of Crowley and Halt. Halt urged his horse forward a few paces to catch up with the man.

"First it's his shrilling, now it's your whining," he said. "Will this noise never stop? What's your trouble?"

"My leg hurts," the soldier whined.

"Of course it does," Halt told him. "I put an arrow through it. Did you expect it not to hurt?"

The soldier was taken aback by this pragmatic answer. Crowley, listening, smiled to himself. From what he'd seen of Halt so far, if the soldier expected sympathy, he was talking to the wrong man entirely.

"I need to rest," the man complained. "This riding is jolting my leg."

"No," Halt told him. "You need to shut up. But if you can't bring yourself to do that, I'll do something to take your mind off that leg of yours."

The soldier looked at him fearfully. He was reasonably sure that Halt was not proposing to alleviate his pain. "What'll you do?" he asked.

"I'll shoot you through the other leg," Halt told him. "That'll spread the pain around."

"You'd shoot a helpless man?" The soldier cringed away in his saddle as far as he could without losing his balance and falling off.

Halt regarded him steadily before he replied. "Don't ever forget that you threatened to cut off my friend's nose while his hands were tied behind him. That's not likely to win you any sympathy from me."

The soldier opened his mouth to reply, looked at Halt and shut it again with a slightly audible *clop*.

Halt, satisfied that he had got the message, nodded once and reined in his horse, falling back to ride beside Crowley once more.

The sandy-headed Ranger grinned cheerfully at him. "So I'm your friend, am I?" he asked.

Halt looked straight ahead for a few seconds before replying.

"As long as you don't start whistling again."

They camped that evening in a small clearing beside a stream of fresh, cold water. While Halt disappeared into the woods with his bow, Crowley untied the prisoners one at a time, then refastened their hands behind their backs with thumb cuffs. He sat them beside one another, leaning against a fallen tree. In each of their saddle-bags he found a blanket, and he draped these over the men.

"Aren't you going to give us something to eat?" one of them asked in an aggrieved tone.

Crowley shook his head. "Shouldn't think so. A night without eating won't harm you."

He poured water into a tin cup and let them drink as much as they wanted, however. When he had finished with the men, he lit a fire. He had some potatoes in his cooking kit and he set them to boil in a blackened pot. As the water began to bubble, Halt reappeared carrying a plump rabbit, already skinned and cleaned.

"Just the thing!" Crowley said happily. "Nothing like a fresh rabbit to take away the pangs."

The soldier who had spoken earlier looked up hopefully. "Can we—"

"No," said Halt and Crowley together. They quickly jointed the rabbit, rolled the pieces in flour with a few dried herbs mixed in, and then melted butter in an iron fry pan over the fire. As the floured joints went into the hot butter and began to sizzle, Crowley sighed happily. He enjoyed food.

"Much better way to do it than putting it on a spit over the fire," he commented. "Takes far too long to cook it that way."

When the rabbit pieces were golden and cooked through, Crowley added a heap of greens to the pan, covering it so they would wilt down quickly. Then he and Halt enjoyed their meal together, sitting opposite each other across the campfire in companionable silence. From time to time, one of the prisoners moaned as the delicious smell of fried spiced rabbit drifted to them. Crowley and Halt ignored the sound.

When they finished their meal, they licked the last traces of rabbit, butter and potato from their fingers, then wiped them on the grass. Crowley made coffee and watched as Halt added a large dollop of honey to his cup.

"Doesn't that spoil the taste?" he asked.

Halt looked up at him, considered the question, then replied. "No."

Crowley smiled at the one-word answer. "You don't talk much, do you?"

Again, those dark eyes lifted and met his. "I say what needs to be said."

Crowley shrugged good-naturedly. "Probably a good thing. I tend to talk too much sometimes."

"I'd noticed."

"Does it bother you?" Crowley asked. He felt an instinctive liking for this dark stranger and he sensed that Halt thought well of him in return. Halt shrugged now.

"It keeps you from whistling."

Crowley snorted with laughter at the reply. Halt maintained a bleak and serious facade, but Crowley could detect, deep down, a deadpan vein of humor in the man.

"You said earlier today that you wanted to talk about something," Halt said.

Crowley nodded, gathering his thoughts before he began. "We seem to share a lot of the same skills," he said. "And the same weapons. I noticed you carry a saxe knife and a throwing knife like mine. I wondered where you came by them."

Crowley, of course, carried his two knives in the distinctive Ranger-issue double scabbard. Halt's were in separate scabbards, placed close together on the left side of his belt. He glanced at them now, where the belt was draped over a rock beside the campfire.

"My mentor gave them to me," he said. "He was a Ranger, like you."

Crowley sat up at that piece of information. "A Ranger?" he said. "In Hibernia? What was his name?"

"He called himself Pritchard. He was an amazing man."

"He was indeed," Crowley affirmed, and now it was Halt's turn to look surprised.

"You knew him?"

Crowley nodded eagerly. "I was his apprentice for five years. He taught me everything I know. How did you come to meet him?"

"He turned up at Du . . . Droghela, some three years ago. He took me under his wing and taught me silent movement, knife work, tracking and the rest. I could already shoot, but he tightened up my technique quite a bit."

Crowley noticed the hesitation and correction when Halt mentioned the name of the place where he'd met Pritchard. But he let it pass.

"Yes. He was very big on technique."

"And practice," Halt agreed.

Crowley smiled at the memory of his old teacher. "He had a saying. *An ordinary archer practices until he gets it right. A Ranger—*"

"*Practices until he never gets it wrong.*" Halt finished the saying and they both smiled. They sat in silence for a few moments.

"What became of him?" Crowley asked. "Is he still in . . . Droghela, did you say?"

Halt shook his head. "He moved on. I had some unpleasantness there and I had to leave. I decided to come to Araluen to see if I could contact the Rangers—perhaps join the Corps and complete my training. Pritchard moved on to one of the western kingdoms in Hibernia. He said he was unable to come back here."

Crowley nodded sadly. "That's right. He was hounded out of the country—on a totally trumped-up charge, of course. But sad to say, that's the way the Ranger Corps has become these days. It's all changed for the worse."

"How do you mean?" Halt said. "You seem pretty much like the Rangers that Pritchard told me about."

"I'm glad to hear that," Crowley replied. "But things have changed."

He reached for his quiver. He'd noticed that the fletching on two of his arrows was working loose and he set about repairing them. Halt watched him, then rummaged in his own pack and passed him a fletching jig.

"Here. Use this. It'll make it easier."

"Thanks," said Crowley, stripping the old feathered flights from the shaft. He settled the shaft in the fletching jig, which would hold the shaft and the new flights in place until the glue had set, and began to repair the first arrow. After a minute or two, he addressed Halt's earlier question.

"Things have changed," he repeated. "These days, the Ranger Corps is little more than a social drinking club for lazy young nobles. There's no training, no apprenticeships. You buy your way in now. I'm one of the few remaining Rangers who were properly trained. And they're trying to squeeze me out."

"Why would they do that?" Halt asked.

Crowley shrugged. "I suppose I'm an embarrassment to them. I've just been to Castle Araluen to have my knuckles rapped over a ridiculous complaint. It's happened to others before me. Pritchard was one of the first. But since then, others have been squeezed out as well. I figure there are maybe only a dozen properly trained Rangers left in the Kingdom these days—and we're widely scattered."

"But why? Who would want to destroy such an effective force? Can't the King do something? You're King's Rangers, after all."

Crowley smiled sadly. "The King doesn't know what's going on. And as for who would want to destroy the Rangers, the answer's simple. There's a group of barons, the Royal Council, who have the old King completely under their influence. He's sick and senile and has no idea what's going on. It's my belief that they're maneuvering to take over the throne. They've got him to agree to virtually exile Prince Duncan to the northeast coast. The King is powerless and they're making sure that there is no cohesive group who might support Prince Duncan when it comes time for him to assume the throne."

"Who's behind it all?" Halt asked.

Crowley gestured to the three men tied up a few meters away.

"You'll meet him tomorrow," he said. "I can't prove it, but I'm pretty sure it's Morgarath."

4

Halt reined in his horse as they crested the final rise and Castle Gorlan came into view.

It was spectacular. There was no other word for it. Soaring, graceful towers surmounted by pointed spires thrust high into the sky. The spires themselves had been faced with white marble that gleamed in the midmorning sunshine. Several of the towers were linked by graceful arched walkways, their balustrades finished in ornate carved patterns. The same carved patterns were in evidence on the many balconies that were a feature of the castle.

From a dozen points, long, brightly colored pennants and flags drifted on the light breeze, some of them three to four meters in length.

At the base of the hill in front of them, sloping up to the castle, was a carefully manicured park. The green grass and carefully tended decorative trees were interspersed with white-gleaming, elegant statuary. Paved paths meandered through the park, and there were benches and tables set in bowers among the trees. Freshly painted jousting lists and grandstands stood just outside the main wall and portcullis. The huge castle complex was surrounded by a dry moat, with access via a drawbridge. Currently, the bridge was lowered and the portcullis was open.

"It's something, isn't it?" Crowley said. He crossed his hands on his saddle pommel and leaned forward, easing the stiffness in his back.

"I've never seen anything like it," Halt said. And it was true. He had seen castles before—in fact, he had lived in one most of his life so far. But the castles he was familiar with were grim, heavy buildings, designed for strength and impregnability, not sheer beauty as this one was. Yet even as he had the thought, he was studying the walls and noting their thickness—disguised by the graceful lines. Gorlan would be a tough nut to crack, he thought, in spite of its almost ethereal beauty.

"It even puts Castle Araluen in the shade," Crowley continued. "And that takes some doing, believe me. Pity that it belongs to Morgarath," he added, a sour expression on his face.

Halt glanced at him but said nothing. He'd decided he'd make his own judgment of the Baron of Gorlan.

He didn't have long to wait. They rode down to the castle, Crowley's rank as a Ranger gaining them admission. He delivered their prisoners to the guardroom and requested an audience with the Baron. They were shown into a small anteroom in the keep, adjacent to the Great Hall where Morgarath conducted his official business. Crowley frowned at that. It was his first time inside the walls of Gorlan and the practice of doing business in a large audience hall smacked of would-be royal behavior. Most barons maintained smaller offices where they met with their staff and with visiting officers such as Rangers. Morgarath's vast audience hall was reminiscent of the similar room maintained and used by the King at Castle Araluen. Or more correctly these days, Crowley thought, by the Royal Council.

They were kept waiting for forty minutes—little enough, the Ranger thought, since they had arrived unannounced—then shown into the massive hall.

The ceiling was high, supported by vaulted arches set on buttresses. Down the eastern side of the wall, there were windows of multicolored glass. The sun shone through them, creating exotic patterns on the interior of the hall. Altogether, the Great Hall was as impressive as the exterior of the building.

They entered through tall double doors, which were opened by men-at-arms wearing the lightning bolt sword device that Halt had seen on the three men in the tavern. Morgarath sat at the far end of the hall, in a large, thronelike chair made of blackwood, on a dais that placed it a meter higher than its surroundings. Crowley and Halt marched together down the length of the room, their soft boots making little sound on the flagstone floor. Just short of the dais, the floor surface changed to one of marble tiles set in geometric patterns.

Taking his cue from Crowley, Halt stopped at the foot of the dais. Crowley stood at attention. Halt's stance was more relaxed as he studied the Baron of Gorlan Fief.

Morgarath sat casually, one leg draped over an arm of the chair. He was toying with a broad-bladed dagger, admiring the silver-chased hilt and crosspiece. He looked up at them as they stopped. His expression was one of total disinterest.

Even seated, it was apparent that Morgarath was an exceptionally tall man. He was handsome, with a longish face and a strong jaw. He wore no beard or mustache but his hair was long and straight. It was a pale blond color—a color that would probably go white rather than gray as the man aged. His skin was pale and he was dressed entirely in black, throwing the pale skin and light-colored hair into stark relief. A heavy silver chain hung around his neck.

But his most surprising features were his eyes. With coloring such as his, Halt would have expected pale eyes—blue or almost colorless. But these eyes were black—deep black, so that it was impossible to see where the irises ended and the pupils began.

Dead eyes, Halt thought to himself. He had no idea where the thought came from. It simply appeared in his mind as he studied the Baron.

Morgarath put the dagger down on a small side table by his chair. His jogged his foot up and down as he studied the two men before him. Their rough, practical traveling clothing and equipment was at odds with the elegance of his hall, and he frowned at them as if they had somehow defiled the beauty of Castle Gorlan.

"Your name?" he said to Crowley. His voice was deep and resonant. He didn't seem to speak loudly, but the voice filled the room. Crowley shifted uncomfortably. The Baron's disapproval was painfully obvious.

"Crowley, sir. King's Ranger Number Seventeen, attached to Hogarth Fief."

"The correct mode of address, Ranger, is *my lord*. Not *sir*."

Crowley flushed red. Morgarath was wrong. As a Ranger holding the King's warrant, Crowley was a senior officer and was entitled to address barons as *sir*. Only the King, or members of the royal family, merited the title *my lord*, and it was usually reserved for formal occasions. Morgarath seemed to have an exaggerated idea of his own rank. There was no point, however, in arguing with the man here in his own castle.

"Apologies, my lord," he said curtly. Morgarath held his gaze for several seconds, measuring him. He nodded to himself and turned those black eyes on Halt, dismissing the sandy-haired Ranger for the time being.

"And you are . . . ?" He was puzzled by the Ranger's companion. He seemed to be equipped as a King's Ranger, with a longbow and two knives on his belt. Yet there were small differences. His cloak was dark green, all one shade. It wasn't mottled green and gray like the Ranger's cloak. And the knives were in two separate scabbards, pushed close together.

"My name is Halt." The Hibernian accent was unmistakable.

Morgarath raised his eyebrows. "Just Halt? No second name? Were your parents too poor to afford one? Or do you not know who they were?"

Halt regarded the man without reacting to the implied insult in his words. "My apologies. My full name is Halt . . . Arratay." On the spur of the moment, he came up with the pseudonym that he would use for the rest of his life. He smiled inwardly at the mockery inherent in the name—mockery that Morgarath failed to recognize. "Arratay" was Halt's pronunciation of the Gallic word *arretez*, which meant "Halt." In other words, he had just told the sneering nobleman that his name was Halt Halt.

"I'm a forester from the court of Lord Dennis O'Mara, Duke of Droghela County, in the Kingdom of Clon—"

He got no further as Morgarath held up a dismissive hand. "I asked for your name, Hibernian. Not your life story." Halt bowed slightly, a mere inclination of the head. Morgarath turned his attention back to Crowley. "Now what's this all about, Ranger? I believe you have arrested three of my men?"

"That's right, sir. They were drunk and causing a disturbance in a tavern, terrorizing the innkeeper and his serving girl."

"Terrorizing them?" Morgarath said, his eyebrows rising. "Threatening their lives? Slicing off parts of their bodies with sharp knives? Torturing them with red-hot pokers?"

Crowley shifted uncomfortably. "Perhaps *terrorizing* is too strong a word for it, sir . . . my lord. Intimidating them might be a better way of putting it. They were bullying them and causing a disturbance. The girl was frightened, sir."

"It sounds like nothing more than high spirits to me, Ranger."

"You could look at it that way, my lord. But when I told them to stop, one of them threatened me with a knife. They tied my hands and he threatened to cut off my nose."

"After you struck him, I believe."

"I hit him, yes. But only in retaliation. He was roughing up the girl and I pulled him away. He swung a punch at me. I ducked and hit him. Then his companions grabbed me and he drew a dagger, then threatened to cut off my nose."

"So how did you escape this terrible peril? What persuaded him to stop?"

"I shot him," Halt said, interrupting. Morgarath's sneering was beginning to annoy him. The Baron now turned his mocking, wide-eyed gaze back to Halt.

"You shot him? Where did you shoot him?"

"In the tavern," Halt said, keeping his face completely straight. The sally cut through Morgarath's affected air of bored disdain and Halt saw a sudden flare of anger behind those black eyes. The man was obviously toying with them. Halt was sure that, while they had been kept waiting, he had already sought a full report of the events in the inn.

"I meant," Morgarath said, with icy precision, "whereabouts on his body did you shoot him?"

"My apologies. I shot him through the leg. He said you'd be angry at me if I killed him."

Morgarath locked eyes with the Hibernian for several seconds. Halt's calm eyes met his gaze without wavering. Eventually, it was Morgarath who looked away, feigning a lack of interest.

"Then it was as well you didn't kill him," he said.

"I thought so, my lord."

"Still, even a leg wound seems a severe punishment for simply annoying an innkeeper and a serving girl."

Crowley cleared his throat and interrupted. "Excuse me, my lord. The men's treatment of the innkeeper and his girl was insufferable. But the fact that they laid hands on and threatened a King's officer is a far more serious matter."

"They offended your dignity, did they, Ranger?" Morgarath sneered.

Crowley shook his head. "It's not a personal matter with me, sir. They showed disrespect to the uniform and the Corps and they threatened a superior officer."

"And you expect me to punish them, is that it?"

Crowley shrugged. "I thought it best to report the matter to you for action, sir. They're your men, after all, so it's better to deal with it unofficially, as it were. Otherwise I'd have to report it to Ranger headquarters."

Morgarath's brows lowered. That was the problem, of course. He had no idea how this Crowley was regarded by his superiors. The idiots who ran the Ranger Corps these days were an arrogant bunch. Even though they were technically aligned with Morgarath and the other members of the Royal Council, they tended to stand on their dignity if their pride was offended. If they felt their organization had been treated with disrespect, they could demand all sorts of retribution. And ineffectual as they might be as fighting men, they had a lot of influence. They belonged to some of the more important families in the Kingdom and Morgarath wasn't yet in a strong enough position to alienate them. He forced a smile.

"I appreciate your discretion, Ranger Crowley. As you say, it's better to keep these matters among ourselves. I'll have them flogged."

Crowley was startled by the words. "No need for that, sir! I think demotion and a few months of unpleasant duties would be enough."

"You're too softhearted, Ranger. I think a flogging is merited.

Fifty lashes at least. After all, they offended the Ranger Corps, and we can't have that. What do you think, Halt Arratay?"

Halt had to force himself not to smile at Morgarath's unwitting use of the ridiculous repetitive name. He sensed that the Baron, by proposing such a cruel punishment, was attempting to keep Crowley off balance and to undermine his resolve. He was playing a sadistic mind game. Crowley was a decent man and the thought that he had caused three men to have their flesh torn from their backs would sicken him. Halt, however, felt no such qualms.

"Flog them by all means, my lord. A good flogging never hurt anyone—certainly not the flogger, anyway."

Crowley glanced quickly at him. Halt gave him an almost imperceptible nod. Crowley wasn't sure what Halt was doing, but elected to follow his lead. "As you see fit, my lord," he said.

Morgarath considered the two men before him in silence for some time. Then he stroked his chin slowly.

"Quite so. As I see fit. Very well. You can rest assured that I will see to their punishment—and it will be appropriate to the crime they committed. That's all. Get out of here."

He made a shooing gesture with one languid hand and turned his gaze from them, picking up the dagger and examining the design work on its hilt once more. Halt and Crowley turned and walked quickly away. For a moment, Crowley was inclined to back away from the dais, then he took his lead from Halt and turned smartly, putting his back to the tall black-clad figure on the throne. As they walked away in step, Morgarath abandoned his feigned interest in the dagger and stared after them, his gaze unblinking. The Ranger was predictable, he thought—one of the last of a rapidly disappearing kind. He was of little interest to Morgarath.

The Hibernian was a different matter. He was bold, resourceful and difficult to cow. Surrounded by yes-men and toadies as he was,

Morgarath had need of a few strong-willed lieutenants. The Hibernian could be a useful person to have on his side.

Crowley and Halt spent the night at Castle Gorlan, eating in the main hall with the castle senior staff and knights from the Battle-school. For the most part, the locals ignored them. Morgarath chose to eat in his own quarters and made no appearance.

They were assigned comfortable guest chambers in one of the towers. The rooms were big, airy and well furnished. After he had blown out his candle, Halt lay, eyes open, thinking over events of the day. Long after midnight, he heard a light rap at the door. He slipped out of bed. His belt with the two scabbards was looped over the headboard beside his pillow. He drew the saxe knife and moved quietly to the door. Opening it, he found a castle servant, who recoiled in fear as his candle's light reflected on the heavy blade in the Hibernian's hand.

"Lord Morgarath wishes to speak to you," the servant said nervously.

"Wait here," Halt told him. He dressed hurriedly, debated whether to leave his knives behind, then shrugged and buckled on the heavy leather belt, replacing the saxe in its scabbard. He followed the servant downstairs to a lower level. They crossed to another staircase, this one leading to the central tower, and the man led him upward again. After four flights, they came to Morgarath's private quarters. The servant knocked apprehensively on the massive door. Faintly, they heard Morgarath's voice.

"Come in."

They entered. The Baron was sitting behind a massive desk, leafing through sheaves of parchment. One solitary candle lit the room. Shadows pressed in around the black-clad form and Halt stopped in front of the desk. Morgarath glanced at the servant.

"Get out," he said, and the man scuttled away. Halt was put in mind of a cockroach hurrying for cover when a light was shone upon it. He heard the door close behind the man. Morgarath had kept his gaze fixed on Halt while the servant left. Halt returned the scrutiny.

The Baron waved him to a chair.

"Sit down," he said, and as Halt complied, Morgarath leaned forward on his elbows, pushing the candle closer to the Hibernian so he could see his face more clearly.

"You interest me, Halt," he said finally.

Halt shrugged. "I'm not a very interesting person, my lord," he said evenly, but Morgarath shook his head.

"Oh, but you are. You're a man who knows his own mind, and who's not afraid to speak it. I value that. You're resourceful and, from what I've heard, you're a skilled fighter."

Halt said nothing. The silence between them grew. Finally, Morgarath broke it.

"I could use a man like you."

A faint smile touched the corners of Halt's mouth. "I'm not sure I like the idea of being used, my lord."

Morgarath waved the statement aside. "A figure of speech. Let me put it another way. I'd like to have you working for me. I pay well, and as you can see, conditions here at Gorlan are extremely pleasant. A lot of men would be honored to work for me."

"Regretfully, sir, I don't think I'm worthy of that honor." There was no trace of regret in Halt's voice.

"I find that those who aren't for me are usually against me, Halt," Morgarath said. Halt recognized the warning implicit in the words, but he was unmoved. He remained silent, meeting Morgarath's basilisk stare without any sign of wavering or uncertainty.

Morgarath tried one last time. "I'd rather have you as an ally than as an enemy," he said.

Halt stood abruptly, pushing the chair back with a scrape of wood on wood.

"That choice may not be yours," he said. And before the furious Baron could respond, Halt turned on his heel and left the room.

5

CROWLEY AND HALT LEFT THE CASTLE THE FOLLOWING MORNING.
Halt made no mention of his late-night meeting with Morgarath
and they rode in silence for several minutes. Finally, inevitably, it was
Crowley who spoke first.

"I wonder what he'll do to them?"

Halt glanced sidelong at him. "Who'll do to who?" he said, ignoring strict grammar. Halt was never a stickler for rules of any kind.

"Morgarath. I wonder how he'll punish those three men-at-
arms we brought in."

Halt's lip curled in disdain. "I doubt he'll do anything to them.
I suspect they were throwing their weight around with his full
approval."

Crowley frowned at the statement. "Why would he encourage
them to do that?"

"He's a tyrant. Tyrants like their subjects to live in fear. Helps
keep them in line."

Crowley nodded sadly. "I suppose you're right." He sighed
deeply and Halt looked at him again.

"What's the trouble? You're normally such a cheery fellow."

Crowley allowed himself a faint grin at that description, coming as it did from the grim, unsmiling figure riding beside him.

"I was just thinking what a terrible state the Kingdom is in," he said. "Men like Morgarath treating their own subjects so badly, the Royal Council doing their best to undermine the King, and the Ranger Corps nothing more than a group of vain, indolent loafers. I wonder where it will all end?"

"You're a Ranger, and you're not vain," Halt pointed out. "You may be indolent, of course. I can't be sure about that. And you said there were others like you." He was obviously trying to cajole Crowley out of his gloomy mood. But the Ranger shook his head and made a hopeless little gesture.

"Only a few," he said. "A dozen at most. And we're widely scattered. The Corps Commandant sees to that. They'll get rid of us one by one, with trumped-up charges and accusations—just as they did with Pritchard and the others."

"Why not get in first?" Halt said. "Get the others together and fight back. From what you say about the current commanders, they wouldn't put up much of a fight."

"I think that's what Morgarath is hoping we'll do," Crowley said. "He'd like to see the last traces of the old Ranger Corps totally destroyed. If we rebelled against our own leadership, technically we'd be rebelling against the King."

"It's a problem," Halt said thoughtfully. "Band together and they accuse you of treason, stay separate and they can pick you off one at a time."

"Well, it's not your problem, anyway. Have you any idea what you might do?"

Halt shrugged. "As I told you, I had a vague idea of joining the Rangers. But that doesn't seem like an option now. I suppose I'll head south and east and cross over to Gallica."

"Well, we can ride together for a while longer. The highway south is farther along this way. I'll be glad of some cheerful company."

"First time anyone's said that about me," Halt replied.

They came to the fork in the road some forty minutes later. The south highway branched off to the left, heading across rolling countryside and farmland. The north road, the road Crowley would follow, entered a large forest half a kilometer away. The two men shook hands.

"Thanks for your help," Crowley said.

"And my cheerful company," Halt added, straight-faced.

Crowley smiled. "Yes. That too. I hope things work out for you."

"Same to you," Halt said, and the Ranger shrugged with mock cheerfulness.

"Oh, I'll be fine, I'm sure."

There was an awkward pause. The two men had enjoyed each other's company and each sensed the other was a kindred spirit. But they didn't have a long history of friendship to smooth out the parting. Eventually, Halt broke the silence and turned his horse south.

"Well . . . I suppose I'll be seeing you," he said, and Crowley nodded, raising one hand in salute.

"Be seeing you."

They rode away from each other and Halt considered how ridiculous their final words had been. We won't be seeing each other, he thought. Why do we say we will?

His path led down a long incline, then up a slope on the other side. He reached the crest and stopped to turn in his saddle, looking after Crowley. But the Ranger had already disappeared into the thick forest that straddled the road. Halt pursed his lips. He had a vague feeling that he should have offered help to the Ranger. He had a sense that he was letting Crowley down. He wasn't sure what else he could have done, but the uneasy feeling remained.

He was about to urge his horse on again when he remembered his fletching jig. He had lent it to Crowley on the first night they were camped and he realized now that the Ranger hadn't returned it. He could manage without it, but the process of fletching an arrow was much more time-consuming without it. He clicked his tongue and turned his horse, setting him to a canter, retracing his path and heading after Crowley.

The gray had an easy, long-striding gait, and they covered the distance to the forest in short time. They rode into the dim coolness under the trees. Over the years, branches had grown across the path from each side so that the road resembled a green shaded tunnel. The road turned sharply to the right a few hundred meters ahead. There was no sign of Crowley. He must have covered more ground than Halt had expected. He tapped the horse with his heels, urging more speed from him. The hoofbeats were cushioned by the soft surface of the road under the trees. Shaded constantly by the over-hanging foliage, the road had never dried out and hardened. In addition, a thick carpet of leaves had built up over the passage of the years.

As they neared the turn in the road, Halt became aware of a faint sound—the sliding, scraping clash of steel on steel. He felt a tightening of apprehension in his stomach. He slipped the bow from his shoulder and flicked back a corner of his cloak to leave his quiver unencumbered.

The horse's rear hooves skidded slightly on the damp ground as they made the right-hand turn around the bend in the road.

Sixty meters away, Crowley was backed against a large oak tree, surrounded by a group of armed men. As he took in the scene, Halt counted four attackers, with a fifth a few meters away, out of the fight, on his knees and crumpled over, holding his side. Crowley's horse was limping awkwardly on the far side of the road.

Without conscious thought, Halt's hand flew to his quiver and sent two arrows on their way in the space of a heartbeat. The first inkling that Crowley's attackers had of his presence was when two of their number cried out in pain as the black-shafted arrows drove into them, slicing through their chain mail as if it were no more than linen. After the first cry, one fell and lay silent. The other continued to moan in pain, crawling on hands and knees away from the scene of combat.

The others turned to see what had happened to their comrades. It was a fatal mistake. Crowley lunged at one and the saxe knife bit deep into the man's body. The other was sent flying as Halt's horse slammed its shoulder into him. The man thudded to the ground, skidding on the damp leaves, then lay still.

Halt reined in and swung down from the saddle, dropping the bow and drawing his saxe. There was a smear of blood on Crowley's forehead.

"Are you all right?" Halt asked.

The Ranger nodded breathlessly. "Thanks to you, yes," he said. He glanced down at the man he had just run through. He was sprawled on his back, eyes open, staring sightlessly at the sky. "Recognize him?"

Halt looked down. He saw the familiar lightning bolt symbol on the man's surcoat, then looked more closely at his face. It was the stoutly built man he had shot through the leg at the tavern. He looked quickly at the others. The man doubled over on his knees, crying in pain, had also been in the tavern, as had the first of the attackers Halt had shot.

"Morgarath has a strange idea of punishment," he said.

Crowley gave him a tired smile. "Oh, I don't know. It certainly didn't do them any good in the long run. What should we do with them, do you think?" He gestured at the three surviving wounded men.

"Leave them," Halt said briefly. "No use taking them back to Morgarath. He obviously sent them after you. Five of them," he added. "He thought they'd need more than three this time."

"Probably thought you'd still be with me," Crowley said, and Halt nodded thoughtfully.

"You realize that Morgarath can't afford to let you live now, don't you?" he said. "He'll probably trump up some charges against you—say that you were responsible for the death of two of his loyal soldiers."

"That thought had occurred to me."

"Then come with me. We'll head for Gallica. There's always work for good fighting men there. And I can see you're a good fighting man." Halt indicated the bodies scattered across the road. But Crowley was already shaking his head before Halt finished speaking.

"I was thinking about what you said—about organizing the remaining Rangers and fighting back. I've decided that's what I'm going to do."

"You're not worried about being declared a traitor?" Halt asked.

"I'm going northeast to find Prince Duncan. As the heir to the throne, if he'll give me a royal warrant to assemble the other remaining Rangers and re-form the Corps, I can't be charged with treason. And he might find it useful to have a dozen or so highly trained men in his service."

Halt considered Crowley's words for a few seconds, then nodded. "That might be your best course," he said. "And I like the idea of your re-forming the Ranger Corps. Mind you, a dozen men isn't a lot."

"A dozen Rangers," Crowley corrected him. "And it may not be a lot, but it's a start." He paused, then added, "It'd be thirteen if you'd consider joining us. I'm sure Prince Duncan could be persuaded to give you a commission in the Corps."

Halt shook his head, a frown bringing the dark eyebrows together. "I don't place a great deal of trust in princes," he said.

"This one you can trust. He's a good man," Crowley told him. But still the Hibernian was reluctant.

"They're all good men until they get a taste of power."

"Not this one. You can trust Duncan, believe me." A long, steady look passed between them.

"So you say," Halt said.

Crowley nodded emphatically. "Yes. I do. Do you trust me?"

Now Halt looked deep into Crowley's hazel eyes, and he saw nothing there but honesty and dedication—no sign of deceit or underhandedness. He recalled his earlier moment of unease, when he felt that somehow he was letting Crowley down by simply riding away. The sandy-haired Ranger sensed that Halt was wavering.

"All our ancillary services are still in place—our horse trainers and breeders and armorers," he said. "They're just waiting for the chance to be reactivated. In a few years, we could build up a force to be reckoned with. I'd be happy to help you complete your training— not that there's much you have to learn. You're already a far better shot than I am."

Still Halt said nothing, and a mischievous smile crept over Crowley's face as he played his final card.

"And wouldn't you like a chance to tweak Morgarath's skinny nose for him?" he asked.

In spite of himself, Halt smiled as well. A faint smile, it was true. But a smile nonetheless. From him, that was the equivalent of helpless mirth.

"Now, that is an attractive offer," he said, and this time Crowley laughed out loud.

"Then you'll join us?"

"You say this Duncan is a man to trust?"

"I do."

"And a leader a man would be proud to follow?"

"I certainly do. You have my word on that."

There was a long pause. Crowley sensed he had said enough and waited for Halt to make his decision. Finally, the Hibernian nodded slowly.

"Then . . . why not? I've never really been fond of Gallica."

He held out his hand and Crowley took it. They shook hands, each man noting the other's firm and positive grip. Each man sensing that this was the beginning of a long and remarkable partnership.

"Welcome to the Corps," Crowley said.

THE WOLF

1

THE WOLF WAS A BIG ONE.

He was a full-grown male in the prime of his life who should have been the dominant male of a pack. But some months prior, he had been caught by the right forefoot in a trap set by hunters. The steel jaws held him firmly, so that no matter how hard he struggled and twisted, he could not get free. And since freedom to a wolf is life itself, he had taken the only course open to him. He had gnawed at the broken limb until he severed the remaining flesh and tendons, leaving his foot and half the leg still in the trap. Then, trailing blood, he had limped awkwardly into the deepest part of the forest, finding a secure hiding place under a large rock outcrop, overgrown with shrubs and bushes, where he could wait to recover.

Or to die.

Racked with pain and trembling with shock, he had made not a sound. Instinct told him that the sound of whimpering or crying was the sound of an animal that was injured and vulnerable. Similarly, he made no attempt to rejoin the pack he had belonged to—the pack where he would have become leader within the next few months. He knew the injury would see him driven out by the others. Wolves are normally sociable and affectionate pack members, but the rule of survival of the fittest is a harsh one, and an injured pack member would be a liability—unable to participate in hunting and putting the pack itself in danger. He knew he would be driven out, or even killed, by the others if he approached them.

So he lay silently in his hiding place, licking constantly at the dreadful wound until the bleeding stopped and he recovered, although the pain of the severed leg never left him. But his former speed and agility had forsaken him and he faced another potential danger—starvation.

He couldn't hunt as he used to. He had tried to chase a small deer when the leg stopped bleeding. By then, his flanks were gaunt and the ribs were visible beneath his thick coat. But the deer evaded him with apparent contempt, springing to one side to avoid his clumsy rush, so that he went sprawling when he tried to follow. Then it had bounded away, the white markings on its tail visible among the trees for a few minutes before they were lost to his sight.

Rabbits, which he used to catch with ease, were beyond his skills now as well. His former hunting patterns would no longer serve. He took to waiting in ambush by those places where animals came to drink, lying motionless for hours on end as he waited for them to come within range of his awkward leap. Sometimes he was successful. More often he was not. And once he had attacked in this way, he was forced to abandon his ambush site and move on to another. He became a wanderer, moving from territory to territory and, for the most part, forced to satisfy his hunger with small, slow-moving animals.

There were never enough to satisfy him, and as the hunger grew, he broke the cardinal rule by which he had always lived and moved into territory inhabited by man.

Now he discovered a new form of prey. The domestic animals and birds that were raised by farmers had none of the survival skills of wild animals. He took ducks and hens and lambs with relative ease.

As he recovered his strength, he adjusted somewhat to the missing foreleg. He was still clumsy and slow compared to the way he had been, but he was more than capable of catching this easy prey that he had found. He filled out. His coat grew thick and heavy once more. But unknown to him, there would be a price for this new form of hunting.

Eventually, he chanced upon what was surely the easiest prey of all.

Small and clumsy in his movements, the toddler had found the door of the farmhouse left open and had escaped into the dangerous world outside. He was sitting, looking uncertainly around, when the wolf saw him. Slowly, the huge predator limped across the farmyard, teeth bared. The infant saw him and recognized danger. Where an animal, even one as stupid as a chicken, might have tried to escape, the human child simply began to cry.

The sound registered with the wolf. It was the sound of helplessness and vulnerability. He crept closer, belly low to the ground, a deep snarl rumbling in the back of his throat.

But other ears were attuned to the sound of the child's crying. The mother heard her son and came to find him. And found the wolf, huge and black and menacing, moving toward its victim.

She screamed. The sound pierced the wolf's ears, shocking him. He had never heard that sound before. It mingled rage and fear and defiance in one complex note. He looked up from his intended prey and saw a figure running toward him—a figure that ran on two legs and seemed much taller and larger than he was. In the wolf's mind, dominant creatures ran toward. Victims ran away. Now this new and unknown animal was running at him, ready to attack, and he hesitated.

The woman had no weapon. But when she had noticed the open door and heard the baby crying, she had been in the act of putting a large iron skillet on the hob of her stove. As she came out into the farmyard, she still had it in her hand, and without conscious thought, she threw it at the black shape stalking her son.

The heavy pan whirled through the air, struck the wolf on its left rear hip and fell with a dull clang to the hard-packed ground. The wolf howled briefly with pain, then turned and ran, limping, back into the forest that skirted the farmyard.

The woman gathered up her crying son as her husband came running from the field he had been plowing. He had heard her scream and he feared the worst. Relief surged through him as he saw his wife and child safe. She looked up as he vaulted the fence into the farmyard paddock and ran to her, gathering her and the baby into his arms.

"A wolf," she said. "A big one. He nearly had Tom." She was racked with sobs at the thought of what might have been, and she buried her face against his chest. He nodded thoughtfully, holding her, patting her to comfort her. Something had been taking his animals in the past few days. Now he knew what it must have been. A fox or a marten he might handle himself. Even a lynx. But a wolf was a different matter. And if this one was attacking humans, it must be a renegade.

"I'll send for the Ranger," he said.

Will liked wolves as a general rule. They were courageous and loyal to their pack and usually they caused no trouble for humans. But if, as the farmer had surmised, this one had turned renegade, then it must be dealt with.

By sheer chance Will was on one of his regular patrols and was less than an hour away from the Complepes' farm. The farmer found him in a nearby village and led him back to study the scene of the attack. Will examined the tracks in the farmyard. They were relatively fresh and easy to follow and he frowned as he noticed an irregularity in them.

"You say he ran awkwardly?" he asked the woman.

She shrugged. "I was more concerned looking at Tom, but yes, he seemed to lurch a little."

Will scratched his chin as he looked at the tracks once more, idly tracing them with a stick he had picked up.

"Never seen wolves here in twenty years or more," the farmer told him. "Usually they keep their distance."

"Well, this might be the reason why this one came calling," he said, tapping the stick on one of the faint marks. "He seems to be crippled. He's lost a leg." He glanced at the woman once more. "What was he up to when you first saw him?"

"He was snarling and growling," she said, her eyes wide with the remembered horror of the moment. "He threw his head back and howled. His teeth were bare and he was all frothing at the mouth. He came at Tom like a streak of lightning—"

Will interrupted her with a raised hand. "But you said he was lurching?"

She hesitated, looking confused. "Well, mebbe he was ... but he was lurching fast. Real fast. And howling and snarling and tearing at the ground with his teeth."

"Hmm." Will regarded her thoughtfully. He didn't believe she was consciously lying to him, but he wasn't convinced that her account was an accurate one. He knew that a mother's protective instinct would have been aroused the moment she saw the threat to her child. And her instinct would have magnified the potential threat tenfold. The wolf could have been rolling on its back, wagging its tail and asking for a belly rub and she would have seen it snarling and slavering.

The woman sensed his doubt. "I'm telling the truth, Ranger."

Her husband moved to stand beside her. "My Agnes doesn't lie. She's an honest woman," he said stoutly.

Will nodded apologetically. "I'm sure of it. I'm sorry if I offended you, Mistress Complepe," he said. "I certainly didn't mean any insult."

She nodded, looking mollified by his apology. Simple farm folk never expected an apology from lofty characters like Rangers. "No offense taken, I'm sure," she said, with the hint of a curtsey in his direction.

He glanced to where the sun was dropping low over the trees around the farmhouse. "Well, there's little I can do tonight. I'll find a place to camp and start tracking him tomorrow."

He moved toward Tug.

Agnes Complepe put her hands to her face in alarm. "You'll not risk camping out in the open with this wolf around?"

Will grinned at her. "I'm sure I'll be safe enough. My fierce horse will keep watch over me," he said. If her account was even halfway accurate, there was a big difference between a wolf attacking a helpless baby and an armed Ranger.

"You're welcome to stay with us, Ranger," her husband said. He indicated the small farmhouse. Will hesitated. With three adults and a baby, it would be crowded in there. And he suspected that the Complepes would probably bring some of their more prized animals inside as well. It would be cramped and stuffy and he'd prefer to spend the night in the open, with Tug for company.

Agnes sensed his reluctance. "At least we can give you a meal," she said. "I've got a lamb stew simmering on the fire. And fresh baked bread."

"My Agnes is the best cook in the district," the farmer said.

Will smiled at them and the expression transformed his face.

"Now, that's an offer I'd be delighted to accept," he said. "I couldn't refuse a lamb stew from the best cook in the district."

Tug tossed his head and shook his mane.

You've never refused a lamb stew from anyone.

2

WILL WOKE AT FIRST LIGHT. HE MADE A HURRIED BREAKFAST OF coffee and toasted flat bread, with wild honey added to both. The night had been clear and he hadn't bothered to pitch a tent. He had made do with the oiled canvas bedroll that was a new part of Ranger equipment. Waterproof on the outside, it contained a thin but comfortable woolen mattress and a blanket inside. It was far superior to the old system of rolling blankets on the ground, and in the event that it did rain, there was a waterproof hood that could be raised to keep the occupant dry.

Tug eyed him curiously as he packed up the camp.

So, are we hunting the wolf this morning?

"Not immediately," Will said as he tied the bedroll behind Tug's saddle. "I want to ask around some of the other farms first."

There was always the chance that the attack at the Complepes' farm had been an aberration, he thought. But by the time he had visited three of the other farms in the immediate area, he knew that wasn't the case.

Two of the farmers reported stock losses in the past weeks. One thought he had seen a large dog in the area. The third farmer hadn't remarked on any missing stock. But his farm was farthest to the east.

"Maybe the wolf hasn't reached this far yet," Will said to Tug. The horse shook his mane. That passed for a shrug in horse body language, Will thought.

By early afternoon, he had retraced his steps to the Complepes' farm and was casting about for the wolf's tracks.

They were fairly obvious for the first hundred meters. But then, as the panic had subsided, the wolf had regained his cunning and reverted to his natural ways. Missing leg or not, he was a clever and resourceful opponent. He had backtracked several times, and headed across hard ground, where little sign of his passing would remain. But Will was a skilled tracker, as all Rangers were, and he quickly discerned a base course in the wolf's movements so that, when he lost the trail, he could cast around in that general direction until he found signs of the wolf's passing again.

"I wish we didn't have to do this," he said as he swung down from the saddle for the tenth time to study the ground ahead of him. A short while ago, the wolf had sidetracked through a rocky patch to the right. Will had continued heading in his original direction, taking a slight detour to the right. Halt would have frowned at him for taking such a shortcut and trusting to luck that he would cross the wolf's trail once more. Normal practice was to move forward slowly, sweeping in an ever-increasing arc until the tracker caught sight of the wolf's tracks once more. But by now Will was fairly sure of the direction the wolf was heading and he thought he could take the chance.

"He's probably got a lair somewhere up here," he said to Tug.

The horse said nothing. Tug knew he was taking a shortcut and he wanted Will to know that he knew.

"You're as bad as Halt," Will said, then emitted a low cry of triumph when he caught sight of a paw print in soft sand just ahead of them. Then another.

"Told you so," he said. Tug remained silent. A few meters farther along, a tuft of black fur clung to a thorny vine and Will knew he was on the right track once more.

In fact, the wolf did have a lair in the area. It was on a small, rocky hill that commanded a view of the surrounding countryside. A shelf of rock jutted out from its neighbors and provided a sheltered hollow that the wolf had taken for its base. He had returned there the previous day and spent the night. Then, earlier this morning, his stomach rumbling with hunger, he had left again to scout the area for food. It wasn't long before he became aware of a foreign presence close by—two presences, in fact. He sensed that they posed a danger to him, and instinct told him he must not let them discover his home. Moving carefully despite the limp, he swung in an arc that took him beside and behind the two creatures. He noted their direction of travel and confirmed that they were indeed heading toward his lair. He retraced his steps. There was a deep thicket ahead of them that would provide cover for him. He could lie in wait for them there.

He moved into the thicket, crouched belly to the ground and wriggled forward until he could see the trail down which the two creatures would come. The wind was behind them and he soon caught their scent. It was one that he had experienced only in recent times—the scent of humans. Satisfied that they wouldn't scent him, he lay still, his amber eyes unblinking, as they came into sight.

For a moment, his eyes narrowed. He could smell two foreign scents, but he could see only one intruder. It was large and four-legged. He had seen a smaller creature with it earlier, when he caught sight of them from a distance. He could smell the second presence but couldn't see it. The four-legged creature stopped and the wolf emitted an almost inaudible grunt of surprise as he realized the smaller figure was riding on top of the larger. As he watched, it detached itself and swung down, moving forward a few paces, head bent, studying the ground. The larger animal followed it, staying a few paces behind.

The larger animal posed the greater danger, the wolf decided. He flattened himself even closer to the ground, concealed by the bushes and the shadows beneath them, as the two creatures came closer to his hiding spot.

The smaller one was making noises now. A strange thing to do when you were following a dangerous enemy, the wolf thought. And he was definitely their enemy, and decidedly dangerous.

"Here we are again, Tug," Will said, tracing the outline of a canine pad print in the dirt. "Still heading northwest."

Tug emitted a low rumble. He raised his head and sniffed the air, trying to discern some foreign scent that would explain the overwhelming sense of danger he was feeling. He didn't like this situation. He didn't like Will going ahead on foot when there might be danger present. He never did like that. Tug wanted Will safe in the saddle, where Tug's speed and agility could protect him from a sudden attack.

"You're a worrywart," Will told him. He had heard Tug's sound and knew exactly what his horse was thinking. "Just settle down. I'm safe enough. This trail is half a day old. The wolf is nowhere near us."

The trail was an old one. But Will had no way of knowing that the wolf had left his lair again, discovered them approaching, and was now intent on protecting his home territory.

The wolf's tensed muscles trembled slightly in anticipation, then he calmed himself and lay motionless again, his eyes unblinking, locked on the two figures. The smaller animal was nearly level with him now. He knew if he attacked it, the larger one would be able to rush to its defense. Better to take care of the bigger one first.

The crouching figure moved past his hiding place and its large, long-legged companion moved forward too, until he was almost level with the spot where the wolf lay concealed. In spite of himself, another tremor of anticipation ran through the wolf's body.

Tug looked up suddenly. He had heard something. Or sensed something. He wasn't sure. But there was something close by. Something bad. He rumbled a low warning again.

Will looked at him and grinned. "What is it now?" he asked. "It can't be our friend the wolf. He's definitely heading this way." He pointed in the direction the wolf had been following and moved forward.

Ears pricked, senses screaming a warning, Tug followed, stepping nervously.

A blue jay darted away from a low bush nearby with a sudden flurry of wings. Both Will and Tug started nervously. Then Will laughed at his old companion.

"Happy now? It was nothing but a big bad blue jay," he said.

Tug shook his mane angrily. He had been sure there was something . . .

The wolf attacked. Tug was aware of a sudden, violent rush of movement from a thicket behind where he stood. He whirled to face the direction of danger, spinning on his rear hooves. But the wolf, now clear of the bushes, was already leaping for his throat, fangs bared. Realizing the danger, Tug reversed his spin awkwardly, turning away from those slashing teeth.

The wolf crashed into his right side, sending him staggering for a second, and Tug felt those fangs raking down his shoulder, gouging deep into the muscles there and sending hot blood cascading down his foreleg. The wolf hung on, his fangs ripping and tearing deeper and deeper into the muscle as he shook his head savagely.

Tug whinnied. As his front hooves came back to earth, he tried to bring his rear hooves up to kick at his attacker. But his right front leg was badly injured, muscles and tendons torn and lacerated, and it faltered under him. He lurched away, stumbling as it refused to bear his weight. Finally, the wolf tore free from its terrible grip. It hit the ground and rolled, then crouched beneath Tug, teeth bared for another attack.

Will's arrow slammed into its side, with all the force of his bow's eighty-pound draw weight behind it, from a range of less than four meters. The arrow ripped through the wolf's body, tearing organs and rupturing blood vessels and destroying its heart on the way, killing the beast instantly. It fell to the ground, eyes glazed and lifeless, with nine centimeters of the arrow protruding from its far side.

"Tug!" Will's cry was almost a scream. At first, he thought Tug had evaded the wolf's attack. Now he could see the torn flesh of his horse's shoulder, the gleaming white of exposed bone and tendon, and the bright blood streaming down Tug's right foreleg. Will threw the bow aside and rushed to his horse, tears forming in his eyes and coursing down his cheeks.

He threw his right arm around Tug's neck and reached clumsily with his left to touch the terrible wound.

Tug balanced on three legs, placing no weight on the injured limb. He whinnied in surprise as the shock wore off and he felt the first throbbing pain from the injury.

"Oh god, Tug! Oh god!" Will was momentarily helpless at the sight of his injured horse. In all their years together, he had never seen Tug so badly wounded. Now, faced with this terrible, red-pumping gash, his mind froze, refusing to accept what had happened, refusing to think about what he must do next.

Then his training reasserted itself. He had a medical kit in his saddlebag. He relinquished his embrace around Tug's neck, patted him gently several times, and then reached for the saddlebag.

"Steady, boy. Steady. Take it easy. You'll be fine."

Will opened the medical pack and studied it for a few seconds. He'd need a bandage pad to stanch the flow of blood, and a long pressure bandage to hold it in place. He found both items and placed them ready. But before he could bandage the wound, he'd have to clean it. He took out a gauze pad and a small jar of the pungent ointment that would cleanse the wound and dull the pain. He never liked handling the medication, as it was derived from warmweed, and the smell reminded him of an unpleasant episode many years ago. But he knew it was a highly effective treatment for any wound. He also took his canteen from the saddle pommel and unstoppered it, pouring a large amount of water over the wound. The blood continued to flow as the water hit it, the color diluting to pink at first, then turning deep red again. He dabbed at the wound with a linen pad, trying to be as gentle as he could, yet knowing he had to use some firmness. Tug flinched once, then stood still.

"Good boy. That's it. You'll be fine," Will crooned. His eyes narrowed. As he cleared the blood momentarily, he could see how deeply the wolf's fangs had torn into Tug's flesh. This was no superficial wound, he realized. He might be able to render first aid, but Tug was going to need help far beyond his limited skill.

He pushed the negative thought aside, then smeared a liberal dose of the painkilling cream into the wound. Again, Tug trembled slightly but made no complaint. Soon, Will hoped, the analgesic properties of the cream should take effect. Now he braced his largest bandage pad over the wound and held the end of a rolled linen bandage against it. He tossed the rolled end over Tug's withers, leaned under him to retrieve it, and wound it under his body and up over the bandage pad. Then he repeated the process over and over, until the linen wrapping held the pad firmly in place. As he watched, the bandage slowly turned red with seeping blood. But then the coagulant mixed into the ointment took effect and the blood flow slowed.

He stepped back and surveyed his work. Then his eyes blurred with tears again and he moved forward, embracing the horse—careful to avoid the area of the wound—resting his head against the rough, shaggy coat.

"Oh god, Tug, please be all right."

Tug shifted awkwardly. The pain in his right shoulder had lessened dramatically with the application of the salve. But when he tried to put weight on the right foreleg, it gave way under him.

"I'll have to get you to the closest farm," Will said, thinking desperately. It would be a long walk, with Tug limping on three legs, but Will had already realized that he would have to go for expert help, and he couldn't leave Tug alone in the forest in this condition. He took Tug's bridle and began to lead the way back toward the second farm that he had visited earlier that day. It was the closest to the spot where they now found themselves, and he remembered there had been a sizable barn there where Tug could rest while Will went for help. With any luck, the farmer might have a horse he could borrow.

The thought saddened him. Many times over the years, he had ridden to fetch help. But he had always done so with Tug. Now he would be leaving the little horse behind while he rode a strange horse to bring back the expert help that Tug needed. The realization only served to heighten his fears as Tug hobbled along behind him.

3

"It's a bad 'un, young Will, and no mistake."

Old Bob straightened from where he was crouched beside Tug, studying the deep wound in his shoulder. It had taken a day and a half for Will to fetch the old horse breeder. It had nearly broken his heart when he rode off on a borrowed horse, leaving Tug in the care of the farmer.

Relief had flowed through him when they returned and he opened the barn door to see Tug standing in a stall, ears pricked, nickering a greeting to him. Maybe it was going to be all right, he thought. After all, Old Bob was reckoned to be a near wizard when it came to horses.

Now, however, Old Bob was shaking his head doubtfully. "It's a bad 'un, young Will, and no mistake."

Will's heart sank. He felt an enormous lump forming in his throat.

"He's not going to . . . to . . . ?" He couldn't bring himself to finish the question.

Bob looked at him, shaking his head, as he realized what Will was trying to ask.

"To die? No. The salve has done a good job keeping infection out of the wound. You did well there. The question is, will he recover completely? That shoulder muscle is badly damaged and he's not a young horse anymore."

"But ... what will I do if he doesn't ...?" Again, it was a thought that Will couldn't finish.

Old Bob patted his arm gently. He knew only too well of the bond that formed between a Ranger and his horse. He remembered the first day Will and Tug had met each other and the almost instant rapport they had developed.

"Let's not worry about that before we have to," he said. "I can't really tell here. We need to get him back to my stables, where I can work on him. Help me get him into the cart."

Bob had a specially designed cart for transporting injured horses. It had high sides and a ramp at the back. Will led Tug up the ramp, going slowly as the little horse hopped on his single working front foot up the sloped timber. When he was in the cart itself, they passed a canvas sling under his belly. The sling was then attached to the high sides of the cart and they took up tension on it so that it was supporting most of Tug's weight, taking the strain off his uninjured legs.

As he took his place beside Bob on the driver's seat of the cart, Will felt a familiar nudge against the back of his shoulder as Tug butted him affectionately. He reached back and fondled the horse's muzzle as Bob clicked his tongue to the burly cart horse and the cart lurched forward.

"How long have you and Tug been together now?" Bob asked. Will thought for a moment.

"Must be about fifteen years," Will said, smiling to himself as he cast his mind back over the period they had spent together. They'd seen so much together, he thought, from the mountains of Picta to the burning waste of the Arridi desert.

"Hmm," Bob said thoughtfully, and Will looked at him, concerned by the old horse breeder's tone.

"What?" he said. "What is it?"

But Bob shook his head, unwilling for the moment to say any more on the subject.

"Nothing," he said. "Just wondering is all."

But Will sensed there was something behind the question, and he wasn't sure he was going to like it.

Back at Bob's farm, they carefully helped Tug down from the cart and led him, limping on three legs, into a warm, dry stall in the barn. There, Bob gently removed the bandage, crooning apologetically as he did so and taking care not to cause the little horse any undue pain.

Will watched in an agony of uncertainty. There was nothing he could do to assist Bob, nothing he could do to lessen Tug's pain. He forced himself to stay silent, although the temptation was to question the wizened old horse handler at every shift of expression or muttered comment. Now that the heavy bleeding had stopped, he could see how deeply the wolf's fangs had savaged Tug's flesh. There was a large torn flap hanging loose. Bob screwed up his mouth as he examined it and assessed it.

"Have to stitch that," he said. "But we need to clean the wound completely first. Don't want any infection getting in there."

He set about applying salves and ointments to the raw flesh, dabbing gently, speaking to the horse as he did so. From time to time, Tug would flinch, and instantly the gentle hands would stop what they were doing and instead soothe the little horse, stroking his nose and neck. Old Bob glanced around and saw the drawn expression on Will's face.

"Nothing you can do here for the moment, young Will," he said. "Why don't you go into my cabin and get us some supper? I'll be through here in fifteen minutes and you can come and see Tug then."

"I'd prefer to stay," Will said awkwardly, and Bob nodded, smiling at him.

"I know you would. But with all respect, you're distracting me. Every time I make a sound or Tug flinches, you start forward, and then you stop. Just let me do my job and make yourself useful getting supper ready. All right?"

Will hesitated. He was loath to leave Tug, but the thought that he was distracting Bob, that he might cause him to make a mistake while he was tending to the horse, settled the matter. He nodded and turned away, then turned back and patted Tug's muzzle.

"I won't be far," he said.

Tug snorted. His normal reaction would have been to shake his head and mane violently. But such a movement would have caused pain to his injured leg.

I know. Now let Bob get on with his job . . . worrywart.

It was the expression Will often used for Tug. The young Ranger smiled now that it was being applied to himself.

"I'll be back," he said, and left the barn. As he reached the big double doors, he heard Bob say softly: "I thought he'd never go."

Tug responded with another snort.

4

EARLY THE FOLLOWING MORNING, BOB FOUND WILL IN THE BARN, where he'd slept in the hay beside his horse. The old trainer nodded to himself. He'd heard Will get up in the middle of the night and leave the cabin, and he'd guessed where he'd gone.

Knowing that Will desperately wanted to care for his horse, Bob allowed him to check the wound for any sign of inflammation or infection. Thankfully, there was none. Then he supervised the Ranger as he put a new bandage on. The flap of torn skin had been neatly stitched back in place and now there was only a slight flow of blood to be stanched.

When that was done, he dropped a hand onto Will's shoulder.

"Come on now," he said. "Breakfast, and then we'll talk."

They sat outside Bob's kitchen in the early-morning sunshine. But the sun did nothing to raise Will's spirits. He sipped his coffee, without his usual relish, and morosely broke pieces off a sweet roll on the platter in front of him.

"I won't lie to you, young fellow," Bob said. "Tug's hurt bad. It's a terrible wound. It's much worse than a simple bite. The wolf hung on when he bit into him, shaking his head and pulling with all his body weight, and he cut deep into the muscles and tendons."

"But he will recover?" Will asked, and his heart sank as the old horse trainer hesitated, his gaze sliding away.

"I hope so. But we won't know for four or five days at the earliest." He saw the fear in the young man's eyes and hurried to give him what little reassurance he could offer.

"He's not going to die, Will. He'll recover in that sense. But the leg may never mend properly. I just don't know. I'll do all I can for him and he's a strong and healthy horse."

"So we just have to sit and wait?" Will said. But Bob was shaking his head before Will finished the sentence.

"I have to sit and wait. You've got work to do back at Redmont." Bob eyed the young man shrewdly. In truth, he had no idea if Will had pressing work to do back at Redmont. The probability was high that he did, as Rangers were constantly being called on. But he knew that the worst thing for Will would be to sit here brooding for the next four or five days. It would be better to get him back to work, to take his mind off the situation here.

Will stared at his hands on the table. He did have a lot of urgent work waiting back at Redmont. But this was Tug! He looked up at Bob.

"I don't have a horse. What can I do without a horse?"

Bob smiled reassuringly. "I'll lend you a horse. I have plenty of retired Ranger horses here. Not as spry as Tug, maybe, but good enough for a few days." He saw Will wavering and he reinforced his argument. "Will, there's nothing you can do here. You'll sit around watching Tug and worrying about him. And he'll know you're worried, and that will affect him." He paused, then added, "It could delay his healing."

That did the trick. The thought that he might have an adverse effect on his horse's convalescence was enough for Will. He came to a decision.

"I'll pack my gear. Would you get the horse ready?"

Bob leaned across the table and gripped his forearm.

"Good lad. And I imagine you'll be wanting to say good-bye to Tug."

It took an enormous effort to leave Tug in the barn. Will stood patting his neck and muzzle for some minutes, speaking gently to him. Old Bob stayed out of earshot, giving them privacy. Then, finally, sensing that Will didn't know how to tear himself away, he coughed to attract his attention.

"Time to go, Will Treaty. Cormac is ready and waiting for you."

Will hugged Tug's neck one last time, gently touching the bandaged wound with a forefinger.

"I'll be back in five days," he said.

Tug shook his head, but it was a more gentle action than his normal, boisterous movement.

I'm not going anywhere.

Will's eyes filled with tears and Tug nudged him with his head.

That was a joke.

Dashing the back of his hand across his eyes, Will turned quickly and walked out of the barn into the bright sun.

Cormac was a chestnut, with a light-colored mane and tail. He was somewhat taller than Tug, but with the same shaggy coat and solid, muscular look that all Ranger horses shared. Old Bob had put Will's saddle and bridle on him and tied the Ranger's camping gear in place behind the saddle.

Will judged that he was a few years older than Tug. But he still looked fit and energetic—and he was vaguely familiar. Will had the sense that he had seen him somewhere before.

"Will, this is Cormac. Cormac, this is Will," Old Bob said as he handed the reins to Will. He slapped the chestnut on the neck affectionately. "He's a good horse, this 'un. He'll serve you well for a few days. Mebbe not as fast as he was five years ago, but he'll still run all day for you—and keep going into the next day as well."

"That's the way you train them, Bob," Will said, with an attempt at a smile.

Bob noticed and slapped him on the shoulder. "That's the spirit, Will Treaty! Off you go then. I'm sure you have all sorts of important work to do. And never fear, I'll take good care of Tug."

Will nodded his thanks and went to put his foot in the stirrup. Then he hesitated.

"Do I need a permission phrase?" he asked.

Bob laughed. "No. I told you, Cormac is retired. Once we retire them, we teach them they don't need a permission word."

Will swung up into the saddle, albeit a little suspiciously. He sat for a second or two, waiting to see if Cormac would react. But the chestnut simply turned his head and looked curiously at him. Bob let go a wheezing cackle of laughter.

"Don't trust me, eh?" he said. "I told you. He's retired. Now get going!"

Will touched his heels lightly to Cormac's side and the horse responded immediately, moving off at a trot. His gait was a little different from Tug's, but it was smooth and even. He had a spring in his step too—as if he were glad to be back at work.

"I'll see you in five days," Will called over his shoulder. Bob waved a hand in acknowledgment, then nodded approvingly as Will, with only the slightest touch, set Cormac into a smooth, easy canter.

The horse's tail came up as he ran. *This is fun.*

"Glad you think so . . . ," Will began, and then stopped, surprised that he was talking to his temporary mount. Maybe all Ranger horses responded this way.

5

THE NEXT FIVE DAYS PASSED IN A BLUR. IF HE HAD BEEN ASKED TO recount what happened or what he had done, Will would have been at a loss.

Halt and Lady Pauline were both away from Redmont, attending to a diplomatic problem at one of the fief's subsidiary castles. The mayor of one of Celtica's largest towns had absconded with the town's treasury and was claiming diplomatic immunity in Redmont Fief. The Celtic king had sent soldiers after him to bring him back. This was understandable, and while Baron Arald had no intention of protecting the thief, the Celtic king's action was technically a breach of the treaty between Araluen and Celtica. Neither country had the right to send armed troops over the border. Baron Arald had sent Halt to escort the miscreant back to Celtica, and Lady Pauline to persuade the Celtic troops to keep their hands off the criminal until he was back in their jurisdiction.

Halt could have convinced them himself, of course, but his methods were liable to be a little more direct than Pauline's and Arald was hoping to avoid piling one diplomatic incident on top of another.

With Lady Pauline thus engaged, it had fallen to Alyss to attend the biannual Diplomatic Service meeting at Castle Araluen. Will found a note to that effect on the table of the little cabin in the woods.

But if Will had thought he might spend a lonely week in the cabin, worrying about Tug, he was quickly disabused of the notion. A report came in of a band of brigands preying on lone travelers in the northern part of the fief. Accordingly, Will set off in a borrowed wagon, disguised as a peddler of household goods. He traveled through the area where the bandits were known to be operating, selling his wares at remote farms and building up a sizable amount of money in the process. The bandits were watching him, as he knew they would be, and once they were satisfied that he was ripe for the plucking, they stopped him on a lonely stretch of road with heathland on either side.

There were four of them, so Will had them seriously outnumbered.

He gave them one warning, identifying himself as a King's Ranger, but they chose to attack. Within seconds, three of them were on the ground, nursing arrow wounds to arms and legs. The fourth, his eyes wide with terror, tossed his sword away and fell to his knees, begging for mercy.

Will allowed them to bandage their wounds, then tied their hands together. He strung them in a line behind the peddler's cart to walk back to Castle Redmont for trial. One of them pleaded for gentler treatment.

"Please, Ranger, we're hurt bad. Can't we ride in the cart?"

Will glanced at him coldly. In his present mood, he had little sympathy for the bandits, who had left several of their former victims wounded and bleeding by the roadside.

"I'm doing you a favor," he said, and as the man frowned, about to ask a further question, he added, "I'm letting you enjoy the fresh air and open spaces. You'll see little of either for the next ten years."

So the time passed and the fifth day found him cantering Cormac back to the farm where Bob trained horses for the Ranger Corps.

The horse shook his head, enjoying the freedom of the road and the opportunity to stretch his legs. Ranger horses loved to run.

I've enjoyed being back at work. I'd be happy to keep serving you.

Will smiled. "You've been a good companion and I'm grateful," he said, patting the chestnut's neck affectionately. "But I'm hoping Tug will be on the way to healing."

Cormac tossed his head. *I can understand that. But if you ever need me . . .*

"I'll come calling," Will said. As they rode out of the trees and followed the long track leading up to Bob's cabin, Will eagerly scanned the paddocks on either side. At first he saw nothing, then his heart lifted as he spotted a familiar gray shape in the distance, running for the sheer joy of it in the crisp autumn sunshine.

"Tug!" he shouted eagerly, and touched his heels to Cormac's sides. The chestnut responded instantly and broke into a gallop. The gray horse heard the drumming hooves and swung to run toward them, cutting diagonally across the large paddock.

Will reined in, waiting for him.

The gait, the movement, the way the little horse tossed his head. It was all so familiar. Will actually laughed out loud at the sight of his horse as the shaggy gray came up to the fence that delineated the paddock.

Then he frowned. It was so like Tug. Yet it wasn't him. This horse was considerably younger. There was no sign of the white hairs that had begun to show around Tug's muzzle over the last few years. And now that they were closer, Will could see a small diamond-shaped patch of darker hair on the little horse's left front leg, close by the hoof. It wasn't Tug. Yet, in so many ways, *it was.*

The horse nickered a greeting, then shook himself, rattling his mane in exactly the way Tug did. Cormac returned the greeting. The gray looked expectantly at Will, but Will was too confused to speak. Finally, tossing his head, the gray horse turned and galloped off, going back the way he had come.

You hurt his feelings.

Will didn't reply. He tapped his heels against Cormac's sides and they cantered up the track to Bob's cabin.

Here, another surprise awaited them. Another chestnut was standing outside the cabin, almost identical to Cormac. But he was younger, Will realized, much younger. The two horses greeted each other like old friends and Will realized where he had seen Cormac before.

"You were Crowley's horse," he said to Cormac. "But your name was Cropper."

As he said the name, the horse outside the cabin raised his head in recognition.

"This is Cropper now," said Crowley as he emerged from the cabin and walked toward them. "That's the way we do it. When we retire a horse, we change his name, and we give the old name to the new horse."

Cormac moved eagerly toward the Ranger Commandant, and he fondled the horse's muzzle affectionately. "Hullo, old friend," he said softly. Then he glanced up at Will. "Step down, Will. We need to talk."

Will swung down from the saddle, a vague sense of unease growing within him.

"Crowley?" he said. "What are you doing here? How's Tug?"

Crowley put a reassuring hand on the young Ranger's shoulder.

"Tug's doing fine," he said. "He's a lot better than when you saw him last. In fact, here he comes now."

404 RANGER'S APPRENTICE: THE LOST STORIES

He pointed and Will turned to see Old Bob leading his horse out of the stable and toward the cabin. At first sight, he seemed totally recovered.

"Tug!" he called, and the horse looked up and whinnied eagerly. Bob released the lead rein and made a gesture toward Will. Without further urging, Tug trotted toward his master and Will's heart suddenly sank.

"He's limping," he said. The limp had become evident as Tug increased his pace.

Crowley nodded. "He is. Bob's done all he can, but the muscle damage was too great to heal completely. I'm afraid he'll always limp, Will."

Tug butted his head against Will's chest in his familiar way, then he began nosing around his pockets, searching for the apple that he knew would be there. Will helped him find it and the little horse crunched it blissfully. But Will's head was still whirling as he absorbed Crowley's last statement.

"He'll always limp?" he said. "But how can I . . . ?" He couldn't finish the question. Suddenly, he sensed what was coming. The talk of retired Ranger horses; the two chestnuts, virtually identical; and the young gray he'd seen in the paddock—all those facts came together to form one obvious, terrible conclusion.

"We're going to have to retire him," he said dully. It wasn't a question and he saw Crowley and Bob nodding in confirmation.

"It's the way we do things, Will," Crowley told him. "Our horses can only serve us for fifteen or sixteen years. Then they begin to lose the speed and agility and stamina that we rely on so much. So this would have happened in the near future anyway. The injury has only brought the inevitable a little closer."

"But . . . this is Tug!" Will said, his eyes blinded by tears. "This is no ordinary horse! He's Tug!" He came to a sudden decision and raised his head defiantly, angrily wiping the tears away with the back of his hand. "I don't care if he limps. I don't care if he's not as fast or as agile as he used to be! He's my horse and I'm keeping him!"

He reached for Tug's bridle, but Crowley caught his hand gently and stopped him.

"That's not possible," he said. "It's not the Ranger way."

"Then I'll retire as well. If I can't have Tug, I no longer want to be a Ranger!"

They all started with surprise as Tug reared back, his ears flattened against his head.

Don't you dare say that! Not after all I've done for you!

"Tug?" Will said, bewildered by the horse's anger. But Tug shook his head now, rattling his mane.

Quit if you want to! But don't make me the reason for it!

"But . . . I need you, Tug. I can't imagine going on without you," Will said.

Old Bob and Crowley exchanged a glance. They were familiar with the uncanny bond that formed between a Ranger and his horse. Both of them knew that a strange form of communication grew up over the years. Crowley experienced it himself with Cropper. They withdrew to allow Will to talk to the horse without embarrassment or awkwardness. Tug butted him gently once more, the anger gone now.

Don't you see? I can't serve you properly like this. I can't keep you safe. That's a job for the new Tug. But you have to give him a chance.

"The new Tug?" Will said.

Crowley, sensing the time was right, nodded to Bob. The old horse breeder turned away and walked back to the stable. When he had gone, Crowley answered the question.

"Bob's just one of our horse breeders, Will. We have many of them and they do an amazing job. They keep track of the bloodlines of all our horses and the breeding records from our herds. Tug will go into that breeding process now, just as his ancestors did. He'll be well looked after and he'll be safe. And he'll ensure that in the future, there will be other horses like himself available to Rangers. Did you see that little gray in the front paddock when you rode up?"

Will nodded. "I thought it *was* Tug for a few minutes."

"As well you might have. His sire was Tug's grandfather. And his dam was a mare whose characteristics were almost identical to Tug's mother. When Bob saw this one foaled, he set him aside specifically for you. Of course, we had no idea you'd be needing him quite so soon. Normally, we would have prepared you for it over the next year or two. But this came out of the blue. That's why Bob sent for me to explain it. Sooner or later, we all have to go through it."

He looked sympathetically at the younger Ranger and his horse. Will had moved close to Tug. His left arm was around the horse's neck and his right hand was stroking the soft muzzle.

"Couldn't I just keep him at Redmont anyway?" Will asked.

Crowley smiled. "We all ask that. But think about it. He's not a pet. And he's needed here in the breeding program. He's one of our best horses. On top of that, it wouldn't be fair to your new horse. You wouldn't bond properly. And it wouldn't be fair to Tug either. He'd have to watch you going off on missions without him."

And you know I'm a worrywart.

In spite of himself, Will couldn't help smiling at that. "So what will your new name be?" he asked.

Tug hesitated, his head to one side. *I've always fancied myself as a Bellerophon.*

"Bellerophon?" Will said, surprised. It was an unexpected choice.

Crowley grinned. "Not bad. We should mention it to Bob. And here he comes now."

Will turned and saw Bob approaching, leading the gray he had seen earlier. Now, however, the horse was saddled and bridled. Every inch of the horse was familiar, even the way he held himself as he walked. Except for the small patch of black hair on his leg and the lack of white hairs around his muzzle, he was identical to the Tug who had served Will for the past fifteen years.

Now that's a decidedly good-looking horse.

"You would think so," Will said. Then, as Bob handed him the reins, he stepped forward and scratched the young horse's muzzle. The horse moved his head in appreciation, then nuzzled against Will's pockets, searching for an apple. It was such a familiar action, such a *Tug* action, that Will was startled for a second or two.

"I'm sorry," he said. "I gave my last apple to . . ." He hesitated, then said, with a grin, "Bellerophon."

Bob reached into his own pocket and tossed an apple to him. "Thought you might have," he said.

Will held the apple out on the flat of his hand to the horse, who took it gently, his lips tickling the palm of Will's hand, then crunched it happily.

"Why don't you two get to know each other?" Bob said, gesturing to the saddle. Will nodded. Suddenly he was eager to know just how much like Tug this new horse really was.

"Good idea," he said. He stepped his left foot into the stirrup and swung easily up onto the horse's back. Crowley and Bob exchanged wicked grins.

"Now," Will said, "let's see . . ."

He got no further. The horse beneath him suddenly exploded into motion, bounding off all four feet, twisting and spinning in the air, heaving his hindquarters up as his forelegs came back to earth. Will shot into the air over his neck, turning a somersault, feeling several seconds of weightlessness, then crashing to the dusty earth so that the air was driven from his body. He lay groaning, trying desperately to refill his lungs. The horse stood by him, its head cocked curiously to one side.

Bob and Crowley stood by, laughing helplessly, as Will lay there, propped on his elbows, gradually getting air back into his lungs.

"This one ain't retired, Will Treaty!" Bob told him cheerfully. "You need your code phrase for him, same as for old Tug here."

Will looked up, his mind flashing back to an identical incident many years ago. He realized old Tug, now Bellerophon, was watching him, shaking his head.

"He bucks just like you, too," Will said breathlessly.

You'll never learn, will you?

As they cantered home later that morning, Will continued to be amazed at the resemblance between the two horses. It was as if Tug had suddenly and inexplicably been rejuvenated, and he realized now that Crowley and Bob had been right. In the past few years, Tug had become fractionally slower, a little less sure of foot. This new Tug was a reminder of how his horse had been in their very first days together.

He thought about those times now. About how Tug had stormed to protect him when the wild boar had charged him. About the desperate race with the Bedullin stallion, Sandstorm, when Tug showed him a blazing turn of speed that Will had never known about. As he thought about that day, the new Tug shook his head, rattling his mane.

I would have beaten Sandstorm.

Will looked at him with surprise. "How do you know about Sandstorm?" he asked. Again, the horse shook his mane.

If it's in your mind, I know it. Now, do you want to keep to this crawl or shall we pace it up a little?

"You sound just like Tug," Will told him.

I am Tug.

"Yes," Will replied thoughtfully. "I believe you are."

> *Author's note: The preceding story came about after I received an e-mail query from Laurie, a New Zealand reader. She pointed out that the practical working life for Ranger horses couldn't be much more than sixteen or seventeen years and wanted to know what happened after that period. I couldn't bear the thought of Will without Tug, so I devised the ingenious breeding program mentioned here.*

AND ABOUT
TIME, TOO...

WILL LOOKED DOWN AND CHECKED HIMSELF ONE LAST TIME. His jacket was neat and uncreased. The open collar of a spotless white silk shirt showed above it, and the silver oakleaf that indicated his rank was just visible in the V formed by his collar. His pants were free of any stains or marks. His boots were clean and freshly worked with oil. They weren't shiny. A Ranger never shined his boots. Shiny boots could reflect flashes of light and make it easier for someone to spot a concealed Ranger. He buckled on his broad leather belt. Like the boots, the buckle itself was a dull, mat black and the hilts of his two knives were bound in plain leather. Only the blades would have caught the light had they been exposed. They were kept carefully honed and they were of a fine grade steel, harder than the swords carried by the Kingdom's knights.

He wished he had a mirror. This was an important day, after all. But mirrors were wildly expensive. Only someone as wealthy as Baron Arald could afford such a luxury. A Ranger's pay didn't stretch to that sort of thing.

Ebony was lying by the door, her chin on her outstretched paws, her eyes riveted on him. He glanced at her now and held out his hands.

"How do I look?" he said. She thumped her tail twice on the floor, her eyes never moving from him.

"As good as that?" he mused. *Thump, thump* went the tail again.

He glanced out the window. The sun was well down, below the tops of the trees that surrounded the little cabin.

"Time to go," he said. He pulled back the curtain that covered the hanging space in his simple wardrobe and took out his cloak.

This time, Ebony showed some interest. Her head cocked to one side and she looked at him curiously. He hadn't selected his normal, workaday cloak. He had taken out the formal uniform cloak, with the stylized silver representations of arrows set diagonally across its back. He swung it around his shoulders and grinned at her.

"Special day," he said. Ebony let her head slump back onto her paws again. He moved to the door and made a shooing motion for her to get out of the way. With a sigh, she rose to her feet and took a few steps to the side as he opened the door and moved out onto the porch. He paused and looked back at her.

"You coming?" he said. "You *are* invited, after all." Tail wagging once more, she sidled past the open door and joined him on the porch. She looked up at him in that way that border shepherds have of constantly looking to their master for direction.

Where are we going now? the look said. Will didn't answer but instead let out a low whistle. Ebony's ears pricked up at the sound. A few seconds later, they heard the soft *clip-clop* of hooves as Tug appeared around the end of the little cabin. He had been resting in the stable behind. But since Will never needed to tether him, he was able to answer the whistle immediately.

Unlike Ebony, Tug seemed to know where they were going. He glanced once at Ebony, standing ready beside Will.

Is she coming too?

"Of course," Will told him. "She's part of the family, after all. You don't object, do you?"

Tug shook his mane explosively. *Not at all. But she does sometimes lack a sense of decorum. I don't want her to start scratching herself in the middle of things.*

Will grinned at the dog. "Hear that, Eb? No disrespectful scratching." The dog's tail moved with the mention of her name. Tug looked sidelong at his master.

The same goes for you.

"I'm glad we have you along as chief of protocol," Will said. "Are we going?"

Waiting on you.

Will shook his head. After all these years, he thought, you'd think I'd have learned that I'll never get the last word with this horse.

Never.

He looked at Tug suspiciously. If a horse could be said to have assumed an innocent air, that was what he was doing.

He clicked his fingers to Ebony and stepped off the verandah. She fell into place immediately at his right heel. Tug walked on his left, his head alongside his master's shoulder. The three of them made their way across the small clearing in front of the cabin to a track that ran through the woods. Space was restricted on the track, so Tug fell back to bring up the rear.

It was dim under the trees, but the path was a familiar one. It meandered down a slight slope, taking the line of least resistance, to a small stream that was a tributary of the Tarbus River. There was a deep pool where he and Halt had fished for trout over the years. There was a grassy clearing by the pool as well, and in more recent times, he and Alyss had often picnicked there on summer evenings— like this one.

The air was soft and warm on his face, and a few birds rustled around in the trees and bushes as they settled in for the night. He glanced off into the darkness among the trees and saw the tiny, darting pinpoints of light that marked the movement of fireflies. One strayed out of the trees, the light in its tail dimming as it moved out of the comparative darkness. It came close to Ebony and there was a sudden *clop!* as her jaws snapped shut, then she shook her head and pawed at her tongue to remove the debris of the dead insect.

"You'll never learn, will you?" he said affectionately. Ebony could never resist the temptation to snap at flying insects. This was inevitably followed by frantic efforts to get rid of the results. Somehow, they never seemed to taste as good as Ebony expected.

As they came closer to the clearing by the stream, he was aware of a low buzz of conversation.

"We're the last ones here," he commented. But Tug shook his head.

She'll be last. It's traditional.

They emerged from the trees. The clearing was lit by torches on poles driven into the ground, and lanterns in different colors were strung among the branches. A small crowd of people was waiting for him. As Will, Tug and Ebony stepped out into the clearing, there was a low smatter of applause and a few softly called words of greeting.

He looked around with a warm sense of pleasure. There weren't many people here, but they numbered all of those who were important in his life.

Halt, of course. And his beautiful wife beside him, standing half a head taller than he did. Since Will's sixteenth birthday, Halt had been a father figure to him. And in more recent years, he had begun to think of Lady Pauline as a surrogate mother.

He glanced to one side and his face lit up with a smile. Horace was here. Well, he'd assumed that he would be. And with him was Evanlyn, his wife.

I'm really going to have to start calling her Cassandra, Will thought. He was touched that they'd made the long journey from Castle Araluen to be with him today. It didn't occur to him that he would have done exactly the same for them without a second thought. He looked keenly at the Princess. He'd had an excited letter from Horace telling him that they were expecting a child. So far, there was no sign of the pregnancy. Evanlyn—Cassandra, he corrected himself—looked as slim as ever.

Standing by a podium set up beside the river was Baron Arald, grinning widely at the most famous of all his wards. Will nodded a respectful greeting to him, and his gaze scanned the rest of the people assembled. Jenny and Gilan, he noticed, standing hand in hand, Jenny beaming proudly at him and from time to time looking up with adoring eyes at the tall, handsome Ranger by her side.

You'll be next, Will thought. Gilan seemed to read his thoughts and smiled widely at him. The prospect didn't seem to bother him at all.

He stopped in midstride as he made out the next two guests, standing back in the shadows behind Gilan and Jenny. Two totally disparate forms—one small and slightly built, looking as if a strong wind would blow him away, the other tall and broad. Huge, in fact. And between them, a black-and-white shape that rose from the ground and advanced toward Ebony, her heavy tail sweeping back and forth as she came.

As Ebony and her mother, Shadow, reacquainted themselves, tails wagging slowly, heads lowered, Will stepped forward quickly to embrace Malcolm, then to be crushed in return by Trobar's bear hug.

"You made it!" he said, delighted to see them. "I wasn't sure you'd come so far!"

"Wouldn't have missed it for worlds!" the birdlike healer told him, smiling fondly at the young man.

Trobar's huge voice rumbled as softly as the giant could manage. "Co'gra-lashuns, Will Treaty."

"Thanks, Trobar," Will said. "The day is better for the fact that you're here."

The Baron coughed meaningfully and Will realized that it was time to get matters under way. Disengaging himself from the healer and his giant bodyguard, he moved to where Arald was waiting, a sheaf of official papers on the podium before him.

Tug and Ebony followed him.

"Well," said the Baron fondly, "it's a beautiful night for a wedding, Will Treaty."

"Can't think of a better one, sir," Will replied.

"I'm reminded of a rather amusing story . . . ," the Baron began. But his wife, Lady Sandra, made a low warning noise—subtle but unmistakable—and he looked at her guiltily. "Eh? Oh . . . yes . . . of course, my dear. Perhaps later, young Will."

"Later would probably be better, sir," Will agreed, hiding a smile.

"Right . . . well, you're here. We can all see that. Do we have a best man?"

In answer, Horace stepped forward and stood by Will's side, putting his hand on his best friend's shoulder. The two looked at each other—a look that spoke more than any number of words could convey.

"Excellent," the Baron continued. "Excellent choice." He looked at the shaggy horse and sleek dog standing behind Will. "And these are . . . ?"

Before Will could reply, Horace spoke up. "Best horse and best dog," he said.

"Excellent!" said the Baron. "A little unconventional, but

excellent—so long as they don't have to sign anything!" He laughed at his own witticism. Tug pushed his head forward to study him more closely. The Baron became aware of the horse's scrutiny and looked down, hurriedly rearranging his papers.

"Behave," Will said quietly to the horse, and Tug withdrew. Will was sure he was smirking.

Arald took a few moments to recover his normal ebullience, then he rubbed his hands together and scanned the assembly before him. Without being asked, those present had moved to form a loose half circle, facing the podium.

"Well then," he said briskly. "It seems we're all here. Groom. Best man. Witnesses. Celebrant." He paused and looked sidelong at Tug. "Best horse and best dog. Now all we need is the bride."

And suddenly, without warning, Alyss was there. She stepped out of the trees to stand in a pool of light thrown by a lantern hanging from a branch.

Will caught his breath at the sight of her. She was beautiful, there was no other word for it. She was dressed in a simple white gown, with one shoulder bare. Her long blond hair, surmounted by a circlet of yellow flowers, gleamed in the lantern light, seeming to have its own light from within.

Later, thinking about it, he realized that this must have been a prearranged piece of theater on the Baron's part. And a very effective one too. Sometimes, he thought, Arald got it right. Alyss caught Will's gaze and smiled at him. He felt his heart turn over.

Quickly, Cassandra crossed the clearing to stand before Alyss as her matron of honor. Halt moved to Alyss's side and took her arm. Since Alyss was an orphan, she had asked Halt to act in place of her father and to give her away. He beamed at her. She was one of the few people who could elicit a smile so easily from the dour gray-bearded Ranger.

Seeing that everyone was ready, Baron Arald made a signal with one hand and a trio of musicians from the castle, previously concealed among the trees to one side, moved into the clearing and began to play. Alyss had selected the song and Will smiled as he recognized the gentle strains of "Cabin in the Trees." It was the unofficial song of the Ranger Corps, the one they sang at every important event. She couldn't have chosen better.

He continued to smile at Alyss as she walked gracefully to stand beside him. It was a day for smiling, he thought happily. Halt took her hand from where it rested on his arm and placed it in Will's hand, then withdrew. Cassandra and Horace stepped back a pace to leave the bride and groom standing alone before Baron Arald.

"Well then," he said, a huge smile on his face as he gazed at the two young people. "What a day this is! What a day indeed!"

The vows they spoke were simple and to the point. There's no need to repeat them here—suffice to say that they concerned love and loyalty and honesty. And duty to each other and caring. They came from the heart and their direct simplicity caught at the hearts of all those in attendance. Lady Pauline smiled gently as she noticed Halt surreptitiously wiping his eyes with a corner of his cloak.

She nudged him with her elbow. "You old fraud," she whispered, and he nodded sheepishly. Halt had spent his life maintaining a bleak, forbidding demeanor. On this day, he simply couldn't keep it up.

Once the vows were exchanged, Arald pronounced the official, legal words that sealed the marriage. It seemed that only seconds had passed before he stepped back, smiling at the young couple, and spread his arms to them. For a moment, Will was nonplussed. He'd gone through the ceremony in a sort of a daze, captured by the presence of Alyss beside him, amazed at the thought that this day had come at last.

Now, he realized with a jolt, the day had come, and the ceremony was done. He and Alyss were bound to each other and he felt a warm, comforting glow deep within himself at the thought of it.

The Baron had said something, he realized, and people were looking at him expectantly.

Arald leaned forward and said, in a stage whisper that everyone could hear, "I said, *you may kiss the bride.*"

Will did so, with a degree of enthusiasm. He was delighted that Alyss responded in kind as the cheers and applause of his closest friends rang around the clearing.

Slowly the sound died down, and in the ensuing silence, one voice rang out.

"And about time too!"

Halt meant to say it jokingly, but before he realized it, there was a lump in his throat and a catch in his voice and he had to disguise it as a small coughing fit, turning away as he did so.

That way, he hoped, people would never notice the tears running so freely down his cheeks.

Hal nudged the steering oar gently and swung onto a diagonal course away from the coast, heading to the left, away from Hallasholm. *Heron* rose and fell smoothly under his feet as the swell rolled under her keel. The other boys had settled into a smooth rowing rhythm—one they could maintain for hours if necessary—and he exulted in the feeling of being under way, at the helm of his own ship.

Stig glanced up at him from his rowing bench.

"How does she handle?" he asked.

Hal grinned back at him. "Like a bird."

AFTERWORD

MACFARLANE GENTLY PLACED THE FRAGMENT OF PARCHMENT ON the surface of his desk. The other nine stories found in the trunk had been carefully assembled, copied and preserved. Now this was all that was left—a tattered fragment with a few words written on it—barely a hundred words. In places, the ink was so faint that he could barely decipher it.

He had left this one till last—partly because it was incomplete and partly because, after his first quick inspection, he sensed that this was something different.

Using a long pair of tweezers, he moved the page until it was underneath his magnifying lens. Then he leaned forward and peered at the words, his lips moving soundlessly as he read them, hesitating when he reached the fainter sections and grateful for the strong light and the magnification.

Finally, he sat back, drumming his fingers on the table.

Audrey was sitting opposite him, in a fever of anticipation. As she had been the one to uncover the trunk, he thought it was only fair that she should be here when he finally transcribed this, the final piece.

"What is it, Professor?" she asked. "Is it important?"

There was no need for the second question, she thought. His

expression and body language told her that it was. He looked at her.

"Yes, Audrey. As a matter of fact, it is."

She waited, knowing that he would elaborate. After some seconds had passed, he continued.

"For some time now, those of us who have studied the world of Araluen and its heroes have been aware of another legend from that time. It's a legend of a young boy, half Araluen and half Skandian, who revolutionized the design of the Skandians' wolfships. But we've known little about him."

Audrey frowned thoughtfully. "I think I recall a brief mention of him in the chronicle of Will's journey to Nihon-Ja," she said thoughtfully, and the professor smiled at her.

"Precisely. But aside from that one fleeting reference, we've known nothing else about him. Now, it seems, we might have discovered a further clue to his story."

"This fragment?" she said, nodding toward the tattered page on the desk between them.

"This fragment," he said, nodding. "And if there is one page, there must have been others. And perhaps they still exist somewhere."

Her eyes widened in excitement. "Do you think we could find the rest of his story, Professor?" she asked.

He smiled indulgently at her, enjoying her youth and her enthusiasm.

"Well, I certainly plan to try," he said.

Turn the page for a preview of

BOOK TWELVE: THE ROYAL RANGER

1

IT HAD BEEN A POOR HARVEST IN SCANLON ESTATE. THE wheat crop had been meager at best, and the apple orchards had been savaged by a blight that left three-quarters of the fruit blemished and rotting on the trees.

As a result, the share farmers, farm laborers, orchardists and fruit pickers were facing hard times, with three months before the next harvest, during which time they would have nowhere near enough to eat.

Squire Dennis of Scanlon Manor was a kindhearted man. He was also a practical one, and while his kindhearted nature urged him to help his needy tenants, his practical side recognized such an action as good business. If his farmers and laborers went hungry, chances were they would move away, in search of work in a less stricken region. Then, when good times returned to Scanlon Estate, there would be insufficient workers available to reap the harvest.

Dennis had acquired considerable wealth over the years and could ride out the hard times ahead. But he knew that such an option wasn't available to his workers. Accordingly, he decided to invest some of his accumulated wealth in them. He set up a workers' kitchen, which he paid for himself, and opened it to the needy who lived on his estate. In that way, he ensured that his people received at least one good meal a day. It was nothing fancy—usually a soup or porridge made from oats. But it was hot and nourishing and filling, and he was confident that the cost would be more than repaid by the continuing loyalty of his tenants and laborers.

The kitchen was in the parkland in front of the manor house. It consisted of rows of trestle tables and benches, and a large serving table. These were sheltered from the worst of the weather by canvas awnings stretched over poles above them, creating a large marquee. The sides were left open. In bad weather, this often meant that the wind and rain blew around the tables. But farm folk are of hardy stock, and the arrangement was far better than eating in the open.

In fact, "kitchen" was a misnomer. All the cooking was done in the vast kitchen inside the manor house, and the food was carried out to be served to the hungry tenants and their families. The estate workers understood that the food was provided free of charge. But it was a matter of principle that any who could afford a small payment would do so. Most often, this was in the form of a few copper coins, or of produce—a brace of rabbits or a wild duck taken at the pond.

The kitchen operated for the two hours leading up to dusk, ensuring that the workers could enjoy a night's sleep without the gnawing pains of hunger in their bellies.

It was almost dusk when the stranger pushed his way through to the serving table.

He was a big man with shoulder-length blond hair. He was wearing a wagoner's leather vest, and a pair of thick gauntlets were tucked into his belt, alongside the scabbard that held a heavy-bladed dagger. His eyes darted continually from side to side, never remaining long in one spot, giving him a hunted look.

Squire Dennis's chief steward, who was in charge of the serving table, looked at him suspiciously. The workers' kitchen was intended for locals, not for travelers, and he'd never seen this man before.

"What do you want?" he asked, his tone less than friendly.

The wagoner stopped his darting side-to-side looks for a few seconds and focused on the man facing him. He was about to bluster and threaten, but the steward was a heavily built man, and there were two powerful-looking servants behind him, obviously tasked with keeping order. He nodded at the cauldron of thick soup hanging over the fire behind the serving table.

"I want food," he said roughly. "Haven't eaten all day."

The steward frowned. "You're welcome to soup, but you'll have to pay," he said. "Free food is for estate tenants and workers only."

The wagoner scowled at him, but he reached into a grubby purse hanging from his belt and rummaged around. The steward heard the jingle of coins as he sorted through the contents, letting some drop back into the purse. He deposited three pennigs on the table.

"That do?" he challenged. "That's all I've got."

The steward raised a disbelieving eyebrow. He'd heard the jingle of coins dropping back into the purse. But it had been a long day, and he couldn't be bothered with a confrontation. Best to give the man some food and get rid of him as soon as possible. He gestured to the serving girl by the soup vat.

"Give him a bowl," he said.

She dumped a healthy portion into a wooden bowl and set it before him, adding a hunk of crusty bread.

The wagoner looked at the tables around him. Many of those seated were drinking noggins of ale as well. There was nothing unusual in that. Ale was relatively cheap, and the squire had decided that his people shouldn't have a dry meal. There was a cask behind the serving table, with ale dripping slowly from its spigot. The wagoner nodded toward it.

"What about ale?" he demanded.

The steward drew himself up a little straighter. He didn't like the man's manner. He might be paying for his meal, but it was a paltry amount and he was getting good value for his money.

"That'll cost extra," he said. "Two pennigs more."

Grumbling, the wagoner rummaged in his purse again. He showed no sign of embarrassment at producing more coins after claiming that he had none. He tossed them on the table, and the steward nodded to one of his men.

"Give him a noggin," he said.

The wagoner took his soup, bread and ale and turned away without another word.

"And thank you," the steward said sarcastically, but the blond man ignored him. He threaded his way through the tables, studying the faces of those sitting there. The steward watched him go. The wagoner was obviously looking for someone and, equally obviously, hoping not to see him.

The servant who had drawn the ale stepped close to him and said in a lowered voice, "He looks like trouble waiting to happen."

The steward nodded. "Best let him eat and be on his way. Don't give him any extra, even if he offers to pay."

The serving man grunted assent, then turned as a farmer

and his family approached the table, hopefully looking at the soup cauldron.

"Step up, Jem. Let's give you and your family something to stick your ribs together, eh?"

Holding his soup bowl and ale high to avoid bumping them against the people seated at the tables, the wagoner made his way to the very rear of the marquee, close by the sandstone walls of the great manor house. He sat at the last table, on his own, facing the front, where he could see new arrivals as they entered the big open tent. He began to eat, but with his eyes constantly flicking up to watch the front of the tent, he managed to spill and dribble a good amount of the soup down his beard and the front of his clothes.

He took a deep draft of his ale, still with his eyes searching above the rim of the wooden noggin. There was only a centimeter left when he set it down again. A serving girl, moving through the tables and collecting empty plates, paused to look into the noggin. Seeing it virtually empty, she reached for it. But the wagoner stopped her, grasping her wrist with unnecessary force so that she gasped.

"Leave it," he ordered. "Haven't finished."

She snatched her wrist away from his grip and curled her lip at him.

"Big man," she sneered. "Finish off your last few drops of ale then."

She stalked away angrily, turning once to glare back at him. As she did, a frown came over her face. There was a cloaked and cowled figure standing directly behind the wagoner's chair. She hadn't seen him arrive. One moment, there was nobody near the wagoner. Then the cloaked man appeared, seemingly having risen out of the earth. She shook her head. That was fanciful, she thought. Then she reconsidered, noting the mottled green-and-gray cloak the man wore. It was a Ranger's cloak, and folk said that Rangers could do all manner of unnatural things—like appearing and disappearing at will.

The Ranger stood directly behind the wagoner's chair. So far, the ill-tempered man had no idea that he was there.

The shadow of the cowl hid the newcomer's features. All that was visible was a steel-gray beard. Then he slipped back the cowl to reveal a grim face, with dark eyes and gray, roughly trimmed hair to match the beard.

At the same time, he drew a heavy saxe knife from beneath the cloak and tapped its flat side gently on the wagoner's shoulder, leaving it resting there so the wagoner could see it with his peripheral vision.

"Don't turn around."

The wagoner stiffened, sitting bolt upright on his bench. Instinctively, he began to turn to view the man behind him. The saxe rapped on his shoulder, harder this time.

"I said don't."

The command was uttered in a more peremptory tone, and some of those nearby became aware of the scene playing out at the table. The low murmur of voices died away to silence as more people noticed. All eyes turned toward the rear table, where the wagoner sat, seemingly transfixed.

Somewhere, someone recognized the significance of the gray mottled cloak and the heavy saxe knife.

"It's a Ranger."

The wagoner slumped as he heard the words, and a haunted look came over his face.

"You're Henry Wheeler," the Ranger said.

Now the haunted look changed to one of abject fear. The big man shook his head rapidly, spittle flying from his lips as he denied the name.

"No! I'm Henry Carrier! You've got the wrong man! I swear."

The Ranger's lips twisted in what might have been a smile. "Wheeler . . . Carrier. Not a very imaginative stretch if you're planning to change your name. And you should have got rid of the Henry."

"I don't know what you're talking about!" the wagoner babbled. He began to turn to face his accuser. Again, the saxe rapped him sharply on the shoulder.

"I told you. Don't turn around."

"What do you want from me?" The wagoner's voice was rising in pitch. Those watching were convinced that he knew why the grim-faced Ranger had singled him out.

"Perhaps you could tell me."

"I haven't done anything! Whoever this Wheeler person is, it's not me! I tell you, you've got the wrong man! Leave me be, I say."

He tried to put a sense of command into the last few words and failed miserably. They came out more as a guilt-laden plea for mercy than the indignation of an innocent man. The Ranger said nothing for a few seconds. Then he said three words.

"The Wyvern Inn."

Now the guilt and fear were all too evident on the wagoner's face.

"Remember it, Henry? The Wyvern Inn in Anselm Fief. Eighteen months ago. You were there."

"No!"

"What about the name Jory Ruhl, Henry? Remember him? He was the leader of your gang, wasn't he?"

"I never heard of no Jory Ruhl!"

"Oh, I think you have."

"I never have! I was never at any Wyvern Inn and I had nothing to do with the . . ."

The big man stopped, realizing he was about to convict himself with his words.

"So you weren't there, and you had nothing to do with . . . what exactly, Henry?"

"Nothing! I never did nothing. You're twisting my words! I wasn't there! I don't know anything about what happened!"

"Are you referring to the fire that you and Ruhl set in that inn, by any chance? There was a woman killed in that fire, remember? A Courier. She got out of the building. But there was a child trapped inside. Nobody important, just a peasant girl— the sort of person you would consider beneath your notice."

"No! You're making this up!" Wheeler cried.

The Ranger was unrelenting. "But the Courier didn't think she was unimportant, did she? She went back into the burning building to save her. She shoved the girl out through an upper-floor window, then the roof collapsed and she was killed. Surely you remember now?"

"I don't know any Wyvern Inn! I've never been in Anselm Fief. You've got the wrong—"

Suddenly, with a speed that belied his bulk, the wagoner was on his feet and whirling to his right to face the Ranger. As he began the movement, his right hand snatched the dagger from his belt and he swung it in a backhanded strike.

But, fast as he was, the Ranger was even faster. He had been expecting some sudden, defiant movement like this as the desperation had been mounting in Wheeler's voice. He took a swift half step backward, and the saxe came up to block the wagoner's dagger. The blades rang together with a rasping clang, then the Ranger countered the wagoner's move with his own. Pivoting on his right heel, he deflected the dagger even further with his saxe and followed the movement with an open-palmed strike with his left hand, hitting Wheeler on the ridge of his jawline.

The wagoner grunted in shock and staggered back. His feet tangled in the bench he'd been sitting on and he stumbled, crashing over to hit the edge of the table, then falling with a thud to the ground.

The wagoner lay there, unmoving. An ominous dark stain began to spread across the turf.

"What's going on here?" The steward moved from behind the serving table, with his two assistants in tow. He looked at the Ranger, who met his gaze steadily. Then the Ranger shrugged, gesturing toward the still figure on the ground. The steward tore his gaze away, knelt and reached to turn the heavy figure over.

The wagoner's eyes were wide-open. The shock of what had happened was frozen on his face. His own dagger was buried deep in his chest.

"He fell on his knife. He's dead," the steward said. He looked up at the Ranger, but saw neither guilt nor regret in his dark eyes.

"What a shame," said Will Treaty. Then, gathering his cloak around him, he turned and strode from the tent.

Keep reading to discover
John Flanagan's

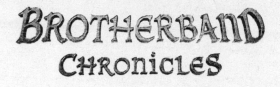

BOOK 1: THE OUTCASTS

Twelve years prior . . .

olfwind emerged from the predawn sea mist like
a wraith, slowly taking physical form.

With her sail furled and the yardarm lowered to the deck, and propelled by only four of
her oars, the wolfship glided slowly toward the beach. The four
rowers wielded their oars carefully, raising them only a few centimeters from the water at the end of each stroke so that the noise of
drops splashing back into the sea was kept to a minimum. They
were Erak's most experienced oarsmen and they were used to the
task of approaching an enemy coast stealthily.

And during raiding season, all coasts were enemy coasts.

Such was their skill that the loudest sound was the *lap-lap-lap* of
small ripples along the wooden hull. In the bow, Svengal and two
other crew members crouched fully armed, peering ahead to catch
sight of the dim line where the water met the beach.

The lack of surf might make their approach easier but a little
extra noise would have been welcome, Svengal thought. Plus
white water would have made the line of the beach easier to spot

in the dimness. Then he saw the beach and held up his hand, fist clenched.

Far astern, at the steering oar, Erak watched his second in command as he revealed five fingers, then four, then three as he measured off the distance to the sand.

"In oars."

Erak spoke the words in a conversational tone, unlike the bellow he usually employed to pass orders. In the center section of the wolfship, his bosun, Mikkel, relayed the orders. The four oars lifted out of the water as one, rising quickly to the vertical so that any excess water would fall into the ship and not into the sea, where it would make more noise. A few seconds later, the prow of the ship grated softly against the sand. Erak felt the vibrations of the gentle contact with the shore through the deck beneath his feet.

Svengal and his two companions vaulted over the bow, landing catlike on the wet sand. Two of them moved up the beach, fanning out to scan the country on either side, ready to give warning of any possible ambush. Svengal took the small beach anchor that another sailor lowered to him. He stepped twenty paces up the beach, strained against the anchor rope to bring it tight and drove the shovel-shaped fluke into the firm sand.

Wolfwind, secured by the bow, slewed a little to one side under the pressure of the gentle breeze.

"Clear left!"

"Clear right!"

The two men who had gone onshore called their reports now. There was no need for further stealth. Svengal checked his own area of responsibility, then added his report to theirs.

"Clear ahead."

On board, Erak nodded with satisfaction. He hadn't expected any sort of armed reception on the beach but it always paid to make sure. That was why he had been such a successful raider over the years—and why he had lost so few of his crewmen.

"All right," he said, lifting his shield from the bulwark and hefting it onto his left arm. "Let's go."

He quickly strode the length of the wolfship to the bow, where a boarding ladder had been placed over the side. Shoving his heavy battleax through the leather sling on his belt, he climbed easily over the bulwark and down to the beach. His crewmen followed, forming up behind him. There was no need for orders. They had all done this before, many times.

Svengal joined him.

"No sign of anyone here, chief," he reported.

Erak grunted. "Neither should there be. They should all be busy at Alty Bosky."

He pronounced the name in his usual way—careless of the finer points of Iberian pronunciation. The town in question was actually Alto Bosque, a relatively unimportant market town some ten kilometers to the south, built on the high, wooded hill from which it derived its name.

The previous day, seven of his crew had taken the skiff and landed there, carrying out a lightning raid on the market before they retreated to the coast. Alto Bosque had no garrison and a rider from the town had been sent to Santa Sebilla, where a small force of militia was maintained. Erak's plan was to draw the garrison away to Alto Bosque while he and his men plundered Santa Sebilla unhindered.

Santa Sebilla was a small town, too. Probably smaller than Alto Bosque. But, over the years, it had gained an enviable reputation for the quality of the jewelry that was designed and crafted there. As time went on, more and more artisans and designers were drawn to Santa Sebilla and it became a center for fine design and craftsmanship in gold and precious stones.

Erak, like most Skandians, cared little for fine design and craftsmanship. But he cared a lot about gold and he knew there was a disproportionate amount of it in Santa Sebilla—far more than would normally be found in a small town such as this. The community of artists and designers needed generous supplies of the raw materials in which they worked—gold and silver and gemstones. Erak was a fervent believer in the principle of redistribution of wealth, as long as a great amount of it was redistributed in his direction, so he had planned this raid in detail for some weeks.

He checked behind him. The anchor watch of four men were standing by the bow of *Wolfwind*, guarding it while the main party went inland. He nodded, satisfied that everything was ready.

"Send your scouts ahead," he told Svengal. The second in command gestured to the two men to go ahead of the main raiding party.

The beach rose gradually to a low line of scrubby bushes and trees. The scouts ran to this line, surveyed the country beyond, then beckoned the main party forward. The ground was flat here, but some kilometers inland, a range of low hills rose from the plain. The first rose-colored rays of the sun were beginning to show about the peaks. They were behind schedule, Erak thought. He had wanted to reach the town before sunup, while people were still drowsy and longing for their beds, as yet reluctant to accept the challenges of a new day.

"Let's pace it up," he said tersely and the group settled into a steady jog behind him, moving in two columns. The scouts continued to range some fifty meters in advance of the raiding party. Erak could already see that there was nowhere a substantial party of armed men could remain hidden. Still, it did no harm to be sure.

Waved forward by the scouts, they crested a low rise and there, before them, stood Santa Sebilla.

BOOK ONE: THE RUINS OF GORLAN

The Rangers, with their shadowy ways, are the protectors of the kingdom who will fight battles before the battles reach the people. Fifteen-year-old Will has been chosen as a Ranger's apprentice. And there is a large battle brewing. The exiled Morgarath, Lord of the Mountains of Rain and Night, is gathering his forces for an attack on the kingdom. This time he will not be denied.

BOOK TWO: THE BURNING BRIDGE

On a special mission for the Rangers, Will discovers all the people in the neighboring villages have been either slain or captured. But why? Could it be that Morgarath has finally devised a plan to bring his legions over the supposedly insurmountable pass? If so, the king's army is in imminent danger of being crushed in a fierce ambush. And Will is the only one who can save them.

BOOK THREE: THE ICEBOUND LAND

Kidnapped and taken to a frozen land after the fierce battle with Lord Morgarath, Will and Evanlyn are bound for Skandia as captives. Halt has sworn to rescue his young apprentice, and he will do anything to keep his promise— even defy his king. Expelled from the Rangers he has served so loyally, Halt is joined by Will's friend Horace as he travels toward Skandia. But will he and Halt be in time to rescue Will from a horrific life of slavery?

BOOK FOUR: THE BATTLE FOR SKANDIA

Still far from home after escaping slavery in the icebound land of Skandia, young Will and Evanlyn's plans to return to Araluen are spoiled when Evanlyn is taken captive, and Will discovers that Skandia and Araluen are in grave danger. Only an unlikely union can save the two kingdoms, but can it hold long enough to vanquish a ruthless new enemy?

BOOK FIVE: THE SORCERER OF THE NORTH

Will is finally a full-fledged Ranger with his own fief to look after. But when Lord Syron, master of a castle far in the north, is struck down by a mysterious illness, Will is suddenly thrown headfirst into an extraordinary adventure, investigating fears of sorcery and trying to determine who is loyal to Lord Syron.

BOOK SIX: THE SIEGE OF MACINDAW

The kingdom is in danger. Renegade knight Sir Keren has succeeded in overtaking Castle Macindaw. The fate of Araluen rests in the hands of two young adventurers: the Ranger Will and his warrior friend, Horace.

RANGER'S APPRENTICE

BOOK SEVEN: ERAK'S RANSOM

In the wake of Araluen's uneasy truce with the raiding Skandians comes word that the Skandian leader has been captured by a dangerous desert tribe. The Rangers—and Will—are sent to free him. Strangers in a strange land, they are brutalized by sandstorms, beaten by the unrelenting heat; nothing is as it seems. Yet one thing is constant: the bravery of the Rangers.

BOOK EIGHT: THE KINGS OF CLONMEL

When a cult springs up in neighboring Clonmel, people flock from all over to offer gold in exchange for protection. But Halt is all too familiar with this group, and he knows they have a less than charitable agenda. Secrets will be unveiled and battles fought to the death as Will and Horace help Halt in ridding the land of a dangerous enemy.

BOOK NINE: HALT'S PERIL

The renegade outlaw group known as the Outsiders may have been chased from Clonmel, but now the Rangers Halt and Will, along with the young warrior Horace, are in pursuit. The Outsiders have done an effective job of dividing the kingdom into factions and are looking to overtake Araluen. It will take every bit of skill and cunning for the Rangers to survive. Some may not be so lucky.

RANGER'S APPRENTICE

BOOK TEN: THE EMPEROR OF NIHON-JA

Months have passed since Horace departed for the eastern nation of Nihon-Ja on a vital mission. Having received no communication from him, his friends fear the worst. Unwilling to wait a second longer, Alyss, Evanlyn, and Will leave and venture into an exotic land in search of their missing friend.

BOOK ELEVEN: THE LOST STORIES

Some claim they were merely the stuff of legend: the Rangers as defenders of the kingdom. Reports of their brave battles vary; but we all know of at least ten accounts, most of which feature Will and his mentor, Halt. There are reports of others who fought alongside the Rangers: the warrior Horace, a courageous princess named Evanlyn, and a cunning diplomat named Alyss. Yet this crew left very little behind, and their existence has never been proven. Until now, that is . . . behold the Lost Stories.

BOOK TWELVE: THE ROYAL RANGER

Will Treaty has come a long way from the small boy with dreams of knighthood. He's grown into a legend, the finest Ranger the kingdom has even known. In this series finale, Will takes on an apprentice of his own, and it's the last person he ever would have expected.

BROTHERBAND CHRONICLES

Join the Herons
on all their adventures!

BROTHERBAND CHRONICLES BOOK 1: THE OUTCASTS

Hal never knew his father, a Skandian warrior. But unlike his esteemed father, Hal is an outcast. In a country that values physical strength over intellect, Hal's ingenuity only serves to set him apart from other boys his age. The one thing he has in common with his peers? Brotherband training. Forced to compete in tests of endurance and strength, Hal discovers that he's not the only outcast in this land of seafaring marauders.

BROTHERBAND CHRONICLES BOOK 2: THE INVADERS

As champions of the Brotherband competition, Hal and the rest of the Herons are given one simple assignment: safeguard the Skandians' most sacred artifact, the Andomal. When the Andomal is stolen, however, the Herons must track down the thief to recover the precious relic. But that means traversing stormy seas, surviving a bitter winter, and battling a group of deadly bandits willing to protect their prize at all costs.

BROTHERBAND CHRONICLES

Journey onward
with the Herons!

BROTHERBAND CHRONICLES BOOK 3: THE HUNTERS

Hal and his fellow Herons have tracked Zavac across the ocean, intent on recovering the stolen Andomal, Skandia's most prized treasure. And though a fierce battle left Zavac and his fellow pirates counting their dead, the rogue captain managed to escape right through the Skandians' fingers. Now, the Herons must take to the seas if they hope to bring Zavac to justice and reclaim the Andomal.

BROTHERBAND CHRONICLES BOOK 4: SLAVES OF SOCORRO

Hal and his fellow Herons have returned home to Skandia with their honor restored, turning to a new mission: tracking down an old rival turned bitter enemy. Tursgud—leader of the Shark Brotherband and Hal's constant opponent—has turned from a bullying youth into a pirate and slave trader. After Tursgud captures twelve Araluen villagers to sell as slaves, the Heron crew sails into action . . . with the help of one of Araluen's finest Rangers!